ANCIENT HISTORY:
A Paraphase

Also by Joseph McElroy

Cannonball
Night Soul and Other Stories
Preparations for Search
Actress in the House
The Letter Left To Me
Exponential
Women and Men
Plus
Lookout Cartridge
Hind's Kidnap. A Pastoral on Familiar Airs
A Smuggler's Bible

ANCIENT HISTORY:
A Paraphase

JOSEPH McELROY

Introduction by
Jonathan Lethem

DZANC
BOOKS

DZANC
BOOKS

5220 Dexter Ann Arbor Rd.
Ann Arbor, MI 48103
www.dzancbooks.org

ANCIENT HISTORY: A PARAPHASE

Book design by Steven Seighman.

Published 2014 by Dzanc Books
First edition published 1971 by Alfred A. Knopf

ISBN: 978-1-938604-23-2
First Dzanc edition: February 2014

ART WORKS.
arts.gov

This project is supported in part by awards from the National Endowment for the Arts and Michigan Council for Arts and Cultural Affairs.

Printed in the United States of America

10   9   8   7   6   5   4   3   2   1

In memory of

DAVID SEGAL

Remarks Perhaps Of Some Assistance To the Reader Of Joseph McElroy's *ANCIENT HISTORY: A PARAPHASE*

1. At the center of Henry James' writings, forming a sort of hinge in James' shelf, perhaps, stand a handful of tales in which someone contemplates and abides with the mysterious and supervalent absence of a dead or dying writer: "The Lesson of the Master," "The Figure In The Carpet," "The Aspern Papers," "The Middle Years." Joseph McElroy's shelf is double-hinged (at least), with two narratives that resonate with this archetypal plot, in *The Letter Left To Me* and *Ancient History: A Paraphase*. In *Letter*, as in the examples from James, the narrator/ protagonist is a vulnerable recipient, a would-be interpreter or medium, left to contend with an opaque address from the dark side. *Ancient History* reverses these charges. It takes the form of an eloquent, garrulous, obsessionally digressive, tender and yet rebuking address to a dead genius.

2. I've just heaved out my effort at categorical description—"a reverse-engineered Jamesian address to the dead"—at great cost. For, like most—all?—of McElroy's fiction, *Ancient History* stymies the categorical impulse to an extreme degree. McElroy's prose, coming on less like a street-gang than like a storm-cloud of evocations, intimations, and signifiers, robs the reader of his guidebook and compass. McElroy doesn't shirk clarity, or particularity; he's a great bestower of *intensely* clear descriptive and conceptual moments. His writing consists of almost nothing else. But there are few writers less interested in standing to one side, in the role of ringmaster or stage manager, to interject with comparisons, framing remarks, or encompassing descriptions. For a reader hungry for announcements as to what he or she is experiencing, before, during or after the experience of it (and we are all this reader, sometimes, most especially at the fraught start of a new relationship to what fiction can do, the kind a first encounter with a master necessarily entails), a plunge into McElroy can be vertiginous.

3. It is worth it.

4. Another Advertisement for McElroy, while I'm risking those: like most writers who throw up such explosive challenges to ordinary narrative "sense," McElroy's at heart an adamant realist. A realist, that is, in the sense that his discontinuities generate, it seems to me, from a single pure impulse: to sort out what consciousness—our interval as minds trapped inside bodies on Planet Earth—really feels like, when pushed through the strange machine of language. *Like this, damn it, not like you've been told before!* It is with such self-appointments, rather than any desire to innovate in narrative or language *per se*, that a writer like McElroy sets out on a life's work. And that, in turn, is what makes it (see #3, above) worth it: McElroy is demanding that his machine of

language *think*, with each sentence it sets down, about what life on earth really consists of (*hint*: it can be vertiginous).

5. Anyone seeking further such general encouragement ought to consult, as I have, Garth Risk Halberg's eloquent "The Lost Postmodernist" (on *Women And Men*), and the invaluable McElroy festschrifts in both *Electronic Literature* and *Golden Handcuffs* Review—perhaps most especially Mike Heppner's defiant *envoi* "The Courage of Joseph McElroy," which itself gives a reader courage, too.

6. *Ancient History* consists of an address, then—to whom? The famous dead writer, a suicide, bears a striking resemblance to Norman Mailer (in as much as he gives speeches in put-on accents, runs for office, writes about outer space, divorces spectacularly, punches and bleeds in public, etc.). The narrator, Cy, lives in the same New York apartment building as the Great Dead Man; he's snuck into the famous writer's rooms during the police investigation, there to deliver the text as a monologue both written and spoken, with a brief interruption during which he hides, like Hamlet, behind a curtain. Monologue consisting of what? Of centrifugal meditations on Cy's coming of age in the company of two friends, one—like the narrator—a native of Brooklyn Heights, a city boy. The other, a friend from summers spent fleeing the city, a country boy. The two friends have never met, but may be on the verge of doing so; this possibility is for the narrator strangely destabilizing, and supercharged. So: two sets of men in erratic conjunction. Around them: women, children, careers, fame, public events, the world, outer space. McElroy is a specialist in matters of spatial relation: neighbors upstairs and down, passersby on the street, the eerie distances contained inside nuclear families—generally, he makes a subject of the power of adjacency and proximity in our intimate lives.

Yet why should the Mailer-like writer be made to listen—if the dead can listen—to Cy's stories of his two friends? The answer is that for all the intellectual and political force of the addressee's public career—and these forces are respected by Cy as considerable in themselves—this monologuist may be seen to believe that the addressee has missed something. Missed something of life as it is actually lived, missed a thing as elusive as it is essential. It might even be supposed that it is this absence, this oversight, which has driven the addressee to his suicide. "You thought only the thirsty media cared for you, Dom—to drink you down and piss you out: the meteoric you at San Gennaro taking a flap in the face from one of those flag-exposing twin guinea hens who run Empire Hardware while yours truly watched through the fence with Joseph and Mary and their boy behind me; or you not quite upstaging sweet Seeger on the Hudson babbling huskily over your bourbon to a black news-chick while the skipper and his banjo sang us down the stinking tide; you bleeding right onto a hand-mike a raincollared TV reporter darted to you like an electric prod, against a field of dark Barrio stone the edge of live gunshots one summer night when you were supposed to be not in Spanish Harlem but giving a big birthday party for Dot in Edinburgh; you getting mugged all alone on Brooklyn Bridge a month ago by three kids who it turned out didn't know who you were then or even by name later in some station house; you vomiting on a TV talk show, pointing at the eggy pool and calling it 'Magma,' and after mopping your mouth and tongue-tip, answering the host's original question straight and mild.... And those excuses posted in the kitchen for any and all callers? And what about 'EARTH = SPACECRAFT'? That addendum hardly seems an excuse for anything. Would you use it to put off a media representative? Or is it a hot-line excuse for the President of the United States to whom if he phoned you to congratulate you on being you you could say, 'Sorry, can't talk now: the Earth is a spacecraft.' I'm losing you, Dom…"

7. So, maybe *Ancient History* is a kind of secretly-not-too-late intervention: Mailer was, after all, still alive. McElroy's argument with his titanic soulmate (for I believe McElroy may have felt Mailer to be his rare equal in curiosity about the existential implications of the new technology and media that had altered the scope of our planetary understanding, and, assuming I'm right, I believe he would have right to feel this). One Brooklyn boy calling to another to reconsider his "Manichean" (the word is McElroy's) exaggerations in favor of a view more grounded in awarenesses of bodies in time, bodies in their places, in rooms and in streets and in nature, and most of all as bodies in relation to others rather than existing in solipsistic outer-space vacuums of ego: "As on the educational channel last week my small Emma was watching the thin man Mr. Rogers from his own private outer space end his kids' show 'You make each day such a special day. You know how. By just your being you' the gossip column Eagle Eye said that your wife Dorothy had got her final decree but that you were sitting around these days enjoying your life in your 'vast elegant' living room running your slide collection round and round your Carousel projector—mostly 'candid news shots involving himself.'" McElroy's narrator persistently feels the uncanny call of his life as both a child and a parent, as well as a resident of the specific and intimate cultural space of midcentury Brooklyn: "I take the measure of my Heights street's space partly by my two-sewer line-drive which Hugh Blood backpedaled to catch without coming within thirty yards of the harbor-view dead-end whose lamp-post and black-iron fence were roughly in the same plane as the street window of my parents' third-floor bedroom…"

8. A speculation, doomed to be incomplete for many reasons, not least my insufficient grasp of literary theory: Joseph McElroy, with his ecstatic depiction of consciousness as a thing incarnated in the unstable but gorgeous *relations between* humans and their companions here on spaceship earth may be exactly the great writer who most needed—most *needs*—the terminology of what is currently called "Affect Theory" to come along and account for what he's getting at.

9. *Ancient History*, then, because of the clarifying urgency of its mode of address, is possibly McElroy's manifesto, a master key, even—the hinge, I called it earlier, of his shelf. At the least, a precursor to his two most daunting (and divergent) masterworks: the densely economical *Plus*, that outer-space deconstruction of the absolutes of solipsistic estrangement, and *Women And Men*, McElroy's symphonic and encompassing depiction of the vast field of human proximities. The way such proximities bind us to the permanent mystery of *presence*—in our bodies, and in time— despite how consciousness and recollection seem precisely designed to escape such limits, much as a space voyager escapes the field of earth. The way our thinking, no matter how abstract, takes place inside, not outside, our lives.

—Jonathan Lethem

ANCIENT HISTORY:
A Paraphase

My luck you're not here.

For once, dear Dom, both elevators were healthy, so without being seen or if seen thought worth interrogating I came out of the east elevator just in time to hear way down to my right an Irish voice call, "No, lady, you're purrfectly safe, he did it himself," and to see at that end of the long hall your door being held ajar and a fully blanketed stretcher moving out of sight certainly into the west elevator. The same voice called, "I mean he was all by himself, lady, O.K.?"

A patrolman as he let your door close gently heard the high Irish voice presumably in the elevator say, "Let's gaw," and wheeled and with his hand out took two running strides to get the elevator door. I turned away feeling in my jacket as if for my key in case they wondered why I was up on this floor. But so far as I could see at my east end, the cop hadn't locked your door. But did he think it locks itself? The west elevator ran shut a second after that east I'd just stepped out of, and unless the inspector had left a man on duty inside your apartment the door to which the cop closed so gently he seemed bemused, why then unless you had guests or contrary to my information weren't living alone, the coast was clear and I had a kind of welcome, if not from you in person. So I went down the long hall to your door, where as I expected another hall came into view to my right. Standing on your mat, I swear that for the long moment during which I looked to my right to check on the nervous woman, somehow your apartment watched. I turned your knob, pushed, and stepped in.

The Irish voice said you did it yourself, I'm sure that's what it said.

How can I begin to take the measure of this living room of yours? With my story of Al and Bob?

I came to see you tonight just in time to see you carried away, if that navy-blue form was you. But at least your place was open, and with your new fountain pen between my thumb and first two fingers here at the south end of your living room, dear Dom, I could if you were here assure you your door is now locked—an inside job by yours truly. But I didn't put on the chain, for a chain means someone's inside. A square claim-receipt card from the typewriter repair shop lies here, but you never typed on *this* beautiful table. I might well have said to you last week, "In the event of disaster call me," for at that very private opening where we barely met I saw that as all I knew of you led me to expect you were the kind of man I could say that to lightly, "in the event of disaster call me." Cora introduced you as "Don" or "Dom," a rare use of your given name; the public knows you as you appear on this benighted old building's crowded directory-board downstairs where now for half a year my name has also stood. The very day we moved in the super had our name up, mint white grooved in velvety black.

Hearing the west (or from here the near) elevator open again at this high floor, I've just put down your gray pen to zip across the carpet between the long white leather couch to the east and your neat desk to the west near a window, and then shift gears to tiptoe the foyer tiles to the peephole.

Which was already open. In the coarse light within its scope I could see only three cocoa doormats along the hall I'd come down from the east elevator. Peace be with the super. I'm getting to know him (though not on *this* floor)—a bulky, statuesque black man with a quality paperback in his hip pocket. He was left by his chic-suited wife about the time I and my family moved in. He looks too young to have those grandchildren he sometimes in conversation seems to free-associate with the ailing elevators and the steel in his shin. Peace be in the old apartment house, Dom, this night you've taken leave. I saw nothing but doormats and an amber scum on the peephole glass. No cop came from the near elevator area, the elevator itself just outside my scope. This irrepressible west elevator simply on its own came back here to twelve; and then from the peephole I heard its door run shut with a bump that may also have been the fresh descent commencing. Last week the west elevator came untracked and was "Under Inspection" for two days and we had to use the east. And now, having slipped shut the peephole's pendular lid, I'm back at the cherry dropleaf in your living room's south end. This wall of steel-casement windows reveals the inclement night sky's blank shade as well as the top floor of an office building right across the street, and in it a red EXIT sign like a face with its vectors askew.

Didn't the cops know they left your door unlocked? Did they mean to? Or did they not have the key. Has someone gone for it? What could this space mean to them? Yet, as you yourself said, measurement is not to be sniffed at.

Your late door was left unlocked as if for me, but I don't flatter myself. I didn't phone, lest you be not home. I just came up, as once before when I stood on your mat and identified your Eagle lock and heard typewriter keys slot-slot-slotting interrupted by the firm under-bump of the spacer. But I hadn't the courage to buzz. I couldn't be sure I'd be of interest to you. Tonight I told my wife Ev I was going to the basement lockers to see if I could appropriate some andirons. Now in your late apartment I feel that each advancing sigh of the west elevator may be bearing police shoes up here. Would it do for me to hide if they came in? This living room is so open if I used my head I could hide right here. At either end of the traverse track running above the wall of windows here at my elbow, your estranged wife's earth-colored curtains which you probably took for granted are drawn back to form a pillar of folds. This was her room too, as I might easily forget. Since you are dead, she can be called your late wife. The light Irish voice said you were the victim of suicide. I guess the space under the police blanket was you all right.

I flipped your pickproof Eagle. If the cop comes back won't he know he left it unlocked? Does he know that an Eagle doesn't lock itself, that you flip it from inside or use a key from outside? Or will the cop say what the hell maybe the super locked up, or a neighbor. But would you have trusted anybody with one of your registered keys, Dom? I feel I know the answer to that one, if I stick around here long enough. My going in here and staying is a trick I played on myself that may take hours to explain. It is nine p.m. It may take other than hours. It is open-ended like a circle that's only a moving point whose centrifugal trail fades behind it. I wanted to speak to you of Bob and Al. I knew all about even events in your career I hadn't actually witnessed, like upwards of three years ago taking a jump with paratroop trainees in Georgia. Not even the Base paper much less the local weekly ran a picture of you, in harness or out, but you told a woman representing a wire service that parachuting was like nothing else, and then instead of telling what it wasn't like you went on about finding that morning in your motel that when you doused cold water on the right side of your jaw to clean off shaving blood and close the cut you couldn't help dousing the left side too. For ages I'd wanted to know you, and then last week I learned that Cora knew you and that you'd be at that opening; and I found that I could get asked.

Last year landing an apartment here was even trickier. I needed a cover for my acts on your behalf. Fortunately my wife Ev had also had her eye on this old building. She, too, thought it might be just the ticket if we could keep below the control ceiling. Real space at a sane rent. Now the city has made it illegal to have a fire in the fireplace. Jumping into the sky you were hooked up like your slimmer comrades the trainees to a static line that opened your pack automatically. Until you got into the plane you thought your rip pin would be controlled by you. Here in New York the week before, you were quoted saying what could one know about jumping if one didn't jump. My father hoped I'd go into science. I was one of those only children who go into other people's lives. I could have used a tape measure tonight, Ev would be interested to know the coördinates of your long brown living room. I see I said coördinates. Your place is roughly like ours downstairs. Which now you'll never see. Ev was expecting some very nice people any minute, I should go back. She tends to mix people without thinking, so you could find yourself facing two who don't get along, which can kill an evening.

She asked Bob the weekend he was last here. We were just settled in. Bob preferred the Biltmore.

We could put both Al and Bob up, our place is spacious. But they're on the eighth and tenth floors of a westside motor hotel for this (I now suppose) extraordinary weekend. You see, I received independent letters from them saying we'd all meet. Al and Bob have never met, or at least to my knowledge hadn't until their respective arrivals in the city yesterday. Yet each worded his note almost as if *he* were arranging to have *me* meet the other. Till now their sole bond has been me. I haven't phoned the motel. I've known them both for years.

Summers I knew Al, a country boy. Soon after Labor Day I turned to Bob, who spent summers at the ocean. Yes, after fields of goldenrod and the serial flow of bugs finely buzzing above the warm tar road that Al and I wildly pedaled, my friendship with my Poly classmate Bob returned as cleanly exercising as new kinds of math problems and as alien and promising as the paint smell in my parents' city apartment.

But Dom I meant to start with your career and its meaning. Instead I interrupted with Al and Bob, and must now announce, dear Dom, that over the years by design I've kept Bob and Al from meeting. Not that this took much care. I've told you too soon, without preparation. Maybe I couldn't help it. "Hopefully"—as our super begins his grand answers to tenant questions—what I have to tell you Dom will occur like those confectionary bomblets in capsule staggered to go off at equal intervals keeping our common cold occluded. "Occupation?" the police recorder asks, if by some awkward chance I'm called to the precinct in your death. Pre-amping him I reply, "When I was six or seven and had a headache my mother would take my head and press it fore-and-aft then transversely, which helped to relieve the pressure." The police recorder says, "Occupation: Head," and writes.

You, Dom, I could ask, "What's my line?" and your notorious grasp of the times could let you coolly bear my quip back to me on a sliver of neutral wit. With civil rhythms what I have to say will slowly come—occluding, yes, our common cold.

Bob wouldn't touch one of those two-a-day specifics. He'd tell one of his kids to take a pill if he had to but stop the sniveling and suffering. I saw Bob once look into his and his wife's medicine cabinet with wincing wonderment at salve and powder and spray, cosmetic, medical, marital. If like one of his lobsterman neighbors he'd toppled into that northern bay that he drives the way he used to play lacrosse, and been then tracked by his empty, circling outboard till pitching the frosty swells it found him and came back at his naked head and he ducked but came up too quick and lost the main part of a hand, this huge result would bring out of him not a frail finality of breathless cries but a Whoop of epical amazement, before he died of shock. Bob no longer lives in the city.

Imagine Al and Bob head-on. Al, who has barely lived in Maine, could say, "Bet you didn't know that four hundred and sixty-eight people died in Lewiston in 1961."

"I'll bet *you* I didn't," Bob may say. "The number doesn't do a thing for me." He'll grant some mild whimsy in Al but doesn't see that Al meant fact for fact's sake, not even when Al adds, "Four hundred and sixty-eight died there in 1962, and four hundred and sixty-eight in 1963."

"Local pride," says Bob rising, and takes Al's empty; "local pride," moving toward the kitchen, where he calls out, "In the heart of the State of Maine is a mystery you and I will never be able to put into words. And it's an American mystery too by Christ. All the rest is sheepshit, Al, pure and simple." A dew-stained can cracks. The weekend is snug and gray. Country rain seals Bob's self-made house.

But Bob and Al have not met. And if I say they wouldn't have got along at all you with your well-known knowledge surely know my not bringing them together was no simple social precaution, Dom. (Dom for Dominic?) For I don't after all boast many friends and so you'd think I'd want my friends to know each other. But Al and Bob? Enough for them to have in common me. It's not my fault that apparently in these last weeks they've been in correspondence and apparently this weekend have left their families and come to the city to a midtown motel with better elevators than ours: Bob on the tenth floor, Al on the eighth. Were they two men who would stir each other's worst colors? Apart, they are dreadfully alive for me.

It's raining. I have just stood at one of your west windows and seen far below me the sealed beams of a long car stopped at the light headed east. The wipers pace parallel on the windshield. A second slick length racing up behind braked to fall just shy of the lead car's prompt take-off as the light turned, the second car's wipers are different, they meet and part like the ribs of a fan. On the corner a black man with a plastic bag over him down to his chest looked in the framer's window which I know says, "To the Trade Only."

But now here at this old beautiful table I can't hear rain. News of your impromptu death won't hit the streets for a few hours. A mobile unit is sliding you downtown I imagine. My only fear of death, Dom, is of losing my approach to it. I must say suicide's old stuff. I will scratch some of this out, it seems to take you to task for what you've done. When Cora invited me to the opening where I met you she said she'd heard from the blind actor's former girlfriend Kit Carbon that you were taking marijuana for migraine. How far will I go? By one view, Dom, I cannot lose your audience even if I try. A minute ago passing in your foyer the large white mirror whose uncertainty and depth you devised by superposing four sheets of windowglass, I looked into it as if it held a hint of your late form suspended like the odor of an orange or a cigar that meets you in the empty elevator. Why don't I get back what I give?

As if absently, Bob stands in the middle of a living room he himself built far from this dark city. Gold rims ring the eyes of man and boy caught between contemplation and violence; this midpoint equals speech, and he asks if I recall how in the Poly days he could stun Akkie Backus the Spanish-teaching lacrosse coach.

Wait, Bob, and I put my hand across my eyes to rub it down over my nose and cheeks—but he can't sense I know better than he, I not only recall but having often observed Bob's famous window-leap from the fifth-form study hall I know better than he what it looked like and what Akkie the proctor looked like once again surprised by Bob's savage run at the bright sill, feet then up at the last careless instant in the silent room, the air-borne body slid proneward through the open third-floor window and Bob's arms neatly up from the body so the hands catch the cross-frame and stopping him ram him back in.

That happened. He recalls applause and far away on the podium Akkie's trapped grin behind his desk, but I recall also Akkie's *Times* spread to the sports, and at his elbow as solid as if I could see them from my seat at the back of the room his scissors with black finger holes; and I silently recall after a long second a great caw of irritation in the spring air outside as our school's hairy blond athletic director with the fearful and powerful limp, having heard Bob's hands slap wood and looked up to see headless flannels extended and then legs retracting from the third-floor window, condemned the encroachment. Our geometry teacher Mr. Cohn got wind of these leaps and said if Bob tried it again he'd get him suspended, it was just plain unfair to the school.

Yes, your suicide tonight is almost a blow, Dom. Almost the last thing I meant to address myself to. The biggest bore of all. Though a subject inevitably in the air when Cora introduced us last week. The heartfelt sinews parted stiff. The brain's tentative disorder resolved to absence. No, Dom, suicide was not in my plan tonight. I think Cora doesn't really know you except through her dig friends. Returning from my trip to the peephole I was diverted to the kitchen. I heard the drip. But you have a stainless steel sink and this drip lacked that special *plank-plank*. I tried each tap, but both were tight, yet now the drip was behind me, and turning back toward the kitchen door I saw that what I mistook for a drip was coming from the kitchen wall phone you'd left off the hook. The white receiver straddles the top of your Admiral portable TV. You should have left a movie silently on in this dark kitchen to complete whatever the effect is. I'm doing the best I can explaining.

Today's bizarre events aside, I'd soon be normally in bed with Ev facing an easy assault on the palisades of sleep. My puzzle with sleep, Dom, was never falling into it but out. I wake too soon, I sleep too fast. My fall from sleep—I'm a *de*somn—brings not just the solitary shock that, as I pivot from one locus to another, I can't ever get ready for; no, in all fairness to the rhythms that be, this pivotal precipice reveals, often for as much as a minute or more, my chairs and walls, shadows and shelves, optical irritants or my favorite print, as if they were newly unknown. And that unholy plummet-swing of waking revalues these phenomenal possessions of mine by wily new balances. Am I making it out of my head, Dom? making it any place? making sense? In winter dark, to think I'm seeing from my hollow of our bed a long glimmer of the River Lune as Gray described it

with its "hanging banks" to his sometime friend Wharton—this is
nothing compared to some of the pre-dawn finds I feel sure I shall
dig you up. But a likelier truth about these desomniac alarms is
how these *scenes* respond to *me*. (I've never told a soul, Dom, but
I tell you now and am no doubt glad to write it in lieu of speech
and in a way that asks at last no answer from you, you are a great
man and no doubt have suffered inhuman taxes on your time.)
My eye—*one* not *two* it often seems—seems when I fall thus out
of sleep to have been open for a long while upon, let us say, a
livid bone profile arrested at the point of, and on account of, my
fall from sleep. It is no addict thief or random murderer there in
Ev's kitchen, but it honors my paralyzed alert as if it were. I tell
myself the profile leaning across the wedge of kitchen available
to me across the front hall from our bed must be something else,
I even will it to be, but there it hangs from a body whose dark
or unseen hands hold its angle of arrest by gripping the sink or
refrigerator I can't see, or Ev's ten-foot butcher-block, one of her
admirable acquisitions which can age—unlike the off-lime walls
and appointments of my step-son Ted's classrooms which soil
but never grow old in the old way. When after half a minute I've
given up willing the intrusor-profile to be something else—which
in my precipitately pivoted state of just-waking I can't conceive
could be anything but the profile—he pivots, like me coming out
of sleep, and I see instead a familiar perspective spread by night
and moonlight on the glass that covers a small drawing the lines
of whose delicate wood frame have faded into the live dark and the
moonshine, and at that pivotal dissolution of illusion into truth
(as if I willed it, though unsure what it was I wished to will) one
last new signature of that illusion appears in what my waking eye
stares at, a heretofore unseen hand's shadow above the intrusor-
profile slyly fixed so rigid as to go unnoticed, and as I see Ev's
quilted potholder, which is all this hand in fact is, I now again
can't see the hand. Look, Dom, I meant to speak of Al and Bob,

it's what I was aiming to do even I think when I set out for your apartment telling Ev I was headed for the basement. Your places begins to get into my head but nothing is displaced.

Over that pale phone-box in your kitchen were words which in the pearly verge of light from your hall I didn't really see. But I'm now aware some of them are quite alive, almost a message.

Well, I got up and had another look, and this is what I found, Dom, over your kitchen phone penciled on a sheet of this paper:

CAN'T COME NOW   CAN'T TALK NOW

aged cousin staying night prior to entering Memorial for
   exploratory
busy last-minute writing memorial tribute for former Zionist
uncle to meet copy deadline for inclusion in Bulletin of
Association of Regional Casualty Assurance Managers

A. called for help with gushing faucet OR for electric drill to
   make holes for wing-nut screws

(the pencil softens, the hand is erratic)

B. just phoned at Underground intermission to ask me to meet
   right away in Chinatown

cut arm on sharp hunks of ancient paint
   stretching around window to tear off hanging
   strips of insulation; going to doc downstairs
   in building

about to receive overseas call Energy Release
   Committee Geneva/Brussels/Cairo

(then, irrelevantly though with a freshly sharpened point:)

EARTH = SPACECRAFT

So I gather people were getting to you. Yet such ready excuses aren't the mark of the man who in last year's book argued that we must welcome Interruption. But if I've met you only once, I know you not so much from what you've publicly said as from your person. Today our super had a book about Egypt on his hip, but what's in his head is something else.

Al, unlike Bob, courted interruption. Bike tread furrows the shoulder gravel, then as if to underscore the skid his rear wheel slides sideways (though in fact diagonally because of forward motion). Al is springing from his right pedal vaulting as off a horse from left to right and before I can glance back to see if a car is coming he's down in the ditch scrambling up into the thick sweet field after a brown woodchuck bumping away—but no: a little American flag. Al trots back through goldenrod, his flag held up on its stick.

At the edge of the ditch he stops short pretending to lose his balance. He whips Old Glory back and forth: "We had a parade before you come up from the city."

He thinks my parents are rich.

"*We* had a Decoration Day parade," I say.

"We had the Legion." But in Heatsburg, not here in the village.

"*My* dad took me to Fifth Avenue and you could hardly see the soldiers."

Al drops the flag into the ditch. "*We* don't want that fucker."

Back on the road cruising and coasting, he calls over his shoulder to me did I know what the Marine Committee in 1777 said the thirteen stars on the blue background meant and he quickly adds he does not mean the thirteen states—*that's* not what he means. Bending sharp left across the road to come around at me broadside, "A new constellation" he calls without giving me a chance not to answer; and rising I press ahead like a slow-motion runner as Al cuts skidding in just behind, and then coasting I call out, "Sure, all you got to do is *look* at the flag to see that. Hey, how fast you going?" The next year my parents sent me to camp thirty miles from our summer house for three weeks of July, which deprived Al of a pretty fast pitcher to practice catching, and when I got home Al let himself seem impressed one night I dragged him away from a sink full of dishes in an empty house and showed him Arcturus and Spica to the west and green Vega overhead.

Careful even at nine or ten not to be lured into discussing with Al's father my advantages, like private school, the Planetarium, the Yanks, the subway, the docks, or summers in the country, I did want to be the man's friend. And not because I was, as my mother more than once put it, "devoted" to his son. When she and I drove in to Heatsburg we might pass Al's mysteriously free-lance father parked by the lake chatting up to a telephone lineman, or in the middle of nowhere directing traffic around a big yellow earthmover or along a line of marker-cones, or going the other way with a couple of dingy refrigerators in the back or some bags of feed I knew he had no personal use for. In his house his tone with me—while I smoothly appropriated my father's views on Landon or Vandenberg—was like a host's equality, adult to adult, even proprietor to patron. Then Al's father with one foot up on a leather ottoman would make some remark that seemed instead to surround me with the scale of all our differences—"Dad takin' the train up Fridays?" But at once he'd resume that incurious equality unsettling in that it seemed to relegate Al to the corner of the divan where without a word to us he worked neats foot into his DiMaggio glove or as if to remind me snapped a hardball into the steep hole of his catcher's mitt, but unsettling too, though I hadn't the words for this then, in that the father seemed to keep the son incommunicado in a kind of class childhood. Al's dad was always arriving or leaving in his pickup, the tailgate hooked on one side, the bed strewn with tow chain, wrenches, match-books, sand, a sneaker, grease-tracked pages of *The Heatsburg Hour*, one of whose weekly issues in June would carry, thanks to a local lady who played sonatas with my mother, a social note to tell subscribers my mother, my father, and I were once again summering in the area.

Dom, here are some probable facts: you died tonight, I think shortly before I got to you, even if I didn't get to *you* but only to the place you left; and now I'm filling you in.

Ev is so alive for me she's virtually here in your late apartment carrying against her substantial hip my own small Emma, who *can't* be here because she's down in her own dark crib asleep but who holds her arms out to me and designates in her low-pitched voice, "Dad-dy" as Ev's deep-turquoise eyes stare and she asks, "Why would you want to write to somebody dead?" Yet Ev's tone is not a woman's blank challenge, but simple query. It's not a question she'd ever have had to ask her first husband. He, I may add here, cost her the mitigating status of widowhood by accidentally not dying till after the divorce was final. But I, it could be argued, gave her what she always wanted, a little girl. But I offered dark-haired, blue-eyed Ev exactly what else? You may say, Luck, a new list of friends...dot dot dot. And I should add, not subtract, that she believes me to be funny, and this after all is something, the mortar for a bridge of sighs, in private I embrace you Ev, your doom.

In the affectionate household of my only childhood I was used to seeing hands held, embraces, my father interfering with my mother at the sink, even if (granted) this isn't the whole story. Al was called "Alvin" by his father, "Brother" by his mother; he was held upside down by the one, clouted and sometimes kissed by the other— pulled, pushed, elbowed, sometimes kissed by his older sisters, whom he clouted back and hurt. However, though I wouldn't have said it—certainly not in one of my overpopulated, unnecessarily clear sentences that made Al's father shake his head and smile—morning, afternoon, or evening I never saw Al's parents touch. The summer I was nine—which ended with my father ending his vacation slowly nodding to the radio's bad news across which cycles of static broke inside my imagination like swells upon a half-submerged sub from whose open conning tower Chamberlain grayly spoke—Fridays often I'd stand with Al around five by the low, sagging armchair and watch his dad do two puzzles at the bottom of *The Heatsburg Hour's* comic strips. Even before this singular man had given up on the word-puzzle and gone on to the other, Al would be after me to have a catch or come put mustard water down to bring up the worms we were going to fish with tomorrow. Instead, I stood by that armchair staring at the other puzzle and forming a dozen pictures in my head—Charles Atlas in a still shot hauling a train, Bob and I roller-skating on the Brooklyn Bridge pedestrian boardwalk, a city tug's taut hawser squeaking under strain—and I smelled what I felt must come straight from this country father's muscles: sawdust and motor oil and something else that carried sweat in it but so overmassed the dry sweat that what was left was the intimate schedule of the man, not at all that unmanly B.O. threatened by our athletic director at Poly in his talk "Personal Hygiene Comes First" or embodied in radio ads for Lifebuoy Soap by the eerie promise of that two-note harbor foghorn I and my city schoolfriends echoed in our changing voices. Then Al's mother said from the kitchen that he wasn't warming any worms with her mustard because he was going to wash up for supper; and Al's father, whose stomach suddenly moaned, did not look at him straddling the window sill whispering Come *on*; and as I watched Al's father draw the last line of that second puzzle, Al wasn't there at the sill in the corner of my eye, his sneakers were pounding away around the house. I smelled hamburgers crusting, and now the humid honey of corn. No one said anything to me and I knew I should go.

My mother and I would meet the seven-thirty and have dinner when we three got back from the Hillsdale station. And at (as my father put it) the crack of dawn, Al would be outside our glistening screen door very quietly asking, "Aincha had yer breakfer' yet?" The fresh space waiting for us outside was huge because it was passionately known. But I seldom in those days stopped to think that the village was Al's year-round home.

How did the authorities get here tonight, Dom? You said you smoked because Berkeley's Sheriff Madigan gave you high blood pressure, but the New York Narcotics Squad hasn't time to go hunting for pot. Here in your long living room no mess marks the spot, no contour of your fallen form. (I did not count on your suicide tonight.) But why assume you did it in the living room? Will it become necessary for me to look elsewhere? Will it be an open-ended contour? Will tonight be?

My father brought work with him in his pigskin bag those luminous Friday evenings when he came sideways like a sailor down the high steps of the New York Central coach to set foot in New England. He always had something for me, and I received his energy with a need I cannot merely express here, compounded of an only child's intact though contracted privacy plus certain excited filial misgivings that may well be the true ground of religion or even the writing of history. I kissed him until I was twelve.

Tomorrow for the afternoon papers, Dom, select peers will "take a look at" you—your disappearance from the scene pivotal history for the real estate of all of us, a space impossible to fill. Tomorrow night a televizier in his molded swivel measures the broken summer of your achievement—"Virtually a natural force...created a new dimension in personal action"—swings thirty thoughtful degrees to ask his panel quintet, "Was this then an extension of that dimension? Why *did* he do it?" Mmm minimal response from the public sector, says one. Overwork, says two. Tangent syndrome, says a direct female voice flavored with twenty-dollar-an-ounce Persianelle. An English voice says, Oh I would argue loss of familioidentity. But (say I) what about the generous paranoia of those who pursue themselves? Ah Dom, such stuff as this is ripe to help tell your tale, the pre-neatened, pre-recoded, pre-shrunk annals of a radically active man who wrote key books *in* the selfsame field-situation he foretold and filled.

Well, let my step-son Ted quote you; but I know where you live, and know too as if my life hung on it the ancient trick of figuring a future by inspecting sacrificial victims, Dom. But a priest of any class or order needs privacy to do his line of work. He needs it even in this very home of one who once addressing The Population Institute flatly proclaimed Collaboration as, henceforth in our century, "the corner-module for any appropriate creative dynamic." Your recent mode, Dom, moves in piecemeal vector-sights up and down your chance page, though still across the same terrain. To forcibly thus modulate, you risked indeed entering your postulate field of neutraline equatics through a commitment such that I must confess I saw this suicide of yours weeks ago as one newly viable valence in that field or field-situation. These last are largely your words. Does Ted think that if he quotes you—though I haven't heard him mention you lately—the more he'll be like you? You live with miraculous privacy in this building—Ted doesn't know and I think neither does Ev.

I of course am kept wholly private from, though I'd love to know, the crowd with whom my Ted, my step-son, sits, smokes, shares awareness, and sometimes lives. ("C.C.," he stops me, "for God's sake!" Well what did I say wrong? "Not *what*," he goes on gnomically; "*how*." He says I sound like I ran my words through some old-fashioned computer—"I mean C.C. let them come spontaneously (right?).")

Do Ted's lotus-limbed crowd even know what a fight is? Al and I those summers never quite had a fight, but I think we both felt it was always possible. On the other hand, in the august quiet of our Brooklyn Heights neighborhood where Bob and I and Hugh Blood and the Smith twins and one interloping girl Perpetua Belle Pound and others of our circle played rough touch and practically professional stickball weekends and now and then a weekday afternoon, it seemed that a fight was not *ever* possible. From Bob's cut cheekbones and gray-and-yellow hip bruises and the strawberries on his knees and elbows you'd say that as he climaxed his shifty charge past defense-specialist Hugh Blood with an arms-out leap as if imploring the gods of the air to give him the clean spiral the minister's son fired halfway down the block, Bob forgot the position of the parked car he was about to hit. But the way that in one turning unit of force Bob caromed off that gray fender or pale blue door possessing himself of the football, and then staggering against gravity plunged to the goal-line sewer—this might have suggested to you that Bob trusted his body and knew where that paltry beach wagon was even more exactly than the minister's son who'd said he'd aim for it, though not than Hugh Blood, who was right there waiting but despite his skinny height was always out-jumped. Or if, with your lethally weightless broomstick, you pulled or sliced a cute pitch (from me say) round to the left sidewalk or away to the right, you might just miss a dowager black Persian lamb trudging over those great slate slabs of walk tilted and individual and someday to be replaced by flat grooved cement—or you might bop the Bohack delivery boy lifting a carton out of the deep steel carrier built onto the front of the bike; or the deep or short centerfielder down this street whose single axis made the only field center field might go onto a car hood for a mad-banging one-hander, or spring up off the running board onto the sparrow-limed top for a gracefully aspiring, rib-killing one-hand miss. But why do fist-fights now seem always to have been unlikely among these veerings and velocities? Elsewhere, twenty years on, Al perhaps answers, simpering, "You were Brooklyn Heights kids." The colored superintendent in my parents' building, Mr. Washington, had three sons out of high school but also a little girl seven whom we called A.B. or Abra which wasn't her real name who hung around the railings hoping for a fly no one else could catch. Once, Petty Pound to spear a fly slipped between two bumpers, then instinctively took the high brownstone stoop two-four-six-eight-ten-twelve steps to get the ball just before it hit the next step at the level of the vestibule one of whose outer doors was open, and then she did tumble but in my opinion never lost the ball as she disappeared inside. One—I forget which—of the Smith twins calmly refused to believe she'd held it. He was umpiring that day, self-appointed; yes, he had water on the knee, swollen ripe and sprinkled with raw pimples, and while he'd pulled up his pant to show us I'd taken his shiny blond crutch and we'd all tried it, yes it was *Bill* Smith, the stingy twin, stingy Bill. Well, though big Bob himself had hit (off me) that long ball, he ignored Bill's decision, gave up halfway to first (which was a car fender), and said "Jesus" two or three times partly to congratulate himself on his respect for Petty's spectacular catch, if catch it was. We consented to play with her because she was good, she was "terribly well coördinated" as my mother was more than once told by Perpetua's father, a museum curator who played court tennis. But it was something else too about Petty, and she knew it, and Bob and I did too in our little preoccupations even well before whatever age we were that Saturday of Petty's famous feat. "Get on with the game," Bob called, taking the chalk from little Abra and squatting in the gutter to add a zero to the boxscore, though actually no one was stalling. Petty underhanded him the ball as she bustled in to bat, she had on blue sneakers and an official Poly T-shirt Hugh Blood had gotten for her, and her dark braids came down to her waist. Bob stood ready to pitch, and without interrupting his concentration to look at the Bohack delivery boy he said, "Hi, Joey." Then Hugh Blood, who it occurs to me was the only one I ever heard call Perpetua Pound a tomboy, said to Joey, "Bohack isn't paying you to stand around and watch us play stickball." But Joey, who had been about to push off, didn't hear the levity in Hugh's words, for the levity was an afterthought. The moment was a nasty nub for Joey, who now of course had to wait for something new to happen. Bob, pitching to Petty and, as he let the ball go, straining the last syllable, said to Hugh, "That was a stupid *remark*," and Petty lined the pitch over Joey's head into the Vande Lands' areaway. There it ricocheted around and became a ground-rule double by rolling under the grating door. The other Smith twin lifted himself backwards onto a fender and sat waiting. Then while the minister's son was ringing the Vande Lands' delivery bell, Joey put his foot through onto the far pedal, rose to the saddle of his bike cart, and lounged off. Picking up the broomstick and heading for the sewer cover we used as home, I found myself thinking why didn't he have a swastika on the steel bin rather than a skull and crossbones.

Ah Dom, if I'd died yesterday what would you have known about me? For that matter, what would Ted? Every suicide demands a survivor, and it's the survivor who foots the loss and breaks or bricks up the code. But think if you were the last person on earth—the others all suicides. You could play golf. You could pray. Would you spend your time on suicide? Ted's textbook says, "The quotient common to all societal breakdown-tabulations is Interdependence." It is not my fault Ted got me for a step-father. We are open ends. Ev understood Emma when Emma said, "Ong Zeus." Ev has so much time to do so much that I wonder if she doesn't to begin with have more time. One of those old Friday evenings my father stepped off the train with two cases instead of one, and though nothing had been said about a typewriter for my birthday I'd wished for one, and carrying back across the station platform that density of independent weight I was reduced to dumb labor by knowing what was in that black, square-sided case whose gravity I now know I was exactly equaling. I would not receive the machine for two days yet, I wouldn't be eight till Sunday—Sunday evening, to be precise. Well, Saturday Al's mother heard me tell Al what I was getting, and she asked him why he and I didn't play with Tony and another of Al's schoolfriends, and when he said he didn't have to if he didn't want to she slapped his left cheek with her right hand. He ran into his room, and I went in there too, he had more things than I did including a Norden bombsight, but his mother told me I better go home. As soon as I got my typewriter Sunday my mother made me pick out a letter to my grandmother, who was so sick she couldn't write legibly any more—you couldn't even tell her *p*'s and *k*'s apart. It was a junior machine, it had about everything except a margin release, a back space, and a single-quote for an exclamation. With the top off, it was bigger, and I would slowly click the drum around secure in the endless energy of the cylinder's clear soft black and I would rest my fingertips along the silver-ringed celluloid-topped letters and let its authority touch a mass of merciless future behind my eyes.

Al's birthday was in January—a bad month for a birthday it seemed to me then. It was on a Sunday, the year he was twelve, and he was going to spend the weekend with me in the city, the first and last time we asked him. I was so excited I had a stomach ache and didn't go Thursday the fifteenth to the Brooklyn Ice Palace with Bob and Petty, and I even forgot to phone the Norwegian girl from Bay Ridge who was meeting us at the rink and who two or three years later when I'd walk her home through her very different neighborhood (where the stoops went up grassy embankments) gave me a soft kiss at each streetlamp. But Al's mother phoned person-to-person that Thursday to tell my mother Al had pinkeye and couldn't come down, and it was his birthday Sunday the eighteenth also and she hoped we'd understand, and I confess I was relieved even if I did not understand. I wonder which fooled my step-son Ted more, the divorce or his father's sudden death? He is only now coming out of an orbit of filial distraction he went into at fourteen; it kept him from knowing where he wanted to go to college. He stands today in my living room downstairs and Dom he says things like "Oh, books are so *linear!*" But he doesn't read. He wants an 8-millimeter movie kit but hasn't asked for it. When I was his age—and that's only twenty years ago—I worked a couple of summers on the ranch of a business friend of Perpetua's father's, though granted it wasn't all digging postholes and shifting aluminum irrigation pipes in fields of Sudan and forcing Herefords into chutes where they could be stuck with needles. I'm a doer, in any case. Ted tells me there's nothing left to do, and not even time to. One morning he came in and looked at us in bed and said he wanted to be a writer not a doctor, but Ev and I hadn't even known he was contemplating medicine. I was able one night to state and illustrate for him the parabola principle. What I think stops Ted is locus, all points equidistant from point F and line D. He is not exactly an only child now, but I suspect his receptors were always different from mine. When I couldn't solve a problem at the end of a chapter in his Analytic book he said it didn't matter and thanked me for clearing up the theory in, like, creative quik-trips (right?) like my old friend Bob's cross-stick boomerang that he got for Christmas 1946 or the diver's flight from springboard to strobe-water oh wow—

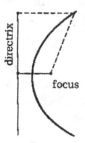

But Ted couldn't see parabola as conic section—

and when I said what good were my analogies if I couldn't do the problems in his book, he said the point was the *concept* of focus-directrix-vertices, upon which *I* said mildly that at least I could demonstrate why only a ninth of an iceberg is exposed—but Ted says, I don't *want* you to demonstrate that—Or, say I (remembering Ev his mother happily waking once in the middle of the night when I'd fallen from sleep and was willing a thigh suspended on the wall to turn into something else), is it a seventh of Archimedes' iceberg or an eleventh?, you divide densities—Which doesn't *matter*, interrupts Ted, its irrelevant (right?)—*Which*, I therefore shout, does too matter and by the way irrelevant to what?

Oh if our ends, Dom, were only open at the same point.

Mass is energy: granted, natural Lucretius couldn't have divined *that;* but redefine mass both at rest and otherwise, as our old Einstein did, and lo! Lucretius is saved: or (and does my father nod approval?) to be more precise Lavoisier's eighteenth-century axiom "in all the operations of art and nature nothing is created" can now by grace of Einstein's artful Mass insure that grave Lucretian clue "Things cannot be born from, nor once born restored to, nought" (in my English a syntax over-neat). Terrible Ted bolts out the door, an incident which lends itself to multiple reproduction, and I hear the stair exit slam in the long hall, for in these moods he'll never take the elevator.

Would I like to feel *I've* done some of all this to Ted? And am I initially disarmed by his willingness to shut his eyes, shake his head, successfully try to smile, then so expertly recount the waiting room sequence? Yes, Dom, I indeed am initially disarmed. For I want to believe he's resisting. So I think, What? is he inventing it all? No, that sideways sag of the combed head denies he is. The waiting room serial strains my brain. Would he tighten truth into a puzzle to prove to my satisfaction my adult poverty, sitting here ruling parabolic axes with your typewriter repair shop claim card? No, he's too natural. Yet this high-priced interlude composed over the secret weeks of certain half-hours in his psychiatrist's waiting room shrinks out of reach. I can merely listen to the kid and pay his bills. His doctor, a plump but distant Hungarian highly recommended by poor old thirty-eight-year-old Hugh Blood, came often late for appointments or even forgot and gave two patients the same hour. *So* often that Ted thought he meant to. But he produced excuses, like incredible morning traffic coming down from the hospital, or an empty squad car double-parked blocking the nonetheless vacant space he always parks in, or then somebody broke into his buxom Mercedes and he had to go to his garage to order a new burglar alarm, which was the only thing tampered with. Or he'd blame the time-lag on his secretary, who operates from someplace else and serves several doctors. Three or four times, the person waiting with Ted was a girl who at first when the plump Hungarian finally showed was glad to dislodge her pending congruence with Ted and go out for coffee. Ted teased himself that she was the plump Hungarian's plant testing Ted's capacity for healthy selfishness; but on the other hand, Ted's appointment Monday was for no less than nine a.m.

During the first wait with Betsy, when he rose to change *Look* for *Time* or the other way around—I forget—his shoes felt like diver's boots, his jeans like bandages. But subsequently he found that she felt the same way, and he guessed that, sitting on one blue-foam length of the L-shaped couch leaning against the whitewashed beach-house wall-planks whose raw hairy pine a decorator had scored with a random design of gouges, Betsy likewise felt financially embarrassed by the bandanna'd black char whose brown, stockinged soles below her kneeling bottom lay over the lavatory's threshold as she applied Lestoil to the floor and seemed to explode the toilet every minute or so like a persistent throat-clearing. Ted in self-defense began to talk to Betsy. And she, who at first seemed relieved when the doctor would at last appear and remove his six-button jacket and neaten the great knot of his wide tie, seemed the next time content with Ted, till one day she read Ted's mind and led him to suggest they not stand for that grave Hungarian's absence any longer but leave a note canceling these costly hours, and they did and never looked back, though as they came out onto the sidewalk Ted detected across that tree-green street something which, should he and Betsy discuss it, might smudge the dimensions of what they believed they were leaving, so he kept it to himself. But listen, Dom, when the suppositious secretary billed us a whole month's two hundred and eighty dollars we paid only what my step-son told us to, and we've heard nothing since. Nor have I seen Betsy, though I've had her on the phone. Three's a crowd, yet that strain the waiting room sequence put on me seems to even that odd fear of meddling I have. So after telling Betsy that Ted'll be right here, I idly ask if she thinks their doctor contrived their conjunction; but Betsy's gentle "Brought us together? I suppose so" softly adorns surely her alarm at the chance I'm right. Or maybe like Ted she doesn't like the phone. I gather it's not exactly dates they go on. Is he playing the field? He wouldn't put it like that. Betsy was phoning all day today. Ted was in and out, and didn't call her back on our phone.

And I, Dom, what do I do about Bob and Al? You might accuse me of bringing them together. Ev if she'd seen their notes to me could have picked up her beige phone and dialed them with magic dispatch. No one dials like Ev. But unless Al and Bob have called me in the last how many minutes and been asked over by Ev, they may still not have met. I can afford to feel that here in your apartment I'd almost rather tell the tale right to your face. But you are not here, yet granted thus not able to judge me a harassing crank. This great fountain pen came fresh from its art shop gift box which lay on your desk near the west window. Your daughter Lila's birthday note lay under the box. The bottle of black ink in its box beside the pen may have come from Lila also, for you don't write in longhand.

As I read this room, once your redoubt, I do not find in your things mere expressions of you. They don't need you. Which might be precisely why you should have been able to need them. With the north book-wall behind it, a tripod-based shaft, extensible but not extended, supports in the intermediate position a horizontal case containing a standard 40 by 40 projection screen. I have space, if not time, to explain, and I will, uninterrupted by Al or Bob or Al's father's number two puzzle or the cross-stick boomerang Bob fired off Brooklyn Bridge in April of '46, or Bohack Joey and the fight. Where's your projector, being fixed?

Did you make a wish as you killed yourself? Did you wish to be friends with the black, blind Hamlet who in an interview on educational TV condemned you for caring more about technology than for poor people, and for telling a black militant breakfast their only hope was intermarriage? Was suicide your way to say to present friends and former wife, You never knew me, now you know? But Dom, what *was* this that these minds surrounding your life could now know at last? I am also one of your survivors, maybe your first unless some neighbor here who heard the high Irish voice is close enough to you to claim such. I'm the Unknown Survivor. What if I put your phone back on the hook? For the busy signal may bring someone over here. Having much to do, I put Al and Bob right out of my mind, be they limpid parable or lame fact. If, Dom, you couldn't stand the solitude which others' views of you enforced, these crowding distances are still to be preferred to what your suicide says, namely that these wrong views must now be supplanted in your absence by the clear blank vision that you weren't what these persons thought—say, a hero ideologue, or an idea devoted to a man, a creature who tolled new rates of time on one hand but on the other swore to all the ages old and young, thirties, forties, that time was overrated and could be controlled, you were a prophet of the present in a superland of plans, you had something for a retired cop on jury duty or a tired post-adolescent feeling obsolete, though now nothing for a Zionist uncle who said he hadn't heard you right when you said to him on a prime-time talk show that you weren't interested in the death-camps any more. Well, if everyone missed the point of you, you alas won't be here for the review. Yet something worse, your quondam wife Dorothy and your dear, if adult, children Richard and Lila won't be able to turn this faithful event, your suicide, to any purpose; for their idea will be not to let grief turn to death but to get along, just get along. Suicidal satisfaction better not be the locus of somebody *else's* feelings, even if that would sound better rendered in Latin. You know so well how people don't pay attention.

But you couldn't have known where my fugitive circle crossed yours, and your suicidal satisfactions can have had nothing to do with me. But I've had much to do with you. All worlds are real, but yours seemed realer than mine.

The day we moved in I learned from the magisterial, patient super the kind of thing I had almost forgotten I wished to know. My encounter with him—first in our new apartment, with Ev busy and half-listening (and Emma saying, "Ong Zeus"), then in the hall outside our front door, then in the west elevator whose ID button the super pushed to illustrate a point, then in the dim basement and its corridors where we pretended to look for a vacant storage locket—led to two conclusions, his and mine, distinct yet seemingly congruent in the one rounded shadow we combined to cast in the light of two dusty bulbs, one of them behind him one behind me. Ma'am the answer to that is there's *no* space in the basement. Yes sir you sure have got a lot of books, I see you have a book on Islam, very interesting, I don't know it; have you read all those? It's going to be a splendid apartment in my opinion we get them bathrooms finished. Sure the fireplace works, long's the City don't crack down. Plastering (plastering-plastering) well yes and no, the house painter will do plastering if you ask real nice, he's very busy. Over the shower? In the window? He's very busy, I got him on a pretty extensive operation all this week but next week who knows—*who knows?* Basement (basementbasement) oh we going to *look;* but like I told you there *is* no space; hopefully we can allocate a spot for the trunks, yes sure we could take this one now. The east elevator down the hall there's under inspection. Leggo I got it. *This* button? The ID! Funny I never thought of that. No it means "One Down," but it don't work, push it all you want the only way to go one down from eight is press seven. No I got what you meant, oh the *id*, sure; no, it's one floor down, *that's* the meaning not the id. Don't you strain yourself, what the missus leave inside, cinder blocks? O.K. watch out, I got her. We can leave it up against these newspapers. Sure, sure, we can *look*, but those lockers belong to people been here twenty thirty years. Oh yes he's got one all right; oh you know him; his *first* name? Funny, I don't know either, but he's a pal of mine, two night owls at the all-night deli, even give me an autographed book he wrote. But he's got trouble, y'see. See?, *there's* no lockers for you. Hopefully one could become vacant and then I might arrange for you people to get it but people live here till they die, big apartments for the rent, we don't have the wherewithal to provide the services we once could before I come here. B' I think we might make a special space back there where we left your trunk, move some of those stacks of papers, I could give you a spot all to yourself, you couldn't store a bedroom set there but hopefully some of your luggage kind of thing y'see. The trouble? What you expect?, the man's controversial, the mailman needs an extra box for him is what he needs he gets so much mail. Made these speeches all over the country—see, what happened he asked for an unlisted number he was getting some crazy calls after he went around the country and said all that about the Religious Leaders—oh you know?—somebody let it out he was in for an unlisted number, and Christ if the papers didn't get hold of the number before *he* did. Yes I know him personally, he's a real gentleman, and a brilliant man in my opinion; a little extremist but you got to respect him. Thank you sir that wasn't necessary, thanks (thanks-thanks), we clear them stacks off this week so you got your own space. The space you save may be your own. No he's not presently in the city. Got some land down in the Islands—Exuma? Well, I couldn't say, but he got land on two of them down there—no taxes—went there for a long weekend, he's got pirates from—Haiti I think coming over there they say; it's undeveloped, just one hotel, he'll be back Monday Tuesday; mail's piling up, stacks of it, I think he better get a secretary, had one a few years back then he fired her and she got married all of a sudden and very next month lost her baby, some of his mail just laying around in the mailroom, he never comes down till noon. He's after me to buy down there.

Still, the super through the next two weeks maintained a kind of equidistance between our apartment and the course of my movements. When I said, Dom, that I had space to explain, did I mean among others the superintendent's space I have just for this inflated moment occupied? I dislodge myself, Dom, from the super's space of hopeful vacancies, Haitian pirates, a derelict plaque in the basement emblazoned "OUR CODE," stacks of papers and (on the main floor) mail, and confess it's been some years since I presumed either by parabolic passage or creative congruence to lose myself in other lives. In short, I tipped the super an opening five for his idioms and the eerie equivalence each item of his talk seemed to have with each other item, and before the week was out ascertained the mailman's schedule and acted on it.

Saturday you never know; but eight-fifteen Monday through Friday he's at the boxes with the two canvas sacks of house mail slumped on the floor. In ranked banks of twenty per official lock the eighty boxes are tilted out like bins and top-loaded. Now, that early in the day tenants don't bother unlocking the front of the box but reach in the top while the mailman's at work. My box, though remote from yours by floor, is right under yours, for one thing because we've the same letter apartments (though judging from the scale of this room not exactly the same apartments—did I say scale?). With a sigh and a matutinally murmured pardon I bumped the mailman and reached. Reached, removed—then perhaps turned with gracious surprise to greet the man who has half a Bermuda onion first thing before he walks his obese Corgi. My own mailbox I could unlock later, if Ev didn't.

Now a public man not only rates more junk mail than a man like me but may oftener feel obliged to answer it. And it isn't only junk mail that costs pointless intersections. Your recent wife was of the opinion your attack on Religious Leaders might lose you that new conservative interest you'd elicited from the vast para-urban constituencies even if you and I (in our separate but like-lettered apartments here in this old benighted building) knew that these constituencies merely used you as entertainment. It was clear to me your wife wanted you to sense that even going around in circles you were still the man she once took you for, and that if you took each other back, you two might now finesse an open-ended truce in this great apartment I've as yet not had time to case. Three of her letters misconstrued your work so subtly I almost resealed them and sneaked them back into your box. But I trusted my hand and deposited them in our floor's incinerator chute whose little room at ten a.m. can fill so with back-up fumes due to the landlord's failure to replace a defective baffle that the bulb above the porter's deep slop-sink can be seen through the smoke only in sulphuric blur. My censoring in any case lessened the pressure on you. Perhaps not enough. Tonight something happened. I will need more than time to explain it to myself. I don't have to raise the extensible rod and pull up your projection screen out of its case and hook it to know it's a silver-gray lenticular. The DA-LITE label tells me.

What's my line? Maybe you. But be warned, my course is partly coördinated by certain points and lines it never touches, it runs between them in a way and misses them but is derived from their distances. Take my paternal uncle Coolidge along the Potomac and my step-grandfather John stuck in Flatbush.

Yes, Dom, maybe you. But I've neither striven nor wished to be someone else. My complaining step-son Ted will read of your death and never guess my connection. A generation of complainers seek now from all those over thirty sweet peace as right rather than privilege—as a fringe benefit on the magic map of cost-to-cost plenty. But better off complaining than borne on mild old grass to some poly-deceleration of the head. Ted, thanks to the rhythms that be, isn't interested in smoking (*period*) much less in syncopating his charismosomes. Oh for God's sake, C.C., he says to me, pausing head down at the front door one evening he knows I wish he'd stay home, for God's sake the way you *talk*—be spontaneous. Then back home at the crack of dawn he's staring out the kitchen window pretending he didn't hear me get up and no doubt hoping I'm still sunk in dense sleep, which shows you how much he knows about this desomniac dad of his (right?). *I* didn't have to follow *you* to the other side of the country, Dom, to know what I know. But just the same, I went.

On the way out I stopped for the Intercontinental Rotary AGT, like you. We flew quickly into Chicago's O'Hare on the same Astro-Jet. The lapel card I'd had laminated in a New York subway station before leaving here admitted me as a member of the Working Press and with barely a glimpse of the Loop's broad and massive streets I made the select and newly sprayed Early-Bird Session of The Inner Group in time to grab the last of the Non-Participant chairs along the wall. Two leggy "Hi"-saying beauts from Utah U.'s U-shaped campus passed coffee and crullers to those sitting seminar round the frame of long leather tables, and after two Religious Leaders with hairy wrists led us in prayers (the second silent and in some instances secret), you were introduced by past-President Dr. Dave Dickens, a carrot-crested insurance mogul, whose inter-fingered hands on the table completed the comfortable corral of his fore-arms surrounding his coffee cup. Eventually you finished staring at your white-powdered chocolate cruller and stared at Dickens who was by now calling you "virtually a national *re*source, a thinker yes, but a thinker meriting our particular attention in terms of his special field of moral cost-consciousness, the coördination of overall aims. How, that is, can we underwrite in our young people our nation's ancient priorities?" You looked right at me and I let go the ghost of a grin. It was Tuesday. As you bit off half your cruller and at once began to speak muffled words, I thought two things: This man may do himself in; but what has his life to do with mine?

But long before you'd downed a leisurely length of sentence while chuckling (bitterly and I think even humming) through an initial premise that the U.S. heads for a field-state superposing new levels of both dilution *and* density, I was seeing again a prospect in acts of yours I observed during the year or two before we moved into this building.

It was back here in New York, and you had come from a platform where toward the end of your spiel the loyal abstractions Courage versus Love that you were squeezing springily together to the ritual shock and wry amusement of black and white leaders from the Old Settlement, Inc., began for me to fade among and become equal to a number of vivid physical distinctions: the woven kink of your hair like sea or land penetrated by the clean pale promontory of temple receding either side; the glass of yellow fluid you reached for and sipped in mid-peroration so a small part of its perspicuous self dripped to the floor delicately splashing your black wing-tips; the nail of your left little finger you hooked into your nostril turning away from the audience, and then at the mouth of that nostril the dot of blood you discovered when you put your nail up there again to try to finish the job. Appalled, you left the stage and just as you passed out of my sight you looked it seemed right at me as if startled by applause *I* had set off; for they were clapping, they thought you'd really finished. Well, an hour later I had followed you to B&A's, where you spoke of the failure of your attack on liberal dogma but then were flattered by a denizen of that bar who with an erroneous east-coast Anglo-vowel called you "after all, a polymoth, a polymoth, no matter *what*." But in a high state of nerves you said you now saw you had not added to the Available Energy and then said, "My own medicine, my own medicine," drank three Topaz Neons, picked off the brown clot and put it on the dark varnished bar at the right elbow of the denizen (from Scituate, Mass.) who said really he could hardly see it. Leaving your tie and billfold beside the blood, you passed behind the denizen and strayed out the door just missing my extended saddle shoe. The Life Insurance dome banged five p.m. and as I and the denizen behind me coming to the doorway watched the odd, though neatly duate, game you were playing with the premature witch who had just written VAYA CON EDIS on the hoarding next to the ocelot shop and who was on her daily way to collect free leftover macaroni salad before the business deli closed, we saw beyond you two the four insurance clerks advancing. If I interrupt this scene of interruption near its end just as the denizen pushes in front of me and before the four clerks arrive at B&A's, it is in order to make best use of the much later event of Dickens' Inner Group. Dr. Dave smiled privately. Several of the Inner Group were bending this way and that, and so was I in my Non-Participant chair, and my stomach roused.

One hairy wrist didn't want its cruller and gave it to the hairy wrist that had led the silent prayer. I wonder, Dom, if you recall the last thing you said, and with a poignant lameness looking down at your untouched coffee some of whose good Chicago cream I saw a short time later had surfaced in a cool arabesque: "We *owe* it to our children to make mistakes with them; but let our mistakes be pivotal, let them be exciting." You seemed set to go on, but then after a moment looked up surprised, as if imprinting—and too late—a delayed exclamation point.

During Question Time you attacked Religious Leaders. The attack exploded westward toward the setting sun and its afternoon papers, and you (you devil) managed to catch the setting sun that day by accidentally eluding me and not attending the night congress of the I.R. Annual Get Together where, in my laminated dinner jacket, I sat in vain till past-President Dickens whispered to incoming President Deirdre Reardon, Nun-at-Large for some regional religion, who then announced that "prior commitments on the west coast" had forced you to cancel. And I was off (as quick as thought) across a toe or two along my aisle, then to hotel, cab rank, O'Hare, and via neutral skies to the brink of the Pacific.

But I foresaw. For I had seen. Your morning performance in the Inner Group did not amaze me, for the simple reason that almost two years before as the denizen from Scituate or did he say North Scituate and I noted the advance of the four clerks that afternoon of your self-styled failure before the black and white leaders of Old Settlement, you teamed gratuitously with the premature witch. On the corner was the red fire alarm box she was accustomed to go around three or four times and this afternoon of your bloodied nose on the wry platform and the prematurely applauding audience and, left on the bar inside, your tie and billfold, you caught the premature witch as she reached her ritual alarm box preparatory to crossing the street, and you said something I infer must have been "Let's go halves." Whereupon you each did semi-circles about the box, meeting first on the curb side then on the inboard side once and twice—but the magic didn't work—till like a virtually sane person she stopped you and said, "Friday I go round here just three times before I cross the street; can't get to the deli too soon; *you* got better things to do." You said, "No better things, no worse—*many* things." Your prior mutterings about "medicine" demonstrated plainly what your trouble was: you were failing to keep a clear passage at least between if not equinear a couple of your ideas, Field-State and Commitment. You were becoming uninsulatable.

By the time I got to the coast you'd been there since three p.m. If to plot your truth I do not need exactly *time* here tonight in your late apartment, so I did not that Tuesday night of Sister Deirdre's Rotary Congress when though tardy catching up with you on the coast I naturally foresaw what had happened, I mean your telegraphed challenges to students, to faculty, to one or two sheriffs, to the governor, though nothing for the college administration. You were photographed in *The Examiner* with your mouth tortuously open as in one of your accents, Irish, Italian, southern.

Wednesday in a squared spiral you climbed the flights of tiled stair-halls in that official edifice the occupation of whose top few floors students had signaled weeks before by accidentally jamming both elevators. You lost interest and paused at the sixth floor for a sight of the twilit sea and a slight press conference. *Yes,* you said, your blast in Chicago yesterday *had* been intended; and yes, Religious Leaders for once *had* better be poured all on the same griddle if only to see if their differences disappeared. But feeling the pull from above you were off up the stairs again, summiting at last among an occupation squad who had read some of your books, knew your later positions on the Mickey Mouse watch, followed your campaigns for archery, undersea farming, marriage, trains, highway de-organization, and the House of Representatives, rocked onto your one musical composition "The Song of Kuwait" which had unexpectedly taken off and not as satire but as a reversible area of open yearn—and having had a suppertime wrap-up on their synchronized transistors they at once asked what might come of your Chicago blast. Answer? If my step-son Ted had watched me, Dom, the way I observed you, he'd have been just as able to foresee that I'd be awake at that dawn hour when he was looking out our kitchen window, as I to foresee your response to those student demonstrators nine or ten levels above the Pacific coast.

You were baring your teeth to speak, when a harmless fub-lubber blurted out a mere matter of fact: "You, you—led-a-march-on-Santa-Barbara." He might as well have said you'd been divorced or had a daughter Lila and a son Richard who didn't like his sister's husband or in New York you'd kept a trampoline on your upstairs neighbor's penthouse terrace. The fub, who twice told newsmen it was tough making a revolution, making a revolution made a man thirsty—admired that 1966 cause of yours.

On what ensued student testimony seems consistent if not wholly factual. You said (winded from your climb), "You kids think you're tough. Where I come from there's tough guys and tough guys." You told them when you went to Harvard the last thing you'd have thought worth your sweat was administrative reform. You told them if they had to use a logical counter like "relevant" better be clear what wasn't relevant to what, and—look, one term of the relation was themselves and the other term was (you name it) a book assigned or a policy promulgated or what one of their own number right here in the clerical wreckage of this room high above the Pacific had just last week cryptically designated "ancient atmospheres." Yeah, where *are* you Darla Fasinelli? ah *that's* you, sweetiepants, nicer than the U.P. shot, yeah well then let's say ancient atmospheres are not relevant to you heads, but how *many* atmospheres? and just which ones? you can't cry "irrelevant" if you don't know both terms of the relation. But (as, Dom, you briskly unsealed one of their dark jugs of Paisano) *tough?* Why who up there knew about *tough?*, and how come no niggers?, and what's your paramillinery yearning power?

Dom, you might at this point high above the campus and its Pacific cliff have brought up the street fight in New York, Christmas of '67. You'd been on a platform a few stones' throw south of San Gennaro—Hester it was. You held a succulent sheep's head half out of its brown paper bag and beside you was a starched-ribboned child whose papa pushed her up the steps to you while you were praising your friends the Iacco boys home from Air Cavalry duty, the younger missing a hand. You were trying to end your celebration speech and get a drink, and at last suddenly said that the talk against the war made us forget that in any war men could be brave as well as weak, and had true chances to be tested unlike almost any other chances in a man's life. I trailed your group north, and so did that last remark, and so did two giant sisters who own Empire Hardware off Canal: three girls with knapsacks stopped chanting "Hardware *No!* Software *Sí!*" to accuse you of glorifying the war, and you grinned and called back to them, "It's a stupid pointless war, *that's* my position" whereupon the giant Duono sisters caught you with your back to the church fence and shouted, "I got a brother over there!" and thrust at you cute metal flags prettily painted fifty stars and all—and with your back to the wire-mesh and through it behind you the lifesize Christmas crêche, you—

your pen seemed for a moment to run dry just as I was forgetting your retort and as your tale here in one long square corner of your living room was rushing into it a host of facts like *me*, innocently standing by on its banks hoping none will ask me what's my line—

child, sheepshead, hand, sisters, hardware, church, crêche: you required all your old craft to defend yourself without (a) attacking the giant sisters, or (b) understandably bolting. How well I myself know that riddle, the contour determinable yet in the mind of its exact describer open. Just how many equidistances locate my only parabola not even I the parabolist know. Your back against the fence, you retorted to the Duono sisters but to the knapsack girls too and with troubled pompous eyes to the crowd: "Look, you can't insure yourself against life, you can't insure yourself against interference, not even against being a hero."

High above the Pacific you might have cited San Gennaro for toughness, but these students wouldn't have understood. Or you might have described the toughness needed at the end of the Santa Barbara Anti-Abstraction March the year before. Granted entry at last to the sunny Think-Tank, you changed your mind and left the initial mission interrupted and spoke to all and sundry dispersed and gathered there *outside* the cloister. (Your ink runs fast, and I am nothing and the only way you can understand these sentences maybe is if I read them aloud to you but there isn't time and you're not here yet.) A prime speech indeed, it led to your risky trick, a gappy calculus to test young auditors by tossing them a dear dogma to gnaw. Darla, the others, even (if he was there) the blurting thirsty chub, could not have seen through that one either, though maybe they thought it more nearly relevant than the (*sic*) threadbare conservatism of your Hester Street climax—"the wonderful world of war" you were disquoted underground the next week in *Manhattan Hash.*

What you did say about true toughness there above the blue Pacific before what the papers called your "surprise defenestration" was as easy to foresee as, now in retrospect, your exit from Chicago that noon. I hear our west elevator again moaning near, perhaps bringing force, cop or super or curious, incurious or furious tenant, or a field of smells, Dom. The *ideas* in your response to the occupation crew high above the Pacific in rising dusk seem not now vivid, but wrong too in their too prompt association with your (come now, *surprise?*) de-fe-nes—I confess I confess (yes suddenly we've gotten somewhere tonight) that in the virtually narrative length of that ancient word that means "throwing out of a window"—*defenestration*—and, more, in the clear slots between its Roman units, I see not your (for me) abstracted and fraternal point but in spite of myself and in no clear order Bob's white-knuckled fist, Al's drenched sneaker, and my venerable but still efficient junior Corona stolen from our downstairs doorway in Brooklyn Heights in April of 1946.

It was never clear to me how he saw my relation to him at puzzle-time Fridays. I refer to Al's father. Leaning over him as he held his yellow stub above his twice-folded *Heatsburg Hour* I believed he might be including me by waiting for me to say what the next line should be or just to think it out silently before he drew it in. I usually knew the next line, and every particle of my being focused so on what absolutely must come next that, as I now know, my mouth would open. Once, I couldn't keep quiet, for I had a hunch Al's father was going to connect the wrong two points, there was a melony air of cut grass coming straight up from his hand to the roots of my tongue, I was going to speak when ye gods at my lower lip an unusually welling mass of spit had moved. Impelled, I got out most of the word "No" but could tear free of it barely enough to drag in my lower lip and with it luckily my dripping drool just before it reached a length of no reclaim from which it would have fallen finally to Al's father's smudged, brown forearm. "Got a cold?" he murmured, and made the wrong line. But I've gone too fast, even for an ideal audience like you.

Some pages back if you'd been here you'd have said, "Hey wait, why did you have to keep Al and Bob from meeting? That's pretty fussy stuff."

Was I afraid they'd become friends or tell each other things innocent until joined? Your questions almost equal Ev's "Why write to somebody dead?" I solved parabolas for my father quite a while before I saw for myself what a parabola is, which made it a whole new solid puzzle disturbing as it hadn't been before. And this was probably two years before the parabola came up at Poly in Mr. Cohn's brisk, afternoon class that made me forget the dreadful challenge and pointlessness of ten o'clock chem.

I wiped my mouth with the back of my hand replying to the brown arm that no *I* didn't have a cold. Al's voice came very close to the house, beside a window in the west wall of their living room a dozen feet from his regular exit window on the south side; and intensely and low he said to his small dog Archy, "Jesus Christ, Arch, I told you don't dig there, Jesus peezus." His mother's flowers.

As he then raised that rather husky voice and complainingly called me to come out and give him a hand, and from the kitchen his sandy-haired sister Gail said, "Oh *he'd* rather do *puzzles*," Al's mother's steps crossed the kitchen floor with an emergency firmness, and the kitchen door slammed: "*All* right, Brother, you're gettin' it now! I don't know where you hear that language and I don't care."

Pork loin hissed as the oven came open with a snap of the catch and a crank of the hinge, and staring at Al's father's mistake so close to the completion of the puzzle, I could imagine off there in the kitchen my secret Gail holding her head to one side lifting the pan onto the stove top and turning back to the table to finish mashing, they didn't have a potato ricer. I called her Gail but Al and his

father in their own different tones called her by her real name that
she disliked. She was one big year older than me then, when I was
nine or ten. Al didn't run away from his mother, he took what she
thought he had coming.

But when I was twelve, the year Gail had on me was different—
both more and less to both of us than before. She was a natural
swimmer and Al wasn't, though he pulled strong and deep with
his wide, growing shoulders, and when he remembered to kick, you
could hear it for a quarter of a mile on a still day. Gail didn't swim fast
but she breathed without much roll and she had that strange skim
of the instinctive swimmer who seems not held in the normal way
by the water's friction. Up in the hills south of the Heatsburg road
and below a small mountain, was a granite quarry long abandoned.
The corner of it that had been filled by converging springs was said
by Al's father to be too deep to measure. My parents took Al with
us on a picnic there one Saturday when a business friend and his
wife and my uncle Coolidge were visiting us. It was the summer my
grandmother died and it was the summer I got my typewriter.

No one ever again found it convenient to take us to the quarry,
and Al and I were forbidden by my parents and his mother to go up
there alone. So for four summers we went secretly, and until the end
of the third not even Gail knew.

Al and I biked up the unpaved mountain road, coasted off into
a gorge, then went higher and around, and eventually wheeled our
way along a needly, root-ridged path dark and full of the thick, mild
growth of pine sap that made me want to lay out a poncho roll for
the night.

One spring evening the year I was thirteen my parents argued
about going someplace else that summer, trying the ocean where the
Pounds went and Bob's parents. And as I listened in my city room
confused by a tone I'd never heard, the extreme essence of all those
inland summers was for an unsharable moment the quarry far away.
Oh to be sure back in the village was the Old Blacksmith Shop,

where they sold old stuff that my parents' friends up for a weekend would look at for it seemed hours after a long lunch at the tavern— ancient farm tools, wooden spoons, blue goblets with tiny bubbles blown right into the glass, hymnals, a churn you wanted to grab hold of and work, and scented soaps I figured must be practically the oldest of all. And oh yes, behind the Blue Grille of the Major Talcott Tavern there was the pleasant swimming hole you had to have a member's ticket for with sandy beach and mucky bottom. And there was an inn my father said had been a station on the stagecoach route and was restored; and in its low-beamed lobby they had a typed menu on an easel. And the rest, the road past the goldenrod, the gas smell from our laboring refrigerator, the flat lake as you went toward the town of Heatsburg, our village barber-postmaster who made twenty-six flavors of ice cream, a roster of possibility for me even though, through my six-hundred-odd cones there, there were twenty-five flavors I never tried. The goblets, the swimming hole with its diving board by the rocks and cat-tails and the swinging rope down at the dam end, the goldenrod, the stagecoach route, the lake, the ginger (the baked apple, lemon-peel crunch, or peanut brittle) ice cream, oh yes. But losing all this by going to the ocean for the summer instead, meant the quarry that Al and I had taken secret possession of, though I told Al I was sure Gail had found out. And losing it would have meant losing one afternoon the August I was twelve and it meant a wind that passed through the quarry over our deep corner of it.

It was uniquely open to the sky, which seemed slanted because of the shoulder of mountain that hung over one tier of the quarry. Yet by its cliffs and, above them, the steep retreating banks of fir and birch, it was as secluded as the tight-sealed play of our echoing whistles and calls, Al's and mine. "OH: OH-Oh-oh-oh," "HEY: HEY-Hey-hey-hey," then louder and answered one or two echoes longer "SHIT: SHIT-Shit-shi-shi-shi," eventually succeeded by the lone boldness of "FUCK," fading all around that beautiful mountain

quarry into the mysterious prospect of "FUck-FUck-fuh-fuh-fuh."
Lying out in the cold water and, as if you hung at a great height,
imagining the water's density suddenly gone, you might spot a small
hawk coming over or a stone-chip bombed at you so thoughtfully
that its arc would end at a point never nearer any part of you than
a yard. But nothing else, not a woodpecker tapping or a squirrel's
rustling weight in a bough.

Al dived again and again off one ten-foot-high setback from
which you had to stretch and arch to miss a lower ledge. I did some
of that too, but I saw myself rather as the submariner of the team.
Al wasn't interested in my kind of dive, but he listened politely when
I came up gasping to report (a) how far down I estimated I'd been
(: over fifteen feet one day with earplugs, the second of the quarry
summers), and (b) what exactly I'd seen (: nothing—except in the
deepening blue-brown shade a pale strip in the granite wall).

Dom, we let Gail come with us because she'd found out. I didn't
mean to get onto Gail tonight, I came almost unprepared for her
lithe intervention in these pages. But now I think even if we hadn't
let her come she wouldn't have told on us; and I believe I knew this
even then. Who could she have told? Maybe her sister. Not her
mother, who she thought was too hard on Al. And not her father,
with whom she played dominoes every night after supper. No, not
her father.

Why? Well, if love is style, then "not her father" because that
wasn't the kind of thing they said and did together. He'd have felt
obliged to beat Al if she *had* told; on the other hand, this wasn't why
she refrained.

She was beside her father in the pickup once when he came
to look at our gas refrigerator, but she wouldn't come in; I kept an
eye on her out our kitchen window as our fathers knelt together.
My mother offered Al's father a bottle of beer before he was ready,
and opening it and standing it on the counter she told him she
was terribly grateful to him because she had houseguests coming

that weekend; he said, "Y'have, have you?," and she said two friends
and her cousin-in-law. My father asked how to get to the quarry—
though the postmaster had already told him—and was it still active,
and Al's father murmured, "Active?," why no it'd cost too much to
get the stone out. "Marketing problems," my father said pensively—
did they plug and feather?, was it dimension stone they were after?
And Al's father didn't say anything for a few seconds, rubbing some
part he had pulled out of the back of the refrigerator, then said no he
guessed not, guessed they just blew it out in pieces. My father said it
wasn't true, was it, that there were rattlers in the caves?, after all you
didn't *really* get rattlers in New England, did you?, and Al's father
fitted on the panel and stood up and looked at my mother and then
my father, and quietly said, "*There's* rattlers, yuh." And he wouldn't
take a cent. Gail sat perfectly still in the pickup so far as I could see;
and, Dom, I'm not getting any closer to the quarry three summers
later. My father, who didn't join Al's father in a beer, asked what he
thought about the war, and in return Al's father asked if Roosevelt
would get us into it; to which my father replied by asking, "How
can he not?" but his warm, reasonable voice was suddenly so dim he
might have been speaking from inside the freezing compartment:
for Gail was out of the pickup and was standing on the far side of its
bed with the end of the goldenrod field behind her and, if she'd only
known, she was looking right at me across our green lawn. "My little
girl's waitin' on me," said Al's father, and wiped his mouth along his
index finger; then he nodded, and went. The summer sun combed
into Gail's long sandy hair a sharper, crystalline light. It is ten p.m.,
Dom, and I'm still a long way from Al's drenched sneaker, much less
Bob's white-knuckled fist, but I need something other than time
tonight. Her mother somewhat inaccurately called her "Goldilocks,"
but I bet her dad never did.

Great distances at which forces in a field occultly but exactly
work—aren't they, Dom, like those silences love knows it does not
have to fill? For instance, you knew I hope that your son Richard,

a creative actuary, loved you even if he did derive his nurture at the breast of Henry James and even if you didn't receive his monthly letters. And I knew precisely how much my father loved me even when he asked emotionally vague questions like "How many miles was it around Babylon's walls, probably?"

Tomorrow night panel pundit number five—great head sunk on twin chins, hands between his legs—having subordinated clause to phase, the pressure on you Dom to the talents in you, then having winnowed the four preceding diagnoses and suborned them to his own, is at last called on by the pivoting televizier. Whereupon, raising the heavy head, hauling his idea off the ground like the great Karnak shaft, he spreads himself and, aiming a sightless elbow at his armrest, leans. And apparently misses, for in the pre-shrunk TV picture his head now drops sharply at an angle. But to discuss effectively the generous paranoia of those who pursue themselves, this emergency pandit must keep back down that narrative tube such sure-fire capsules as, unearthed or not, will soon melt away their own clear solvent coatings, Dom. I mean two crescents of aquamarine satin lastex sealing the top of Gail's barely thirteen-year-old thighs, all but one crooked pale hair; I mean three bikes wheeling back down the path from the quarry with now and then a domestic clink belying the sense of our terrible silence; I mean Al's drenched sneakers in Gail's basket behind me; and Al in the lead but not leading us, his sopping dungarees puckered to his legs, and brown needles stuck to his bare heels. What predatory watcher would have guessed the truth?

Even dimmed by close breath or smudged then by wiping fingers, these small slides of being when blown up by a projector have a bright volume. Ten years later a temporarily bearded Bob says, "The mountains are different from the seashore." But the truth is not always in good taste, and leaving the quarry for a moment I might add that Al's sneakers were—one of them—soon to be drenched in more than these granite waters.

The summer I was eleven the Number Two puzzle in *The Heatsburg Hour* began to change. I noticed it all through June and after I got back from camp the end of July. We had already seen one change the summer before: the puzzle's deviser had stopped numbering his points. But though this looked like a big change, it wasn't, for the shapes were still so easy (if inevitably curveless) that, except for a line or two of rigging on a frigate or a musket muzzle above the right shoulder of a Colonial militiaman, or, in the square field of its design, one or two of the swastika's horizontals or verticals, the Number Two remained a cinch. Al's father's little errors—like the halyard, the musket muzzle, or the swastika—merely confirmed him in his preference for Two. Eventually he stopped even trying the Number One. It was the word-puzzle, and you had to find a certain number of words at least four letters long in the letters of, say, *vestibule, perpetual,* or *celluloid.* He'd fall short of the minimum sometimes by as much as half; he'd ask me and I'd politely (if quickly) think of two more, then say I gave up, and on we'd go to Number Two. Here you drew lines from point to point to make a mystery shape. If Al's father missed a couple of early connections he'd erase and go back and try to join other sets of points. Once or twice I'd feel Gail watching from the kitchen doorway and look around to find a neutral, close attention in her eyes and (I now realize) her mouth. But the new change in the Number Two was in the shapes themselves, now so much trickier that, at least for Al's father I could see, the lack of numbers had become an insult to his intelligence, and he'd do a slow burn. He might close the contour correctly but then, his stomach now distantly crashing, he wouldn't know what to call the shape, and he'd mutter that he'd like to cold-cock the guy. One day outside I told Al I was sure there was a new person making up the puzzle, and Al shrugged and called for me to pitch; without having to move an inch he caught what we called my curve, thrown with a hopeful sidearm sweep, and he said, "Prob'ly a new guy does the puzzle every week." But aside from my instinctive rejection of this view, I'd already seen something in the changed puzzles that I knew related them. I couldn't pinpoint it, so I wouldn't have discussed it with Al, but I said I knew someone who got things printed in the *Hour* and I could find out if I wanted. "Oh I bet," said Al.

The swastika, though, was different, and one Saturday right out of the blue we almost got into a serious fight. I said it was a Navaho friendship sign, our social studies master said so, but last winter the chiefs had met in council out in New Mexico and banned the swastika. Al said that was a stack of shit, maybe pirates used it—who knows!—but it was a Nazi insignia, and I said for God's sake that was the whole point, and he said balls and walked around the other side of our house where the big gray stone heart was that the Dutch people who built the house had made right in with the red brick, which was why my mother had originally wanted to rent it.

Dom, if you can hear me, have you ever thought that maybe you're simply a subconscious and that you belong to some unknown person far around you? Or in that unknown being a small central empty space.

The first time we ever let Gail come to the quarry was a Friday. Up on Al's diving level I measured them back to back to settle an argument. Al seemed to do an unusual number of dives, one after the other in almost a hurry; anyway he was bushed when we got home and instead of grabbing his mitt and going outside snapping his American League ball into the pocket, he sat on the couch and looked at *Child Life*. After a while he threw it at me and we were about to fall off the couch trying to get hammerlocks when Gail and her mother stopped their bickering about the peas that were already shelled when Gail got home. Al's father came in and took up the *Hour* from his armchair's antimacassar when I'd had my eye on it. Al joined us for the whole puzzle and he even kibitzed and his father told him to keep his shirt on. That Friday it was a whale spouting a fine symmetrical umbrella, there was an unnecessary cluster of points for his eye, an uncertain series for the water line, and long grooves in his side like the whale at the Museum of Natural History. The final Friday of my stay that summer, the dots were the contour of The United States with one state singled out inside. Al correctly identified it as Utah, though one point remained a problem; Al's father tried one or two impatient radii, but I said the point was not to be connected to anything, it marked the state capital, and I proved it in their atlas.

It had been a satisfying summer. Al followed the Red Sox but we both followed Joe DiMaggio's hitting streak. I had told Al about going to Yankee Stadium and the view down over center field from the IRT elevated platform, but it all may have been a jumble to him and I doubt if he cared about the fans advancing on the ticket booths or then the long stone ramps inside that you raced up faster than your father wanted to go and with an expectation that exploded as you came up into that old stadium so much bigger than the city it was in. But Al would listen anyway. And with her sister waiting on at the Major Talcott, Gail had been around more that summer; and if I didn't know just how to treat her I figured she didn't know how I should either. At least, I was much taller than she. Al caught up on me during the winter, but the next summer when I turned twelve the bridge of Gail's nose still came just to my mouth.

You know—like some ideal listener, Dom—that I could describe her if I chose, locate exactly the two raisin moles dropped as if on caressing perpendiculars each side of her collar-bone about halfway to each hidden bud; you know I could find on your shelves behind your tripod and its cased screen a dust-jacket the same cherry magenta as her toenail polish that summer, or *in* one of these books the words to hit off the prim coördination with which she slid her strong narrow hands ahead into the water, fingers always (unlike Al's) tight together in a plane whose grace seemed to deceive the water into—well, with or without the interruption a second ago of four feet stepping climactically past your door then on down the hall in the direction of the nervous woman's apartment (among others), I could capture all that early time if I chose, as easily as tell to the tenth of a mile the distance clocked by Al's much consulted speedometer from his driveway to the beginning of the quarry path.

Cora's a good listener, curled up among her pre-Columbian treasures.

The summer I was twelve my father said he didn't feel like paying for me to go to camp, I'd been there two years running and probably wouldn't get much out of it. Secretly I was glad, for camp would have been at least as dull as the village, and of course newly impossible. Yes, as if between that summer's static banks, the current of my fall toward Gail rushed and returned and silently slowed and then in private throbs rushed toward nothing but restless return. I think that even during the summer before, I'd hardly thought of Perpetua Pound.

During this twelfth summer I typed long letters to Bob reporting how I rose "from me downy couch" at dawn to bike "through the dew with Alvin, my rustic guide who seriously you must meet"; later mowed our lawn, caught a green snake in my mother's flower bed "coiled perfectly" (I lied) "about a tulip stem," and "as an appetizer for my meridian repast and with the canny aid of Al's ancient lore, skinned said unsuspecting ophidian concentric e'er 'twas e'en well waked from its sun-drenched dream." Bob at last wrote back that he had read my letters to the gang at the beach and everyone agreed they were side-splitting; when, exactly, I wrote them during that dry summer I don't know. The morning of an incredibly long round-trip to Boston to see Tex Hughson pitch, I found myself almost physically unable to go. My mother said I'd be all right when Al and I and his school friend Tony and Tony's dad the Heatsburg druggist got on the road, and I was. But sitting through the smoky afternoon back of first in Section 15 of Fenway—whose single deck seemed to give the crowd a small-town sound—I kept wondering pitch by pitch if Gail had gone up to swim without us, and in my lap my fingers on my scorecard typed an anonymous note warning her she was in danger; and Al got mad when Tony's father had to ask three times if I wanted more popcorn, and leaving Boston Al and I got into a dispute which, if I'd only cared, was worse than a fist-fight, about who was the best hitter, Ted Williams or Babe Ruth, and after our closing silence of some seconds Tony's father inadvertently slowed down as he tried to ease things, observing that this would be Ted's last season till after the War. Friday of that week coming back from the Hillsdale station my father, in his gabardine suit that made me feel so palpable in my bare brown arms and legs and my sneakers, asked me about that game and I gave back information automatically, most of which he'd noted in the *Tribune,* and he said Boston and New York were almost equally far from where we were right now. My mother took her right hand off the wheel to pat his leg, and said, "Equidistant, dear."

Gail scooped ice cream three days a week, Al often didn't want to go to the quarry, he'd come pedaling hard up our curving road after lunch with his mitt in his basket, his mask already on, and strapped above his rear wheel his new chest-protector without the old-fashioned crotch-tongue. He talked about a pitcher in Heatsburg, the policeman's nephew, for whom the Legion had wangled a tryout with the A's even though he was about to be drafted. At the quarry I'd tried and discarded goggles; I'd been able to see only that as you descended the quarry pool its sides seemed to funnel in, but my inner eye spiraled clear down to a tiny circular floor.

Sounds trivial next to those two or was it three oceanographic jaunts you got onto last year, Dom: you in sunglasses at the rail of a small vessel, and a briny beard which in the U.P. shot seemed to grow a hair less thickly on one cheek than the other—the papers weren't clear whether or not you'd dived, but you found a lot to say about nitrate concentrations in Friday Harbor, Washington, and one late February you were off the Peruvian coast observing the dreaded El Niño (Christ-child) Effect that comes with the equatorial counter-current displacing the cold Peru current soon after Christmas killing everything from plankton on up, and later in print you told grimly how a ship's paint can turn black overnight in this area from the mixture of seafog and the foul hydrogen sulfide stewed up by fish rotting on the beaches. Oh yes.

But my quarry was no more trivial than the *Heatsburg Hour* puzzles. The first time I suggested to Al that we go ahead on the Number Two puzzle without his father, it was a ziggurat. Al thought it was like the side of the quarry, only too regular, but I said it was a ziggurat and probably Babylonian. Al's father came in and looked at what we'd done and said it was an easy one today. But another time that we went on without him, it was—as I asserted—a minutely detailed Swiss phalanx seen from a low aerial perspective. Then another Friday there was a sub, but seen head-on, which made it difficult, and Al's father came in as we were finishing and said we didn't know what we were doing but said he couldn't be bothered to erase it. He and Al both doubted me when in the course of our brief discussion before I had to leave them to their dinner (though my own father wasn't coming up that weekend), I told them that in '39 they gassed all the snakes in the London Zoo just in case, though all I knew for sure was that there'd been a plan to.

Halfway through the summer Al's father finally ceded to us his Number Two puzzle. The immediate cause was the carelessly executed—or anyway sloppily dotted—picture whose solution I didn't really see how I'd known: an angular cow being milked—but "Cripes! from *behind?*" asked Al's father—ah yes indeed, a bell rang in my mind, an ancient custom, milking cows from behind—and Al's father said he'd be glad to see the paper when we got finished marking it up, but that that wasn't any milk cow, he bet it was part of a geodetic survey map, probably some place round here.

It was a Thursday that Al had an infected ear and had to stay in. I rode by, looking casually for Gail. Up the hill the barber-postmaster told me what he knew I already knew, that this wasn't one of her days, but also that she was waiting on for her sister at the tavern. I rode around behind the Blue Grille and saw her through the screen. And remembering her sister's schedule and from another distance virtually hearing each complex stroke of piano and violin coming from a certain Heatsburg dame's vanilla-scented chamber four miles away from two to five that very afternoon, I came by our village tavern again when Gail, in her sister's pale brown uniform and white apron and low white shoes but without the white cap her sister wore, was walking home for a rest till five-thirty.

I asked her to come home with me and play badminton, there was no wind so it would be just right. Instead of a gently serious no, which I could have worked with in one way or another, I saw another mouth and heard a powerful harshness that, had I been vulnerable, I could not have believed: "Well jeez, *that* all you can say? Yeah'n then we'll skip up the quarry for a swim, *yeah!* When I got eight tables at the *ta*vern and a sick *brother* and *sister!* Maybe you'll pay me to play with you, what'll you pay me?"

Although I calmly mumbled, "Tell it to the Marines," and coasted off, I was thinking of how the warm, protective warnings I imagined anonymously typing to Gail elicited from their imagined recipient never more than a frail shudder, a brave smile, and a longing look out her bedroom casement to the short road that half a mile north curved past cows and then the goldenrod on the left and the rather remarkable writer's stone heart house on the right.

It was Friday of another week that we swam at the quarry for the last time. It was getting cold. It is something other than hours I need tonight Dom. (What about years?, my father jibes from his grave.) Al's parents had bought Al new sneakers the night before in Heatsburg, and he wanted to spend the afternoon with me practicing signals pitching to the Red Sox batting order. I don't know where Al's mother was but suddenly Gail was at the window of her and her sister's bedroom upstairs saying quite low to Al Let's go swimming up the quarry. Her tone struck me funny and I laughed, I guess

because we weren't allowed to go and a certain absurd seriousness
was imparted to her by the dusky shimmer behind which she spoke.
Then she appealed to me, and I stopped my windup and Al said,
"Jesus peezus," and I said well we won't have much more chance
to go—thinking Gail was making up for her harsh words the day
of Al's infected ear. Well, then I pitched an indecisive let-up that
looped right over Al's head, Dom, if you can believe that, but a
tree stopped it, and Gail said louder, "I'm going myself." I caught
a shadow of aquamarine lastex, and as I turned to try to persuade
Al, he pitched his mask hard into his mother's snapdragons. He
said he wasn't letting Gail go alone, but today it's more puzzling
than it was then, and you can perhaps sympathize with my inability
to get at last to Al's drenched sneaker which is merely one passing
step toward Bob's white-knuckled fist, for remember how you ended
your Hester Street speech thirsty?

We didn't say much up there. Al dived his dives and I dived mine,
and on the other side of me Gail did a lot of serious swimming. It
seemed a long time before she side-stroked over to me at last and
asked me to show her the life-saving dive I'd learned at camp.

There was nothing to show her that she hadn't seen me do every
time I began a descent. But I did it anyhow, and this time she started
to follow me down and I had one of my finest descents and when I
came up, feeling rather magnetic, I said it was fabulous down there.
When Al called, "How deep'd you go?" I said without thinking,
"Too far down to measure." The clouds began to move but there
were then so many that the sky was simply overcast and the wind
seemed to have no effect on this mass above us. But let me go back
a second to say what had just been so great I'd gone so far down that
Gail had faded back to the top and my eyes had begun to pound;
well, I'd thought some lower light had been released—like deep air
forced out of a cave trap—or I'd simply reached a depth at which
I could see this lower light which maybe was always there. What I
thought I'd seen by this new access of lower light coincided with a

strange wind in me like some bodily inspiration, that can't have been as great as I thought but seemed to be a thousand new air-sacs, or like juicy kernels podding power into my linings. (Just your second wind, Al's dad would have said.) Astounded, I resolved to interrupt myself, go back up, and test this new reserve deliberately with a fresh start from the surface. The parental village and other points were far away, and Al equally far, and in between were Gail and I.

"Southeast wind," Al said from his ledge. "We better go home. Come on, Abigail." He'd toweled off, and turning away he changed into his dungarees. "Abigail?"

I said, "I can hold my breath five minutes, maybe ten."

Gail watched. I did my half-somersault, stuck my legs up into the cool afternoon, and breasted downward. The thousand new sacs were there, but now so was Gail. But in the blue-brown dusk at not more than ten feet, she pulled me around by the knee. She got her feet behind me with a scissor on my hips, and as I winged my arms upward again and again fighting my buoyancy, she kissed me. When I kissed back, she held it, and instinctively in the interests of unforeseen experimental knowledge I tried and tried to keep us down. I won't say it was a lifetime, because her embrace is so hard to recall all I remember is its permanence, and a small hissing concussion way above us.

It wasn't till we surfaced I saw I was out of breath. But not Gail, whose mouth opened a little as I moved my hand down the small of her back and found myself. I heard a gasp, it was Al in the water with us, and as Gail with the minty spear of her tongue broke our kiss and turned toward him, that damned southeast wind rolled like occult frost right through my opening eyelids then my gelid white eyeballs, and before Al turned to swim for the rock he said, "What're you doin', screwin'?" Well, she moaned so complexly I don't to this day know what it meant, and just then I felt her legs inadvertently still clamped round my hips. I was steadily treading water, the moles appeared for a second, each delicately raised.

I called to Al, "We *were not*," but I'm sure he didn't hear above his kick; anyway he was over ears trying to do the regular crawl. I said it again, when like a shot he had neatly levered himself up onto the ledge two feet above the water, and there were his dungarees on him dark—"We *were not*." But he just squooshed a few steps in his sneakers up a couple of levels, as Gail, scissor-kicking backwards sweeping slowly with her arms, said to me—and I wished she had smiled—"How would *you* know?"

She looked around when Al cursed, he took off his sneakers and threw them down on the ledge he was on and one flopped down to the lower ledge and right to the edge two feet above the water. He picked up a 5-cent pack of peanut butter crackers Gail had saved for the trip home. Then he threw it down and started up around the rocks toward the bikes.

When we got home Al didn't try to hide his dungarees, and when he mother asked, he said where we'd been, and went on upstairs. Looking at me standing on a flagstone outside, she may have understood something, whether worthwhile or not, and she let him alone. She had a plastic apron on.

"I guess you been up there too," she said, and Gail said yes, and looked back at me.

And then Gail came back out of the house. To me. Through a corner of a downstairs window I saw Al's father sitting with the paper, and for the first time wondered where he'd been at the long instant of the kiss. I didn't say anything stupid to Gail; I raised my eyebrows wrinkling my patient, experienced forehead, and eased onto my bike and lounged off.

Past the "restored" stagecoach inn and the eight or nine shiny cars there, I became aware of Gail just as I became aware of something else I'd forgotten about. She overtook me as we were leaving the village about a hundred yards from my house—

to this day the Red Sox record for a consecutive game hitting streak is twenty-two shy of the Yankee Clipper's all-time mark. "But which state gives condemned men a choice?" I asked Al right after he identified the lone corral of points within the Number Two's U.S.A.—

So I stopped on the left shoulder by the ditch. Remembering that my father was again not coming this weekend made me mad at Gail but made me want to tell her any lie that would keep her here with me though I wasn't at all clear what I would do. But she wasn't really alone, for as she stopped beside me and seemed glad, I saw Al pedaling up the road in his drying dungarees and bare feet.

He said approaching, "I didn't come after you. I come for my Keds."

"There's *one*," said Gail dropping it out of her basket. Then laying her bike down she took the other sneaker.

"One down one to go," said Al walking toward her as she backed away; but there way up the road behind Gail standing at our picket fence like one of the mind's indelible spectators was my mother in a white sweater. "Give it *here*," said Al and lunged, but Gail got it off in time and it hit my front fender, and holding my left handlebar I stretched down to pick it off the gravel.

Al didn't say a thing. He walked toward me with his quick hands now out in front a bit, and when he was two thirds to me I underhanded the sneaker but ye gods underhanded it over his head right to Gail.

And when he ran at her she sweepingly backhanded it high into the cowfield and we saw so precisely where it had gone that it wasn't till a lonely week later I visualized the Guernseys and Jerseys that had been there watching at a distance.

Through our rain tonight cars point tubes of light ahead from sealed-beam headlamps two by two.

From one of these twelfth-floor windows the arc of fall to a point in the street is the locus of which focus and directrix?

Looking into that enclosed field that we had more than once been told not to go in, and then at Al, I heard Gail lift her bike.

A finger-tip in my rib, and I heard her ride away, but I continued to look at Al staring at the sneaker where it lay in bad taste near a brown Jersey cow.

A field-situation was what you called the moments of force at Santa Barbara. To go ahead into that sunny Think-Tank and be seated around a famous table would have finished the Anti-Abstraction March, not completed it. So you said a huge hoarse *No* into a fresh bullhorn and, not knowing that your daughter Lila was there with her husband, you used and kept (even better than you could actually see) your many distances. You stayed close to student supporters and within range of intrusible passers-by, and not so close to the prestige waiting seriously inside the gates as to suffer palpable neutralizing contact with those profoundly funded Fellows and end by being tabled. You maintained vector variety.

Al said, "I didn't want that sneaker anyhow," and I said, "What a lot of shit—you just bought them." Again he was interrupting himself. A fight there then would have been terrible. I saw Al beat up Tony's fat older brother, an unsuccessful bully. Al could not fight me over Gail, any more than she in her way I thought would fight me over what she thought I'd done to her father or his puzzles.

You said, through your Santa Barbara bullhorn, "Let's *fight* the Center, not talk to it. I'd be selling you out if I accepted now what looks like their come-down and went on in there to the Center to discuss in realitsik" (*sic*, for you were tired) "dialogue even the true issue—not how classrooms or the family can be rewired, not how to defray the cost of generalized frankout, nor how to speed the processing of legislative packages, but the true issue, namely how pass from one space to another without wearing your own protective pressures, why retract from interruption into a quiet that's divided (if at all) only in bisection by the coolest of cloisters. Oh, here at the Center they're into a by-blow kind of onane teletaping, they're into what doesn't commit them to risking the next moment."

(Someone near me said, "He's so abstract, I thought this was the *Anti*-Abstraction March," and someone else said, "The March is over.") You were saying, "Because they know all their well-funded moments can just be rerun, cut, spliced, fixed—look, we'll come back to this—" but heckling began from a team of older tourists placarded as the first polar bear club in Coney Island "EUREKA, CALIF OR BUST," but you hadn't lost *all* your audience.

Your vector variety, Dom, is nothing so simple as the leaning Heatsburg triangles pyramidally sharing me as apex. You ask what are the base corners? They are Gail, Al, and their father (he now in undivided possession of his paper, soon to be drafted, ultimately to achieve membership in the Heatsburg Legion post); but who's at the pyramid's fourth corner?, and if Al's mother is not the only candidate left (yes, if (say) we include as other triangulating corners my parents (as one or separate) and even Bob), then unless I drop utterly my parabolic guard I'll end up not with carnelian beads and unguent vases obsidian and gold, much less their probable, albeit mummied, owner the Twelfth Dynasty Princess Merit, but through some unspeakable mortuary labyrinth a pyramid of another water, some hopelessly polyfaced crystal. When in 1953 Bob came home from Europe with, after all, the bride of his late childhood, his mother and father invited thirty-four of Bob's old friends, many inevitably also his bride's. But Bob the morning of the party learned of the impending surprise through a phone call from one of the guests, and thereupon compelled his dark-braided bride to absent herself with him, leaving his poor parents and her "pappy" (as he was often called) to face all but the honored guests plus an evening through which with cheerful inventions I if I say so myself led the way adopting myself in effect host.

Dom, just as you in the generosity of your genius couldn't see the insidious debilitation offered by your son Richard's warning letters, so too you inevitably will see what evil valences Al has plus Bob and Bob has plus Al.

Had Al that odd evening in '53 turned up at Bob's parents (invited let's say by me once I knew Bob wouldn't be there) it needed an eye not half so fine as yours to see Al's problem. And I don't mean the civvies lent him out of my closet—they were a near-perfect fit. I mean the distance from Al's game shoulder to Bill Smith's stiffly regular nod and behind Al to a blue morocco copy of Gray's letters. Al would have put an index finger on it and on the Murphy *Johnson* running along beside it (though he would not have known for three or four more years who Murphy was), and Bill would have introduced himself in order to ascertain precisely how far from Brooklyn Heights Al's origins were. Al will not be savaged by anyone, genteelly or any other way. Bill frowns discovering that only once, and then just for a minute from a bridge, did Al see the ocean before joining the Coast Guard, from which he is now in '53 shortly to be excused. Hugh Blood's tall, shy, lascivious sister Tracy appears at Al's side just as Bill, still apparently (though slowly) nodding, inquires if a Reserve ensign will make j.g. in two years; Al inclines his face toward Tracy slightly underestimating her height, and by the various listeners at their different distances is heard to say at the precise volume he wishes, "I just got busted back to Radarman Third." And just as this Bob-less scene that never was comes to a sort of end in a hearthlit soirée that did occur, the other Smith twin "Freddy" alert across the room calls without thinking, "Tracy, hey Tracy," who's murmuring in answer to Al, "Is that good?," while I at this really Al-less scene watch Bob's mother's brave fumbling with a dip-hubbed plate of raw cauliflower and carrots and a slanted rank of little curling pumpernickel rounds she brought up from the basement kitchen—she and Bob's father don't normally go in much for hors-d'oeuvres—and I take in Tracy's clear rosy tan and think that if Bob and his dark-braided bride didn't drive out of town, and if of course Al stayed on for a while in our apartment after I left for this party and my mother for hers, Bob and Al (who was indeed wearing my civvies) could both be at this moment on Brooklyn Heights.

I must open another route to Bob's white-knuckled fist. From Gail's fingertip I had thought to bend into a mellow Monsanto ad during the War that Perpetua Pound and I flipped past one Sunday lunchtime; it described uses of cotton in the vital chemistry of plastic and showed a mellowly half-submerged group of cotton-picking blacks medium dark (or light), a very team, a fine-toothed family of pick-together stick-together social studies. But that scene within a scene is for the moment as far out of sight as our common premise Brooklyn Heights indelibly is for Bob.

Somewhere in the late '50s—his face all screwed up concentrating in the bright sun—he's checking the oil in a two-year-old lemon, a station wagon. His younger son is in the living room of this largely white, largely improvised house staring into the fishtank, and Bob's ever-loving wife, her bouffant of last night dropped and tightened into a frontier bun, stands at the window and repeats the beginning of a question, merely his name: "Bob?"—for he doesn't answer, he draws his rag down the measuring rod, runs the rod back into the sludgy tank, and does not answer. He twists off the radiator cap; the rotted gasket hangs.

Food the little boy has sprinkled in descends like weather; his is a scholar's dumb absorption, an inch-long neon tetra hangs while one flake passes the silky zinc-green lateral and another lands and sticks on its feathery tail. "Have you got your suit, John?" his mother asks, knowing he hasn't. He whirls out of his concentration and grinning yells, "No, I got nothing!"

Bob brings down the hood and leans on it to lock it. "John B., you get ready."

John B. saunters to the open window near his mother, and calls back, "I *are* ready."

His father's face sags happily. There is a universe around, by *Je*sus there is. Bob looks across the hood at the house, staring at the insolent five-year-old blonder than he. "Then you get out here, dear, 'r I'll fetch you such a wallop your fanny'll sizzle when it hits the water." His accent has moved north.

Six-year-old Robert with a towel and two pairs of trunks wanders into the living room Bob built.

"Robby's got my stuff," John B. calls challengingly out the window, but Bob goes across the grass to the cellar hatch. He calls to me to come help with the cement. Holiday labor at the island today: being his guest is a hazardous responsibility: I foresee a swell and forelean to a spumy pitch and forehear the scuff of a badly perched sack of cement as it slips into the racing bay, and my New York imagination wonders what salt-water cement is like. I prefer Robby, though John B. is more fun. When Robby walks past you you don't instinctively reach out to grab him. John B. is used to people doing this.

Faraway on Route One a truck double-clutches. I still taste rich Welsh Rarebit.

I step off the grass down steep cellar steps and can't see. "Can you take this alone?" Bob asks as I see him. And back past two shelves of preserve jars I find my recently dead step-grandfather, back to me, chiseling that wooden catapult-fire rifle that looked so real when I was thirteen.

I get the stone-stiff sack up into the sun.

The boys are wriggling and giggling in the second row of seats. Robby's voice whines out, "John B. threw my suit out the window." His mother begins to say something but Bob, emerging with a sack, says with a simplicity more humorless than final—

Dom, why am I writing this in the present, it drags at my throat-strings, you're not here yet, is there anything to drink in your icebox near that busy phone?—

"Then Robertum you get out 'n get it, and *quick*," and Robby ignores another jab from little John B., gets out, walks around behind me as I push my cement further in over the tailgate, and is handed his trunks by his beautiful mother who, about to get in the front seat, has picked them up and started to toss them in the window on that side. When she tells the blond charmer simpering pertly at the window to stop bothering his older brother, Bob says, "And wipe that suffering look off your puss, Robby. Did you *hear* me, dear?" "I heard you," the prophetic assertion dimly overlaps the ambiguous question.

"*He* heard you," I say, and Bob's wife is grateful and says to me, "We didn't mean to leave so late." Against the high, gray garage-annex lean two planks.

My step-grandfather John, whom I once called "Zo-an," then "Zwan," and whom in '43 I believe I taught the Australian crawl (and who is neither here nor there), was almost the only one of the bunch on my mother's side who knew how to leave me alone. At three, four, five, six, seven, in their overheated living room within walking distance of the Bedford Presbyterian Church I'd sometimes find the trip from my step-grandfather's wing-chair to the no-longer-tuned upright, to the window or the sofa imperiled by intercepting hands, though the hands grew fewer and fewer. My great-aunt, for example, even once fought over me with "Zo-an" when I'd been sitting on the rug trying to reglue the wing into the groove in the strip of balsa that served for my plane's body along either side of which ran the rubber band that powered the prop; and having dripped a glob of that banana-sweet cement on the rug, I'd stood to go get a newspaper to put over the spot when Sue surprised me savagely from behind. She was hugging my shoulder blades to her stomach and she was all perfumed, when my step-grandfather threw down *Field and Stream* and blew up at her and when I struggled she let go and I fell forward and stepped on my plane but didn't break anything because I hadn't left the wing grooved into the body and the pieces lay flat. "Don't you like Aunt Sue?" she said—she stood tall and straight, her blued hair tight-permed—and John and I in unison said, "No!" and she said, so promptly I felt in my chilly intestines (though I couldn't understand that I felt) that she'd had this in readiness for a long time: "You're not the same baby they had at the hospital, they exchanged that baby for you." But what I neither understood nor felt was that in truth she adored me.

Doing sixty on Route One, Bob is answering a question of mine that I've forgotten. "Leo's a lyrical man, he just *has*n't found a *cen*ter." Bob's wife staring straight out ahead from the right front seat says gently, "Now what the hell does that mean?" Behind them Robby slides a hand through my arm as I gaze into the familiar dark hair ahead. Bob races the light at the new shopping center, risks fifty yards of red, and after braking a hundred yards past the intersection accelerates left into the narrow blacktop that leads to the landing. "I told him we were buying Schick for everybody. He's been researching electronics just duplicating data we already had from the New York office, but without my saying a thing he dropped it and went back to his phone. Leo veers between being a really remarkable customer's man and fighting to keep the 1800 barn from being destroyed, and getting his girls out soliciting door-to-door to tempt some Finnish tympanist away from some other symphony and some young conductor in Salt—"

"It was a Hungarian violinist."

"Well you should know, Christ I'd rather listen to records; and not *Carousel* or *My Fair Lady* either—"

"I don't just listen to *Carousel*, Bob—"

"Did you," I intrude, "ever think about the corn is as high as an elephant's eye?" Bob guffaws, "*Beau*tiful! but close enough if you're measuring—no, the point is it's melody with Leo, not harmony; horizontal not vertical—"

"He's horizontal all right," adds Bob's wife, "you walk right over him."

"The point is, he's doing all the right things but doesn't *feel* how they come together in one life. But—"

"But Bob—"

"But"—the chuckle *sub specie mysterii*—"he's *just* amazing, he goes out to some of these towns he's never heard of himself, The Only East Otisfield On Earth, and an old gal gives us an order for two hundred Ohio Oil—oh in the heart of the State of Maine oh Jesus—always hankered to be in the market but thought there was some trick to getting in, and Leo found her. I had him to the island last week—"

"Breaking his lyrical back, dear—"

"I'm going to build him a house on the nubble."

"You haven't finished ours," the familiar voice breaks in again.

But "Daddy" (Bob removes his arm from mine) "do we have to go camping next summer too?"

"Dear, you don't know what camping is, you fellows have your own beach...and—"

"And a house" (I interrupt) "that Bob will build for the rest of his life."

Not to be confused, Dom, with the mainland home in whose cellar I have just taken up a hundred-weight of cement and seen my step-grandfather's shoulder blades curved in thought, a man as factual as my father was and my country friend Al became, though Al never learned that *I'd told* his sister Gail about our quarry. I want to reach Bob's white-knuckled fist and I can't even get to the island his lovely wife (who thinks of everything) got her "Pappy" to buy Bob part of for their fourth anniversary. I'm telling Robby and John B. about Buck Rogers and John B. isn't impressed, but they're both silent after I tell about the spaceman who was on a metabolic microsupport system out beyond the moon for decades and when they finally vectored him home to Earth and he stepped from his spacecraft, he hadn't aged a year.

If I veer forth into some madness tonight in this space of yours Dom that I'm only beginning to use, I hope I've brains to make something of it. Of madness or of space? Is that where this night is taking me? You're not here yet. My head and chin were heavy,

but not now. Below in that place I pay rent on where the water
in the johns sways in and out as if we were at sea, Ev instead of
phoning the police will have indiscriminately phoned her friends.
She'll have scouted the basement boiler room and laundry and
even, with gingerly decorum for the rats' sake, checked the super's
workshop. It is so overhung with pipes multiplying on the whole
horizontally lower and lower from an obscure ceiling, that if you're
like me you'll infer certain earlier pipes aren't used now, or more
have been added maybe because besides the daily load the *past* in
some modest style is being accommodated here too, waters caloric
or residual centrifugally if not quite cleanly contained in this
benighted pile's once elegant system that connects not so much with
the city as with itself. Ev may have phoned Cora, whose party she
didn't attend last week because at the last minute Ted decided not
to babysit, perhaps a lucky break for me. Is our building doomed by
Mafia timetable? So claims the florid Austrian music teacher who if
the east elevator stops at five is invariably there in her old dressing
gown styled somehow of pink quilt and blue (or is it gray) chiffon,
and she is always dismissing some male student of almost any, or
indeed even of indeterminate, age or instrument. And the gent who
smells of dog and onion who gets off sometimes at ten sometimes
at eight promises me that the city has forgotten about us and that
the inspector whose signature at three different dates in a framed
proviso protected by ancient plastic up above the button panel is just
a landlordly whim, for the hazards of these shafts are wholly in the
landlord's power not ours.

Dom, I looked for you in vain at the tenants' meetings. You did,
though, sign the complain I helped the venerable TV scriptwriter in
11F word, for later there indeed you were among the others in two
columns beneath our grievances. You rarely write even your name
in longhand.

Pure information now lacks for me the exercising power I
once breathed out as well as in, yes the grand intercostal lights

spreading a vernal gulf whose source I was. In Utah, where you
have a choice, a condemned man in 1912 chose hanging because
it cost the state more. But the year I received my typewriter the
first electro-cardiograph ever made of a man's heart action while
being executed proved that John Deering, who took the other Utah
option, would have died even if the squad had fired blanks. His
heartbeat rose to 180 just before he was shot. His heart stopped
15.6 seconds after it was pierced, a remarkable muscle even if
you pierce it with pure information. Oh I knew every point of
interest around the Fertile Crescent from Jerusalem the Golden
to the suburbs of Ur. Think, Dom, of 1940, a trip to Washington
and to my uncle in Alexandria, my father and I playing "Capitals":
and just as my mother, having negotiated a rotary, climbed onto
a bright concrete span I answered my father's "Honduras" in one
intaken breath "Tegucigalpa!," my brutal éclat as reveling as my
exam answers at school which were delivered in densely correct
sentences about (say) the stargazer Pytheas who my teacher said
only *probably* invented latitude, or about the Great Northwestern
Quadrant containing the Great White Race which to judge from
James Henry Breasted's words apparently did not, like "the black
world" to the south, "teem"; or sentences about (say) the eye-for-
an-eye, death-for-a-death (life-for-a-life?) legal code dictated by
the Sun-god to that creative Babylonian king Hammurapi (whose
dates at that time were 1948–1905). I knew the Nile as I knew
the Potomac, backwards and forwards. I can never again, Dom,
command the joy with which on an exam I exemplified that tidy
code (preserved, I knew and would someday see in the Louvre on a
block of diorite) by telling my tale from Breasted of the house that
fell down around its owner's son whose terminal concussion was
then according to Hammurapi's system answered for by, not the
"guilty builder" as Breasted put it, but unbearably the builder's son.
I drew engaged columns with darkly incised capitals to illustrate my
stolen views about those puzzling buildings A and B next to Zoser's

Step Pyramid—lotus, papyrus, Upper and Lower Egypt. I saw with my own brown eyes sun-fired bricks, hills of silver coin, I saw more than you can imagine—the incensed beauty Ishtar with terrible grief seeking her fellow god Tammuz through seven precincts of the Underworld, and in one of Breasted's plates a fedora'd scholar with double-jointed legs standing stoutly in tweed plus-fours on a wall of excavated earth, toes pointing out; and I on these exams proudly reported the twenty-percent interest rate under Hammurapi and the organic link between commerce and religion. When Ev is lucky enough to find me a pound of lamb's liver—though I guess those days are over now—I call up that classroom past like a future found in omens. No one else is partial to liver in my house, and yet we all foretell the future. At the tenants' committee meeting I suspect it was felt that I took on too vividly my mantle as annalist of this building. I told the super's tale of the defective baffle, and then I described the incinerator-room on our floor and told about holding your breath as you move between a deep, grimy basin and two cartons of empties to the chute and the door slams behind you, and still holding that breath (such as it is) you pull back the trap like the lid of the big mailbox on the corner that's always too full to trust a letter to in the afternoon, then tip your stuff in holding your hand up to keep bits and even ash from blowing back; then letting the trap slam you stride back bursting to the door. But I couldn't very well tell them I was disposing of your letters.

A slick accumulates in a flat swirl of purple green, I'm holding a pint of Budweiser for him as Bob snaps the outboard again and then it turns over and he chokes it, it is to be replaced in 1960 by a rebuilt job with automatic starter. Now Dom, not all of this fits: I mean *Al* knows about machines too, although (credit card in hand) he hardly seems to. And Al has a brunette beauty too, though her interests, unlike those of Bob's angel, are almost wholly indoor. And, with seconds of sun splitting up out of racing bay spume into my eyes, it is also true—though I don't belie my irrevocable knowledge that

Al and Bob shouldn't have met (if at last they have)—true, yes, that Gail's mother visited her that year on Memorial Day (her thirtieth birthday) the same May day Bob's wife was visited by her "Pappy."

Robby and John B. are fighting over the blue Maxwell House bailer. I'm trying to forget priorities and let my face drink the spray. I haven't been alone with Bob's wife this trip since at the little airport she shook my hand and kissed me. "That letter..." I said, and then I saw Bob's gold spectacles through a swinging door, and he pushed through, springy in tattered tennis sneakers and khaki shirt and shorts—"Oh Christ," she said to me as if changing her mind, "give me a break." But I think—but here's Bob—Hi: Hi—I think I'd meant not exactly in that letter her tantalizing clauses flirting with the past here and there like a hand on my cheek; no, I think I'd meant her veering recollection of what I once years ago told her.

If (as I believe) you're like me, Dom—as like me as Al and Bob are unlike each other—some personal letters make you indelible promises; your son Richard's weren't the only ones that threatened your sensitive career.

Bob, with his hand on the outboard's rubber-handled tiller, probably doesn't know she wrote me, and so thinks *my* letter was just my regular wish to see them and their house and their island. Well, the island's only about one tenth theirs, but turning in out of the bay's main mass with now the full Atlantic astern and Bob still at full-out, the sight ahead—widening as the approach pass narrows—makes the place seem all theirs. (For some financial, some prudential reason this land isn't in Bob's name.) Its titular owner beside her older child on the thwart forward of me, turns halfway round and smiles with the wind. In her letter she said she'd had a dream about her "*first* husband; *first* was what the dream said, but who on earth was he?"

Their crescent of beach gets bigger and we pass between white lobster buoys twenty-five yards apart, then rocks even closer, the left flat shelves now barely under high water. Bob's cove opens, substantial. The left pincer curves landward rising to black boulders, then to a higher nubble of ground strewn with cinder blocks. Bob throttles down. The beach drops to the water, and you know that if I chose I could catch its candid surface as well in my words as you those unidentified *loci Americani* in the tall thin book of photographs you published December of '63, more than four years after this scene. The long beams lying near the upper grass that runs around from the nubble to the ledges on our right where Bob's phenomenal camp stands, were not washed up; he acquired them by night, passing under moonlit clouds to a silent pair of isles where the government once did some kind of training and storage.

Bob wants these beams for floor joists in the next extension. John B. ignores his mother's cry and jumps off the bow before the motor cuts. On his feet shoulder-deep, he strokes himself ashore, and as we crunch sand and gravel he's scrambling to lay hold of the old whaleboat's bow and beach her himself.

The two boys and their mother will take the boat back to the mainland after supper. Bob and I will stay the night and work tomorrow first thing.

Unloading the cement, the beer, moving three of the four beams up to the extension, hacking down lawn grass with a dull sickle— in this scene Bob's priorities aren't mine, and then beyond even mine for a dissolute moment like a vision which you Dom were soon to expound for the modern unready world and for certain few graduates of only-childhood, all the afternoon's points, objects, and deeds spread to a coördinate equality. But putting Bob and the fourth beam off for a minute I follow his wife and the boys into his two impressive improvisations somehow timbered together to the varying ledge angles.

She is changing in one room, I in the other. I'd like to get rid of the boys so I can find out how much she told Bob. What she recollected in her letter if it got to Al could only *undo* the truth. I hear rustling on the other side, scuffing on the sandy floor, springs as someone (probably she) sits down. "Hey cut it *out!*" cries Robby, and John B. with his suit in one hand steps naked into the low doorway to see me. I hear springs next door, John B. had been giggling but now keeps looking at my nakedness quite soberly. His mother says, as he turns back into the other room, "Pick up your underpants." Robby's dark head pokes round the doorpost smiling silly and interested. And I try to find in his brown eyes what they saw in the other room. "Why don't you put on your bathing suit?" he says, and I obey at a distance of many years: no, Dom, no neat ushering from present to past, it's all equal.

Wait, I said to her in her father's library in Brooklyn Heights hearing my father in the dining room happily agreeing to attend a court tennis match and displaying quite a considerable knowledge of that absurd game, *Wait* don't go so fast, turning back to the Monsanto ad she turned her head to look at me, and I slapped one on her with such a rush she had to help us into a warmly leaning balance: "You didn't really want to look at those Negroes picking cotton," she said six months later sitting outside the bathhouses at the beach club the summer I was thirteen. My father loved swimming in salt water, especially when there was no surf. No (I told her), it was spontaneous. (She and I heard Bob singing "God Bless America" while he changed from tennis.) I'm not always spontaneous (I said); listen (I said to Petty) one summer at Heatsburg where we used to go and my mother says we'll go again, I used my friend's sister to blackmail him into going up to a quarry because I liked her, but he'll never know.

But I wasn't afraid Petty might spill this. No, that wasn't why I hadn't taken Al along to the Welcome Home party which the honored guests Bob and Petty skipped in '53. Yes oh of course it's *Petty*, Dom. If you were here in this room of yours you'd no doubt have asked more about the dark-braided bride, the familiar voice, the strong angel—Pert, Pet, Petty: Perpetua, Petua—ye gods let it be one of my substantive liberties with you, Dom, that I did not initially condition this maritime precinct of my past with her name. *The Examiner* identified your former girlfriend Kit Carbon as the "well-known black archaeologist" and Darla Fasinelli in her column in *Manhattan Hash* condemned the adjective's bias.

Petty's wiping a vast black stove Bob found somewhere and cemented here to a mountainous ledge. She flicks her eyes at my bathing suit and murmurs, "K.P." She's putting magazines on a cable spool table in the north extension where I changed; under the plastic-paned window an Army blanket covers a cotful of pillows, another cot meets it at right angles along the adjacent wall; she's asking if my mother ever bought the place near Bob's parents, and if she still plays the violin and piano; Petty hopes Robby is musical; she hesitates to ask me about my work, then says she was trying just the other night to describe to Leo's wife Irish what it is I do and that Bob interrupted saying you could call it social anthropology—but she didn't think that described it exactly. I'm about to ask her if she ever told Bob what I said to her about Gail and Al in '43, but Bob stops hammering and yells to get the hell out here, and John B. comes in to get the yellow plastic bucket to facilitate construction of the pale city he and Robby are molding. He steps sideways down the rocks and leaps onto the sand.

"—not often," she says, and I forget what I asked here, I'm in the doorway looking left at the bay and the cove and, thirty-odd feet from here where the new extension is being floored, at Bob's calf, yellowed athletic sock, and high army shoe, and now the second shoe slides into view; some eastern scent sticks in Petty's hair, in the doorway her right breast is firmly against my left tricep, but this isn't why I forgot my late question ("Do Bob's parents come up?").

When he came back to New York after almost finishing his M.A. in philosophy, it was only to leave again. He followed the east coast way up beyond the summer place his father was getting ready to retire to. Missed it completely.

He will indeed continue his own camp at minimal cost and build Leo one on the nubble.

Hindsight eases out of Bob's life seeming interruption, to make a life as seamless as the unspeakable.

John B. is off in the grass peeing, now grabs a huge rotten plank and tries to haul it down to the sand.

"That man's there again," Perpetua says looking up from her knee that's stabilizing the end of one joist Bob's hammering. "Comes and sits in his Land Rover above the next beach at our line and looks. No he's over our line."

"Maybe I can use him," murmurs Bob.

I've hauled up a fourth, fifth, and sixth beam; the seventh lies across the eighth, which leans on an overturned driftwood stump.

I've been in the water and I'm having a beer, I don't know what time it is.

You can see Bob's two lobster pots out there past the pincers. But he likes to raid a summer neighbor's illegal pot within this cove, Bob knows exactly where to put down his boathook for its submerged line, Brandeis professor of economic geography who thinks he's quite a salt according to Bob. Bob knows he wouldn't do a thing if he caught us, it's funny to Bob like sex.

The question isn't *what* but *who* Bob takes seriously, or maybe no one or everyone. In the vaunted order of his life maybe everyone.

Robby to Bob: "That man's going on our nubble." The man's contour against the deepening southeast sky is still.

Bob hammers again, then gets up out of his framework of joists and looks away toward the man. What Bob will do is completely open suddenly.

Al wouldn't witness Bob's life without recalling his own father's incredulity when Al brought home a twenty-two dollar encyclopedia one day in '45. Al couldn't witness Bob talking Karl Barth tomorrow night with the Harvard vicar of their local church any more than he could Bob and Petty and the vicar crossing themselves after grace in front of a glistening tower of Liebfraumilch and a blue, willow-pattern platter of hot dogs and the Sunday-night earthenware pot of sweet yellow eyebeans. Imagine Al when the Indian pudding comes, and the jolly buoyant collaboring of the credo's *carnis resurrectionis* and that reverent sense of the true business of Monday and Tuesday, parish debts or the bracing distinction between gambling and a hard-nosed faithful participation in the American body economic, yes it's these mysterious companies that Leo loves to know, the knowing, yes yes and growth prospect the concrete ground toward yes a transcendental Awareness of the Impossible that nevertheless really happened in this synoptic country Ben (while the young vicar nods with palsied speed nay joy); Bob laughs with gay incredulity: the Profit Motive and the Resurrection (and the vicar interrupts: Of *course*, Bob, but by Jiminy our generation's heard enough about the so-called Christian *ethic*, which gets nobody anywhere theologically)—"Kierkegaard," says Bob, squeezing the brown bottle upside down over Ben Sedgwick's glass.

Were Al present he would flex his right bicep in anxious scorn, and his game shoulder would jab him.

Yet when I look from Petty to her vulnerable Robby to the man on the nubble a hundred and fifty yards off now staring apparently at its effective owner Bob, to John B. to my own bare foot, my arc between Bob and Al seems to have been crossing a field of force as indescribable, Dom, my normal way as Bob's harmonies are merely warm.

The finished city lies between Robby and John B. They make no move to wreck it. Bob's been staring at the man; now he contemplates his dark-bunned bride of six years close by, who knows Bob is looking, so doesn't break her gaze at the man on the nubble.

Bob's low laugh is way off in another mood. "Why you just go a*head* and be Lady Pound but you and *I* know." The laugh rises and John B. looks around for a second. Bob would not touch her now. Petty is still looking at the intruder but is surrounded by Bob. He says to me, but not so Petty can't hear, "Oh you hang around her you know you been somewhere, and you won't find it in *National Geographic.*" It's a big joke, but again also under the aspect of mystery.

"Please stop it," Petty says without shifting her gaze from the man on the nubble, but her primness is flickeringly tickled and she tries to keep back all she thinks she shows. The unknown man on the nubble seems to give her something to protect her against the exciting doubts that Bob's presence assaults her with.

He turns away and looks at what he's been doing. He says, "I'll never get to the bottom of *you*, woman, not in a hundred Maine winters, by *Je*sus," and the low laughter is again under the aspect of mystery.

As he jumps on down to the sand to get the last two joists, Petty calls, "You can get the lobsters any time," and preoccupied he doesn't answer. She follows down and heads for the water.

Robby says to Bob as Bob goes to take up the two beams, "Daddy, look at our castle," and Bob turns and squats to look at the low but monumental oblongs, their walls here and there in the Egyptian style steeply "battered" like the great outer barrier. John B. has his hand on the Number 7 joist: "It's nawt a castle; it's a city."

"Whatever it is," says Bob, "it's beautiful." He means it and his sincerity embraces both boys, they come together in the sound of their father's word.

"Whatever it is," says Robby, "it's a castle."

Still squatting in the space between the sand construction and the beams, Bob looks up again at the man on the nubble. "*It's* a city too."

"I said it's a castle," says Robby. And then as John B. says, "It's a city," in four stamps Robby levels the buildings, kicking down the outer wall for good measure.

"Gawd damn you!" shouts John B.'s high voice and with his palm he claps the end of the Number 7 beam, which pivots on the flat slant of Number 8 so the other end turns smartly into

Bob's temple and he tips right over onto the wreckage of the city-castle. His hand doesn't move to his head, he doesn't move.

Robby is lifting Bob's head and John B. is running in a sort of sideways dance away from his father and nearer Petty, who, up to her hips, turns and rushes powerfully out of the water and runs to Bob.

The man is leaving the nubble for his Land Rover, and as the radial line between us because of his motion sweeps across the family scene at the edge of the tough beachgrass, I am able to move swiftly. Bob is out cold.

When Hugh Blood and Bob got into an argument between stickball innings, I stepped between them and shoved Hugh. It was over an issue of fact which, despite what our English book at Poly said, is always more gripping than a matter of opinion because you know the true truth is there waiting. Hugh said his argument was with Bob not me, but we all knew he'd never try anything with Bob and I just stood facing him. It was the year before we graduated, so it must have been Saturday or Sunday—probably Sunday because we'd have been at Poly for practice almost any other afternoon. It was either DiMaggio's record streak or the walls of Babylon, games or miles, I forget. And after Hugh did not shove back, Bob said let's let Joey settle it. So Bohack Joey must have been there, so it couldn't have been Sunday, and as I shall explain later it must have been before May. And it must have been DiMaggio not Babylon. And for a moment, here moving surely to Bob's unconscious side lying on the ruins of Robby's castle, I have moved all too swiftly to his white-knuckled fist which ultimately Joey Neurohr's mouth and spine sought and found. Today Joey is in a real estate agent's on Cobble Hill and if we met we wouldn't dare speak. Joey had the right answer—I wondered how Hugh could even imagine it was fifty-*four*—and then Bob, as if Joey were *about* to give the answer he'd *already* given, said to all of us, "Joey knows." And Joey knew he'd been rooked again somehow and he sneered a grin and went off on his bike-cart.

As the nubble man backs around I think of asking him to help us and take Bob down that next crescent of beach to the island's one short road that bends past the general store and ends smack at the ferry landing.

Bob is coming around. I don't know how long it's been, I don't wear a watch. Dom, what is happening here is beside time. Bob has gone yellow. Petty holds his shoulders back but he pulls up and stands. And then without having time to bend forward he vomits yellow all over himself.

So we're all five of us going back to the mainland tonight but not before Bob swims it off; and then I pole him out to the Brandeis professor's lobster pot but to get enough we start the motor and go out to Bob's own buoys, while Petty watches from the beach, arms akimbo. Bob is remote. Petty watches us haul up the wood cages. The small lobster is too small to take and of the four others one is missing a claw; we take them all. There's little talking at supper, Petty isn't happy. The beach is ours.

Back on Route One she's at the wheel.

We'll cut to Bob's living room, the boys in bed, John B. with a sore behind to go with his sore hand.

"No, I'm all right," Bob calls going out through the kitchen to the bathroom.

"Listen," I ask Petty quietly, "*did* you ever tell Bob what I told you about Al and Gail in Heatsburg? The quarry?"

"Oh yes, maybe; yes, years ago. Maybe the same day *you* told me. I went out with Bob all those summers. I used to tell him everything. But before I wrote you that silly letter last week he'd just been talking about that very thing, which must be why I mentioned it to you."

So I learn even more than I wanted. He told Petty I mixed emotion with biology, and why get mixed up in a ploy to a girl that compromised my friendship with a guy?, but it's water under the dam, and Petty said she thought all that about emotion and biology was typical Bob.

But ask for reproof and you'll get it.

Bob has a fresh bourbon when he comes back. His forehead has been rubbed and there are still some drops in his hair in front.

Petty is worried about him and wanted to cancel the two couples Bob phoned as soon as we got home, bump on his head and all.

Bob is almost eager for me to meet Leo and Irish. I find I can't imagine them. Why can't I?

I ask Bob, Have they children? Yes, a girl three, a boy two, and something on the way. Do they come to the island? Yes, of course they come; say have you read Beckett? Only his novels, I reply. Well, *I've* only read his plays, but—now the seismic pause, and Petty frowns, she's had a hard day; she murmurs Which plays did he *write* besides—Ben Sedgwick and I talked this out all night last May after they did *Krapp's Last Tape* at the church: by *Jesus* he's a religious writer, Beckett. Bob's guest is tired. Final things maybe, I say, but *things,* just *things.* Bob shakes the same head that commended Joey and got badly hit this afternoon: *No* s'r, I think you've got a problem...no two ways about it, Beckett's religious, why he's God-obsessed. He seeks him because he's found Him, that's how Father Sedgwick puts it. It's a problem of commitment, Cy, commitment.

Do I hear tires on gravel? "Was it a castle or a city this afternoon?" I ask Petty.

Bob says, "Which said which?"

"John B. said a city," I answer. Do I hear a car motor die?

Petty sighs. "And Robby said a castle."

"I know, I know," Bob says. He looks at me, Dom, and I feel Al behind me, and Bob says slowly, "I just don't *love* them the same. John B. is more lovable. I don't love Robby as much."

We're silent, and then Bob claps his hands to his eyes. He is weeping.

He jumps up and with one hand holding his distorted face he rushes out through the kitchen, and Petty follows him. A door shuts, probably the bathroom.

The bell goes, Dom. My great-aunt Sue said a terrible thing once when I wouldn't kiss her after she'd taken me to a double-feature. But though my other great-aunt Kate looked over her crossword at me and said, "Nonsense, he's a lamb," I took it to heart and got to work thinking about it.

The bell goes? No, not your buzzer. (I took a break for orange juice, I drank it right out of the carton and topped it off with some flaky halibut which besides a half-consumed coffee yogurt was the only other thing in the strangely personal interior of your old medium-size icebox.) No indeed, I've heard not a thing since the four feet passed, or were they the future and my icebox raid further past than I know? Middle-class life goes on.

I don't care how much you were looking forward to your son Richard's next letter (as it began by saying you'd said), believe me most of it was punitive decoration. The core was that you ought to lay off: take Dorothy back, who he said looked better than ever having lost weight living apart from you; get back to your "long-term" writing and your "hobbies," which I assume include that light, fat styrofoam pastoral crowded in front of the bookcase between window and screen tripod; stop trying (he said with a shade of mere intimacy) to throw yourself against odds into the maelstrom of this country's kitsch doom (or was it "century's"?); and get to the barber at once. "For it isn't necessary to *try* every life you imagine in order to be one on whom nothing is lost."

Ten big days in jail right on top of your ejection from that Jackson hotel interrupted your private investigation of the Mississippi Mystery and left you visibly weakened but visually more vivid. In jail, time is very different, you told reporters. Who smirked, no doubt recalling that the hotel management hadn't had to lean toothpicks up against your door to know that you and your secretary used only one of the two rooms you booked.

What odds would Richard have given that you'd bump yourself off? I made sure you didn't get enervating letters from an actuary who reads James, happens to be your son, and loathes the phone.

To keep on top of your mail yet be at those public exhibitions of yours that I foresaw would be significant, I had to play percentage. So from Mississippi I didn't go direct to Point Mugu to start the March, but flew here to check.

From your daughter Lila's note I learned that during the week at the end of which the Anti-Abstraction March would hit Santa Barbara she and her husband would be in San Francisco. Their address was in the Mission District with friends. Why not in a hotel? (Well now I'm going to stop in Melbourne with *retired* friends on the way to Naples where I'll put up with an old *friend*— if she'll put up with *me!*—whence I mean to combine a look at Tamiami Canal (I know a skipper with a side-trip to look up a full-blooded Seminole Al served with in Ike's Coast Guard).) And plainly, Dom, Lila hoped you would call on them there at their *friends'* in Frisco when your March was over. Her husband's drug therapy conference would end Friday but they'd stay on hoping you'd fly up. (Prudential provisions! Thursday afternoon we leave the St. Francis conference early to meet some friends who want us to see an ancient site; then sunset and sweet-and-sour duck with Sam, did you ever meet Sam?, he's a beautiful old man—sort of everybody's uncle: then early to bed 'cause Friday's a big day.) But then for some reason Lila and husband came on downstate instead of waiting for you to come up, and were suddenly right in front of me in your open-air audience when through your bull-horn you startled Darla Fasinelli's crowd with that veiled gamble, what I called earlier tonight a "risky trick," a "gappy calculus." Lila's plump spouse turned to stare around, and whether or not his eyes found mine he seemed fed up.

"We came here," you called, "not really to penetrate a Think-Tank but to confront ourselves. Not till the missile-man finds himself on the end of his own vector, no not till the pickers became the growers"—here a dramatic shift to grapes—"will you get what you think you're seeking with your boycotts and your marches. I found as I wended my way from breakfast to teatime in a gentle curve up the coast" (you didn't on this word veer into your brogue), "that this march is itself an abstraction. So whyn't you kids become capitalists and change things."

Well in the space between the Marxist pap and the black-capitalism-for-white-kids stood a charge of paradox that Darla first (through 180 degrees) cheered, then in her *Manhattan Hash* column next week attacked as the "threadbare neo-conservatism" of a would-be body-contact head who was "ultimately" little more than an "artist." (Her personally asterisked footnote: "See his minor styrofoams said to be in private collections in Boston, Salt Lake, New York, and the legendary preserve of a rancher-recluse in extreme northeast Montana.")

But I saw your greatness as your will to interrupt yourself, to be a hero who would not de-oscillate the dialectic. (And yet, Dom, oh the Field-Truth that sometimes seems to surround!) At Cora's you interrupted my remark about space by gazing past me.

At your climactic equations your patronizing son-in-law the doctor shook his head in despair. Their cameras on straps round their strong tan necks, he and Lila turned to go and they parted to pass either side of me but as if they didn't see me, which I found peculiarly pleasurable. You called those equations the beginning of a science called Structural Activism—"which," you added, "is a bit different from a hard-on on a boycott, Darla."

I could have added a twist of humor to my mouth to honor Lila and her husband's voluntarily entering my Dom-scope and staring at me in total ignorance of who I was; but I couldn't, because your equations suddenly so restructured my priorities that I had to review my Force-Field. That is, I found in your ABC's reason to think I better crystallize your kinship with me. Silence accumulated as through your bullhorn you slowly said, "The relation between altruism and balls will always be to that between collaboration and division exactly the reverse of what the relation of Art or Babel to Commitment is to that between Collaboration and Commitment." (My father would ask for a paraphrase.)

Simplified in my secret Centrifuge, and subjected there to certain separations and simulated gravities, this equation of yours I saw could mean that as the gap between Bob and Al closed, the one between you and me would widen. Which confirmed me in my long-time preference for keeping Al and Bob apart.

Yet I knew even then what my step-son Ted was to mean when he later said he was trying to buck rid of dialectic. He, if not Betsy, may have sensed a similar trap of forces when after canceling their appointment or appointments they left the doctor's building and as they came onto that leaf-gray sidewalk Ted spied their doctor reading the newspaper in his car up the street. That night Ted shrugged and said to Ev, "Well it was your friend recommended him," and Ev without thinking said to me, "Hugh Blood's *your* old friend, not mine," and Ted said gently, "Oh that shrink's more interested in research." Downstairs Ev may be washing her face and thinking what to do next. Emma's speaking in her sleep, reviewing her day, the red light we had to wait at when I was in a hurry to get home, and the things we saw while waiting for the light to turn—she is dreaming of her dad, who seems to be expanding the old parabolic course he follows among his disturbances. But the red light doesn't turn green, the red light goes off and the green goes on.

My parents were good. I could ask them almost anything. I didn't ask about the terrible thing Sue had said, that I'd been a beast all covered with hair at birth and I was still a beast sometimes. My parents didn't try to divide me, I soon knew I was the only one. One

Saturday in June of '39 or '40 a moment after I'd been telling Al
and Gail that I wasn't my parents' real kid because I'd been changed
at the hospital, my father came around the house and heard me say
that because my head was so big when I was born my mom couldn't
have any more pups. My father took me aside later and could not
explain exactly why he hadn't liked the way I put it, but anyway he
didn't like the "pups" part. Any more than I like transitions. Gail was
emphatic: "*Course* she can have more." But Al loyally said, "Cripes,
he oughta know." May Emma's dreams always show legged, armed,
smiling anatomies, not the linenfold abstracts facing Tracy's young-
est when that tan, listless, suburban child opens her coloring book,
while her mother—phoning me for the first time in years—tells me
she's worried about her brother Hugh and can I recommend a psychiatrist. There is time, though no need, for Emma to come someday
to her father's terrible delight in the Force-Field. Its overpopulated
commonwealth of distances can be ruled only in the exercise of a rare
gift. This consists in that ripe triangle arcing between (a) the poly-
linked Pons Varolii, (b) the point in the Spinal Bulb where winking
is controlled, and (c) a point so perfectly between the cerebral hemi-
spheres as to be of neither. This gift, insofar as it is embodied within
the body, I have named the Vectoral Muscle, and I'm beginning to
feel that it is not at home with dialectic. "If you mean," says my father, "just thinking in twos, why not say so?"

"We were getting grass on the picture," said Al, ending his story
and stopping in his skivvies to look out the third-floor window of
the room he rented with two other sailors who were generally out
on weather patrol when Al's cutter was in.

"What's grass?" I asked, still feeling the bear hug I'd given long
lost Gail; and Gail answered for Al: interference lines on the radar-
scope reflecting electronic noise. "Hey," she said to Hal, "where'd
you get *that*?," a dark blue blazer with gold buttons.

"We can't change on the ship," Al said. "In the public library here
if you're in your blues people look at you, and you can't concentrate."

He's begun memorizing poems from a paperback treasury and he reads world almanacs. This small northeast coast city is the same one Bob and Petty will move to the outskirts of a year from now, the living room on the mainland, the island camp a few years later.

"But why not tailor-mades?" said Gail. She rolled her eyes and grinned sweetly. "They're pretty."

"You got to if you don't wear civvies," said Al. "The regulation blues'r like overalls, and tailor-mades don't cost so much but they cost enough. We split the rent three ways, it's only ten bucks a month, so don't give me a hard time."

"*I'm* not saying anything," said Gail, and asked about linen.

I asked her how she knew about radar. It was late afternoon, October, I hadn't seen Gail for three years at least, probably not since the start of Al's hitch.

"I'm the one he writes," she said. "Besides you."

"If you're not saying anything," Al kept at her, "tell me which of your brothers is paying your hotel room this weekend?"

"*I* should phone for a room," I said, but I knew Gail's hotel would be half empty.

We watched Al tie his big cordovans, putting one foot and then the other up on the straight chair. Then he pulled on pressed khakis tucking in the tails of his white Oxford button-down.

"My *only* brother, if you must know," Gail said to Al and got off the bed.

He kissed her on the lips. "Well *you* know what I mean, Ab."

Their father's phlebitis had him in and out of bed, and the leg got so bad he'd been in the hospital but there was nothing to be done for it. Al was out of touch with home; Gail worked in Boston and wasn't sure if she cared about his not writing home but was sure how she cared about him. He'd been to Boston, but this was her first time here.

"Daddy's been impossible, and I do know what you mean. Why *shouldn't* you enjoy yourself when you're not putting in five weeks on

station. Those other two you share with haven't got it as good being
on the same ship. You got this place all to yourself."

"The landlady won't let us have girls up." Al looked at me and
added, "Not with square heels anyhow."

Gail sat back down. "What about me?"

"I told her my sister was coming this weekend."

"I can imagine what she thought." Gail sat very straight on the
bed; she was half-turned toward me. She wore a brown tweed suit,
her trenchcoat lay over her gray-and-blue plaid suitcase on a chair.
She'd done a little too much with her hair.

This is getting out of hand, Dom; to simplify, we'll leave the
plaid case behind.

Well, Crazy Annette was waiting for us in an upstairs Chinese
place just a stone's throw, Al said, from the library. I thought she'd
had a few, even allowing for the notorious whimsy that accounted
for her uproarious nickname with the Coast Guard. On the other
hand, to those boys from Florida and Georgia she wasn't just another
Mainiac, she was oddly, though too oddly, pretty, and she was pretty
smart. At seventeen her dark moist eyes seemed to have been
enlarged not by Nature but by daydreaming or hypnosis. "She reads
Fitzgerald," Al said the other weekend I'd come up. Her father was a
policeman. Gail of course hadn't met her, and Annette, sitting down
opposite Gail, made much of me. When we'd met two months ago
we'd expatiated on my astrological sign. Her father subscribed to a
six-dollar-a-year horoscope. Now, with a quick little hello to Gail,
Annette touching my shoulder and wrist several times gave me a
repetitive account of why I was entering a hazardous period. I would
not be able to rely on friends—she ticked off my situation, touched
my leg with her finger—I'd have to be "circumspect" or I'd lose a
position I'd worked hard to reach. Annette was a bit breathless and
kept eying Gail and punctuating her nonsense about Leos with little
laughs of relief. When the waitress came and was enthusiastically
introduced by Al to Gail and me as having gone to Annette's high

school, Al ordered the Number Four Family for us. I didn't smell alcohol on Annette, but when Al said again that the Number Four was a little bit of everything and this was a good good place and I drily murmured, "This looks like a great place" as I caught the noncommittal eye of a possibly Hawaiian sailor I suspected was a shipmate of Al's, Annette got the giggles and didn't stop even when she put her head on my shoulder.

"Why," said I, "'a most sweet wench,' 'the honey of Hybla'"; in one of my letters a year or two ago I'd told Al we were studying *Henry IV.* Al smiled at Annette but unconvincingly.

"Where's Hybla?" asked Gail.

"Who knows?" I said. "Mythical or made up."

The waitress set down a pink-flowered teapot and Al poured too soon, and the tea was pale and Gail poured the cup back before he could stop her ("No no"). Without looking at me, he said, "It's in Sicily."

"Not really," I said, "not *now.*"

Annette said, "I just want to know is it good or bad," and giggled.

Ignoring her, Al said to me, "'O thou hast done much harm upon me; before I knew thee, I knew nothing, and now am I, if a man should speak truly, little better than one of the wicked.' It's in Sicily."

He hadn't overlooked Annette's queer spark, and it seemed he hadn't figured out if he was showing Gail off to Crazy Annette or letting his farflung sister Gail share his seaport life even if the port wasn't Boston.

Gail was asking Annette if she'd miss Portland next year when she went to the State University in Orono, while I said to Al I ceded to his superior knowledge and stood corrected and he said it was the story of his life but interrupted himself—*and* Annette—to say to Gail (whose high-teased hair seemed too grown-up) that Annette really had it upstairs and would do well at college, the guys on the ship had her all wrong and called her crazy you know just because she had so many smarts and didn't know what she was going to say next to those rebs fresh out of high school.

But Al heard a wheedling "Ann*e*-*e*tte" and it was a second Hawaiian Coast Guardsman who'd sat down with the first. She said, "Hi, Earl," and Al said quietly to Gail, "Ward-room stewards, I got no use for them." The two stewards giggled at something and ordered without looking at the menu the waitress held out to them.

As clearly as I see you, Dom, I hear my step-son Ted patiently say, "But you had an *idea* in keeping these friends apart, didn't you? It wasn't just that you thought they wouldn't get along. And if they took patronizing views of each other, so what?" So it's lucky I never told him about Al and Bob.

But you, Dom, would not interrupt with two such questions, Ted's second derived of course from a set of coördinates other than mine. You cannot; but you would not. Any more than your cased screen above its tripod would interrupt me—or your library—or your phone off the hook, or your list of excuses above it, including the haphazard addition EARTH = SPACECRAFT. You see what I'm trying to do. Because you see the gap between Al and Bob and the kinship system between you and me.

But your forbearance deserves an answer. No, I wasn't in that provincial city with the main street of a town merely to cheer up one of Our Boys, however remote his stake in Korea. And if I say, with due mildness, that I *study* Friendship, don't think my weekend lacked a prudential point. I was just as glad Al was still seeing Annette, because in her rambling reading and her real and wrong sense of her absurdity she was independent.

Or was until faced by me my first visit six weeks before. That Saturday noon for an hour or so Al excused himself. The librarian was lending him a Latin grammar. Annette and I ended down by the Station and my hotel having spaghetti. "You're the one who told him about the encyclopedia, what an encyclopedia!, what a friend!, you should be ashamed of yourself, if *I* had an encyclopedia like his

I'd turn it into a pill and swallow it but I wouldn't swallow you. The way he talks, you're his best friend. Is that right?"

But what she'd settled down to say afterward was what had made me mosey back now for this October weekend, and Gail had come unexpectedly. When the four of us left the High Asia at seven-thirty it was too early to go to the librarian's, where Al had gotten us invited, so we went to a bar and sat in a corner in a semi-circular seat, and I wondered how to talk to Annette.

For during that lunch in August just before Al's little white ship pulled out for Argentia, she'd shown me something. Her voice rose playfully, "Well now what *about* that crazy encyclopedia?" She said Al kept it in sick bay because he didn't have room in his footlocker. He read it in sick bay and he and the Corpsman would smoke their pipes. But "you used to be his best friend," she said, "you must know why he's so crazy on the subject."

I knew his father tried to make him take the encyclopedia back where he bought it and I knew a lot more about those twelve abridged volumes. But from Annette I learned that his father had been so mad at Al for spending twenty-two dollars that, bad leg and all, he'd got out of his chair and in two trips carried all but the last two volumes out to his pickup, he was going to take the encyclopedia back to Caesar Bemis at the Old Blacksmith Shop. Listening to Annette I forgot and with my fork in my soup spoon I wound too much spaghetti to get into my mouth. "But when his father was coming back for the last two—which Al always says were One and Two—Al couldn't stand any more drama and ran out and *un*loaded six volumes and started back into the house, and they bumped shoulder-to-shoulder and his father claimed to have wrenched his leg. Al told me this three, four times, and it's a scream till the end but then he's different."

What the hell. So he brooded over his defense; we all do. It was his money, and if, granted, I was the one who told him I'd seen the encyclopedia at Bemis's and that it was a fair encyclopedia and a

fair price—though I didn't know then what the price would be—
nobody made Al pay twenty-two bucks for it. No one made his
father buy a bottle of whiskey at the Heatsburg Pharmacy that
night and get drunk in his chair and say things Al swore he'd never
forget. No, what stuck in my mind was something else he'd told
Annette, and it didn't come out till I was paying the cashier (while
Annette palmed a pack of spearmint lifesavers), and then Annette
said, "Written inside the cover of Volume One was something
like—'Happy Birthday from Uncle Cooley, August 1942.' Al says
he always wondered about—who it was, who was it?, someone else's
life, *whose* life?, what kind of people?—and then there's something
in a different hand in the last volume he's been trying to make out;
he made an educated guess, but..."

I told the Italian woman to take out a nickel, and then Annette
and I walked back up Congress, through Longfellow Square to the
Public Library right by the State, and you know, Dom, that if I chose
I could tell you what was playing that night at the State, just as I
could tell you the color of Annette's beret and the exact length of
the exciting run up her stocking—"my hose!"—that she discovered
entering the main reading room.

From the High Asia you approach the library not from Union
Station but the other way; but when Annette, Gail, Al, and I came
down to the street we turned not left toward the library but right, in
the general direction of the docks if we'd gone far enough. We took
the fork at the lower square and as fast as it takes to think it, found
ourselves in a bar around the corner from Sears, Roebuck.

A fat boatswain's mate off the buoy tender called from the bar
and Al asked why they'd been out the middle of last night—"not
losin' ya buoys, ah ya?"—and the boatswain's mate said a dragger
had radioed in for a tow. Al said lucky it wasn't the herring steamer,
and Boats said Oh we pulled more than her. He wanted to come
over and see Gail and Annette but when the introduction to that
"Oh My Papa" trumpet solo blared out and three of Al's very

young shipmates came away from the juke box, their uniform cuffs folded back to show the green and orange dragons sewn inside, Al terminated his exchange with the older man at the bar and put his arm around Gail.

"I never *saw* the sea till I enlisted."

"Yes you did," I said, "once going to Fenway."

"Oh yes." He raised a hand off the table and dropped it in acquiescence. Suddenly he seemed not really glad to see anyone tonight—polite but sad.

"Only coming *in*. Because on the way out you and I had a fierce argument. Tex Hughson won his thirteenth that day, shut out the A's on three hits."

Dancing would have helped, but there wasn't any. Al wanted to go to the librarian's house but it was only eight and he didn't want to be even a minute early. Gail was telling Annette about her job working for the Boston representative of a Washington hotel, and how she went to B.U. two nights and was waiting to go to stewardess school. Her fingernails were painted the cleanest pink. Annette put her hand on Al's.

I was back not quite so far as the encyclopedia. I'm quite a fair geographer. After the accident in '48 there was no more talk about the Pittsburgh tryout, only a note from the Pirate front office that Al should get in touch when he was ready again, and they'd see. The scout may have heard the truth from someone at the Heatsburg Legion. Gail wrote me that their father got on Al pretty badly over that accident even with insurance, and Al merely said it was kind of late for his father to be interesting himself in baseball. Al blew his two-hundred-dollar bonus that winter; then he'd suddenly graduated, and that summer he waited on at the inn.

He spend the winter bartending in Florida. One day I got a Metropolitan Museum card postmarked Cape May, New Jersey, where Al was a Coast Guard boot beginning a four-year hitch.

I couldn't speak privately to Annette on the way over to the librarian's either, nor during our not entirely happy evening there. So I'll simply have to tell you, Dom. Or what's relevant, anyway. Over my left shoulder is that giant painting of your face which I need not describe; but I would like to know what time it is. I had indeed told Al there was an encyclopedia at the Old Blacksmith Shop; and partly because I hadn't been around most of that summer of '45, I had a hunch he'd quietly act on my information. He was making six dollars a day suckering corn. I did indeed say that if I hadn't another in Brooklyn I'd buy it myself. As you've probably guessed, my Uncle Coolidge had given it to me for my twelfth birthday, if you've been paying attention to the dates I've mentioned so far tonight in this more and more comfortable living room. But now, three summers later I'd sold the frigging books to Caesar Bemis before I knew Cooley was coming up the next weekend (which as it happened he'd forgotten was my birthday), and I knew that even in a mellow state at two-thirty in the afternoon he wouldn't leave the Old Blacksmith Shop till he'd seen every last thing there from the eighteenth-century well-sweep Caesar had across the rafters the length of the main room, to the last blue bottle in the last of the four dark corners. So it would be wrong to judge me in any clear sense responsible for the blow-up between Al and his dad. Not that you would.

Al was easy with people and after he got out of high school he liked a drink. Bartending in Daytona and Miami seemed to come easy. But his charm with customers was sometimes jolly pedantry which in turn made him interrupt his own view of them and despise them not always secretly for "graduating college" without having read a book. On the *Barataria*, where he was transferred about the time I got my B.A. he was called by two Georgia boys in his berthing compartment "Professor." He spent a month's Search and Rescue in St. George, Bermuda, reading my copy of Breasted, yet if his letters suggest that at sea when not on radar watch he studied German down on the messdeck with the Chief Electronics Technician from whom he began by learning the Greek alphabet, and discussed the Founding Fathers and early American landscape painting with the funny, spoiled little Reserve ensign from Richmond who had a box of oils in his stateroom on the boatdeck, Al if I know him at all spent as much time as I would have at the rail following the sea's gray molten life. Unlike Bob, he never tried to hide the difference between what he thought he wanted and what he thought he was, except to insist on this "story of my life" a bit hard. He never knew it wasn't honesty of that kind I wanted from a friend. I rarely trust a man's account of his own weaknesses, but my doubt may itself be a weakness and on this Ted grimly agreed one night having just come from his three-credit Group Dynamics where they'd all finally gotten "to" the one married woman who they'd all sensed had been holding out on them—and it had been horrible and wonderful, Ted said. Al got looped one night in New London when he was at radar school across the river in Groton, and he failed to make it to Mystic, where I was staying with Tracy Blood. He was lucky the bartender was a moonlighting cop who was impressed by Al's Pirate tryout and didn't want the two OCS boys to get into trouble because of their fight in which over some matter of collegiate fact Al intervened. But at two in the morning back in Groton Al broke into the mess hall and took a half-gallon can of peanut butter, and for this, though he didn't short out of radar school, he got a captain's mast. So three weeks later he *really* couldn't make the weekend party Tracy and I had at her parents' so-called farm.

By the time he got transferred from Norfolk to Maine and a ship full of Georgia farm boys who'd never had it so good, he was wondering what he'd been thinking of in '49 enlisting for four years. On the ship a favorite remark about him which, he wrote me, he couldn't be bothered after a while to contradict, was that he'd had two years of college: because of his encyclopedia and getting through a few USAFI German lessons with the Chief ET who came from near Galveston, Al was supposed (yes) to have had Two Years of College (the phrase went), always Two Years, something to do with requirements for state cop or some insurance training program or some state college aggie qualification.

Well, Dom, I did my farming in Bucks County, Pennsylvania, and don't you forget it. Six almost solid weeks, and so did Bob.

My letters helped Al. In port the ensign from Richmond went to Boone's wharfside lobster house with the exec or a Bowdoin cousin, or he was playing tennis at Prout's Neck. Gail's jibes about money that October weekend late in Al's hitch were just her way of letting him know she understood. He did the best he could on Saturday afternoons not to leave the Public Library. It was where he really wanted to be, but to stay there was like some key abstinence. He browsed. When he walked the streets it was a city; he was living in a city. Not like liberty in Norfolk, when he didn't know yet what he was going to try to get, and where he'd never quite slipped beyond the dragging enclosure of the sailor circuit. Nor like those cramped, soiling sojourns in a bus to get to New York for a stupidly random set of beginnings interrupted by the loneliness that forces boredom— during which I was rarely *in* New York and Al had no idea what he'd say to my parents if he got them on the phone except (say) that he was going to see the Unicorn tomorrow morning. Perhaps dull Portland was the right site for the meditative end of a certain attenuated loneliness that I now see may have arisen those early summers when he and I were the simplest of friends.

Leaving the ship he gave the Blue Moon on Commercial a miss. Ditto the shipmates there, who poured down eight or ten gassy drafts as soon as they got off the ship, then went up town and ate cheeseburgers and french fries at the chrome-tuned skirt-and-sweater center just below Congress Square, but after all that beer they weren't fresh enough to do more than clamp their fresh white hats over their brows and trudge up to the movies and drowse for three reckless hours before making it back to State Pier for a night's sleep. Once he did get caught in the Moon and had to act. But as a rule, it was up India Street to Congress, then the curving length of Congress—I'm boring my*self*, Dom, but maybe not that little pre-Annette student nurse from the boondocks who liked Al too much and, he told me, had worked for E.B. White's family one summer—yes, and I'm no nearer Bob's white-knuckled fist and my stolen Corona junior—all the way, yes, along Congress (he bought his mother a wool stole in Porteous, Mitchell & Braun) up and then down the main municipal hill: past the High Asia, the bus terminal, the Columbia Hotel and its lounge patronized by local magnates and visiting salesmen (Al too, when he was feeling he'd like some authentic service), down past the stale hotel he stayed in during the liberties before he and the two yeomen from the Coos Bay splurged on the tree-screened room on Franklin Street.

It seems such a distance from the delicate raisin moles below Gail's immortal collar bone, while Gail says to Annette (as in the October night they start up the librarian's porch steps, then step aside hoping Al will go first, but I do), "I want to have at least three, maybe four"—

Such a seeming distance to those close coördinate diagrams joining me to Bob on one hand and Al on the other, or to my parents, or to Al and his father, or to Tracy and her prodigal legs, or to Bob and the former Perpetua Pound whose court-tennis-curating "pappy" (the tidy-minded author of monographs on Ryder, Marin, and Dallin) once urged my father to enter me at Groton and who herself was delivered of a third boy the Easter of 1960. Well, must the custodian always contemplate the secret things he protects? And I am no almanac.

But I know that the polio epidemic in the Newtown, Pennsylvania area came right around the Japanese surrender. In our dorm at the family "camp" Bob and I were ready to take on four yokels from Philly over whether or not the Japs would give up, and the tall basketball big shot had called me a damn New York son of a bitch and said I didn't know a Jap from a Jew, the Japs wouldn't give up while there was two of them alive, it was too fucking bad that B25 last week hadn't completely destroyed the Empire State, and Bob and I had moved close to the tall one when his chocolate-milk-drinking friend with bad breath who'd come here straight from a Presbyterian conference at Lafayette and had his bureau drawers stuffed neatly full of Westminster Fellowship hand-outs, said to the tall one, "Don't use language, Hank, there's no need to use language." But how else can I get up past the librarian's amicable porch pillars and through his outer door, his vestibule, his inner door, and through the evening to perhaps Annette and one thing she may know? How can I without damning myself? I don't ask for any help, though. Not for the phone number of her waitress schoolmate Maureen whose father is a telephone lineman; not, Dom, for your instant excuses posted above the phone box here; certainly not for some vile transition, though I might end your phone's endless busy signal tonight and resourcefully take whatever voice first calls. After all, that false busy signal quarantines our space tonight, Dom. And our time, too. Recalling suddenly years later that nasty Barataria Bay incident in the Blue Moon, Al tips down the last of a martini. He's on a crowded, smoky lawn and he says into his smiling wife's ear that if you leave out the prefix the Greek root of "epidemic" means "people." But now he wheels laughing toward someone—"*I heard that*"—and his wife takes his arm and says loud enough, "We have to go, dear," which was what he wanted her to say. A flashbulb blinks in the corner of his eye, a colleague's engaged daughter gently screams; again the flash cube flares, the hostess says, "Gotcha, Allie," and Al shields his profile with his large brown hand then turns to his chronicling hostess—and his wife sees he's decided not to go quite yet.

When I shook your hand at the opening last week and couldn't hear if the hostess said "Dom" or "Don," I told you I'd had an odd sense about your suicide book, to which you too quickly replied (winking over my shoulder at someone) that some of the critics had had an odd sense too. The runner-up for Miss Utah materialized at my elbow and gave you a floppy, vinyl-lined canvas goblet, saying, "One Topaz Neon," and you shrugged. Then later, as I was looking at a styrofoam much like this one of yours here, you were dragged away to a party in Harlem by your former girlfriend the beautiful archaeologist Kit Carbon. You keep late hours. But one evening a week, namely tonight, you're apt to be home.

The atom bombs didn't make much impression on the big basketball player. Maybe they din't remind him of anything. He doubted the Japs would surrender but he was concerned with the nightly game in the gym, where he hipped anybody that came near the key and even though I hit seven times from outside he spent a very satisfying two hours being fed the ball by his friends from Philly. Early in the morning the local farmers let the camp office know how many, and often which, boys were needed; and when I was in the same group as tall-ass I heard nothing all day long but his belly-aching judgments. I was there that summer because Bob's father had told mine, and my father thought it would be an education. Bob was sent because his parents knew of the famous Quaker boarding school where the camp was located; to Bob's mother the tennis courts and ivied dorms made a reassuring base from which to make each morning's foray against the acres of rutabagas and carrot weeds, though Bob was there because he wanted the hardest possible work to toughen him up for the Poly wrestling team. Evenings over that heavy rich earth were dull. No one cared when you got back so long as you got up for work in the morning. We hitched to a fair one Wednesday night. I met a fine girl in a gypsy skirt and one of those loose blouses with the embroidered yolk. Eventually Bob left, and I walked her two miles home to her farmer-father's dark dewy back yard. I was unnecessarily afraid of knocking her up.

Well, the basketball player, who'd been at the camp the summer before, kept saying day after day he was waiting for the tomatoes, that was where the money was. But he didn't make it, and neither did I. One gray August morning he and I and two others went in the back of a pickup to weed an acre or two of something green and heavy, I forget what. And the big leaves were so wet the six-five potentially all-state center called the conditions brutal and walked off the job with the two others. When I went on bending my muddy way through the rest of my first row, thinking I knew what was coming, the big shot as I expected started calling to me that I was a gung ho chicken shit afterbirth of a Japanese gang fuck, a coward and a traitor, and the other two told me I better stop work if I didn't want to get them all in trouble, and the tall one said they were going to notify the authorities the conditions we were made to work in and he said something I couldn't hear about the tomatoes coming in, but when I said Nobody's making you work in these conditions, he started in on me again, and then I stood up at the end of my row, my Levis wet from the knee down and told him he was too dumb to do even this job much less pick ripe tomatoes piece-rate, and then he started toward me. He looked even taller there diagonally across the rows because you knew he wouldn't step on the plants, and I started walking toward him, though indirectly down my row. But there was the farmer in his roomy overalls marching a long pigeon-toed stride down from the house with his little girl bustling beside him. He said if we wouldn't work, there was plenty fellows would at one-fifty an hour, and anyhow he didn't want our foul mouths on his property for his little girl to hear, and when I turned to go back to my rows he said, "You too, Charlie," and that was the end of that, I wasn't going to explain. It was eight-fifteen, a Thursday. The start of a long morning of a long day, especially since the head of the camp told me I'd have to pack my bag. He said he wouldn't send a letter home to my parents but for public relation's sake I had to go. Well, I wasn't about to explain.

Richard your actuary son didn't wish to explain either, though in a way he did and in a way he couldn't. Well, ye gods I couldn't protect you by monitoring your own outgoing phone calls! But Richard's most recent missive said enough for me to know: "you shouldn't have phoned like that": in your present state "a composed letter is to be preferred to an accusing person-to-person call at midnight. And that is not true about not receiving my letters. I *have* written you. And you *have received* them." Then a quiet, abrupt "Yours ever" (and percentally appraising), "Dick."

The odds (a local weekly said) against "contracting" polio that August at the farm camp were considerable. But even more considerable that my parents would hear the news. But they didn't. So they didn't call me home, but by coincidence I'd been kicked out so I was coming home anyhow. Bob's father's message was waiting for Bob that Thursday when he arrived from a ten-dollar day pulling rutabagas; he was to leave at once, train to Easton, then through New York and on up to Providence where he'd be met. He wired his father there was no train that night.

We had a ride the next day with one of the assistants—Doc— who was eighteen and going home to the Cape to be drafted; we'd cross the Delaware well south of Easton and save time. Of course, I phoned my father who was in New York, and he was stunned about the polio and said leave tonight, no don't travel at night, leave first thing in the morning, he'd call my mother in the country; he added irrelevantly that my uncle was coming from Washington the weekend after this. My father was scared; I didn't tell him we were driving. Doc said he had a heavy date in Hartsville and in the morning we'd leave as soon as he could get himself up.

He was liverish in the morning and farted during the whole trip. He knew about my getting booted, I didn't tell him the truth. And Dom, you know that if I chose to forget my timetable for getting the truth out of Annette while Al and the librarian were in the kitchen, I could ramble over to the echoing Quaker gym for that two-hour unrefereed valedictory that night in which on me but more conclusively on the potential all-state big-ass it was proved that basketball is a body-contact sport in spite of what Al's librarian friend said in '52.

"Any friend of hisn's a friend of myun," said the librarian's scruffy friend the goateed bookseller Fred Eagle hauling himself out of his chair and shaking hands with me and bowing to the girls. The stubble on his cheeks was a day or two long, his gray hair looked like a six-or-eight-week-old crew cut. He was somewhere between thirty-nine and fifty, and above little blue pufflets his wild eyes restlessly watched us.

The girls giggled as Al said, "A savant, a great man."

Fred, as if promptly on cue, said, "I am a miscellaneous person full of self-knowledge," and Al laughed and said, "It's better than being a mislaid person," and Fred said, "You're merely misled not mislaid," and they both laughed at that.

When I said I was Al's subversive friend from New York City, Fred became cordially serious and said he'd heard all about me, and when I said "New friends are best," Gail took my hand and leaned her wholesome shoulder against me and said, "Oh you"; and smelling in the house an old sweetness of wine mulling—with raisins, I thought—and not even Halloween yet—I asked myself why the hell I'd stood up Tracy in Northampton and come here this weekend to check how much Al knew.

The librarian had been to Scandinavia for three weeks and was making Glögg. He had a neat gray crew cut and a yellow button-down and belt-in-back khakis. Gail held my elbow and gently pulled me with her onto the sofa as Fred said So I was the famous New York friend. The librarian said to have some appetizers—mixed nuts and pale brown goat cheese—and he went out to the kitchen with Al, telling him the priest in question would be glad to help Al with his Latin. Gail's hand fell off my arm as I made a move for the glass bookcase behind Annette's chair. Annette asked me for some matches but Fred jumped over with his, and his hand shook a bit as he mashed a couple before he got her Kool lit. His nostril-flares were red but he didn't have a cold. He was fifty.

"Here's the Everyman Encyclopedia," I said. "I forget, what's Al's?"

But Fred said, talking very fast, "There's a better one right beside it, the works of Charles Dickens. All you need to know."

"His isn't that one," said Annette turning around in her chair and looking up over her shoulder.

"What you want's the Eleventh Edition of the Britannica," said Fred. "Say, there's Kingsley's *Hypatia,* ever open that book?"

I said no but I knew who she was.

Annette went to the kitchen. I heard the icebox door close. If I keep things apart do I make them equal?

Doc was kidding me about being thrown out of the work camp, but Bob interrupted telling me I'd have time to read *Great Expectations* now for English in the fall, he'd been telling me to read it, it was great, there was a woman in it who was crazy about cleaning because (Akkie Backus had told Bob) she wasn't getting enough from her husband.

Eleven-thirty feet to the near lift. If I were typing, they'd hear. All hands to quarters, I go slow, A and B are side by side, who am I between?, Doc's Plymouth turns into a tense room, the librarian's parlor moves us at devious speeds around the evening.

Downstairs if Ev has made progress in her inquiry I may find on arrival home that I've been discovered dead. She'll leave the guests' glasses, crumbs, ashes, and scurf till the morning or even later, she always does. I love Ev. It does not take time to love. I loved at first sight Tracy's succulent legs each one and Perpetua's plain strong mouth and Gail's collar-bone and sweet moles, though one Sunday when I happened to pass the Episcopal church as early service was letting out, Tracy's hips from behind deceived me I admit into thinking they barely interrupted a tall thin girl, when in fact they were alive all by themselves. An only child dwells upon others with a private thoroughness unmatched even by animal want, though perhaps by art.

Salacious junk! mutters Tracy's brother Hugh Blood, who always knew I'd wind up doing something trivially personal if not treacherously intimate; but Hugh will never know how many U.N. member nations Tracy and I got through, slowly and joyfully, the afternoon of April 19, 1946, honoring each with a differently appropriate kiss from Iraq and Iran to Greece and all the way to Nicaragua and on down to Australia, in observance of the old League's bequeathing its physical assets to the new body the day before.

Out there in the hall the two feet slip away and the arrived elevator closes.

As in the librarian's parlor with its glass-front bookcase and what Annette knew: so in Doc's Plymouth with its windshield and its polio epidemic.

You like such transitions no more than I do, Dom.

"You're not the type," Doc glanced at me in the mirror; I was in the back next to his tan Palm Beach suit hanging over one window, he was making me mad, I don't know where we were in Jersey but it was pretty close to New York. "Getting kicked out, steady type like you—" "He's got a terrific temper," Bob interrupted, but Doc said, "Kids like you just don't *get* expelled from—" "*Expelled!*" said Bob, "from a frigging farm camp?" "What'll your father say?" "He's got other things on his mind," I said. "Like what?" said Doc and at this point I think wanted to let it drop, but without backing down. I said, "Like the polio epidemic, and the stock market, and the *War*." "The *War*." Doc guffawed, "I bet he wasn't even in it. *I'll tell* him about the *War*." "What," said Bob, "about how you kept Rommel out of Alexandria while freeing all those girls in Paris?" "Well who's going in the Army tomorrow, I ask you that," said Doc; "you kids ought to show me a good time in New York today. Especially *you*," he said into the mirror. "Don't do me any favors,"

I said, lamely but bored. "O.K." said Doc, "then I guess your dad better know how his little private school kiddie got kicked out after he spent his summer pay—" "Doc," said Bob humbly, "it's one of the best private schools in the country, every member of this year's senior class made—" "Spent all my money on what, Doc?" I said with careful menace. "Whatever it was, you had a grand total of six bucks in the camp bank yesterday." "That's none of your business," said Bob. I said, "And I gave that to Bob, and I owe him twelve more." "What you been buying, dirty Big-Little Books off the kid from Chester? I'll sell you a Rameses I didn't use last night." "You never touched her," I said.

The librarian came out of the kitchen with a tray almost as soon as Annette went in, and Al followed talking about when the priest could take him, they had anti-sub exercises with the Navy off Newport next week, and the librarian said over his shoulder, "Give it a stir, Annette." So I went in the kitchen, passing them in the unlighted dining room, and Annette was tasting out of a blue enamel dipper.

"There's nothing to it," she said, "sweet and hot." She looked in through the steam. "Got cloves floating around in it." She reached for my hand without looking. "He doesn't like me tonight."

"Were you a little cuckoo at the restaurant?"

"I wasn't drinking this afternoon; I don't, anyway." She held the dipper up to me; the punch was strong. "Well, I don't have that sweet, strait-laced look of his sister."

"He's got a lot on his mind now," I said, though I didn't feel the simple truth of what I'd said. "After you and I had lunch that time I wondered how Al could get so shook about that encyclopedia and the birthday inscription—what was it?—and you said he was making educated guesses about some writing in the margin of Volume Twelve."

"It was Uncle Cooley," Annette cooed softly, crossing and uncrossing her eyes, "and he thinks he knows who *Coo*-ley is, *you're* a little crazy *too*, so why don't you admit it." She put her fingers along the side of my neck, "let me taste the wine," and she rand her tongue side to side between my barely parted lips, and when I opened she moved back. "I guess it's ready."

I said, "Don't think *Gail* is strait-laced," and Gail was suddenly in the kitchen door quietly agreeing, "No, I'm certainly not."

"Well," Annette said to me, "*you* certainly keep your distance," and she began filling punch cups.

Al laughed in the living room, Fred was telling about his cat Epaminondas.

A minute later there would be a toast. Fred would drink off his Glögg and go back to the bourbon. I would feel that my distance to Al was even greater than to Tracy.

But before that, Bob had passed Doc fifty cents for the tunnel seven years south of Portland and in no time we were droning under the high ogival arches of Brooklyn Bridge, and Doc was refusing to look to his right at the vast harbor nor if he'd been around the next year would he have believed that Bob launched a boomerang off this bridge from the pedestrian boardwalk right out over the East River and chop-chop it looped on back and then some. The decision to come to Brooklyn had occurred on the Pulaski Skyway as we passed through the mouth-watering stink of the Jersey flats and were very hungry and saw the Statue of Liberty from behind and standing as if on the mainland on our side. Doc had been saying we didn't sound like we came from Brooklyn but he'd heard Brooklyn was even worse than Philly. Bob said he should see Brooklyn Heights, and I reeled off Riis Park beach, Ebbets Field, Prospect Park, the finest Botanic Garden in the country, Brooklyn Museum with a very good American collection, Grand Army Plaza (to impress him with the sound but he wasn't interested in the arch), and of course the docks—had Doc heard of the Moore-McCormack Lines? "And the Heights," Bob added with quiet obstinacy. "And," I continued, "a population greater than Finland's." So we had lunch at my apartment, Bob didn't have either of the keys to his parents' brownstone.

When the musty dark of our foyer succeeded the deep creak of the front door my ears then pounded me into a near-faint, for the light was on in the kitchen, so maybe my father was taking an earlier train to the country today and had come home for lunch, it was one subway stop under the river from Wall. But he had merely left the light on that morning. There was a dish in the sink with a corn flake stuck to the side, which Dom you know I could precisely botanize for you if I chose.

Doc said we had a lot of funny furniture, and didn't we have any rugs?, and what could I play on the piano. He said he'd never seen so many fucking books in his life and did my father read them all. I said most of them, hearing Doc's casual adjective very solid here in my parents' apartment. For a while I was prepared for someone to come in. Doc wanted to know if there was any brew, and I opened him a Budweiser and Bob had one too. Then Doc wanted to see my room, "my sanctum" I said as I switched on the glaring overhead bulb. In another room Bob turned back the shade to look out into our street and we heard him say it seemed so strange to be here in August, "it's sort of weird"; and in my room Doc said, "Yeah? well I guess dad wouldn't like to know we're sneaking in here drinking his beer when you're supposed to be on the train to Mass." I wondered if they'd put air-conditioning in my father's office yet, there were three women with baby carriages out on that hot street when we got out of the car and they'd made me feel we'd lost speed and been left here in an unrecognizable Heights as if it had been pivoted into a new time, a strange age. Doc moved into my parents' room, let the shade up, and stared across the East River at the mirage of towers where my father worked, and then out left into the broad harbor and to the Statue I'd never been up in though I knew her vital statistics and one night had sat in the dark staring at her while my parents in the living room bickered over where to go that summer. And as Doc ran a hand over the white summer spread my father had neatened over the double bed, and then tapped one of the posts where a pair of undershorts hung, I found myself saying, "On the train to Mass., eh? All right then, I'll make it worth your while to keep quiet."

Doc said, "Yeah," but he was looking at the view.

Bob was somewhere else. Our apartment was so big.

I said, "I'm fed up with your petty threats, I'm going to *give* you—" I went back to my room, the locus of every grandiose plan I'd ever made—"I'm going to give you *this*," and Doc came after me. Yes, I said, if he kept quiet about me when we got to Heatsburg—about my expulsion and the money—he could have this encyclopedia.

Bob came to my door, Doc between us. Bob said, "You wouldn't take it."

"Sure he would," I said, and started tilting books out. I heard Doc's bottle rhythmically draining, and when I eyed him, there was savage reflection around his thick mouth, and he said sure he would. I added, "Consider it a going-away present." Doc hesitated, and I said, "A present to go away." He said where would we be if he *did* go away right now, and I said in that case I'd call my father and take the train with him.

The phone was ringing. I didn't go out to pick it up.

It was after two-thirty when I dried our plates and turned out the kitchen light and we carried the dark red books down to Doc's trunk. The Plymouth was like an oven. Bob looked up the street and we both saw Joey approaching on his bike-cart.

But I seem tonight despite this long memorial arc no nearer Bohack Joey and the fight, much less my stolen Corona.

But as we push north and are eventually pursued by the train that bears my tired father—who (I am to learn tonight) phoned the farm camp in vain this morning to say since I was coming through New York come to his office between trains and we'd go up together—I'm carried at another rate seven years north to that small city where the librarian's yellow Oxford cuff is raised to toast Al's future, and Fred Eagle downing that red confection turns promptly back to his unnursed bourbon.

Fred said that Al was so lit the night before the last weather patrol he hit both sides of his shop door leaving, but Fred said Al didn't have the strength of character to be a full-blown failure. And I said neither did Fred if he was enough in the book business to drive a hundred miles today to buy some unsuspecting old lady's library. Touch, said Fred; yet it was as a beachcomber that he'd found Epaminondas, and next time he needed something as real as a cat he was going back to that beach with a gallon of eight-year-old bourbon and two pounds of wieners and his surf rod and stay till he got whatever it was. What he was going to get one of these days was an English Land Rover, go anywhere in a Land Rover, Panama, any beach, up to the Arctic Circle where men live who sleep four months a year. Al said except for our host *I* was the only one he knew who would ever amount to more than two pounds of hot dogs on a wet beach, and he and Fred laughed about that; but the librarian insisted that Al would go to college, do his graduate work, and (as the librarian put it) teach at the college level someday. Gail said she knew he could do anything he wanted to, which sort of stopped the conversation, but her face from its breathtaking cheekbones down the mysterious secret V-taper to her chin was more than the words of any of us in that parlor. Annette went out to fill a pitcher so we could recharge our cups more easily.

"Now, I can't sleep," said Fred. "Mind's too potent. 'N' I've such a time getting to sleep I dream about it. I dream that I make up stories to drug myself to sleep." Fred took his glass to the kitchen and though he talked louder while we waited it was as if for him we were there in the kitchen with him. "And at the crack of dawn I'm up no matter *how* I feel or look and no matter where I am, heading east from San Diego toward the Chocolate Mountains, or talking to someone in the county courthouse in Jackson, Mississippi, or smack in the center of Manhattan." Fred was back with a glass the color of strong Indian tea.

"A cup of sack, wench," said Al, "a cup—"

"Don't you call *me* wench," said Annette.

"I'll call you what I want to call you, with your Hawaiian friends. A cup of sack to make my eyes look red like old pint-pot tickle-brain. Fred, God give thee the spirit of persuasion."

"Yes, I'll be persuasive rather than exhaustive," said Fred, "better the fleeting melody of the swan than the long-drawn clangor of cranes."

Al nodded slowly to me and winked in honor of the great man, whose Lucretius I chose not to match but to share in the privacy of my smile. I envied Fred's mere good will toward my friend, and I knew that like some Lucretian development my alliance with Al could never turn to nothing despite my strife to preserve it unthreatened.

"One tale I dreamt I made up to put myself to sleep took me up the coast here past Boothbay to look at a houseful of stuffed people, and a big yellow cat showed me around telling me by telepathy all I had to know about each of these stuffed sons and cousins and grannies and servants. I had to walk carefully between them, some were standing, I didn't want to knock 'em over, pretty crowded in there I can tell you."

"I bet," said Annette.

"All dressed up, little boys in wide collars, dames in lace fronts, a ruby-faced uncle leaning on the mantle warming his knees, mid-Victorian matching chairs and sofas, hand-carved medallions— well I'd have to get a loan from the bank to buy, what with the two room of books upstairs. So I said to the yellow cat, I'll take the lot, and named a price. But soon as I did, every last one of that stuffed family came to life stuffing and all and eased on out of that house, furniture too, leaving me with the books upstairs which I soon found I'd after all got a jolly good bargain on."

"I don't get it," I said.

"Why get it? You don't have to get it. It's just a story I dreamed I made up to—"

"I think you trapped yourself and don't know how to get out of it," I said.

"Ought to try it sometime," said Fred. "Very salutary. Maybe there's your trouble. You're young, find yourself a trap."

"He's got you there," said the owner of my old encyclopedia, and Gail looked at me in such a charming way I recalled that her plaid bag was in Al's room, and she said to me, "*You* don't have any troubles."

"But who says I'm finished?" said Fred. "What else did I find upstairs?"

"Your wife," said the librarian, whose name I had somehow missed.

"My wife, is it? O.K. say it was my wife, I don't mind." Al laughed, and said to me quietly, "He married a Deering."

"What then?" said Fred. Let me convey him, Dom, more wholly than mere recollection of his hustling voice. His wife: she was reading Kingsley's *Hypatia* when he arrived among the books upstairs. ("Ever *been* to Egypt?" he interrupted himself to ask me.) She looked up at Fred and instead of silently telling him to shave or silently asking him why he was a day late coming home, for he'd only been up to Friendship, which after all was this side of Rockland, she turned out to be none other than that alluring Alexandrian sage Hypatia herself, though still Mrs. Fred Eagle. On her wedding finger was a *new* familiar ring, its enamel top a picture of the Egyptian desert that grew as you looked till ("You never dreamed this," said Annette whom Al tried to shush with raised hand) you found the great Alexandrian centuries approaching and with them Archimedes staying overnight at the Museum with Euclid, and you saw approaching you the green plots of the Ptolemies and the gymnasiums and basilicas, but there all the time stood the Pharos, the lighthouse four hundred fifty feet high with, centuries behind it or inside its substance, the memory of Babylonian tower-temples. And a mob of Christians mainly clerical including a clutch of those reckless fellows who cared for the sick during epidemics—"What did they call them?"—they were bearing down on the great neo-Platonist mathematician herself but Fred raced in off the desert, stepped across the river from back to back of fat crocodiles lethargic with a glut of recent human suicides, held Hypatia in his pulsing arms, and in short loved her right there in the Alexandrian library, "they won't dig up the ruins today because they're under a building they're using." And this mob bearing down on Hypatia for daring to defend pagan thought are stopped cold by Hypatia and young Fred burning her afternoon oil right there among the tomes.

"And at this point," said Fred going to the kitchen, "I was interrupted. I woke up just as in the dream I was about to talk myself to sleep."

"The Pharos wasn't *that* high," I called, wondering again who might have scribbled in the final volume of the encyclopedia Caesar Bemis sold Al.

"Don't question his facts," said Al a bit too seriously. "He's a walking—"

"Maybe so maybe not," said Fred barely loudly enough to carry in to us. "But it was the ravishing astro-philosopher Hypatia all right."

"It was your wife," said Gail.

"What did you mean—my 'Hawaiian friends'?" said Annette.

"What's your authority for making the Pharos less than four-fifty?"

"Do you forget my Breasted *Ancient Times* you borrowed?"

And read during a month of Search and Rescue in Bermuda: the *Barataria* got painted, the crew were allowed to go ashore in civvies, and Al on the balcony of a Hamilton bar or on the sunset battlements of Fort St. Catherine above St. George or in the Corpsman's presence or absence sought to rescue himself and then strangely was rescued during the last week of this tropical duty by a local teenager wise enough not to send by her brother messages of affection every afternoon as her even darker sister did to Al's Detroit shipmate who was therefore scorned by Al's full-blooded Seminole buddy who slept with a small, Wheatena-colored snake around his shin and never knew Al's girl was black that final week during which the deck crew rolled a second coat of white onto the cutter's comfortable hull and Al gave ancient history a rest.

Dom, the letters from Richard, Dorothy, and Lila would have lowered your resolve, for the less you let yourself sink into your destiny the less could love be displaced by your courage. And those letters were not like one of Richard's actuarially unpreventable acts of God.

Doc said Brooklyn Heights hadn't been much, he thought we'd at least take him to the Club Samoa near Times Square where his brother had gone on furlough last year.

Bob was too quiet; the day had picked up a wearying impurity in its interruption. Bob didn't mention the encyclopedia again, he may have thought the gift reckless snobbery in me puzzling Doc into silly defense.

I woke at a gas station feeling very, very young. Nothing was said about my having been asleep. We were twenty-two miles from Heatsburg and Doc wanted three dollars from each of us, which Bob paid.

I asked them not to tell we'd stopped in New York.

My mother seemed not at all surprised that I arrived as I did. Doc was impressed by her. She just looked at me and said I needed a haircut. Was it possible she didn't know I was supposed to come by train? She isn't a vague person, in the kitchen or at the piano or any place, though she is not unyielding. I didn't want to ask her for money and when Bob at the door of our john upstairs asked me if I could get the fifteen dollars and twenty-five cents from her I said I'd send it to him tomorrow. When he came out my mother was

calling me. Bob started down and I went in the john. Aiming above
the water line I heard my mother say perhaps your friend would
like to use the bathroom. When the cistern filled I took off the
top and disengaged from the hook at the end of the flush-lever the
stiff wire attached to the plunger. Then I replaced the top. Entering
the village I'd seen hilly pasture turn into flat fields and the flat
lake on the Heatsburg road and then I'd seen the postmaster going
back in off his porch following two kids who'd evidently come for
an after-supper cone; I'd seen Caesar Bemis watch us pass without
recognizing me in Doc's Plymouth, and I'd seen Al and Tony
having a catch, and I'd seen four people getting bags out of a yellow
convertible at the inn. As I came downstairs my mother asked if
Bob and Doc would stay for supper, she'd be meeting my father at
Hillsdale pretty soon. Bob said they had to be going. My mother
seemed weirdly unconcerned about our arrival, but did ask about the
polio epidemic and where Doc lived, and he told her why he had to
get home, and she asked if he wanted something to drink. And Doc
took a look at me and said, "You wouldn't have a Budweiser, would
you?" My mother said, "We just do," and when she got the bottle out
and opened it Doc took another look at me and mumbled, "Use the
bathroom" and nodded to my mother and walked out as casually as
he could. Bob was calling Rhode Island. My mother said she'd seen
Al and told him I'd be home tonight and he'd said he might come
over. But I was out of the house before she finished and hoping
that Doc, who loved every inch of that Plymouth, hadn't taken the
keys. I had the trunk open and twelve volumes of the encyclopedia
out and stacked in two piles around the corner of our white fence
and the keys back in the ignition before Bob was finished with his
unpleasant conversation with his father who'd tipped over in a race
that afternoon. Doc was a while coming down.

Before Bob and Doc left, my mother asked Bob if he was sure
he wouldn't like to stay the night. When she and I were driving
to Hillsdale she asked me why on earth Doc had been willing to

detour such a distance from his straightest route, was it that he felt responsible for me and Bob?

And so I was able to mail Bob a money order the next day in the same outgoing post that carried a note from my mother to Coolidge confirming the next weekend. You have to admit it's funny, Dom. Cold, calculating me!

When Gail and Annette were out of the room Fred said, "Emissions recollected in senility"; then, to Al, "Look out how you fool with the constable's daughter."

But the Hawaiians were the fooling Al should not have done. The librarian said television was going to be a great threat to the reader but on the other hand could be very educational, it was probably too early to make a prediction, wait till '54 or '55, and we all nodded. Al said he was already hooked on baseball telecasts, but Fred said baseball was even duller than soccer on or off TV, he for one hated all "manifestations" of physical sport, and when Fred said baseball was an intellectual game and Fred asked Gail if she played chess, the librarian diverted them into the issue of contact and non-contact and he and Al got a bit ruffled when Al said the only reason the librarian could call basketball a pattern-sport not a body-contact sport was that he'd never played it, the librarian said he had played guard in school and he *had* seen what happens under the backboard, and Al said Not only there, and when the librarian though a bit huffy tried to pacify Al and said, "Well we can agree about baseball, baseball is not a body-contact sport," Al looked at me and shook his head. Maybe not for a pitcher.

Annette asked him again what he'd meant before about the Hawaiians. He shrugged her off saying O.K. he probably knew them much better than she did. But she said no he didn't know the first thing about them. "I know they got half the high school girls in Portland smoking tea." "You lie," said Annette in the same moment that I said, "What's wrong with that? The kids are bored." The librarian said, "There's a *lot* wrong with it, it'll *make* them bored is more like the truth." "They don't matter," said Al; "if I've got to pick a drug I'll pick the stuff in the glass with the icecubes tinkling and I'll take Aristotle's intellectual life along with it." "What about sex?" I said, and as I glanced at the librarian he looked at his empty punch glass.

But Annette said Earl and Eddie were fun, maybe they didn't know who Epaminondas was but they loved to dance. And smoke Mary Jane, said Al. Yes, said Annette, yes. Yes, that's partly why they're fun.

"Well, you're getting plenty of fun at this end," said Al, but the evening was over. It hadn't been planned anyway as a long one, and we sensed that we couldn't start a new conversation; it was better to stretch—as *I* did, with a clear crack of the clavicle and with an inward smile—and plead fatigue; I knew it would be well received, if not by Fred and the librarian. (Whose name I did catch on leaving, after having told a puzzled Fred *parabolani* was the name he'd tried to recollect, the reckless tenders of the contagious sick.)

I felt Al was angry at me even though the locked and complete and unresolved fight that happened in my parked car as soon as we reached it in front of the High Asia was between Al and Annette, with Gail and me listening in front looking straight ahead at nothing. "What's Karl to think, you play games with those Hawaiian trash?" "Sandburg's *Lincoln* I can read at home, thanks." "What's that mean?" "Oh God"—Annette was laughing at the tiresome coincidence— "no no no, I meant when I see your stewards I don't bring along a book to read." "I bet you don't take much away with you either." "I didn't *have* anything to leave except a couple of hours, remember?" "You *have* spent time with those useless sons of bitches." "Depends what you mean by time." "Even when *I'm* in?" "Listen, lover, *I* had to call *you* last week to see if you were in from station." "I thought you had a good head. What's Karl going to think?"

I started the car and we turned down Congress in the general direction of Al's rented room.

"Karl's very sweet but I wouldn't pretend with him." "*When* did you smoke?" "This afternoon before I came to meet you. *You* didn't ask me to come around to your place. They were at Noreen's—oh you don't know Noreen. I had a nice time, that's all. And a good appetite worked up for your Number Four Family." "You're being cheap." "Call me a whore." "I though you were a good head." "A *one-man* whore." "Nobody home."

Gail put her hand on my arm and said to Al without looking around, "What's wrong with trying the stuff? What's wrong with *you*, Al?" Annette was right back at her: "Don't give me that *'trying'* stuff, because I know what you're saying."

"I'm not saying anything," said Gail.

When we got to Al's place, Annette said, "What am I doing here?" Al went ahead but turned around at the steps and lowering his voice told Gail he was going back to the ship and she could stay here and I could use the hotel room. I told Annette I'd drive her home. The hotel was the other end of Congress. My bag was still in the trunk. I told Al I'd see him tomorrow. We left him and Gail standing on the sidewalk.

No one was out. Just a hundred wooden houses. Lending themselves, Dom, to multiple reproduction. I turned where Annette told me; she seemed to be staying away from her street, I was lost. I said Al was mad at me too tonight. She said I was out of my mind. I asked if we were getting warmer, I was tired. She said she had an idea why I'd come this weekend. I asked if Al ever talked about Heatsburg and the quarry. She said, "Left here...sure, but he tells me so many things. He's not mad at you, I just think he probably knows you. You been writing Gail?"

I said it was three years since I'd seen Gail. "Rich girlfriend at Smith," said Annette, "I don't understand you. And you just graduated college. And let me tell you dear I don't care about some scribble in a moldy margin beside something about *ziggurat*, I swear

to God I don't. I care about that screwed-up guy." "Screwed up?" I
said, "it's just that he's not settled down yet."

At Annette's house I asked the name of the street and she asked
did I want to know the way to Gail's hotel or Al's room. When I
said, "Congress Square, I can find anything in Portland from there,"
she said, "There's a shortcut, Mister Scientist—that was a science
you majored in, wasn't it?" "I guess so," I said, and she went "Hmph."

Then she said, "Your father's happy, I bet." "Why?" I said. "He
wanted you to be a scientist." "How do you know that?" "Oh Al told
me once." "My father's dead."

Then Annette said, "I know you can find your way to Congress
Square but that's the long way. Aren't you a fellow who likes
shortcuts? Do it my way. Al's walked back to State Pier by now, and
one way or another there's going to be a lot of space wasted tonight."

So after watching her go slowly up the walk, then suddenly
quick up the porch steps, I indeed did it her way. We duly if
disingenuously pay for all our experiences. But you expect to pay
only in tedium and trouble, and you're not told that you may have
to pay by having pleasure: like Gail—like being a conspicuous
absence for Tracy that night.

But Dom, the discovery didn't last. Any more than the space
you occupied high in the hearts of dissentient students. Only last
week when you returned from the Caribbean to your mailbox, you
said (blindly to me) that they didn't want you: there it was, two
mornings after you got back; the *o*'s in "To Whom It May Concern"
sliced right out of the paper, your typed note left in your mailbox
presumably a reply to my insurance note to you the preceding week,
anonymous and anxiously encouraging for I knew how the factional
anomie you'd tried to underwhelm yourself in coupled with the
renewed loosening of family ties might have sucked you into some
new move you might mistake for the right kind of risk. Your surprise
defenestration from the ninth floor above the Pacific twilight was
the right kind of risk, or your bullhorn speech outside the white

poet's storefront children's club in El Barrio (which neither Bob
nor Al would know is uptown and poor and Spanish) saying the
South was like Viet Nam, we should get out and tend to home,
the Mississippi kidnap would remain unsolved but *in an open field*
(that is, frank war). But the wrong kind of risk was to bring your
beautiful black Costa Rican Kit when you met Dorothy for lunch.
You've been deliberately dieting on the most demanding foods. I
was sitting near enough behind you so I heard you order that heavy
cassoulet and so was able myself to order it in time to follow you
bravely bite for bite. But Dot was more demanding still, demanding
of Miss Kit Carbon the archaeologist if she'd yet reached the phase
at which the Chief—namely you, Dom—would be obliged to find
her a husband as he did for his "abortive secretary" a few years back.
Dot had by then swallowed all the Sole Dunkirk she proposed to,
and as she finished this sentence her eye now found me chewing
wild sausage and mealy beans. And she stopped, and I for the space
of one climactic swallow almost thought she knew me. She was
saying too loudly to Kit, "Well I've known him for years, and I'm
sorry—I *just don't get* it." Dom you said something to her with your
mouth full, and she said, "I thought I saw a photographer, I can do
without that today, this isn't my year."

No, the kids who challenged you the morning after your
electrifying defenestration had missed wholly the tone of your
two-year-old book on suicide: What did it add? / It subtracts, you
said. // Suicide's an existential act, right? / It's also an occasion for
measurement. // But we've had statistics, like, we've *had* parameters,
we've had all that. / Where? // Easy to ask me where, but you know
I'm—you know we're right. / I know *nothing* about you. // It's a dull
book; like, who cares if the Hungarians and Finns head the list? / It's
a dull book; I don't really remember what I said in it. // It's a cop-out.
/ No! (the pro lifts his voice, and a newshen scribbles faster) // It's
a sell-out. / (You barely smiled—Jesus what creases!—while *I* knew
that you had endeavored to do a *deliberately* dull book itemizing

causes (like suicide as retort, as revenge, resurrection, publication, /
suicide due to Sphinx syndrome, suicide as time-killer)) and piling
on such numbers of numbers, such calmly provisional percents as
to flatten the subject into its terminal banality. A student asked if
it was true one of your children committed suicide. You said not to
your knowledge. Darla Fasinelli's late boyfriend called from behind
his camera, "You can't prove you were pushed out that window last
night," and you replied, "I *don't* prove I was pushed, I'm not pressing
charges," and he said, "Publicity stunt, you looked before you leapt."
As a lone cornet struck up "Hail to the Chief," you replied, "I'm
stunted by publicity": which, as I hear the elevator door release new
hall steps, hales my eye round to your styrofoam-de-force. When
I her habitual reader interviewed her the columnist back here in
Gotham Friday of the weekend Bob was last in town, Darla for
all her hawk-like loveliness seemed so politic and darkly gentle I
almost could not hear above the laughter jamming my ear pulses
what she gladly gave me, she talked all morning, she was speaking
privately and with surprised comfort. Neither Bob nor Al, even
tonight on the tenth and eighth floors of a midtown motel, would
be able to believe her long tale of your defenestration, and indeed it
is so double Darla by her own admission chose in her *Hash* column
not to report it in its doubleness lest she force her readers to see
so much that they missed the point. At last I looked at my watch,
Bob would be getting into the midtown air terminal. Why was he
coming so late if he wanted to see people in Wall Street?

"The simple point," said this singled-minded directrix Darla,
"is that he's no longer relevant to us except as a fifty-two-year-old
interruption who used to be the hero whose life-style meant do your
thing...thoroughly no matter what it costs in order to restructure
American society...with the humane guarantees that are the only...
feasible possible peaceable basis for community. But he turned out
to mean—like something... abstract and decadently psychosexual,
namely follow your idea out thoroughly no matter what it costs and

no matter what it *is*. That's the simple point. Anyway we don't have stars anymore, we have community, and he wants to be the president of everyone. Left conservative he says he is, but it doesn't fool us. He wants the Nobel Prize for Ubiquity."

"And he'll get it," I said, but did not say *with my help*. Nor could I tell her she wasn't tired enough yet to spot the obsolescence factor in her fixed program for community. She couldn't truly see you Dom, between her line and her point; she could not see how to join Commitment and Field-State. However, to you Dom I confess that when paralyzed from sleep into those moon-shot estrangements transfiguring my favorite print or a quilted potholder that I've mentioned already tonight, I too have often lost your track and instead found myself again comfortably caught in the process of keeping Al and Bob distinct in neat problems like (a) did or did not Bob learn what I'd taken from Doc's trunk (since his case was in the back seat and Doc died at Fort Dix two weeks later of a ruptured colon and probably had no time during those first days of Basic to drop Bob a line), or (b) did or did not Gail report to Al (who woke on the ship Saturday to the bulk smell of steam table scrambled eggs and crumbly home fries) that (waking at three a.m. to the back of her hand) I had asked her if she thought he was angry about the four-hundred-forty-five-foot lighthouse and the ancient history text I once lent him.

But then, as I feel Ev's hot hip and I pivot from my visions, I begin to know again that in '52 in the librarian's living room in Portland, with its cosy Van Goghs and the square-contoured turquoise day-bed and, by a New Yorker Hotel ashtray, a wooden whale with "Welcome to Bergen, Norway" in script on its flank—and in the john a Goya boy—there were livings so fugitive from my petty focus that much was lost, much was lost I firmly sigh. And lost because of the Vectoral Dystrophy chronic I now suppose in only children. My two-year-old Emma may never know Ted; compared to her he's ancient. "Ong Zeus" is turning into "Ange-ooce." At thirty-seven Ev would rather not go through it all again, though I think she would for me. This power over her which I so wonderfully have, I have tonight swapped for that other ex-spatio-vectoral power which I may be only imagining I have and which is not congruent with my power over Ev which itself is not complicated by the fact that Ev is now in an unusual sense looking for me. I was leading, but now the words are leading me. To you? The elevator door has opened again, and now there is an echoing inaudible conversation between two men; they are nearer your door, Dom, and nearer still. I could tell them you're not here yet. Those challenging kids the morning after you descended from that Pacific window positively quivered with pride at having paralleled what they saw as an inadequate monograph on suicide and an inadequately suicidal gesture. Having, with the help of a militant phil major, bumbled onto that parallel, they were high on its logic.

At least I did not keep your letters, Dom, I burned them. Light-years from your real life they could only in their lack of sympathy have lowered your resolve—Lila's one-time psychiatrist who is now her husband would think me mad if I told about voices tampering with my door knob but—

For thirty seconds I've heard you door knob being handled; and accompanying the rattle, ten seconds ago: "Son-in-law's comin' awver, *he* may have a key. Try the super again"—

Now I'm writing again, glad the traverse curtains across fifteen feet of windows at this end are pulled back rather than drawn. Into the regular arc of my legible but distinctive hand so many rates of time collapse: a month in a phrase, interruptions to raid the icebox or listen, a Fred-Eagled hour in three long pages, four summers in the one word "quarry," and now a nearly instant thirty-word response to thirty seconds. Collapse into paraphase.

Not to rule out outside-time is like letting Al and Bob meet or like meanly leaving you Dom unaided. I have no time for outsiders like this detective tenor or Lila's Hungarian husband who will indeed have a key. In her typically loose humid letter yesterday she thanked you for mailing the key—why?—and she complained that you'd never answered her answer months ago to your letter demanding to know why she and her husband had walked out on you after you'd spotted them in the crowd outside the Think-Tank. That exchange of course was long before Ev even heard about the chance of a vacancy in this building. Lila and her plump husband matter to you about half what your son Richard appraisingly does, and let it be said for him that though an actuary (who knows? maybe now a poly-thinker deep beyond such family phenomena as chance), he's not and never was one of these creative salesmen client-oriented to the very root of their courier-case zippers whom (say) Mutual has made not only "Honor Guard" but "Order of the Tower" too by virtue of having each in one twelve-month period designed an umbrella of two million bucks' worth of insurance for relevant families and businesses. And why should you have to think about Lila's thanks—or her gawky reproach, "how easily the celebrity could have switched on his 'secretary' and just dictated a reply." Your dictaphone-secretary bill is astronomical because they do everything; and to judge by a confirming note they sent you I think not only that nothing ever comes back to you, not even carbons, not even correspondence for your signature, but that you encourage variety in your signature. During the slight abstractions which lately have interrupted your public utterances—briefings, speeches, even your printed word—you may have thought you missed and needed your family (from whom I guess it could be argued I was keeping you semi-incommunicado) or missed the old tributes from—you name them—Daley, Dalí, Dellinger, the furry-wristed divine from Des Moines, past-president Dr. Dave Dickens, Sister Deirdre Reardon's far from unrepresentative congressional body, and Darlene (now Darla) Fasinelli (who had tried in vain to keep her ideological activism separate, even distant, from the grad linguistics program famous at I.U. for being a creative one and for attracting almost exclusively girls).

I came tonight to talk of you but soon saw it was also Al and Bob. If I kept them apart thinking they wouldn't hit it off, I kept close to you Dom. Between you and me pivotal affinities occlude such petty tics as my constant distinctive signature with its unforgeable paraph, my not entirely confident dislike of great heights, and my impatience with such idle pressures as the tense Manhattan bragging of Hugh Blood which you'd think healthy self-expression until you discovered that he never interrupts himself.

Often among my books downstairs I've thought of you hitting your trampoline again and again on your upstairs neighbor's penthouse terrace. I've thought, with the only sort of faith that helps now, how your theory (or as you say, your Code) of Welcomed Interruption sprang from your sense that our state is now a Field-State of InterPoly-force Vectors multimplicitly ploding toward Coördinate Availability and away from the hierarchical subordinations of the old tour-de-force anthropols which I feel sure my irreplaceable, late father (were he here) would have the leniency at least to agree could not survive much less embrace intrusor photons and their interruptive barrage. I was with you, but *with* you, Dom, in your proliferating efforts to make yourself a complete image of our time, an actor never unrôled, an open ground of the EquiValences committed as if it were priorities to the spreading Field-State in which all sound is music.

So, in my (I hope polymerged) oscillation between active and contemplative membership in your career's strange arc, tonight had to occur. I had to broach my kinships. But it occurs to me that perhaps to be true kin I must breach my parabolic plan. Certainly your suicide tonight—which earlier I might have dismissed as an underachievement—may be the ultimate disseminal interruption.

Yet to wholly grasp it would be to wrongly fix it.

And it was, as the President says to some poor big-shot he's pressured, "your decision," as my father to me when I elected chemistry but not physics at Poly and he thought I was just protecting my Cum Laude standing.

And did you look through the latest issue of *Newsweep*—which your postman can't get into your box but leaves with other large mail on the ledge beneath? Did you examine the other face or two in the picture in which you appear? I wonder if Lila and her husband connected it with their exit from that Santa Barbara crowd.

I did hear the elevator again, but again the doorknob is being worked.

Imagine anything more alien to Bob's parents' living room on the Heights than that of Al's parents, where in late '53 they had a small party for him and for Goldilocks (as her mother occasionally and inaccurately calls Gail). There was a regular meal and pies and cakes vivid as the three calendars on the walls. There was doubt till that afternoon that Al would come; he had gone hunting in New Hampshire with his Seminole shipmate, also just out of the Coast Guard, and with Annette's father, who had a friend with a camp. At the party I saw Al and his dad speak just once, and it was a brief, hard disagreement over Al's taking legal residence in Maine to get in-state tuition at Orono, a plan Al abandoned. Gail had just become a stewardess and wore her Eastern Airlines raincoat when for a few minutes that evening she and her fiancé and I drove up to see the stone heart house.

The doorknob is moving again, I hear it; they should know that without a registered Eagle key it's pointless. Footsteps are coming from the east end of the hall, probably from the east elevator I stepped out of into another phase.

Bob's sister enraged their father by capitalizing on her fluent French and Italian to land a stewardess job with Pan Am.

Everyone in this benighted building is glad of the elevators. It's good to have the elevator in common, and to talk of its vagaries when we cautiously meet in it.

Only you and I would understand how much you and I had in common, Dom. At the opening where we met, you had no time to acknowledge this.

"On the other hand," my late father breaks back in, still weighing what I ascribed to him thirty lines ago, "if I don't know these new terms InterPoly-force Vectors and Coördinate Availability and the rest, still think of how for the Babylonians the generative force took many forms—polyform if you want—all roughly equal, a falcon, a snake, the sun, a god, a—"

My own parabola thickens. If it's putting on weight, let's hope the process is like yours in that styrofoam across this long room. The template contour fronting your sculpture has been taken back ninety degrees, and though you will say the template contour is the arc of a kind of nineteen-thirties display of neat, banal cypress trees, I would call it clearly parabolic—as indeed that picture article did that called your aging versatility exciting if dubiously derivative.

My father wasn't easy to interrupt. But (as he would say, "on the other hand") why interrupt him? Because—

Petty and Bob and I were in Manhattan all day that Saturday after Christmas '48, all three of us home from college. We stood her "pappy" up at a gallery and saw half a bad movie at a 42nd Street house where posters promised nudity at a health farm but Bob said it was fake so we left. We had whiskey sours in the Biltmore Bar at two in the afternoon. We rented skates at Rockefeller Center, and in long brown wool stockings Petty walking like a dancer across the wood to get to the ice seemed at least as good as the broads taking the cure in that interrupted movie. Bob raced heavily lap after lap, at last missing a middle-aged man on figure skates by so little the man sat right down but not till Bob was past him, as if in retrospect the man had reasoned his way into a collision with Bob. By the time Bob came up with Petty and me he'd come round again toward the sedately uncertain man on figure skates who turned halfway as if he had bursitis and told Bob to slow down or he'd tell an attendant, and as Bob swept smiling by him the man reached for Bob too precipitately and sat down on the ice again as Petty and I made a bridge over him passing. It was memorably cold. We were all late for dinner because we went to see my friend—

Steps. I will not rise. But in my own time. They'll never find you.

I am not responsible for your suicide, Dom, but if I am it's because in the extended privacy of my mind I could see the whole life you were trying to live. But if I pushed you to do it, must I now become you? There are no more like you. Your code, interruptive and silent, obliged you not to answer Darla that you weren't trying really to be a hero, or Dave Dickens that you didn't have any ideals in mind with which to reinvest American youth (two for one), or Sister Deirdre that you thought she ought to try some of her own stuff though you had no program at present though you might next week.

On our way to see my Negro friend Camille who lived south of the Village and whose father came from Andros in the Bahamas and was quite high up in the Motor Vehicle Bureau, Petty kept putting our words into hit songs. Bob told her to cut it out, and she said nothing till we were waiting in the cabbagey apartment hall for Camille to come to the door and then Petty said she wished Bob hadn't persuaded us to go to that dirty movie, pappy'd be fit to be tied. Camille's mother served us jasmine tea and Camille sang Barbara Allen to her guitar but when Bob asked for St. Louie Blues she said she didn't sing that sort of thing. I said she was hoping to go to Bennington in September and Bob said he'd heard fabulous things about what went on in the Bennington graveyard and Camille's mother said she would win a scholarship because she'd been outstanding at Music and Art, and Petty said she must be versatile but I didn't point out that Music and Art was a famous high school. Camille came and sat on the couch-bed beside me and put her arm around my shoulder and asked me to come to a party that night, and I nodded to her, accepting and archly appraising, and no one said anything for a moment. Petty said didn't they have a long time off at Bennington in the middle of the winter, and Camille said yes she was hoping to work for the City. Soon Petty said we had to be going. As we walked down, Bob said, with a grin, "How do you know *her?*"

We didn't find a cab, and after one change and two waits on deserted chilly platforms, we got back to the Heights by subway. My father was up for dinner but wore his bathrobe. He almost at once found out the signal omission of our afternoon and he had something to say about how you simply didn't do that, any more than you walked away while your elders were speaking to you, and Russell Pound was a gentleman and a terribly nice man and a scholar who knew absolutely everyone in the art world. I knew my father was dying. Why did I take his mild lecture so lightly? Not merely because I foresaw that he would not die for three or four years. I loved him in such isolation that everything else by contrast merged—Petty, Al, ancient history, Bob, things like watching the logrolling in the tank at the Sportsman's Show with my frantically nostalgic and displaced step-grandfather John (Zon < Zo-an), or defeating Tracy Blood's brother Hugh—merged, too, with things like the thick smell of corned beef hash from the cafeteria steam table at Poly (and the now unspeakable things we likened it to) on (say) a day rainy and indoor that hence made even more beautifully crucial the prospect of creaming the Solid test at two o'clock and concentrated even more the shiny cool concussions of the basketball court into which I would rush at three—yes, the state all these had of being other than my father gave them a wholesale kinship. But on the other hand ye gods my mother didn't fit into that gross category either. My mother and father didn't know I knew he was so sick. My mother has a class to herself too, in a white cardigan, watering trays of plants on a Sunday morning and drily commenting on the progress of someone's dogged Mozart somewhere above us to which my father would murmur something in reply, absorbed in the current events quiz in "The News of the Week in Review." But if she has a class to herself, hasn't Tracy? Hasn't Bob? Haven't those expensive Christmas vacations? We came down from our country colleges to oratories and *Death of a Salesman* and feverishly to our parents' phones and to bright windy errands round Manhattan—and then after making it home to Brooklyn Heights by cab over a bridge or by IRT under the East River, yes to the reality of southwest winds off the harbor, those serious winds flooding the streets of our Brooklyn Heights slowed us down but forced on us a future that was parental but whole and because of that harbor in some pathetically metaphorical sense maritime. You were Jewish Dom, and a well-to-do Jewish family we knew on the Heights went to Friends Meeting House on Sunday which thus allied them in my early mind with the Red Cross and hence with the Presbyterian Church, for from my room I'd heard my father tell his Cameroons Mission Committee what the Quakers had done in Spain, and my father was an elder in the Presbyterian—the First Presbyterian—Church. The Bloods were Episcopalian.

The super is making a sound again and again in the hall halfway between words and groaning, and the Irish tenor is getting mad. Far away from me he's saying somebody must have had a key to lock the door, his man Donahoe claims he just let the door close and had no key but forgot the lock didn't lock by itself. So who the hell but the *super*? The super says maybe a neighbor and tells the dick to watch his language, but the dick quickly says if you don't like it call The First National City Bank, call your boss, the son-in-law's coming any minute with *his* key—but Dom here *you* are:

From below, with the big rescue mat fifty feet in front of me and the Pacific pink and gray behind me, I kept expecting fire and smoke from the ninth-floor window whose sill you were straddling apparently being jostled. Cops cordoned us back further, and from a window adjacent to yours the FREEDOM NOW poster came paddling down followed by two paper cups. Now your head eased out under the raised window and then your other leg came out too.

Maybe Darla was right, maybe it was double; but it was supreme
and undivided, that sight of you apparently trying to hold onto the
sill behind, so far behind.

Your final lean was abrupt enough to seem pushed, but as you
yelled "No" you twisted to fall out half-sitting, and that was almost
how you hit, bringing with you, I swear, the darkness we all had
imagined the dramatic California twilight postponed.

Dom, the click of heels (in suspense films always the loud prowl
of leather heels) and the near elevator's spindle-engine at the top of
the shaft stimulate your voice in one of its several imperfect accents
to ask—not who's been christening my new fountain pen?, who's
been sitting at my table in my window?, who's been at my cold
halibut?, but—*why*, if I so wanted to keep my friends Al and Bob, I
let myself be so indiscreet.

Talking to you is like talking to me. I see no stars in the rain,
though I'm slipping out past our little cap of ancient atmosphere.
If *you* were me you'd cut the quarantine, tiptoe across a corner of
the foyer into the kitchen and hang up the phone receiver. And
I will. But the sounds are so close outside your front door they'd
hear me pass. You'd approve of the risk and surprise I've played
on myself to bypass the time into an open-ended phase of space.
Space possessed by rent alone. There's room to stand behind the
folds of the floor-length curtains drawn back at either end of this
window-wall. Ted came home from a lecture in the Village and
seeing our bedroom light still on came in and said with loud irony,
"Well big deal, now I know there is no such thing as space," and
Ev shushed him, he'd wake Emma. Ted once told me the plump
Hungarian must be paying three bills minimum for that gouged
and padded wall-to-wall of his with the extra door fitted behind
the regular one to seal the office from the uneasy waiting room.
Poor Ted prided himself on not wanting to keep either of the
doors closed when he was on the couch, but the doc said no, but
not the mysterious harsh No with which my father ripped off the

end of his awful debate with my mother over where we were going that summer. Ted's thirty-five-dollar hour would be interrupted by phone calls about medication or emergency commitment. Then the doctor would tell Ted Ted wasn't being spontaneous, was *preparing* material for the sessions. I foresaw Ted wouldn't last, just as I foresaw the possibility of tonight, perhaps through that ultimate pound of lamb's liver fried tenderly for me last week by a woman I love in spite of all the area codes she has at her firm feathery fingertips. But if you're not here to pin your suicide on me, the thought survives (like me) centrifugally. You wouldn't have expected to get back the art work called Location Piece you mailed Richard plus a key to this apartment and a request that he forget the old differences and do you a favor (if only as a friend) and check the place while you were away trying to break up the misguided demonstrations interfering with work at the Marine Nutrients Station. Of course I intercepted the two items on their return trip, your note and your Location Piece which I gather you offer as some form of documentary event if not art. But your son seems to have kept the key. And you wouldn't have worried about no confirming letter from Dicta-Sec, though your losing track of Dot, Dick and Lila was my fault as much as theirs. But Lila didn't help by telling you her husband thought you were dangerously divided. Well *I* am not split between this pen of yours and the voices tampering with the doorknob. If your suicide book failed, last year's *On Interruption* had a kind of New York success. But then what if I *am* the man who created your suicide or at least caused it? I am. Darla's surprise letter yesterday might have cheered you in the wrong way, I had to confiscate it. I can tell you this much: she says she's changed and now can't wholly condemn (though she still disapproves) your electronic relativism—thinks your mystical Commitment to Field-State and your ballsy talk about absorbing without waste the hottest, spiniest ailments is irrelevant, but thinks you're a lamb with the muscles of a viper. But I couldn't on your behalf invite her attention and even love, for they might have lowered your resolve to probe into the form of some final confusion. Was I wrong? Do not say I did your suicide. Voices from an outer phase gather in. Picture me before my TV with Emma on my lap and my hands on hers, and the Space Program's moon is receding. Well even if the door *was* unlocked when (and if) the neighbor buzzed and entered, there must be other keys even if the super doesn't have one. He and the Irish voice are at it again. I may have to stepacide. It isn't as if this place is sacred. I didn't see how to bring Al and Bob together, and so was drawn to you, Dom, not necessarily because you fused Dialectic, Dichotomy, and Field-State, but because you tried. My parents would knock before coming into my room. I used theirs as indiscriminately as my Ev brings people together. That night in '49, I didn't tell my sick father I was going back to the Village after dinner to see Camille. But he went to bed at seven-thirty bearing his tumbler of acidophilus milk, after we'd made up by reconfirming our suspicions that Herodotus is unsure how the Cimmerian Straits and the River Phasis act as boundaries. And kissing but not halting my mother as she played the piano, I slipped out: much more smoothly than I slipped in after the Bohack Joey fight two years and more before, hoping I wouldn't have to explain the honorable mess on one side of my long face which neither Tracy (an onlooker) nor Perpetua (a participating issue) had been eager to take to *their* houses to clean up lest their parents be upset, and Bob had already gone home with a cut thigh and a thin trickle out of his lacerated scalp coming down his forehead like a crack. I wanted to hide my marks not so much because they'd scare the pants off my parents—the elevator again, now opening—as because I'd had no one to go home with: it was Hugh and Tracy, Wit Holmes and his older sister's boyfriend, the Smith Twins, Petty and at the last minute her father's scrumptious friend Mrs. Bolla, the minister's son and his brother, and others. But I alone was alone. For this odd reason I did not even want to explain to my loving parents. Explain that my fairly fast hands had moved out to answer Joey's insult to Petty but also to seal my suspicion that he'd stolen my Corona—(but *was* it a Corona? or was it, say, a Royal?) stolen two Saturdays before after my father had lugged it back under the river from the repair shop and while he was across the street helping Mrs. Bolla get a huge cardboard carton out of a cab.

We have warped to a soft set of coördinates that are not time, or are beside its point.

Ask me right out, Dom I'll answer Yes I did it I guess I suspect I killed you and I will try to bear it. I could have kept you equidistant from yourself and corresponding and alive but

Where were we? My pages are gone, but on instinct when I got up to hide I put your pen in my shirt pocket. From my curtain-folds and with my back against the glass I heard them walking about this apartment, stopping and walking, sometimes moving into this room more or less toward me, off the heel-clicking sole-tapping bare surfaces of tile or wood onto this almost inaudible and wear-proof dark gold pile of Dot's living room carpet which you told an interviewer last year you'd leave as is because you were afraid if you took the carpet up, the walls would fall in. You did cut out an experimental strip across the room from just south of the white couch to the north corner of your giant portrait leaning against the wall, you ran a tape measurement along the middle of this incision. I thought they'd never finish rechecking the rooms. At a sudden distance of six feet came two sharp rustles, one when the sheets facing up in reverse order were gathered, and one when they were taken up off the antique table. With a gasp I began holding my breath. There was nothing said that I heard except a subordinate voice asking What's the phone number here, and being told to make a note of it, but when the subordinate voice called, "Where *is* the phone?" a new voice with a continental accent said don't bother, and gave the number one-two-three, and then when they were all leaving, that new voice with the accent said, "Leave lights on, officer, in case of burglars," and was answered by an accosting question from the Irish voice, "Got papers there, Doc?," which the other voice (certainly Lila's spouse) answered "Research paper of mine I asked him to read, I *don't* think you'd find it—" "Well Doc why stuff all them papers in your inside pocket like that?," which I heard answered with unsteady pomp, "It is going to be published in...a medical—" "Ah Christ *I* want tell on you, Doc," said the detective tenor—but did he or didn't he suspect Lila's husband of removing documents material to your suicide?—and after that the detective must have been in the hall outside the apartment, for his voice echoed reassuring the nervous woman she was purrfectly safe; and someone else asked what maniac did surgery on the carpet, and the accent, Lila's spouse, your Hungarian son-in-law as the door closed behind him said, "Where is his typewriter?, I did not see his typewriter." Sealed off in the outer hall among echoing voices and the elevator trying unsuccessfully to close, the detective's words seemed to be, "Search *me*, Doc. See any my people touch anything? All *I* saw was them papers on the table you picked up, *you* tell *me* what's been touched, Doc. Apart from the telegram, of course."

My pages are gone, though the pen is willing and the paper is from the same supply, and your silence revives as the door is locked this time by key. Across the street from this apartment the office corridors in that twelve-story turn-of-the-century edifice remain dark except for the glow from a red-and-white EXIT and if I stand up there is also the light at the rear of that room one floor down half blocked by stacks of flat boxes containing no doubt my lady's sleepwear. I watched these through the window while I hid behind the curtain, noting also that the rain has let up. My pages are gone. I'd hardly have reread all those words to you, but anyway now they're gone, I can't go back and simplify.

"O.K., Doc, O.K. Let's get one thing straight, I don't *have* to show you any wire, O.K.? Good. Well, it's signed 'DARLA'—know any Darla?—and it says, 'DISREGARD WHAT I SAID.' And I'll have to ask you for that key, Doc."

"Do not call me Doc."

If the points and lines would only stand still my parabolic arc would be fine. But how can you stay equidistant from something that's cut itself loose from the foreseeable future. You're the one who drank Topaz Neons, Dom, not I. It isn't some unholy cirrhosis in me that has brought Al and Bob unreally together in the same midtown motel, it's not some hardening of polyconnective tissue in me surely that has caused the Hungar shrink oddly to dismember himself from my divining scope—and welcome to those action-packed pages!

I think those men are all getting into the near, or west, elevator. There go my words. My writing, my confession thus far, my Memorial Span, my parallel lives, are gone. I can't recall all I said but feel that we are somewhere we weren't. When Al said he'd give his right arm to go to Harvard I couldn't help visualizing, and I said it was his left the Pirates had once been interested in, and he said, "A catcher does more than throw." (Long ago this evening they slid you downtown.) A catcher blocks the plate. He gives signs that are shaken off. His position embraces the space of the game and team.

We have more than time now, Dom. Did I mention the *Newsweep* shot? No special point—except that the photograph singled you out, you were alone, no competing forces, only your tightly growing dark hair and warm squinting pugnacity, your Neoned chops ravished by big trouble you'd had to go looking for yourself, you had to try to know nothing from other people's say-so but begin it all yourself, and your reward is probably that the *Newsweep* lens failed to detail that various mass behind you—grays mild yet perhaps dead and as if originally blue—faces (three, I think)—lapels, probables— but, of your cowering America, made vivid only in your acts. Your trampoline jumps began long before our hostess at the private

opening last week, Cora, told Ev there was the chance of a vacancy
in this building. And after all let's not forget: mortal risk was always
not just a cost of your way of life but also the coast that guaranteed
the commerce inland.

Supplied the charge that made the movements move, east to
west, and so forth.

You were easy to misunderstand but hard to disregard. You can
misunderstand anyone if you're careful enough. Trace never took
that care with me. She was too shy to fight. But she so well knew—
which was a motor grip on my eyes, my arms, the small of my back
(if not my spinal bulb, for I'd never *wink* at her except surreptitiously
to flinch)—she knew and often knew I liked her legs but the inside
of her curious legs from the wrinkles at the back of her ankle all the
way up, and her blind abdomen, other parts of her, as much because
I liked *her*, as I liked her because I liked all those motional surfaces.
No interruption lapsed between the two likes. As late as last year
near a construction site on Lexington when I came out of the branch
library that was full of uniformed Cathedral schoolgirls whispering
at the main desk or reading *Sepia* or writing plot summaries of *The
Devil's Advocate,* Hugh Blood could smoothly accost me and, as if
we'd been meeting regularly, indeed as if repaying some taunt of
mine a moment ago, ask me (as if he somehow knew of my interest
in your life) what "we poor laymen" were meant to make (Dom, in
last year's book) of your strange bedfellows Interruption and the Act
of Love, for really weren't they strange bedfellows?, after all didn't
Saint Mary McCarthy say *coitus interruptus* wasn't quite *de rigueur*?
(Or something, Hugh boy.) But Dom I didn't have to phone another
of my memorial stations, take a fix and by the plainest trig plot the
ancient motive transiting the scar in poor (though now permanently
tanned) Hugh's transmission. You see, I ditched his sister once—
Hugh hated me for having her and he hated me for not marrying
her and he'd have passed into shock if I *had* married her. Here now,
as two city buses end to end both bound for City Hall passed us and

the gold-badged checker at the curb scowled and shook his finger at the second bus driver, I could only mutter merrily to Hugh that maybe you meant as well to interrupt the *urge* to interrupt, but— and of course I didn't complicate my advice by saying No I didn't know you Dom *personally*—"don't make him be consistent in that crazy old-fashioned way, think of his notions operating in a field-state, Hugh: many forces acting in many directions through many distances that you could call—"

"You haven't changed," he broke in in vain (I think he didn't like my pedagogic "Hugh")—

"Possibilities you see made palpable just by being possibilities but also *by other* possibilities." "Thanks—" said Hugh but I wasn't finished; "Who was it, Hugh, who divided the Tigris into three hundred and sixty channels?" "Thanks," said Hugh, "I'm going across the street for a workout." Faded color photos of his health club were in frames on the brick wall of the hotel. Being aware of two of the schoolgirls in cadet-blue coördinates, vest and pleated skirt, whom I'd been watching before, I chose not to broach with them after all their availability to baby-sit, and simultaneously (a) by seeing Gail's newly softened breast as she lay leaning on her elbow speaking to me with the window leaves dark green that early Portland morning after Annette provoked Al, and (b) seeing tall soft Tracy after a few minutes' absence come back into the nonsense and smoke of some antique Heights living room one gently drunk New Year's noon with her hem caught way up on her garter, I (c) *sensed* contemplating each other (though Dom I swear I did not *see*) Ev naked in morning light and Emma just dressed, I said to Hugh, "Haven't you ever played it by ear in bed—?" "Christ what a thought!" Hugh said with unthinking wit—"like," I said, "you see a part of her you really didn't before and you interrupt yourself? Love is short maybe, but the body is long, I can remember times..." dot dot dot.

With lame reflectiveness Hugh said, "No...no, you haven't changed."

"You still selling space for—that magazine?" I said, and Hugh said, "No," and he said, "Call you sometime," and, mastering himself only enough to not say what he felt, he added, "Ever try the Jap steak house—?" "There's more than one," I said. "As I get older," he went on, "I seem to eat in more expensive restaurants." But he'd said I hadn't changed, and he went back a long way.

I knew we would never get together—unless Ev for no reason phoned him—but I knew we would meet like this a few more times.

Since my pages went, I guess I feel all over again I can say anything to you, Dom. But didn't I feel this when I broke off? They're like Pope Alexander's envoy to Prester John, those pages. But *could* Alexander say anything he wanted to John? I can pick up where I was interrupted, but what preceded *that*? The Pope's envoy never returned, nor with him the Pope's message. Maybe he self-destructed at destination. Or changed. In the shower at the New York A.C. where up to about my thirteenth or fourteenth year we sometimes went on Uncle Cooley's honorary card when he was in town on a Saturday, and he played pool while we swam, my father looked me up and down, we were letting the moderately hot water purify us of our energies and putting off the moment when we'd turn on the cold shock, and we'd been discussing whether it was true that swimming used all your muscles, then we were discussing the magnetized handle of the new knife my mother stuck on the refrigerator door, my father was telling about the electric field, and I finally asked whether you could get fried if you touched a live wire in the shower but were wearing sneakers, and my father said why would you wear sneakers in the shower and continued his former explanation by ending it saying that even if you didn't use a coil or solenoid, even if nothing was there to detect the field, the field itself was still there, and then we turned off our hot taps and turned up the cold, and howled in the searching chill and though

I thought there was something about my father's last remark I should reflect on, I thought upstairs to my uncle and that when we'd arrived earlier I'd wanted to play Chicago with him rather than slog a whole lot of laps crawl, backstroke, and butterfly in the championship chlorine. Did I tell you, Dom, of my brief argument with my father? It was the morning after my date with Camille. Her father was so amused by my embroidered account of how I was named and so startled by my knowing the Exuma islands and his own Andros and its predominant marshes where once he'd slaved for visiting duck hunters—that he'd said she could stay out till one. And my father woke up in the morning more tired than he'd gone to bed and wanted to know more about Camille, whose modest mouth beyond my memory as I sat on the Sunday edge of my cooling bed I found slowly smiling between my thighs. I heard my mother say the father was West Indian and the mother from Detroit, and my mother said to my father, "I promise you you are not going to church today; so you can take it easy in the living room," upon which I said, by now swaying happily in my pajamas in the hall between my room and my bathroom as my mother passed me going to the kitchen, "Only reason to believe in God is it's someone you can tell your side of the story to." An only child doesn't only protect his parents. They lose their lives in his, so he must take care not to lose *his* life. Even including the action theater of your suicide, or my omenoid reflections on history and religion, or the physical witchcrafts of childhood and the kitsch biophysics of your (and my) Americanolysis, is my trick here tonight only the unchidden privateering of an only child? You were one too. Did I talk like this earlier this evening? But in tonight's history we are beyond evenings in a state whose chances—as you yourself Dom if you knew me well might say—seem congruent with the field haunted by my erratic but aforementioned vectoral muscle.

Will your son-in-law come back? He has my words but not the key. Where did that typewriter repair receipt go?

Your son Richard evidently had no use for your peculiar Location Piece, an 8 1/2 by 11 shot of a grid bearing what looks like a plan of this apartment plus dots and dates possibly designating where somebody will be at certain times. The blocking in of little spaces here and there almost makes a picture so maybe the blocks are like picture elements in a TV screen. But who knows whether he used your key and obliged you and came and checked this place for you while, after a lecture-stop at a college, you were helping the phytoplankton people on the Cape? They'd had that strange break-through, but now after protesting that they were non-political they were having to fight off pacifist guerrillas who claimed the break-through research was tied to some of the more belligerent fundings of the space program—and what about the Chemical Bank's investments, what about those?

The Ohio Oil I told Perpetua's father's broker to buy me in '59 changed its title to Marathon in '62 and eventually split, but its holdings are now sixty-five percent in Libya so I'll get out. When I mentioned all this to Bob he said he and Leo were telling their Portland clients about Ohio as early as '58. I think in interrupted scenes, Dom, but there is only one scene here. It is here. It is an arc quite out of time and real not at all like all those good and bad times and those bewildered distances that determine this arc. It is in a field-state, one might gaily say, which is not a proud parable of anything but is the fact of multiruptive bodies acting on each other though rarely in contact.

Though I say so, those vectors know how to slide into the one, albeit interrupted, sinew of my confession.

Since Ev and I were seeing each other long before her divorce, you can imagine what Ted let me feel when she and I observed her former husband's suicide by marrying. You know I could line out the whole damn story: the final five years (for Ev) of nothing; Doug's unclever recessions like "Don't you wish I was an alcoholic, then you'd know I wouldn't dare leave you," and every aging day

a supposition painfully shallowly imbedded in Ev that because
he had to blame his job as a bond underwriter for his gathering
indifference, he blamed her; so that she stopped saying what she
knew was the true truth, that the job wasn't dull at all but..., his
new days of hooky in a sunny rental car, a widening (though not
deepening) weight of implicit nights (an ancient history, another
life, another sex life Ev would not go into, though I didn't ask);
then her efforts to fool them into touch again, starting a fight
when he'd come and sit down with the *New Yorker* movie listings
or a Consumer Report on swimming pool chemicals; puerile
provocation in his announcement that Ted would go to public
school next year for a change, Ted's junior year when the grades
count most—countered by Ev with mere explicit acquiescence
plus then next day her humiliatingly detailed and ye gods helpful
information about Stuyvesant, the best public high school nearby,
maybe the best in the city except Bronx Science—but one spring
day (for after all you can't do this sort of thing on two or three days
unless you want to torture yourself) he rented a Hertz and they
found him on a back road near Croton Reservoir.

This thumbnail contour is perhaps the locus of all equidistances
from Ev's breast and the man's half-recaptured ambitions, or simply
capillary imbalance within and urban noise without.

And Dom, you can tell by now that whether or not you asked me
What's my line (and were answered) I could do that scene near the
Westchester-Putnam line if I had to, and with flair.

But be fair: did *I* have the power to funnel your interests into
suicide? Although you make a point of avoiding losers you survive
on a diet of response, and your children disembodied you. Even if I'd
let their letters through, you'd have felt disinherited, wouldn't you?
By another delivery system, my confession to you comes back to me.
Instead of that DA-LITE screen you could have bought another
lenticular one just as good from Ward for less than half the price.
Bob's conscience is not mine, nor Bob's son Robby, though for some

reason Robby now writes me long letters. My hand has turned sort of scrawly in the last few lines. Bob would, but indeed did, think your life had lost its center judging from what he'd recently read by and about you; there was a day in New York in which we happened to see you. I was still full of the Chicago room where you talked to the Inner Group with your mouth full of powdery doughnut and I suffered (in the graph of our gathering coördination) a drop in faith: yes, for one instinctive moment—did I say this earlier?—I thought what the hell had your life to do with mine, except that I'd moved into your building recently.

Bob didn't know I'd interviewed Darla at the very time he was packing for the plane trip but he read on the plane about your ambiguous defenestration, and he said whatever happened he didn't think you were playing it safe. For him of course you were merely a face on a news magazine. From your angle, Dom, you can imagine how tempted I was to confide in Bob my full dossier if not my (as Darla would say) Involvement. But there wasn't time.

From that eighth floor above Wall Street Bob knew you as soon as I pointed; he said (what of course I knew) that the now mildly famous retired cop had been discouraged by his lawyer from suing you for saying he had a prostate condition. A group had come around you in a parallelogram of late sun down there on the floor of the street's tall chamber, girls in bulging headscarves starting the weekend half an hour early, hatless commuters with attaché cases, ancient gray Mercuries with their stock transfers or certified hundred thousand dollar checks making sure this was the last day's errand. We couldn't hear you; the man Bob had come to see in this office was saying that Donnelly printing, and the publishing stocks generally, hadn't done as well as Connie had predicted in '66; but down there in the street someone reached to push you, and you shoved the wrong shoulder. And eight floors above you Bob—whose old nick over the cheekbone showed white against his tan—was diverted by a nearby secretary holding a phone who called to a man that they were ready with Cairo. Bob said he was ready to go. But it was hardly half an hour we'd been in this his parent office—seats on the Exchange, weekly Market Letter, wire service, informational amenities, all unimportant to my purposes (even to the future of my 100 Marathon that had once been 50 Ohio Oil). Hadn't Bob come all the way down from Maine to talk business? Here we were, headed back over the ticker-to-ticker carpet past desks and file cabinets, past the research library where a lady with rings on her fingers was cutting up a newspaper with black scissors, past a bulletin board featuring a long, crooked graph, and suddenly a doorway through which I saw an ochre conference room with a long oval table clear except for a pad and an ashtray in front of each chair.

When I said you were about to film a political ad in Trinity churchyard at the Broadway end of Wall, Bob said let's have a look. I was wondering if Bob was seeing anyone elsewhere on business that weekend, for I had a ledger full of field results to structure on Saturday. It crossed my mind as we head up toward Trinity that through some fatal trick Bob had learned by way of Dot—and Ev!—that I was under surveillance.

In The Whaler later, when Bob asked if Camille was still around—and for a second I didn't know who he was talking about—I dwelt again on his response to your energy in that city churchyard. It's all one to me tonight, Dom. Why so it is! All one. "*What's* it?" asks my later father—"*what's* all one? Gee, for a Cultured Anthropogromer you're mighty impressionistic."

Don't you want to know what Bob was really doing in New York that weekend? He wanted some illumination postcards for Petty, but we were too late arriving at the Morgan Library, though we'd left Trinity churchyard before you finished shooting. Hard between Fulton's erect slab and Hamilton's topless pyramid, you chatted and hollered and mused to different distances, and the videotapers triangulated your active profile and the unspeakable records of your full face, and there were hecklers and the representative of Bankers

Anonymous To End the War; and while they were trying to film this ad for your forthcoming campaign and the young director was calling Cut, and trying to kid you into being more simply serious, and two cameramen contentedly firing away from Gleaneagled shoulders with (from one vantage) the church and (from an opposite) a clutch of women grinning through the Rector Street fence, I said to Bob that when I'd come here with my old friend Al he'd gotten the sexton's Puerto Rican assistant to trot out the cemetery book showing who and where everyone was; and Bob hardly heard me and murmured something about that sort of fussing over facts, he was grinning at the scene and at you Dom with a kind of readiness that made me think he could easily let go and pop someone. You glanced our way, and I thought you looked twice at my saddle-shoes as if they were odd or even you'd seen them before. Which you had, the day you lost your wallet while sharing the alarm box with the premature witch. And suddenly, as if recollecting more than he could possibly know, Bob turned and said, "Oh yes; *Al*."

In The Whaler, where Bob wanted to go for old time's sake, I answered that I hadn't seen the fair Camille in years, and Bob said that after that Christmas time in the late forties he phoned her once himself but she said any friend of mine wasn't necessarily a friend of hers. Bob would not have accepted Al as an equal.

A couple of hours ago Bob had breezed through that office floor like an up-country millionaire; and on the way to the man he dealt with directly—the lacrosse All-America from Hopkins—Bob had lacked only his old Poly stick to complete in my image the wily broken-field romp that had been his trademark, shoulders going low and then swinging unpredictably, sharp turn at one desk into a lateral aisle, sharp turn then near the window into a longitudinal aisle. Now in The Whaler I told him this, ignoring the query about Camille. I picked up my recollection of Al's intrusive New York data and said Al would do well in Bob's racket, make a hell of an analyst—he'd know how much it would cost in differing circumstances to ship natural gas from Alaska to Japan, and the exact equidistance from a point on the north shore of Alaska's Banks Island to New York, London, and Tokyo—but he'd hesitate to prophesy.

"What *is* this?" asked Bob and tipped his gold-rimmed eyes back and finished his double martini. A middle-aged tar in faded denims came down a toy gangway and passed bearing a tray with a pair of drinks. In the low light they looked like Topaz Neons, but I couldn't turn away from Bob's vague, rough question to peer around that dusky lounge, and of course I couldn't imagine you here in The Whaler Bar among the Fairleigh Dickinson girls and the tourists from East Pennsy. "I mean," he said, "all this about Al. Is it the same Al used to live in Massachusetts? your summer place? where you made a fool of what's-his-name who died in Basic?"

There *wasn't* anything wrong, I said. But Bob said I had a funny idea of what he and Leo did. I asked what Leo was up to this weekend. Lewiston on business, Bob said. I said Yes of course I knew they were committed to the gross national progress, the central notion of America, the individual pursuit of the truth about national enterprise, the life of companies, the coast-to-coast miracle. And Bob said quietly, O.K. that was it if I wanted to put it like that, I saw my irony had made the bullshit sound intellectual; so he wasn't unpleased. And just as the denim tar came to see if we wanted another martini Bob interrupted his bemused—even mystical—concurrence sharply asking if that was "coast" or "cost"— had I picked up a brogue doing field studies in Brooklyn? But when the waiter left, Bob went on from Brooklyn to say that you really couldn't go home again after your "center" had shifted, and I pointed out that though I carried my present investigations into eastern Brooklyn I after all did live in the center of Manhattan now.

And ye gods my words have blown a bell-jar vacuum before me with inside it Bob's white-knuckled fist, and my stolen Junior Corona, and Bohack Joey's horny hand and a dim, slim form in corduroys that should be me coming between that pushing, grasping

hand and its angry object the indescribably supple, now sweaty
Perpetua, just in time for my intervening jawbone to catch Joey's
dim thumbnail: but though Bob's fist is here—and Dom you know
I could describe Petty's neck and arms if I chose—I now see I can't
merely get to that white-knuckled fist

(that has so little to do with those groin-impaled captives who
added savor to my early acquisition of the Assyrian postal system; so
little to do with the hunted lioness, a live relief in stone, dying from
her paralyzed hindquarters on up her great edificial slant to the
fierce head and shoulders above the muscled struts of her forelegs;
so little to do with Sennacherib's library of clay who, though at the
Egyptian borders his iron armies were frustrated to decimation-
point by some Delta pest subsequently identified by the Hebrews
as the angel of the Lord, found cleaner fields on the eastern arc of
the Fertile Crescent crushing once and for all the Babylon of my old
Hammurapi)

no indeed, I find I must earn that white-knuckled fist by
equidistancing such other forces as slipped into my field while I was
merely minding my own parabola.

Bob's idea of you was standard all-purpose, from the media,
and he knows what is said of you. But there in the graveyard I
felt with wondrous Calm and Elasticity the Force and Truth of
your achieved doctrines, Dom, now once more (albeit in jagged
fragments) laid neutrally out. You were putting on your abortive
Italian rhythm: "We gotta get away from *cen*tralized *pri*vacy,
stop try'n'a keep a hold of our *sen*timents—wait I mean—*no*—
our sentiments make us hold onto this crap about our owna
centrality—this city gotta be deunified, everybody gotta see the
city from one big helicopter. If elected that's where I *begin*, pal,
everyone rides that helicopter, see the city as a coördinate field
of force, not a series of kitchens subordinated to living rooms
subordinated to underpants on the bedpost."

Were you faintly Irish answering the first of their questions? Who's financing your campaign? "Cost-to-cost cross-section." What you really running for? "Want win in a walk." A tall thin prematurely gray man in a clerical collar said with a rueful smile, "He's high, the man's high," and in steady Spanish you called him a couple of names and said you were almost in the end-zone and he was still looking around for his balls.

But while I measured the volting ergs of famous future you were pulse after pulse bringing back to homely Gotham from your own moving void your American interior rafting Colorado rapids, judging a drum majorette final, placing (a slightly injured) last in a celebrity trampoline event, and, high in a Houston office complex, cooling a thousand-dollar-a-plate cadre of the underground Counter-Blast Org—somehow the immeasurable familiarity of the bone-white nick on Bob's cheek displayed your daring territory. The same with the tough low moccasin-toe boots that like his father he ordered from L. L. Bean in Freeport, Maine, and the same with the green-gray tweed whose quality he'd have spotted at a sale in Boston, and likewise the tiny edge of roughness where he'd worn his Nixon button last year; yes and your ergs were displaced, too, by Bob's blank gaze behind the gold rims waiting for a violent intuition to take hold (a habit that so sets him apart from my country friend Al that they could never get along). And while these details of Bob displaced the loud wilderness of your life, Dom, I endeavored successfully to remember again what I had in common with you, and simultaneously, or *you* might say "equi-valently," I felt next to me the fatal familiarity of this friend Bob whom I'm so unlike.

Bob shook his head. "He's running for a nomination he doesn't want. Did you read the piece in *Time*?" (I read most of those depth-studies knowing they never come close.) "It's easy," said Bob, "to see where his ideas come from; his wife left him, his son and daughter disowned him, the student movements are dropping him left and right—so he decides to enshrine chaos." Bob lighted a cigarette and said again, "He enshrines chaos."

"Which came first?" I said; "the ideas or the personal screw-up?"

"There's no center," said Bob. "That's the point. Let's go get a drink." So we are not at The Whaler yet.

We had come back to the east porch of the church and were looking into the long turning cleft of Wall Street. I ought to think up some entertainment, but I wondered why Bob had mentioned Al so casually as if Al were some mere matter of fact in (say) that poly-grid of equi-valent phenomena you, Dom, have profoundly outlined for your public if your public would only think and see. People hurried down Broadway toward Bowling Green, some no doubt toward South Ferry, people coming the other way dropped down subway stairs, a man named Breen we'd gone to Poly with and hadn't seen for years saw us and waved, men grabbed their newspapers at the corner-stands without seeming to stop. Bob quoted Nahum—or, as I later learned, Father Sedgwick quoting Nahum in an ecological context: "Locusts and grasshoppers." We had both waved back to Breen. Bob probably regretted missing his regular Friday doubles at the club.

In his pronouncements that Friday afternoon and evening for all their force I felt some absence of priorities puzzlingly similar to what you've preached and displayed (at least till tonight, when you did away with your options). Bob never once acknowledged my comment that our new apartment was still a mess, nor mentioned Ev (who I'd said was home with Emma and painting a second bathroom); in the cab going uptown to The Whaler, he asked about my work in Strictural Anthroponoia; but later downtown in the middle of his second plate of octopus he stared hard at me and said this octopus was "terrifyingly insignificant" stuff. He seemed then to want to get away from the long, strewn table-cloths of Puglia's but not exactly because he was afraid we'd miss the lady archae-ologist I was introducing him to. To you, Dom, I needn't describe

Puglia's, its local posters of combos coming, its grizzled Sicilians chewing roast chicken, and the veteran waitress with brittle-black coif eating her supper out of a carton she's brought back from a Chinese place—for, that platform day of your Hester Street climax, your oil-dark brown-paper sheepshead *came* from Puglia's.

Bob said no one understood the mystery at the heart of the State of Maine or had any visible pride in New York, at least the people he looked at around here, and he said, "Let's go see your friend and ask him what he's running for"—as if you were my friend!—which startled me because I now saw that I'd been treating Bob like a visitor, not a New Yorker, and he really was a visitor.

Dom, to no one could I deny that I did not bring about your suicide. I didn't do it. Bob's conscience is simpler than mine but he too would disown any theory of suicidal influence. He'd say, You do it or you don't, nobody commits anyone else's suicide. Which may have been Bob's refuge from resenting his father's influence.

Your typewriter repair receipt is in those pages your son-in-law appropriated, so at least one of his questions will get an answer.

When we got to her apartment, Bob was surprised when I said I had to go. But surprise was checked by pleasure; and any thanks for my politeness was frustrated by his sneaking knowledge of me. He must not have thought I was heading home to Ev and to what after my words of explanation I could almost smell—the penetrating spread of expensive oil-base paint our landlord had refused to buy or apply since ours was an irregular takeover sublet prior to statutory tenanthood next year. Bob simply said, "You'll come back, eh?"

He and the archaeologist were discussing Robby when I came back two hours later. They were sitting across the long room from each other. She was pinching the last inch of a joint. Bob had a cup and saucer. She dropped ash on her wifely bathrobe of pink quilt. You understand, Dom, I'm following simply a direct if not straight line to a point; hence nothing about her age, her lack of brothers and sisters, her friendship with Kit Carbon, her uncle's stake in New

Mexico natural gas, the equidistance from her of her father's money and her summer dig in Turkey with two equidistant girlfriends of Cora's and so on. Bob had his gold spectacles off and his shoes off.

"Why did I say I'd come back," I said. They chuckled. She said, "Why did you leave?" and I said, "Did I interrupt anything?" and she said, "By leaving?" and Bob laughed again and padded out of the room and then guffawed as if at an afterthought. He continued from there what they'd been on when I arrived. "Robby knows he's kidding himself. *He's* not temperamental any more than I am. He's just lazy. Told me he didn't *have* any homework." Bob appeared in the doorway telling the story as if it were a joke. "Petty tried to cover for him, *I* gave him something to remember by Jesus."

A stranger might not have identified in the picture near Bob that famous stone relief of Assurbanipal just back from Nineveh having a bite with his sweet queen in a bower complete with flowers, fruit, birds, but pendant from a curling bough also the upside-down (hence seemingly bearded) head of the severed king Teuman of Elam often erroneously thought to be a forebear of that greatest Persian a century and a half later who (I once hazarded on a Poly exam) if he owed nothing to the postal system instituted by Assurbanipal's grandfather may yet have traced a dream or two of sway and perpetuity in the track of the Assyrian tiger and its river of blood.

My archaeologist friend said to Bob, "Glad you're not *my* father, love."

As Bob and I left, she told me Cora was having an Accident on somebody's roof tomorrow night—"I think it's going to be just a lot of cotton waste to wade in"—and could Ev and I come, she'd forgotten all about us; but I said it was impossible, and was about to say the apartment was still a mess when she said the paint smell must have gone by now and to me she added, "Ev said Cora got you that apartment. Lucky, from what I hear."

In the cab uptown to the Biltmore Bob said that that woman knew things her mother never learned, and he laughed but broke off sharply. "She's quite a remarkable woman," he said. Just tired.

I said, "And remarkably interesting to compound," and Bob said quietly, "Yes, without a doubt. I should imagine so."

We hardly saw the westbound cab that, jumping its light as we raced ours, nearly hit us broadside. It would have been right by Bob's straightened-out leg, but it was like some vector irrelevantly intruding from another problem.

"Whatever happened to your black poontang? When I asked at The Whaler, you never said."

"She married a strawberry-blond leprechaun. They teach dance at a settlement downtown."

"*We're* into that problem in a way. I mean in Maine. Some are all for getting black students up from Boston, New York—"

"From the south," I said.

"—but it's treating them like things. Friend of mine in the Maine House wants the new program strictly Indian; they're in bad shape."

Bob didn't ask where I'd spent two and a half hours. He didn't say why he'd really come down this weekend, why he'd left his mainland house and family, and his windy bay, and the island beach he'd take a run out to in the glaring raw solitude of winter to check the camp and think. He'd have had to have reasons for coming down this weekend, wouldn't he? But possibles smoothed out to an equality or a hopeless field beyond mere alternatives. He didn't seem to recall that he himself had tipped me Ohio Oil. But as an empty cab bounced past us up the avenue doing fifty, Bob and I seemed to meet in a space devoid of intention—New York not Nineveh, Bob not Nahum, and I not now bugged to be occupying a profound center whose emptiness was at many cubic distances all around it charged with centrifugal and gravitational trivia really fundamental not trivial.

I begin to be the measure of this living room of yours, Dom.

At the Biltmore Bob stopped in the middle of his signature and he and the desk clerk and I stared at the poised ballpoint and Bob said he'd checked his bag at the East Side Air Terminal and we had a laugh at that. History teaches nothing, or so our agnostic Dr. Cadbury at Poly used to say, lowering his rumpled bulk into his chair and gazing up with skeptical apprehensiveness at the board where he had wonderfully reduced, say, the Egyptians and the Assyrians to two somewhat slanted columns of opposites—like, Nile, Tigris-Euphrates; Union of Two Egypts, Conquest of Neighbors; Bull-headed God, Human-headed Bull; Landscape of Bilateral Symmetry, Landscape of Rugged Variety and Hazard. My father demurred, but said there was certainly at least *one* pattern, history was a sequence of moral illuminations so long as you had Jesus Christ. Yet my father's pleasure in sheer fact, like his pleasure in the fact of myth, belied this simplicity. When Bob and I got back from 38th Street with his bag we had a drink in the Biltmore bar, and I have again failed to interrupt myself at an appropriate point to pass ahead to the next rim of my paraphase from early 1969 on to the fight at the Moon in '53, thence to Al's painful part in the student interruption in '68 and then, in a race against sequence, to the truth about the Heatsburg Puzzles and where Al's sneaker landed, much less Bob's white-knuckled first, Joey's guilt, and finally, through this mere pen of yours in words which will open new words, the secret structures I have been working on for months now which may make the continuing scene of my early life plain without doing violence to that vectoral muscle I trust I discussed in those pages that have now been taken from me just as the bartender put down two bottles of Bud.

"Funny, you should have talked like that all of a sudden in the churchyard; I mean about this Al." But Bob was vague. "Ever been to Austria? Asshole question, course you have. Do you know what she asked me tonight? what Robby really thinks of me. And when I said he thinks I'm a hard man, she said wait till he's eighteen. By the way, she misses the whole point of the Dead Sea Scrolls; hasn't even looked at Wilson."

"She tell you about her work?"

"Petty should listen to her."

"Petty has her points."

"Petty simplifies. Child-breeding, it's all some kind of drug, driving a cab, anthropolony, shoveling shards, do-it-yourself house pride. Remember when Freddy Smith cracked up and left Amherst—Stingy Bill said it was because Freddy'd refused to go to Williams with him—and Freddy just drove a cab for six months, fourteen hours a day, made good money, there's nothing wrong with that except it's an asshole thing to do for someone like Freddy, but I don't know that I wouldn't like six months of it right now. Bill Senior told my mother Freddy was driving a cab so he could get material for writing, but Freddy told me that was insane. And I guess he proved it. Old Man Smith was a Williams trustee."

Bob slapped my shoulder with the back of his hand. "Let's go help Ev finish the painting." He finished his beer and pushed the glass to the inside edge of the bar and the bartender opened two more. Bob said, "But if you visualize yourself from behind or above with her lowering and raising her knees and hands and biting an earlobe off—I don't mean Ev, I mean anyone—the thing as I was saying to Ben is so frigging absurd you start breaking up and almost—well I did, not so long ago. Let's call up your friend in Trinity churchyard and ask what he's running for. Tell him he's between two stools; that's it, tell him he's between two stools," and Bob leaned back laughing and almost tipped his tall chair over. "Call up Tracy—who's she married to now?"

"I'll call her and tell her to take a vacation."

"I don't think you really mean that."

"What *about* this Father Sedgwick?" I asked—and as I hear the west elevator near me I feel all the vectors whose sensitive product I am here at a point in your measurable living room, and for a dreadful second I can't remember what you stand for, much less what you look like. And now I don't want to know what I said in those unstraightened pages curled at the long edges as if line by line by my script and your penpoint.

In a sententious drawl almost nasal, Bob said, "Ben's helped us." And as, with the strangest self-congratulatory relief, I saw in the dark varnished wood of the bar the evening years ago with Fred Eagle when I'd oversimplified the rattling, softly live and popping Force-Field into neat dialikes and dislikes, Bob added, "With the Robby thing too." Mild, matter-of-fact, depleted.

"Careful," I said, "I'll make love to your wife."

"Funny," said Bob in the slow clairvoyant way that made Petty impatient, "I don't think I could dare get mad—well, maybe I could. But don't tell me about it."

He didn't ask what Robby's letters to me contained. "I wanted to get him away last summer. Camp up on Sebago. He wouldn't go. But when I was his age Dad tried to shovel me off one summer and I told him to stuff it."

When I'd asked Cora's doorman, who doesn't really know me, to tell her about the apartment coming vacant in your building, I knew she'd pass it on to Ev and almost certainly not guess I was the one who'd given the doorman the message. But I never thought Ev would get inquisitive about my interest in *your* doomed configuration, Dom, and she didn't. That was a year ago, six months before your picture-essay on toilet-bowl divination which elicited from Ev to my knowledge her one comment on you. She liked you. But does she know you live in our building? Probably no, though Bob may have learned this at Cora's Accident which I couldn't make. You, of course, weren't there because you were following your Friday carouse in Harlem with a bullhorn speech around the corner outside the white poet's store-front children's club. You don't need to be told all this except for my sake. I plot myself among our shifting coördinates. Speak English, says Bob, a great exponent of

plaintalk, as three hundred and twenty-odd miles north he replaces
Handel's Water Music on the turntable with the opening Kyrie
of the B-Minor Mass (and now fourteen-year-old Robby shrilly
observes against his will that the fidelity is poor, they ought to get
stereo). But I think, Dom, that this living room of yours does *not*
shift; you and I are so much at one in our sense of the unstable
present. Certainly the length of your east wall stays the same, or
that part of it that seems fixed by the elegant brown tape you've
run from the corner near my table northward to where the lintel
of the wide foyer-entrance begins; you've run this tape just a foot
below the ceiling and interrupted it midway by bold white paste-on
numerals, 24' 2". And various equidistances also remain if I want
them to, like my open-ended parabola now thickening wastefully
but going on; its arc is a section of a coneful of multiplying charges
but a section that doesn't cleave the cone; 'tis a conic section no more
embodied than (for art owes science a disguise or two) the no less
real Vectoral Muscle triangulinking Pons Varolii, Spinal Bulb, and
(I wink not) that point (more like a line) between the two cerebral
demispheres. All of which Professor Al would dismiss more briskly
than he can or would wish to dismiss his eager, charmed classrooms
of undergraduates when the bell ends one of his hours. Al would
dismiss your published view that this handsome measurement facing
me six feet above the floor is art. And in this, Bob and he might
be as one. Yet Al himself today would be indirectly and politely
dismissed by the mystical northern broker Bob, who on the other
hand would never have let himself dismiss Al years ago the January
weekend of Al's twelfth birthday when he got pinkeye or cold feet
and didn't come down to New York to visit us after all; for in those
days Bob would effortlessly and simply not have brought himself to
do what now, if he and Al met, he'd be expected to do: accept Al as
some species of equal.

   Why wouldn't Bob *now*? Is it because, unlike Bob, Al neither
saves his stubs nor often even fills them in in the check book, and

loves dealing his twice-applied-for Carte Blanche to charge Lobster Fra at the motel near the college he teaches at? No, not exactly. Or would it be because Al, unlike Bob, can tell the difference between Antioch theology and the more parabolic Alexandrian, yet cares about Cyril's supposed persecution of Hypatia or Empress Eudoxia's of golden-mouthed Chrysostom only for the reverend learning these violences sprang from.

Why wouldn't Bob accept Al now? Because when he got around to telling Al—as ye gods he's bound to in their midtown motel bar tonight—that if he were back today pursuing his interrupted Master's he'd write his thesis on the figure of the Ordinary Masculine Jesus in Bonhoeffer, Beckett, and the Dead Sea Scrolls, terribly he would feel in Al's cordial doubt the pitiless condescension of an after all in no way limbless boy from Heatsburg who once said he'd give his right arm to have gone to Harvard and who way up in some nook of his mortal soul assumes Bob *could* have gone as if by social fiat. Al lets nothing intrude on his Saturday morning at the new squash courts. Both Al and Bob would be as suspicious of head-shrinkers as Ted's own doctor was of Ted's "prepared material" when Ted was just casually talking about a guy he knows who turns on with 125 mg. antibiotic suppositories taken orally and even hourly.

How, without me, could Al and Bob ever find a way to talk about (granted) the odd (though trivial) *kinships* between them, like how they used to make their wives stay up with them at night till they finished their reading?

Once when Bob did his famous simulated window leap from the fifth-form study hall, "Freddy" Smith sitting as usual way at the back broke the silence with applause and a "Hear, hear" he'd picked up from his father (who played court tennis with Mr. Pound and one muggy Memorial Day said to me with arched eyebrow over bloodshot eye, "It's as *o* double *t* as *e* double *l*"). Well, Akkie Backus up on the podium with his *Times* at the sports pointed his open scissors at

"Freddy" and told him to report after school to do two hundred cubes before he went home. We all forgot Bob's leap and turned varying degrees around to laugh at "Freddy," but because of those endless multiplications he missed his prissy twin Bill's victory in the hundred in the dual meet that afternoon.

Sometimes, though, betraying how much of all this I recall seems to be in me merely the power not to grow up. And I wonder if my memorial dwellings are after all made out of the third little pig's bricky-brick-bricks baked in the warm morning of self-esteem. Ev lets me alone.

For some minutes now, Dom, I have not been writing. *Was* the claim-check from the typewriter shop in with the pages the Hungarian took?

Whether or not you are dead doesn't matter, though you are. It would be outside this apartment anyway. Your pen and your paper make my apparent hand in your suicide easier to bear. Again I haven't put pen to paper for some minutes. What kind of time was that? I waited for *The Heatsburg Hour* all week long and then it was all finished in no time.

I shouldn't have taken your letters perhaps. Maybe so far from ensuring the continuity of your resolve, I interrupted it by increasing your parental isolation, that most assaulting sadness of all, yes maybe more contagious than the masochistic patriotism you told past-President Dave Dickens's Inner Group you sought to embody.

Sometimes she'd murmur in the middle of something wonderful, "I'm so awkward," letting the magnetic tip of my elbow move her weightless wrist or my cheek her long leg, yet thinking that she hadn't been prompt (or something) enough when ye gods she was the kind of prompt that makes love into one waiting mass of near-time. It's Tracy, I hope you've already guessed from what I hope I said somewhere in those pages removed by your weighty (though, from my angle then, spaceless) son-in-law—her whole body every place equal so if I knew in the dark or eyes closed where her head was and where her hair and the live rimlet tucked in the softest pout nearly hiding the navel, they were in no rank of reward or time—well Dom maybe that's slavish but—they were just all always equally there. She murmured "awkward" because she liked to inject that titillating lie—she wasn't the tiniest touch awkward but I never said so to her in words, for bare as I was, that word "awkward" coming through her lips uncovered me all over again as if now she'd grown a third hand, and teeth as kind as reeds. Tall she was, oh yes; but her vulnerable neck was hardly in the same league as that of Parmigianino's Madonna; and in general her proportions and gentle mobility could not have reminded anyone of a giraffe, not even someone who like me lay newly awake at four a.m. visualizing her beside a pale Nubian giraffe (or *cameleopard* I called it on a history quiz) from all sides and in all attitudes, knowing that her father could never have had in mind that persecuted ruminant's rare, remote beauty that the Romans unerringly exploited in their degenerate amphitheaters.

I'm going on to the end of this, Dom, even burdened by the chance that I may have killed you, who now become my ideal listener alive in the space of your things here. Why do Bob and Al want to bring me together?

Ev told me how toward the end she said to Doug her first husband that he should expect less of himself, a little less honor and mind and honesty; have more fun, be less sensitive and—oh she cried for a while; but it wasn't because I was touching her that she was able to say as I was just dropping off, "No, you know I honestly did not drive him to do it."

Dom, *I* tried to know Doug.

She said that too, said it often: "I tried to know him, you know. I didn't let him push me into some fixed household policy of (say) never again mentioning something, oh like having another baby or moving to Phoenix or California (which was one of his ideas once and then he said no it wasn't ever again to be mentioned) or changing his job, taking a real estate course up in Westchester and selling New-York-State-approved lots in Bahama Sound. I mean I didn't go out of my way to bring up what upset him, but I just kept myself from becoming a nurse to his—oh his dreary wet mind (but it didn't *used* to be!)—like resolving to not do some little thing and keeping to your resolve, never letting it get interfered with, interrupted, like you were saying your friend Bob wouldn't speak to Hugh Blood after the big vestibule fight, just sat pat"

Next to him in Problems of Democracy and French, was often in the same car of the Fourth Avenue Local going out in the morning (though Bob and I often drove home with the lacrosse coach) and Bob brought a poem he wrote into the *Polygon* office where Hugh was managing either and Bob still wouldn't speak to Hugh—that's the kind of methodical madness you must never let yourself be a party to inflicting.

"on himself, though you can say I was unyielding. But I did give in often. I sat eating soufflé and a lovely wheaty Arab salad one supper all alone with him and I saw that, gobbling up the tabboule salad which he used to like very much, he wanted to be miserable, so I went against my impulse and didn't interrupt his mood and the sound of his munching. But I stayed human, Cy, don't you see? And say I had that polyp in me that I didn't exactly want to go to Mount Sinai to have excised—even if Dr. Sailor *is* quite a blade— and I was fucked if I wouldn't bellyache to Doug about it, I was not going to treat him like an invalid on a special diet. Say I wonder if gynecologists aren't always pretty dashing. Oh yes I asked Doug that. I was trying to make conversation one night he couldn't sleep, and he said what did I mean by 'dashing,' a cunt-lover?" As if Ev's words were some heretofore unknown tropical or para-tropical vocabulary, they must be honored.

Ev was in bed when she said all that to me verbatim. I said Doug was right about gynecologists, but in the wrong spirit. And after a moment, when I thought she'd dropped off, she giggled. I think at me.

And So Dom this is the last time I try to tell about Al and Bob—distinguish, so to speak, between them, as if by spelling out what keeping them apart meant, I clear up...only perhaps a hypertrophied membrane: I must become less precious, and Ted must become as precious to me as my only child Emma, as precious as my only child's body, whose "Ong Zeus" moves to "Ange-ooce" and toward the reality of orange juice that comes in a Tropicana carton. Ev pays attention, she's one person who pays attention. Is this because what I tell her about, say, Hugh Blood or "Pappy" Russell Pound or Joey Neurohr and learning how to reach in and flip the lock of the Vande Lands' areaway door, does for her what Bob once said my words could do for him, show up as if before an electric field old images sleeping on the inside of his head: a room filling with salt water, a church filling up with winter boats: No. To Ev, Hugh is simply what I've told her he is, she's never met him. I'll add, Dom, that because the touch of Tracy Blood doesn't find another locus—even if I know that at the open end of tonight's confession that lonely loop is to be smudged (like ironic filings lured by an unforeseen polynomial lode from one pattern to another)—I haven't told Ev about Trace.

What did Al not tell *me* about Tracy? She made a pass at him that bad weekend in early '53, as I learned from her not him. That poem Bob submitted in '46 when Hugh was in the *Polygon* room was all about a girl's body found to be like a sort of composite vacation land, and we all thought it was fantastically great though I wondered if he'd really done it himself. Even Dr. Cadbury (the reluctant adviser to the paper) was impressed and took it to his room to read it again, but then, though he said he'd be interested to know who the girl was, he had to veto Hugh, who'd of course instantly accepted it when Bob brought it in because he wanted to get back in good with Bob. I never asked Bob if, in those iambuoys of his, "peaked mounts" and "rolling braes," that "long dividing ravine," "moist *bois*," and "ancient strait" added up to Petty or one of those two Catholic girls on Pineapple Street whose mothers worked, or (for the words made me think of her) my own Tracy.

Dear Trace stammered trying to speak of my secret, whatever in her romantic head it was: "Ev-*e*-*e*verybody's got some...secret. And maybe the guys who talk best are the ones who do the best job of... *you* know." But I said Why *guys*? And that got us onto who talked more, men or girls, and then I cozily conceded she was probably right, men talked a lot more. But from the Biltmore '69 I was bound (wasn't I?) ahead to Al's conservative trap the late spring weekend of '68 but instead have come to my bust-up with Tracy in March of '53. Voices from the near elevator jog my sequence. Around four, Al would be arriving at the New London station with or without Annette, Tracy and I had to meet the train, we had to get up, we had to get dressed. March in Mystic was raw but fresh, the sea and land interrupting each other in rhythms more mysterious than frost and thaw. Before we finally rolled out, Tracy picked up her earlier remark about secrets, and when from the high bed I got my feet down on that cold floor of dark honey boards she said as for secrets it was no secret what *she* wanted, and then said she was sorry but she had dreams of losing me, and I turned around with the ball of my foot in a slight trough warp of one of those magnificent old floor planks and looked at her all snug and anxious under a quilt and said, "We didn't even have lunch." The Bloods weren't coming up this weekend; it wasn't clear who they thought Tracy was entertaining.

She didn't drive in with me to New London after all, and I was late; Al was standing outside the station in his pea jacket with his small blue canvas bag beside his spit-shined black toes and reading what turned out to be *The Iliad*, Dom. I remember, because Al asked what the Thornton Wilder was that Tracy had left on the back seat.

I asked about the ship and Al said he was beginning to have trouble with a couple of the black-gang—enginemen thirds—who played Keep Away in the berthing compartment with his German book, and I asked how Fred Eagle was and how Annette was doing up at Orono and how the librarian in Portland was (whose name I'd forgotten), and the Seminole shipmate and of course the Corpsman who read a lot (whose encyclopedic knowledge of VD, Dom, and of a particular creamy gray meerschaum found in Asia Minor and Thebes and in a certain serpentine mined in Utah I may have mentioned in those pages lifted by your shrink son-in-law) and as I drove away from the center of town toward the bridge that would carry us eastward past Groton (where, as I know I've mentioned, Al once got a Captain's Mast for receiving stolen peanut butter) and thence to Mystic, I was curiously excited returning to Tracy in her car. Al said Annette was wonderful, she should have tried for a scholarship to Smith, Fred Eagle's wife was sick and he was off the sauce and had taken her to Cuba for a week—a *nice nice* man. Al said he was really looking forward to this weekend, and I said They call it a farm, it's a restored farmhouse, they farmed turkeys during the war. I was about to tell in detail how they'd run it while living most of the year in Brooklyn Heights, but Al said, "Eighteenth century?" and said he was looking forward to a few drinks nodding in front of the fender with deep-browed Homer—"and how's your joint?"

About all I could have said for it at that moment was it was clean, but the question's casual insensibility, even succeeded by his asking if I knew any Greek, made me sad. For Trace *and* me. When she said some hours later, "You'll have your way, *as always*" (which was how she signed her surprising letters), she didn't mean sacking in that night (for we had no differences there), but rather my not answering her secret that afternoon when I'd stood up on the cold broad boards and gone to the john.

That night Al had four martinis and half a bottle of Burgundy. Then over some of the Bloods' very special lemon liqueur Bergamot, he and I had a skirmish about how many ships Agamemnon brought against Troy, terminated drily by my remark that the only thing to be said for a college course was that everyone was reading the same thing at the same time. Al went happily up to bed.

Tracy and I were through. Her convexities lived on. We cooperated. I don't know about the devouring and forgetful invention set forth in novels Bob's mother was always urging mine to read, where love has died but the body lives on: but ye ordinary gods I confess it was almost the same as usual, time again recoded, lengths mingling, nothing unheard-of yet a strange gratuity, no moving of pillows though some strange waste, but no cigarettes. My tongue was not in my cheek. I wondered if she'd write. Her letters were dreamy and real and guiltless. For a long time I wasn't aware of Al snoring two doors down, but then I was. He'd forgotten to turn onto his stomach.

: Because you will now, Dom, sleep fast through upwards of fifteen rather quiet years: quiet as if preoccupied or asleep: but in their disappearing act busy proving the locus between triumph and disappointment. Annette's hair draws away from her husband's sleeping hand as in one gesture she wakes startled, rises on an elbow, and in the windowed dawn sees at a kitchen table two or three hours' drive away Al's mother study his pearl-satin scar blazed straight across the slope of four knuckles, and hears her say she used to dream that in the car crash he lost his fingers and his tongue. "Well, he lost his tryout with the Pirates," that deep-seated father would remind any who wished to be reminded: until in 1959 (when, Dom, in a volume containing a chance series of joint press conferences, you called Collaboration the secret of the expanding century) that limping father set out parallel to a green cornfield his last yellow truncated cones to mark where the state was completing a short, beautifully black four-lane by-pass, and after that terminal morning in '59 he continued (but now by his absence) to Remind any who wished to be reminded of anything they wished him (from the grave) to remind them of: by "they" I mean his wife and two daughters, and the desomniac and fancy-cooking daughter-in-law Annette he'd come to like in a manner more satisfying than he loved his scholar-son Al, who passed from a 3.8 "cume" at a state college

near home to a grad assistantship in northern California and by way
of Beeson's medieval Latin primer and two symbolic but misguided
terms teaching at Contra Costa College conveniently located in
nearby San Pablo looped back by way of the Longhorn Renaissance
Collection halfway between Austin and Galveston (though he didn't
visit the Chief ET now retired) and then the sights and adjacent
sands of beautiful Saint Augustine (though he didn't visit his
Seminole shipmate now in conservation near Naples)—at last (with
a good old-fashioned Trivium under his belt) to a berth within range
of (though not quite equidistant from) Atlantic beaches, Harvard's
Widener Library, and those narrow enclosing mountains you'll have
to let me loosely call part of the Taconic system.

You preceded me there, Dom, that spring weekend of '68.
You spoke Thursday morning, afternoon, and night, and just as I
arrived Friday you left for the Marine Nutrients Lab where rumors
of a break-through on phytoplankton efficiency vis-à-vis feces
reabsorption had inspired anti-government demonstrations. I
visited Al and wife that weekend to measure your fresh absence
but also to double-check an inadvertent report from "Pappy"
Pound which in my back-going Heights anthro-dig I saw might
be strangely structurable if not statable, if I could just find out a
thing or two from Al. In memory of my father, who had not been
a member, Russell Pound wanted to put me up for Seneca; the
least I could do was take the IRT over from Murray Hill to lunch
there in an extreme southeast coign of the Heights once or twice a
year. The same old polished black hands helped me to sweetbreads,
crumb-broiled tomatoes, and popovers; and I calmly smiled to other
tables, to old Eben Smith and his permanent committee, and to the
drug magnate Werner Vande Land and two of his chess-players,
and in the farthest possible vantage from us under the famed
Iphetonga Blanket the Presbyterian minister whose son used to
beat defensive-minded Hugh Blood time and again on sewer-to-
sewer pass patterns to Bob and who the January night my father

died came right over to us and sat plump and black-suited in my
father's wing chair and looked at the dark lighted harbor and then
(for heaven's sake) asked our permission and said a very short prayer
which because of his masculine kindness seemed to me agnostically
final and hence honest as I'd never been sure the Christian business
itself really was. And that lunchtime at Seneca years later I amused
myself by amazing my small, trim host Petty's Groton "Pappy" with
my knowledge of Dallin, for Russell Pound always among the deep-
folding rhythms of his self-love forgot that I knew his monograph
on that movingly minor sculptor whose bronze of the Indian chief
Massasoit at Plymouth Bay not only portrays that great Wampanoag
sachem who sold the white settlers the land, but I privately believe
looks deeper still to Dallin's own Utah, which he abandoned for
Paris and Boston though never the Navaho and (I'd guess) Shoshone
tongues he learned in the '60s as a child. "—which is the *only* time
to get your languages," said Russell Pound, whose sons long ago
went off in roughly opposite directions, one to an east Montana
spread with a Harvard classmate, the other with equal accuracy to
an ad concern in Zurich. But somewhere between reminding me
of what it had been like after four years at Harvard to be the only
American cox at Oxford and two years later to just miss Columbia
Law Review, he'd gratuitously delivered an electrifying fact about
what happened after or (depending on your viewpoint) during the
party in '53 whose guests Bob and Petty surprised; and as I split
my way head-on through the meaning of that odd fact—namely, a
phone call made by Tracy Blood—yet believed I saw it as but one
force among forces, and for the moment I could not understand but
only savor the neighborhood of (a) vanilla ice cream shrouded in hot
thin fudge sauce now icing-brittle, and (b) the cracked skin down
one side of the black hand that served it in its silver-plated dish, I
put out of my mind why I'd mainly accepted this lunch invitation
in Brooklyn (*Breukelen*) Heights (called by the Indians *Iphetonga*)
: namely, to observe once more the Seneca's cocktail snacks in the

Library downstairs to add a note or two to my still unstructured
file on Heights hors d'oeuvres—hot versus cold, monochrome
versus versicolored (like eggplant compote), plentiful or scanty,
protein or carbohydrate, female or male (deviled eggs, Greek olives,
with polycollation of these and like indicators to (say) median
annual income, proximity to the harbor, summer habitat (owned
or rented)). If the relevance of the Seneca to all this was curiously
compromised by its public status as a club, Seneca was a situation
private and controlled enough for any lab anthropogromer; my old
Poly classmate Ven (for Venable) Mead was the full-time manager
and had made quite a good thing of it. But calmly receiving in the
very heart of my vectoral muscle Russell Pound's remark about
"some sailor" whom Tracy had phoned late that night of the party,
I'd known that I must take up as soon as I could the open invitation
Al and Annette had extended us to visit them in that college town
of theirs.

Until Russell Pound had sprung Tracy's phone call on me, the
following rough rule had seemed to obtain: "When there is a key
absence at a homogeneously Heights evening, this gap will be
centrifugally ignored with such unbroken élan it will cease to exist."
This field theorem was now under stresses I confess it was never
designed for. I had to try to resense it. I wrote Annette that I was
coming and Ev would try to arrange to come with me.

Dom, I now wanted from Al (a) exactly where he'd spent the
evening of that party I didn't take him to, and (b) exactly what Tracy
had told him. For *he* must be that "sailor" (whose identity Russell
Pound wouldn't have known even if he had known that the phone
call that late evening in '53 had been made to my and my mother's
apartment). But exact or not, I felt after my six-hour trip north to
Al and Annette's that among these evening fragrances of tree-flesh
and damp bushes and bare shingles and the air that made even
the oil drips in Al's garage smell wild and fresh, my arrival wasn't
simply mine. For, like the blandly unmistakable tremors of Sister

Deirdre Reardon's then incipient move to revolve the Presidency of Rotary Intercontinental not to a Dickens man but to one of her own Corrolarian Order, vectors were loose in this college town's spring weekend of '68 beyond the rein of the dialectic spread in spite of myself by my own hermit cavalry.

I drove to Al and Annette's seeking no less than a fresh equation, not armed with the mere fact served up to me from his memorial larder by Petty's dad, to wit: "There they were, Bob and Petty, months abroad, just back from Salzburg, Munich, Geneva, Paris, Oxford; and so after a day and a half home why they calmly wreck their own party and don't come back to Brooklyn for a fortnight. Petty's note to me two days later absolutely refused to blame Bob. And oh she rambled, Cy—how Bob missed Europe and she didn't except the skiing in Austria—more coffee?—then some damn thing about Tracy Blood getting some sailor on the phone by accident late the night of that party, and being *ter*ribly upset by what he said—Cal, Hal, Mal, Val, I forget—Petty was rambling in a way that any alert parent would sense was defensive, Cy—oh Dred, can I sign my... thanks—it was *Bob's* stunt missing that fiasco, not Petty's. There are things you don't do, the rules don't have to be written down, and no words in a pleasant Wellesley hand mailed to Pappy with the right postage can hide the fact. By God, Cy, that awful party. I remember *you*. Your father understood those simple laws and he wasn't brought up with a silver spoon in spite of that rich cousin of his. The nicest man I ever knew, your father. He'd have been proud you're a social scientist. He would have been a professor of chemistry somewhere, who knows maybe Harvard, but—you know the story, he chose safe self-sacrifice and all that. Could have been anything. Charming man."

I resent transition, Dom, though I'm glad your Hungarian son-in-law told the Irish lieutenant to leave lights on.

Professor Al was too keenly aware some of his countryish colleagues thought of him as handy. The department chairman had

called for help just before I drove punctually in Friday night and I
scarcely got onto the back porch and through the kitchen door to
shake hands and kiss Annette and their eldest girl who was still up,
before I was right back in the driver's seat backing out Al's driveway
wishing he had let me catch up on him at least by one little lemon-
peeled vodka martini on the rocks and passing a motorcycle I hadn't
seen up on Al's grass standing near a big bush while Al explained
that "Baba" Babcock couldn't open the trunk of his car that was full
of andirons and Turkish prayer rugs from an auction that afternoon
and phoned to see if Al could jimmy it.

Al said old Babcock had missed all three of your major
appearances, Dom. Al asked had I seen the Yamaha back in the
driveway by the lilac?, that was *your* fault, Dom; and Al said the
bright traffic jam we hit just under the hill leading into Main was
also thanks to you—but then he said no he was stretching a point,
and I wondered if the point was that I was something of an authority
on you, Dom—but I hadn't thought Al knew that.

At his direction I tried to back so I could make a U-turn and
cut around to Babcock's by way of Loop Lane bypassing Main, but
the cars that had come along in the last half minute were so tight
behind me I couldn't wave them back.

"What *about* the Yamaha?" I asked feeling chilly smelling that
sweet liquor.

"Student. *Use*less mother. Fast pacifist named Vance Greatorex.
Pop him one he'll turn the other handlebar. And sue you. He's
litigating his way through college. He was chewing on a one-inch
harmonica in class so I threw him out. Said he wasn't playing,
just breathing. He came over today to be nice to me; he said he
could understand how I'd missed the point about him and our
distinguished lecturer too and a couple of other things, but anyone
could see I was a real person, not some snot from Harvard. He didn't
know how to leave, so he's still there in our living room. Annette's
probably feeding him your dinner by now, which shouldn't goad

his abstemious gones any more than the long seat of his zenocycle. These people think *we're* boring; what are *they* planning to think about in 1980? This one's kind enough to say he finds me interesting. But as a person."

The fancy pickup in front of us moved at last and I stalled.

"Well what were *we* thinking about fifteen years ago?" I said. Three fellows running down the hill veered in front of my car as I got it started again.

"Not being interrupted. And learning something. Being decent. And I guess beating each other over the head, too."

Dom, listen, no one in this building of ours seemed to know what the NS button on the elevator panel meant till I asked the blowsy Austrian in her pink and blue garment dangling her postbox key irritably as we went down one morning. She pressed NS, shrugged, and said it meant Non-Stop but it didn't work now, else the damn thing if there was someone in it would never stop at a floor so low as hers. At the first floor we saw only the bright lobby in the car's diamond window, for the door did not open and instead we started up again. The Austrian woman said, "Have mercy."

This recollection may make you think we've reached the phase of our confession at which the elevator's guillotine-like counterweight gets untracked, or the hoist cable breaks at last and the centrifugal governor fails to close the safety jaws upon the guide rail—at which, in short, life, mass, the uncooked reality, student bulges, effluent spontaneities engulf me. No, not exactly. But in fact a boy and a girl arriving from our rear do suddenly get into the back seat of my car as cars behind honk. Al protests irrelevantly, "Hey look, we're in a hurry to go help out a friend who's stuck." I swiftly take the space behind the pickup ahead, then rockingly U-turn into the opposite lane and head for the Loop shortcut that will take us to Babcock's. The girl leans forward at my shoulder and my vectoral muscle picks up her insoluble age and detects some inner soap she cannot control that keeps rising in her pores; and ye gods in the field of her unperfumed hair I can smell she's nice, and nicely spoiled, and find this even in her incredulous complaint, "Hey where you going? the action's up on Main."

Therefore when I came rocking free of the turn I braked so hard a car gunning down the hill away from it all had to bear half into a ditch beside the dark orange of a brick dorm to miss my back bumper. I said, "Walk it," but as I turned a speaking profile to the back seat and the boy leaned to say something to the girl whom in the glow from up the hill I now almost saw in the lower right angle of my eye, the driver of the other car got out, and as Al said, "Why didn't you knuckleheads walk it in the first place?" the girl said, "That's all right," and the boy, "Go baby," and I did.

Al said, "These aren't typical," but the girl said, "I should hope not," in an accent possibly New York City, certainly not New England. I turned into the silent night of Loop Lane and lost the now dangerous driver I'd ditched. Two high cobra streetlamps lighted us past two hundred yards of two-story houses, college staff mostly. The girl was explaining that the boy had wanted to be *involved* in the traffic jam, so they'd wanted to be, like, inside a car for a start, then later take their equipment into the street with the police and the kids. They knew a paper that would pay for the pictures at least. Al said this was nothing, it was Friday, a few crass casualties who'd never had to work for their education were trying to show they'd got the message of the week's Distinguished Lecturer who'd distinguished himself by telling us nothing we didn't know already. "I'm sorry," the boy said (with a humble precision like Bob's when he merely defined for Doc the excellence of Poly), "but he happens to be a great man"—"and," said Al, "telling it as if the less clear the more profound" (and here for a forty-four-foot second at as a matter of fact our detour's apex I felt chance for all four of us to bust out of our loop into an ambuscade of recognition: and in the boy's words now but not in his spirit the boy seemed to express this too, repeating Al's "the less clear the more profound" yet then subtracting from the possibility by the words "But that's *right*": and the girl clamped a hand on my shoulder and breathed, "That's *it*" and brought her hair near my neck again as I drove through the black-and-yellow STOP and turned out of Loop Lane onto Pond Road that would circle under the new memorial high school over an old, all but invisible bridge to meet a road that on the left was a lower extension of Main Street and on the right led out of town but not before it passed the Babcocks'. I'd do you a map if it would help, Dom, you probably didn't noticed the layout as you were driven Thursday from an ATO cocktail party to a faculty buffet, a fresh batch of New-England-style Topaz Neons mixed for you and screwed into a canteen just back from the DMZ. Your life seems farther away the more public. I didn't cause your suicide. If I didn't cause your suicide, can I have known you anywhere near as well as I know this country friend Al? Seated in the right front where according to the Southeast California Institute of Psychology especially spoiled people like to sit, he is probably contemplating violence.

Al didn't turn around to talk to the boy and girl. He said they couldn't even summarize what you, Dom, had said because they hadn't had the decency to follow it, much less the brains—not even the *strength*. And the boy said melodically True, true, they weren't strong but were trying for real strength not just (like) some old computer code society sleep-teaches for who knows whose material advantage, but's about a much help as a steel cheeseburger—and what's really necessary's to tran*scend*.

Al said they could transcend this car in about half a minute, but the girl said over him, "That's *it*, that's *it*, what we hoped we could do at the traffic jam!"—"this car in half a minute" (Al persisted) "'cause *you're* turning left and we aren't." "Because," the boy said, "like we're occupying part of *your space*, and only through *your* kind of like one-dimensional one-way space can we transcend your *values*, but we emptied our minds of scorn long ago." Without any transition he said, "You teach here."

Al distinguished himself from me. The girl said, "First-generation college?" and "I thought so," before Al could say yes or no, and she added, "Do you *love* learning, I mean the learning *situation*? or is it a tobacco pouch and a long, irrelevant vacation?"

"My father worked for the state highway commission," Al said.

"What's your field?" the boy asked and Al, just as quietly and finally as he'd said "state highway commission," said, "Seventeenth and eighteenth century," and the girl said, "Wonderful." We reached the main road that led (left) back to Main Street and the demonstration and (right) to "Baba" Babcock's and out of town.

"Out," said Al, and I discovered a little road straight ahead and up a hill.

"No," said the boy, "we'll go with you and give you a hand."

Having completed my full stop I experienced a vectoral tremor. Al said, "The old man's probably not even home now."

I said, "It hasn't been that long."

With my right hand I swung the wheel down but Al stopped my hand with his, "Baba's probably out spurring Egypt's flank."

"What?" said the girl. My right-turn signal was winking softly in the bushes across this secondary road and just to the right of the unexpected little one rising almost dead ahead.

"No," said Al. "Go straight through to the landing, I'm sick of being department handyman. Egypt was U.S. Grant's horse. No question about it. It's a fact. Aincha read ya own history, dahlin'?" It was unimaginable that Al knew why I'd come. "And that automated pacifist back in my living room pumping his hair on my antique beams and laying hardwood on my friendly fire."

Without looking, I could guess what our backseat passengers looked like. I straddled the yellow line up the hill and Al mentioned a name or two buried in the cemetery at the top. He asked our passengers if they had anything to drink, and the boy sounded amused when he asked if Al was kidding.

A small, humanly specific beat came with the wind that shivered the tree leaves. Al said it was The Anthropopha-Guys from Boston. The girl said What was he talking about, it was a folk rock group called the Cannibals. Al said the Ed Department had scheduled the concert for last night but by mistake in the hall where, Dom, you'd already been scheduled by History but after filling the field house and later that night drumming up an illegal impromptu on the memorial lacrosse field, the Cannibals had stuck around for the weekend and said they'd stay mobile so long as they weren't bugged by the cops, but if they were, then they'd just settle. Al said he had nothing against blacks but it was tough for people who lived on the landing road and had to get up in the morning.

And we now turned into the landing road. I drove down slowly toward a bonfire and silhouettes scattered out around a small mass of onlookers. Then, arms akimbo, at the roadside edge of his driveway a man flashed into my lights a blank look. The police car near the fire had left its red roof light revolving in time to the measure the Cannibals were evenly rocking out, as we turned into the unpaved parking area. Now I made out some outboards on moorings.

The Cannibals were self-powered; at least, I never saw any lead to an outside jack, if the town had even installed one there on the landing. The Cannibals were up on the hood and roof of their Camper, all but the drummer, whose traps were on the ground. Against the pines and birches on the far bank the pale masts of two early sailboats seemed stuck.

Al said, "Or we have other attractions if you're really from out of town."

"No," the girl said, "we're interested in you."

"Well, I'm not in you," Al said.

"Look," I said, "my bag's still in the trunk and I'd like a drink—what if we leave our friends here and go home to Annette."

We had stopped, but the girl and boy made no move. The music wasn't so loud as you might expect. Maybe between us and it, the wind current veered and took it up the river. The girl said, "How come you're visiting him this weekend?"

Al fingered my radio, then gave up. The Cannibals had a quiet audience. Maybe the two cops, smoking in their front seat, had just forgotten the bright bubble on their roof and its radial red alarm swinging round and round.

I was explaining that I wanted a little fresh air after New York and Al and I were very old friends and I'd wondered what impact you'd had, Dom, on this sort of campus area as yet relatively untouched by ideological tourism—"I mean, how many black students have they, and what poverty is there in a radius of thirty miles, and how many speed freaks are you going to find trooping in in olive-green insulated boots?" ("O.K.," said Al, "so they're olive-green, so what?")

But the boy and girl, whom I still hadn't turned to look at, weren't impressed. I might as well have given them the compulsory VD lecture the Corpsman gave a bunch of seamen and seamen apprentices the week after Al got on the *Barataria*.

Two girls came and sat on my front bumper and Al wanted me to honk them off but there was no point in it. Our passengers wanted to know why I hadn't taken my case out of the trunk but had just been rushed off on an errand after two or three hundred miles driving.

"Because I was being run out of my own house," Al said. "That's why. And if you ask why I didn't tell that student Greatorex to take his bike and go, well don't ask me."

The boy said it must have been something else; and I heard one or both of them there in the back adjust their positions. Al turned my ignition key and jammed in the lighter, and for the moment before it popped out, his mysterious vulnerability caused in me a euphoria that so dissolved all strategies of hesitation that I nearly asked him what he'd said to Tracy in '53 when she—for it must have been she—phoned (for she was assuming I'd gone straight home from the ghastly gathering which Bob and Petty attended more vividly than if they'd come—straight home from Bob's mother's drying pumpernickel and imperishable Danish salami) and I nearly asked Al what, for that matter, he had meant there in my mother's apartment when I checked the guest room at one a.m. and he murmured from under his pillow, "Make out? Nothing like a matoor woman," and so I couldn't tell if he was asleep or not.

A black student came and leaned over my left front fender to talk to the left bumper-girl who took his hand and kissed it and made room for him. Al said he'd passed a black student of his in the library and said, "Slaving away?" and the guy stood up and smiled and took offense.

Dom, can you hear the music blowing like a wind through what I'm saying? And I thought even then—yes, spring '68—that my memory (which didn't need to be aroused by Annette's soft kitchen kiss) is over-sensed, and that other people forget some things merely because they've grown up. Dom, there's so little noise in my paratrayal of this scenic interlude at the old landing!—must be my normal vectorphasia compounded into your settled space and neutralized like a TV grid devoid of sound.

The black boy and the two girls leaned together on my bumper touching one another and talking as if the music wasn't there, but if the music hadn't been there neither would they, much less the fire to our left.

"It's all right," said Al abruptly, "I like this, I like it. We need this." He stretched way back with both arms and continued with one, I guess to touch the girl. "My car the last year in high school had a knob on the wheel," he said.

Our passengers' refraining silence seemed to be politely breathing to us, "Say more, be relevant, give."

"Well," said Al, "if our Big Shot who bailed out this morning with a thousand-buck check in his trousers thinks he's out to change the consciousness of America, why's he talk about shit all the time? That's old stuff, here's our Distinguished Lecturer spending fifteen minutes telling how up here he was shitting country shit, and what am I supposed to think when he leans over the lectern at me and a thousand others in the Babcock Memorial Theater with sliding seats and says, 'Country shit is different from city shit. It smells better and there's much more of it. In the city we don't waste so much.'

I said I thought you couldn't decide, Dom, if you were a heretic or a heretic-hunter, and I pointed out that from here you had left to cover a break-through at the phytoplankton lab on the coast just two hours away, and obviously you were serious.

"Well, Baba called it incredibly bad taste and I agree; but I didn't agree when Baba said with that Mayflower decency of his that he was sorry for the poor chap. The rest about a retired cop on jury duty—you should have heard it, I was counting out the thousand one by one. Our Distinguished Lecturer had jury duty with this retired cop who he said had a prostate condition, so after the cop tried to get on a jury by telling the assistant D.A. he had no prejudice at all against the two Puerto Ricans up for theft and in fact had two grown boys of his own, our Distinguished Lecturer kidded him later because of course the defense challenged the cop who before he got on this panel had been scowling and biting everyone's head off back in the jury pool including the chief clerk who was always joking over the microphone; and our Distinguished Lecturer said the cop should have known no young New York Jewish liberal fresh from his bar exam and appointed by the court would believe such lies even if he misread the constipated creases around the retired cop's mouth and the lack of lines at the corners of the eyes. Cy, it was a lecture in fictive anatomy. I wish I'd said that to Baba."

I said I wished I'd come, and Al told the two in back *they* should have been there if they were going around calling this lunatic a great man—

The boy cut in, "I said he *was* a great man"—

"Why *he's* a New York Jewish liberal himself," Al persisted, "who thinks we all ought to get psychoanalyzed and unhung. Up, that is. You could agree with him at least about the James Bond movies. I throw away *TV Guide* every Friday midnight just like Raymond Burr, the third most important man in the U.S." The girl giggled but the boy, who must have had his camera out of its case and clicked it against something, here spoke up: the Bond-Broccoli films were beautiful, their images were fundamental, like the scrap-iron press that came down on a car and crunched it into one flat jagged pack.

"What they call 'mixer metal,'" I said. "Right," the boy said. "Ninety seconds maximum," I said. "Right," the boy said.

The girl said, "Remember Odd Job?" and the boy said, "Beautiful," and they laughed and when Al said he didn't see what was so fundamental, and I hoped the boy and girl were getting ready to leave because it sounded as if they were handling their equipment, the boy said, "Like what's *more* basic? like the human being crunched into cubic centimeters, what do you call that, a groove?" And the girl added, obviously to Al, "What *is* fundamental for your generation?"

The prowl car was coming back into the landing, and I hadn't even seen it leave. There was only one cop now and his light wasn't popping. The Cannibals seemed to break one steadiness with another, there were endings there maybe but not climaxes. The small crowd had spread over the area, they weren't packed together. Our bumper-three rose and separated.

Al answered the girl, "Plug her and feather her. Bring back steering-wheel pantie-hooks. Let him who is not hung be shot down."

"*You're* not like that," I said. "That's how 'Freddy' Smith used to talk. He straddled a locker-room bench and laid his quantum out on his physics book and challenged anyone to prove it wasn't the longest at Poly, and Akkie Backus came down to his aisle and said didn't 'Freddy' mean he challenged anybody there to *beat* him—"

The girl put her hand on my shoulder and said, "That's tremen-
dous. I mean, it's very sad. You don't know how profound that is."

"If you do, I don't," I said without thinking. "But 'Freddy' said—"

Al interrupted, "I'd give my left cullion to have gone to private
school."

"—'Freddy' pointed at Pat Breen, the skinniest palest kid in our
class who hated all sports except ping pong and never took a shower
there never even took off his underwear, and 'Freddy'—only his
name wasn't quite 'Freddy' yet—pointed at Pat and said, 'Yeah, well
I'm no little Lord Fauntleroy,' and that feisty little Breen snapped
back at him like a prepared answer in Mr. Cohn's Solid class, '*My*
name isn't Bartholomew, so don't talk to *me*' and even afterward,
long after we stopped laughing, years after, Bart Smith was known
as 'Freddy' Smith—"

"I don't get it," said the boy in my back seat, and I heard more
clicking.

"Freddy Bartholomew played the part of little Lord Fauntleroy,
and 'Freddy' Smith's real name was Bartholomew. His twin brother,
the stingy one, loved that day, but 'Freddy' didn't do anything to
Breen, he was always a pretty nice guy, not as well-coördinated as
his brother. *Tracy* said he was *too* nice." I hoped this would do the
trick.

"Wait," Al half-rolled toward me and pointed a cigarette ember
in my face. Something special, the boy in the back seat was right.
"Too fast, too fast, wait..." Al sounded as if he'd been drinking again.

"Yes," said the girl, "much too fast. It's a different generation."

"I belong to the Korean generation," said Al.

The Cannibals were in the middle—or it seemed as if it ought
to be—of a number which was essentially a jaw-breaking jangle-
twang like drawing a giant raw comb down wet fir trees that were
made out of live generator windings. My blood sugar was low and I
thought about Annette and a scent on her as close to Persianelle as
country Topaz Neons are to city, and I wondered if some of those

times Al bombed stone-chips at me up at the quarry his missing me so close had been error not accuracy.

"Don't interrupt," I said to the girl.

Al said, "Wait. The name was Tracy. You always thought I tried to slap one on her—yes, *Tracy:* isn't she the one you didn't marry?"

The boy said, "What a way to identify someone."

"Indemnify you mean," said Al and pointed his ember at me again. "You stayed in bed that Sunday and she got up when I was trying to pour myself an Alka-Seltzer, which made me drunk all over again. We met in the hall between the two johns, she didn't seem so tall in her bathrobe, I thought I'd said something stupid the night before and drunk too much of her father's Cherry Heering—"

"—it was lemon Bergamot—"

"—and she fixed me a second Alka-Seltzer, which made me horny I remember, and V-8 with Worcestershire, and dropped eggs, and bacon she'd broiled—I remember that—and then she couldn't stop, she made me a stack of buckwheat cakes which I ate after all, and I still had an idea I'd been stupid last night—about Agamemnon's ships but I couldn't recall if I'd stated the number or said we didn't know the number—" Al interrupted himself with a little intimate camaraderie: "Oh listen I don't know if it's fourteen ships or fifty-six but she just kept bringing me nums out of the kitchen and sitting down with me and putting those long elbows on the table and watching, and I kept cleaning up the plates that had a couple of hunters on them, and a white fence going out of sight over a hill, and pheasant and woodcock, horses and a fox, and as I was dying to get away upstairs down you came looking bleached and dumb"

(—"That's very good," the girl said as if surprised to be amused; the boy murmured, "Outa sight—")

"and *you*"—Al's ember brightened as he took a drag—"you acted jealous as hell."

"You never wrote to thank Tracy."

"*You* know I'm no correspondent. Anyway I didn't have her address at Smith."

I now knew that the whirring, even friction in back—not the new crackle I was sure was a brown paper bag (out of which to my anthropolvectory defenders came the dry warm meat of a peanut butter unmistakably unhydrogenated, whole, organic, and without dextrose—a Natural peanut butter falsely labeled "Home-made")—was at least one small tape recorder, maybe two. But because Al didn't catch on I didn't mind and decided we'd give the kids a real generational scoop, though their grasping my own anthroponoiarc interest was out of the question but in any case beside the point. And Dom you don't want to hear my verbatim log with every motion on the seat covers, each sigh, click, or stomach static. You recently professed little interest in Space. You said it was what people did to each other in their own rec rooms, kitchens, and johns that interested you.

My opening had worked, but as Al and I entered it—I aware of the busy spindles behind us, he (I think) not—I was again unsure I'd discovered just what, in our joint past, was bugging him. All this matters, Dom. All confessions are fantastically banal—even how I may have mildly affected your end; even how I got together that equation whose form Pappy Pound's gratuitous news had shown me I ought now to seek.

Al sat up straight and said Annette was phoning the Babcocks by now, but I saw he was thinking about what he'd, to his own surprise, said.

Now look: the night of Bob and Petty's party, Fall '53, my mother was going to dinner at the Vande Lands'. She was taking her violin, naturally, and there was going to be an extra man, a Dutch engineer who she'd heard was an accomplished pianist and chess player. When Al turned up at our place in his Coast Guard uniform with his blue canvas bag saying he hadn't phoned for fear there'd be no one home, I told him he didn't want to spend his 72-hour pass watching Mrs.

Vande Land's candles drip or hearing Mr. Vande Land brag how the one time Russ Pound had been so rash as to invite him to play court tennis he'd run the pants off Russ without even knowing the rules. And I told Al he didn't want, either, to sit around listening to a bunch of older people tell him what a nice man my father had been. Al was in the shower when my mother blew in late. She'd bought a new dress she said was all wrong, she never should have taken the minister's wife's advice and gone to the shop in Greenwich Village when, if she couldn't get over to Bonwit's, Martin's right here in Brooklyn on Fulton Street had never failed her, she could have taken the bus from Boro Hall or even walked. Her face had broken out again on the way home on the subway—something new in the last year or so—and she was late leaving for the party because she was swabbing her forehead with milk. She had just time to shake hands with Al and say she'd see him in the morning, and then I walked her to the Vande Lands'. My priorities thus ranged, I had something to eat at Nino's dark bar on Montague that no one I knew on the Heights would ever have gone into. Then I sloped off to the disastrous Welcome Home party at Bob's parents'. Al had said he guessed he'd go to Broadway and try for standing room.

Why tell him I was afraid if he came to the party for Bob and Petty he'd get his back up: up against Perpetua's father's neat gazeteer queries about Heatsburg and environs; up against Bob's father's blue morocco copy of Gray's letters (as indeed *my* back was for five long minutes that very night jabbering to Bill Smith about how glad I was my otherwise meaningless heart murmur exempted me from the Korean thing, while Bill, who was headed for Newport OCS and explained the sextant to me, said three times despite my interruption that he assumed he'd make j.g. before his three years were up); or later in the evening up against "The Banks of the Wabash" harmonized by Mr. Blood, Hugh, and others before the hearth which Al's husky bass would successfully have joined but from which Al would know himself excluded as exactly as the moment's mellowness was vague. If Tracy's phone call had told Al too much, then he would figure I'd spared him that party because I didn't quite trust my four-year Coast Guard enlistee from Heatsburg to have a good time. He wouldn't have known anyone except me. And Tracy.

Now someone slapped my rear fender and The Cannibals broke for a smoke; I told Al he was wrong about that March morning, maybe I was bleached and dumb, but not jealous; in fact Tracy knew I'd just about had it with her, there were only one or two more times.

The boy snickered in the back seat and Al said, "Yeah, maybe so, but as much of her phone call as I remember, *she* said you were jealous."

But Al had to admit she'd been pretty curious about where I was, I'd left the party a good hour and a half before she phoned.

In the space of that one accidental phone conversation with Al, it seemed Tracy had tied me up in my own words and given me away; been fond to Al so he woke up enough to worry that my mother might not be home yet and might walk in and see him in his skivvies; and given Al an acceptable reason for my not bringing him along to the party he thought was at the Vande Lands'. Most puzzling of all was that the next morning Al had not merely not reported the phone call from Tracy, he hadn't denied what she told him she'd told me, namely that when she'd gone up to make the beds, there deep in the drear but refreshening country of March, Al had slapped one or two on her. Dom, you recently professed little interest in space. But what about this parking area by the river landing? what about my rented Galaxie with two beautiful strangers in back? what about what happened to your living room tonight?

Bill Smith had told Freddy that night that I had a Coast Guardsman staying with me who'd been busted back to Third; well, Freddy went across the room and used it to try to amuse Tracy, who always tried to discourage his attentions without being unkind. Anyway Trace guessed it was Al and when she phoned me an hour and a half after I'd left the party and she got Al instead, she said to him he should have come, and he said he thought it was all older people but as far as I could tell hadn't recalled the name Vande Land, and since Tracy was phoning him within earshot of Bob's mother (who was no doubt hoping everybody would go home) Tracy didn't tell about the Welcome Home fiasco and thus apparently didn't name Bob's parents. But your room interrupts me, Dom. I've left something out of it.

"She said if I'd been busted to Third I should have come to the party, she'd have cheered me up. Anyway I said sorry I didn't know *where* you were if you weren't at the party."

The boy in the back seat, who must have picked up a lot of Cannibal music for background to our talk, said, "What are you guys *doing* down here at the landing?" and the girl laughed admiringly. I think the tape recorders were off.

"Annette's mad because I took out a fifty-thousand whole life policy."

The boy said, "*That* won't keep you from dying," and Al said, "Caesar Bemis used to say *death* pays all debts. 'Course he was talking about his *own* death; but *debts other* people owed *him*."

"Insurance is sick," the girl said.

"It's expensive," said Al.

"It's sick," said the boy. "It's sad," said the girl.

Al said, "If it comes from the student it's the uncomfortable truth, if it comes from the teacher it's an up-tight put-down."

But it wasn't just Annette and the student Greatorex bugging him, it was in some way me. I've always forgotten, Dom, that I can't just give myself to a place and fit in—not Bob's parents' living room, not that joint the Moon on Commercial Street in Portland, not (I guess) even my very own rented Ford, any more than our west elevator where your visiting Hungarian son-in-law looked at me with the alertness of a prospective employer one night a week after Santa Barbara, any more than the ninth-floor window out of which you slipped more definitely than the freedom placard.

Now, with more of that battery-powered purr behind us, Al was saying Annette had bought liver for tonight because she knew I liked it even though she didn't like cooking it, and there'd be plenty because they'd thought Ev was coming with me. And by the way, had I told Tracy *why* he'd been busted?

"Of course not, I mentioned it to Bill; I didn't say a thing to Tracy all night."

Beyond the bonfire and the Cannibals' camper a Volkswagen was being fought over, inside and out. Pulled away out of the front seat by his hair, one student suddenly towered over the car; someone was trying to defend the brake against someone else who wanted to let it off, and others were trying to push the VW into the river. The Cannibals' Camper was between the VW and the prowl car, so the cops didn't see what was going on, or in.

Our passengers said they'd had it, yeah they'd had it with us, what they'd got on tape was just gossip. Al jerked around and stared, then shrugged back forward and told them to run something else over it then.

They were getting out, and Al said, "Live now," but seriously. But the boy paused and said, "I'm sick of hearing older people say don't waste these years—my swinging parents are always saying it, it makes me feel *I'm* already looking back too. Well why *not* waste them? I don't know what to do with them and neither do most of my generation. I mean, you blew it and I guess we're going to too if there's anything to blow."

"Hey record this," said Al; "wait." The boy was out; I felt without looking around that the girl had a foot out but her behind on the seat. "'If you shall see Cordelia,—/ As fear not but you shall—show her this ring,/ And she will tell you who that fellow is/ That yet you do not know.' That's Kent, the best part in a muddy play."

"I wouldn't know," the girl said, "but I think you two are going to have a fight tonight and I wouldn't mind taping that."

When they went away and I turned the ignition key right

(noting that Al had left it on battery), Al said, "*We're* not old"; and I remembered another reason I'd left the Welcome Home fiasco at eleven; the "extra man" at the Vande Lands', the Dutchman, had been billed as a Resistance hero.

Annette had the bacon in as soon as we arrived. There was no Greatorex, and the children were in bed. With Annette off in the kitchen, we didn't speak for some moments, which there's no point in confessing because it hardly shortens the line to Bob's white-knuckled fist or my stolen Corona. And you know if I chose I could show wholly the pine sinks and water benches and the half-hidden pins hanging the lower doors of the high jelly cupboard Annette has her blue china and silver and pewter in in the narrow brown and gold dining room. Or if I chose I could show in part the distance, say, from Al's 1750 *Windsor* topped by a fine spindle-comb he's proud of with at either end of it carved ears he's even prouder of:

to (upstairs, and dated from the very early Federal Period) a *field bed*—fair game for coarse jests when Al identifies it for a younger colleague, but the six-foot maple posts a source of joy for a colleague's wife given the tour by Annette:

to (downstairs) the new eye-level *oven*, and on the adjacent counter an oval plate of very promising liver whose dry sepia, now free of edge skin and pale cartilage and dusted with flour, has had five seconds' bath of boiling water poured on it to seal in the blood.

"Where there is a key absence at a homogeneously Brooklyn Heights evening, this gap will be centrifugally ignored with such unbroken élan it will cease to exist." Now, like any distinction you wish to make between hors d'oeuvres lumpy and mealy and/or sticky, I had foreseen *Al's* absence but not clearly Bob and Petty's; yet at that electro-static party in '53 my social senses had been so stimulated by the latter absence that I'd let myself in conversation touch gratuitously upon the former.

Now reviewing in Al and Annette's living room Al's remarks in the car, I found my fresh equational form thwarted not by Tracy's acts alone. But how on earth could I broach to Al the now broken theorem when he couldn't to begin with comprehend why the dialectic inherent in it was insidious, nor believe that it had been a muscular and honest effort to embody field.

Al had often been uneasy or even abrupt about my work. He wanted to know how I'd gotten from Jewish-Negro myth-friction in southeast Brooklyn to hors d'oeuvre ceremony on the Heights. Now (as Annette protested we were about to eat) Al asked me what was the social significance of the pâté de foie gras he was opening; I said goose liver had not to my knowledge had much ancient predictive function but anyway I'd about scrapped my hors d'oeuvres file and was concentrating on you, Dom, and in fact on the anthro-toponomy of friendship.

"That makes you a friendship man," he said quietly, poking the fire. "Still drawing diameters and truncated spirals?"

Annette asked what Baba Babcock had had in his trunk, but Al ignored the interruption. Hadn't we cleaned up on those guys at the Moon that time?, and I said Yes we had—wasn't it '53?

Al said, "You took the little bad-ass striker from the Coos, and I took the big guy. The little one was tougher. Then we finished up with the middle-sized one off my ship."

The SP who'd been standing outside was no friend of Al's. But if he didn't save him from being busted, he saved us both from the Portland cops. "And all because," said Al, "I told them Coos Bay wasn't in Alaska, it was in Oregon, and Barataria Bay was in Louisiana and opened into the Gulf, and you said not only was it in Oregon it was in Coos County and the Coos River ran into it, and the big guy seemed to want to try discussing it but the bad ass said, 'Shee-it' and the middle-sized one said, 'Two years of fuckin' college,' and Cy you turned up the old insouciance and said something about 'Furthermore it's twenty-five-odd miles from *Remote,* Oregon.'"

Did I say that, Dom? That gray Monday, the Coos Bay docked. Gail had stayed Sunday night as well as Saturday and took a morning bus to Boston. Al brought a volume of his encyclopedia on liberty because he wanted to show me a paragraph biography of someone he thought must have been one of those obscure great men, like Fred Eagle. I was dubious, I knew something about the man and when we sat down in a booth at the Moon I modestly scattered into our talk every bit of stuff about him I had, and the three boors were in the next booth, like a force of gravity.

But now Al thought the fight had been provoked by him.

After dinner he told Annette he was sick of ignorant students and wished he could work for a library like the Huntington and be as independent as (he thought) I was, working indirectly for a museum. Then he said he was glad I'd come up. I asked whatever happened to the hospitable librarian in Portland and Annette said, "Al dropped him," but Al said, "Hey wait," as she went through to the kitchen, "he was a bit too unmarried for me," and Annette called, "You never returned the key to his house." Then Al said with amiable but real suspicion he'd have to write this Bob and get the facts on that party I ostracized him from. I said I'd give him the address and Al said without paying much attention to me because he seemed to be thinking of what Annette had said, "It's around Portland, didn't you say?...or *was* it you?"

Later he wanted to know why the hell I was interested in you, Dom, and I with ostensible pomposity beginning and deliberating an answer managed to make Al interrupt. "He's not all wrong, I never said that. He told about two Italian harridans who assaulted him after some speech honoring some Viet vets where he'd said—I almost forget what he said, but I agreed with him. Cy, I hate the war too—Annette knows I do; but tell me why is it most of the time the types who bring me the petitions I can't stand the sight of them, and they're not all students either. It's something about balls. It's not that they need a bath, I just can't help thinking would this one stand up for *me* in a pinch—they've got blackheads inside where you can't see."

"Oh Al," said Annette.

"Anyhow I keep politics out of the classroom. Some want to know where I stand on the Domino theory. I say that's my business and how is it *relevant* to Boswell's *Account of Corsica?* That little teaser tonight never *heard* of Theodore Dreiser."

"Dreiser's coming back," I said. "These kids want accuracy."

"And our thousand-dollar lecturer got asked about his pending divorce and you know what that comedian said? that the real function of marriage was it was a prerequisite to divorce. And you say that's a great man?"

I explained wearily that it was your way of accommodating Dialectic and Dichotomy to Field and Collaboration that induced me to regard you as someone significant.

We all sighed, and a stick of oak that was all coals in the middle burned through and fell.

Al said, "So breaking up is what proves you're alive."

Annette said, "Well I just can't tear myself away." She got up and touched my shoulder and excused herself. After a couple of minutes I heard water in a basin upstairs, then one of the little girls cry out, then the bathroom door close.

"I'm good to her," Al said, "but I get these awful moods."

I couldn't think of what to say, so he added that *I* was no one to talk, speaking of fights at the Moon and the Sunday morning Tracy made breakfast for him; I could be, well, pretty direct myself, like with that poor dumb shit Ev's first husband—wasn't he an insurance salesman? no?—and why in hell didn't I bring Ev up this weekend, Annette had never met her.

I said Doug wasn't a dumb shit.

Al moved the ends of the fire screen in as I was trying to phrase in my head the fresh equation—something about how one coördinated (a) one's field contact with the distal and (b) one's actual contact with the immediate, and I couldn't quite work it into triangulation—and Al asked if Ev had thought he was a goddamn fool to phone up like that to apologize for my being delayed by our encounter with Doug. And I said of course not, my eardrums pounding.

Al of course had wrongly assumed that Ev would tell me right away about his call. I wondered if Al had told her the truth I'd told Doug about himself and Ev and me.

Maybe that girl smelling of vanilla scalp and then peanut butter was right, maybe all this was gossip, and probably their verbatim monitor of that stuff in my rented car was soon erased by the sounds at the river's edge.

We remind each other.

Maybe I'm no Cyrus diverting the Tigris, but ye gods what we don't hear about!

I know I never heard about Al's call to Ev just as certainly as I believe that to this day (this night in or out of that eighth-floor motel room) Al doesn't know that Ev's late husband committed suicide.

Hitting the Cloroxed porcelain slopes so as not to disturb a half-combful of Annette's hair afloat in the middle, I reflected on what the papers had said about the negligible response you'd received up here, Dom, and I wondered what would happen to you.

Tracy wouldn't lie. But Al implied he had *not* made a pass at her that March weekend up at her parents' farm. Perhaps there was what my father would call an honest difference of opinion. The thought that maybe it didn't matter thrust me aside to the thought that my retheorem must issue not only from Tracy's unforeseen behavior the night of the Welcome Home in the fall of '53 but from Al's in March and then now.

"You know," I said to Annette the next noon without fair transition, "the morning of the party in '53 that I didn't take Al to, I phoned Bob."

"Yes?"

"And said I'd heard the good news about his father pulling strings so Bob could apply late to business school or, if he'd rather, he had a standing invitation from a firm in Wall Street to enter a training program. Bob didn't say much, and then I said I'd see him that night, and he said, 'Yes?' and after he'd answered my question about how Petty was holding up, he said he had to go out, and he said a rather abrupt goodbye. He must have gone to work on his mother to find out about the surprise party."

"What party?" said Annette. "I never caught up—who's Bob?"

We heard Al's car and then its doors—well, we're all time-warped centers of attractive force and last night old Al had indeed been bugged by Annette and Greatorex and Baba Babcock, and that was that—and now the three girls came in through the kitchen and when Al appeared he said—to Annette—"Babcock got it open himself."

But old Fred Eagle said over the phone to me when he was in New York on business around the time Ev and I got married, "Annette's a witch, she knows things she's never heard. A beautiful witch, mind, and a rattling good cook." When Fred phoned I'd been mulling over an argument with Ev's Ted that hadn't been quite as understanding as we both pretended—but I may have thought impromptu hospitality from us would merely interrupt Fred's intramural quest for Hypatia. He phoned just before he left—how long he'd stayed I don't know for I'd been living those weeks on another time—and as he was hanging up he remembered he wanted me to recommend a broker and without thinking I gave him Bob's firm right in Portland. For which I have never received credit.

But life isn't like school; yet now I know I welcomed that unlikeness ignorantly when I belonged (I thought) mind and soul to corpulent Dr. Cadbury and wiry, hypnotic Dr. Cohn. I wrote a better hand in those days, though never good enough for my copybook-educated step-grandfather (Zo-an > Zon > John) who revered Poly because it boasted several Ph.D.'s.

But Al never dropped Fred Eagle. Did business with him year in year out. And Fred may have done business with Bob's firm in

Portland. On some excursion with Fred—why not?—maybe up
north at a shop full of old bottles when thanks to Fred Al snatched
for two bucks a mint first of U.S. Grant's 2-vol. *Personal Memoirs*
for Professor Babcock—may not Fred have mentioned Bob? Why
should this matter to me, when so much of my current energy turns
about the vibrations of your American greatness, Dom, who now
like a retreating muse demur at "The Cannibals" and insist I might
have found a better name for them. I've really used your living
room, but it would take ingenuity even I don't possess to show
that I caused your suicide. What will such guilt matter tomorrow
morning when as the first forkfuls of soft pure scrambled eggs pass
her wind-cracked lips the no-less-lovely Darla discovers your death
in the inner spaces of the *Times* and phones in her prediction that
because you were "flirting with a repertoire of other, minor winds
such as the sexicide of skydiving, Japanese undersea husbandry of
the algae *Porphyra umbilicalis,* or what he himself called 'the honest
gut and gentle perspicuity' of a suburban Gary neighborhood that
swallowed Goldwater unanimously," you Dom ignored "the one *big*
wind" and would "ultimately" have in some sense killed yourself
anyway—a syntax *Newsweep's* Prophecy Desk will jump on with
howls of rapine recognition.

I'd almost forgotten where I am and can only guess that had
there been sounds outside your peephole I'd have fielded them. One
of my fellow panel pundits—say, the famous Dr. Polly Ester Sitz in
her short, Persianelle-scented sheath—may if she reads even what is
left of this think I gave you a heartfelt push toward suicide so as at
last to have a firm locus for my own conclusions about your identity.
Your face Dom all know as well as you (though few know so well as
I your major pronouncements, especially the one or two you seemed
to have abandoned unexplained, like your remark at the airport the
morning after your defenestration that America's an only child).

The face I refer to one supposes to be the seven-by-five-foot
black-and-white photo-face leaning against the wall here behind

me. It is miraculously a painting. Up close you can see. Dot bought it for love of you.

Newsweep punned, of course, on "poring over" this painted face of yours..."from some Sea of Tranquillity southeast of one broad nostril, and then dead north (at the mercy of the famous though now absent grin) a liverish pit the artist has blown up into The Great Salt Dimple."

Immigrant eyes, slanting east from Vilna but looking west with the shrewd trust that in the twinkling blank of the great American field your brand of acquisitiveness will work. The more I think, the more I trouble myself to be glad those famous eyes aimed to acquire the whole land, not just the baked or grilled. But the more I look around over my shoulder at this hugely candid photo in paint, the more I measure. Nose, eyes, short convex pugnacious chin silently collabor so I no longer can take for granted personality or, almost, even person. Your reference to this painter last night seemed to me to take back the admiration with which some months ago you found in this kind of painting from photographs an instance of "Field": i.e., "Field" as in your "Neutraline Equatics": a mode that lowers, eases, even coolly ousts ancient hectic hierarchies that have set the mass of us or our parts discretely off from each other or from the mass of our setting. Yet my eyes cry out, Can all that other life I know about subside into some rankless field and lose its poignant fussy orders? Maybe I never knew what you were talking about. Yes, what about my step-grandfather on his desperately discrete vacation up north (where he was born saying First Things First) as he goes back to the barn to get a stone for the hand-mower blades: Or my father upstairs in the stone heart house on a Sunday morning making neat ABC outline notes for his Market Letter, getting the priorities right. Dom, I've closed my eyes, turning away from this amazing picture; then I've turned back opening them, and for a moment I saw you there but also the massive terrain, at most now parafacial, and with it some of your trademark words last night (as reported in this morning's paper). "The secret of concord now is that it doesn't greatly matter if you disappear from the scene—*if* you can come to feel this..." And like your other words these are to be identified with your now renowned last name.

"What a pile *that* is," said Hugh Blood one Sunday twenty-five years ago trying to get into the conversation decisively and thinking Bob and I and the minister's son and Trace would agree, for Petty had said that her father's "friend" Mrs. Bolla's first name Mara meant "the sea." Petty said to Hugh, "Why not?" and Bob said, "What a great name. It's better than Perpetua any day" and I began to feel that the day was turning out not so bad after all—my father had been too blunt at lunch telling me I wasn't going to the movies on a Sunday. Now I said to Hugh, "What about *me*: I'm named for a famous king in Herodotus, ask my father," but while the minister's son slowly said, "Who's Herodotus?" Tracy said quickly and quietly, "You are not, you're named for your uncle Cooley," and her eyes out of that weird shyness of hers got teary. Then Bob said his mother had had their new cat Romeo fixed and his father got her mad by just calling him Cat. Bob said he wouldn't mind having a famous name like mine; then he changed his opinion and said No it was better to get an ordinary Christian name like Bob; the one you had to live up to was your last name. Petty, with a kind of hesitant, proud seriousness, said, "Yes. I think that's right." Then my mother called her and Tracy to come into the kitchen.

What a vast apartment it was! My father was in the back bedroom writing the Market Letter for tomorrow, the weekly long view of what stocks looked good, that his secretary typed first thing Monday; so I couldn't ask then about exactly where in Herodotus, and then I forgot until just as I was dashing out to catch the subway to school the next morning.

He was dusting himself all over with talcum and he laughed and said, "Well, like Cyrus you were a dream first but then you turned out all right. Your grandfather"—he meant my mother's step-father—"said you wouldn't thank us for that name. Why not read the first book of Herodotus, and pick out what you want. But *you* read it; I'm not going to tell it to you. And don't miss the end." He seemed kind of gray and not so frank and open as usual. Maybe I should just evoke the odor of Amolin talcum.

Let me jump time here as naturally as if I were riding your borrowed ink, from the point that ends my preceding sentence to the lines that begin this one, and loop onto that much earlier Sunday some intent lines Bob was busy shading in when two years later I was on the point of turning to something else from the concluding page of my chem assignment—"Ta: atomic no. 73, atomic weight 180.94." It was Akkie Backus's study hall and Bob had his physics book on the desk closed. He finished and passed me the paper. "Know what that is?"

Evidently iron filings, and haired in a neat vertical oval. "Where's the bar magnet," I said, "hidden underneath?"

Bob grabbed it back grinning and said, "Not *what* but *whose?*" Animal and whiskery, say a squirrel's alert but unsuspecting bottom. Kind of a bad joke I thought, but on the other hand to the eye gentle and simple and rather purely animal. Not like some tinkling Turk that long-haired Romeo might sniff (not Tracy and perhaps not Perpetua—I took it all very seriously—and not Gail because Bob had never met her and anyway her hair was too light), but more like a private angle of some inadvertent Heatsburg woodchuck. (Salacious junk!, Hugh Blood may think today from his space-selling desk but *he* was trying to see Bob's sketch too but couldn't from his aisle. Akkie was watching all of us.)

Maybe I didn't mean to confess a thing tonight, merely meant to occupy this space. And all I've done is keep it up. Talking. Or writing. My face isn't like yours; I found only mine in the mirror hypotenused across from your terra-pintorial photo-phiz. But I go on and falling into myself here I've come to necessary next words I had not foreseen. For you I didn't need literally to set the stage, outline this room, scale in (and color) this cherry table

Dot's great-grandfather made with his own fingers that's now warped across the glimmering leaf I'm leaning my forearms on. It's the same room we all saw in *Newsweep's* three-hundred-sixty-degree pan.

(I hear the elevator hall, but not exactly feet.)

Yet there's a difference in this room now, isn't there? Something out of place or phase. Something to do with those two presences in that nearby motor hotel.

"*Our* ancestors weren't immigrants," dreary unbelievable Hugh Blood said to Joey and his two pals the day of the big fight and Bob's white-knuckled fist. And I find shifting away from me bizarre connections not only with your suicide but with your eyes, your fame, your aim, which was to be our fool but a prince, to be in yourself a dangerous and rich walking switchport, an America. "Oh come on, what was he doing around the county courthouse in Jackson, Mississippi," said Darla at the TWA baggage scales the morning after your defenestration, "did he plan to find our kidnapped kids? He just wanted to have a little brawl downtown with some unarmed redneck and get his face on *Time*." Witty, for Darla. But Dom, I'm not calling in your credentials. You're a hero. A real American one, messy though late-model. O.K., that California ninth-floor is part of my head which you said you'd change and did. But the banal peculiarity linking these New York eighth and tenth is what elevates this confession beyond gossip. I paused for some time between "elevates" and "this." My inflamed parabola may need what Bob's dad takes for his sleepless shoulders, injections of gold. I played the field that night in '53 at their house—

oh shit (your immortal voice says from the coroner's coolish table), come on up to '69—

played the field, though only till eleven; concentrated on making Bob's parents' Welcome Home party go, even without its reason showing. But a lapse occurred which I've since come to call Vectoral Dystrophy.

Wait: Tracy was there, talking to a couple of her old Packer classmates and remaining distinctly moist at the outboard angles of her eyes, and doing absolutely nothing with her free hand in that complete yet vulnerable way of which I have no doubt already taken slow measure in those pages lifted by the Hungarian how long ago I can't any longer tell, and she had on low-heeled pumps that as I let myself stare through a momentary clearing of hips and legs she began toe-against-heel to take off.

Twenty-odd more were there. I believe I covered the gap. It was not filled by Bob's small, suddenly round-shouldered mother saying to the Smith twins' father, "I *am sorry*, Bart, Bob ran into schedule problems—you'll just have to catch them at Christmas." I was quite as successful as that evening in Maine in '59 when Bob sat there with a concussion but didn't know it. Petty was glad I ran on and on to Leo and his wife Irish about God knows what—Bob's monthly window-leap at Poly, the cafeteria hash, Bob's cross-stick boomerang fired up off the Brooklyn Bridge that came back, and what all, even some mad quizzing about hors d'oeuvres that scared Irish for a second after she admitted that she always had a bowl of chick peas for Happy Hour. Bob sank slowly. Then he was asleep.

But in '53, there I was in the basement whipping up a dip for Bob's mother and in answer to her distracted inquiry, telling her how my mother was getting along, which seemed almost to take the lady's mind off her own catastrophe. Then upstairs sometime Russell Pound—who to my knowledge said not a word about Perpetua all evening—was telling a pair of my nodding Poly classmates that the point about McCarthy was he was a vulgarian, and Ven Mead drew his fiancée whom nobody seemed to have met into Pappy's group and said very strongly that McCarthy's vulgarity wasn't the point, it was our basic liberties that were being jeopardized, and Pappy replied, "I said *vulgarian*, Venable, *vulgarian*," but I dissolved that little problem turning from another group to this saying that as for my mother she seemed upset by some of McCarthy's young staff, she thought maybe *they* were the sinister ones, and Russell Pound (who always approved of me and had just clapped into his mouth half a handful of sunflower seeds) nodded vigorously and said, "Know zakly wushee means." At another point in the party's arc a bunch of them got a report from me of a Weavers concert (though not, for Tracy's sake, that I'd gone with black Camille), and not one of them knew who Seeger was. Once Hugh and I turned simultaneously toward each other by accident and he said, "I want you to meet my Uncle Victor, he's here from Phoenix, *that's* him," unthinkably tall up against the far wall, white-haired and brown-cheeked—"originally from New England" he was saying to a girl he was sort of hunched over. Trace had never told me about him; I said to Hugh, "Yes, I can see him." Trace was telling Ven Mead's fiancée that Petty had written her that the Parisians never ask you to their homes for a meal, but take you out.

Quite late, I was singing "The Banks of the Wabash" with four elders, including Bob's dad, who kept his hand resting on his mahogany Tantalus just where it barred into place a very special decanter; and thanks to me (though I'd forgotten I knew that song so well) we did not quite forget the least memorable of the Dreiser brothers' immortal lyrics. On my way out I at last was introduced to Uncle Victor, and he said, "This is a wonderful party my niece dragged me to." Hugh and Tracy were hunting for her earrings and when Freddy Smith on his hands and knees jocularly said, "How could you lose *both* of them?," Tracy said she might have lost one down in the kitchen.

Wait: my only self should have told me the vectors that night in '53 weren't merely many (as I simply forgot, thinking by turns of Tracy and Al and by sub-turns of whether she loathed me or loved me and whether he (wherever he was) was put out or not); no, the vectors were also zipping in to many centers besides me—even in some sense to *all* centers *save* me, which understand is not to grant other people there necessarily a vectoral muscle.

So whether or not Petty or Bob told any of the three parents about my odd phone conversation with Bob that morning, no one can say I didn't do my part that night. The party might have turned into one of those Scythian obsequies Herodotus tells of in ghastly detail, an entourage of real men and even horses fresh from the taxidermist and lined up (propped up) outside the dead king's newly occupied tomb.

As I set foot in the venerable vestibule above fourteen brownstone steps and felt the fresh dark air, I was grabbed by Russell Pound: why in hell was I leaving, it was only eleven, and would I lunch at Seneca next week. (Sure I would.) And that Tammuz whom the Goddess Ishtar's love was fatal to, what was he?

I said, "He was the son of Ningishzida, Lord of the Wood of Life, and grandson of Ninazu, Lord of Aquadivination" (a term I'd created on one of Cadbury's exams) "and Tammuz himself was Lord of the Harvest." But this didn't exactly satisfy Pappy Pound, who in his tailored blazer was quite a specimen for his age: "But didn't Ishtar become Venus?"

"Of course," I said, "and as for Tammuz, his harvest in Ishtar was more than corn and less than sacred."

Pappy Pound smiled at me with reflective sentiment. He'd been startled by my father's death, my father had admired him and talked to him about everything under the sun, and of course we had an inscribed copy of his Dallin. I said, "Don't worry, they're going to be very happy." He said irrelevantly, "Your father was a very fair man."

At eight p.m. last night you began your address to the Undersea Press Club by being interrupted by a heckler. To his challenge that you didn't know what the hell you were, ideologue or father-of-your-country or artist or man or what, you replied that in twenty-four hours each person present was to switch on any size TV screen, concentrate on its center simply as a point in a grid, and for any set number of seconds "please fit to the measured length between you and that half-tone or colored picture-element the concept that my unnatural son Richard, a mutual actuary specializing in industrial probability, is not looking at the same point you are." There was glad, clapping laughter at your deceptively spontaneous retort but all this got into the *Times* today rather because at the end you revealed that because a plan of yours for ending the war had been contracted by a major weekly you wouldn't present it tonight except in the hint that it would use (or perhaps even *be*) the Energy released by (a) the dissemination of a certain idea, and (b) all mass-chance juxtapositions with that idea.

Your old Admiral portable was off when I came here tonight. Or is it by now *last* night? But, like water dripping, the phone system was blinking my attention to your TV and thence no doubt to the challenge I have I believe now just faced, for between "challenge" and "I" I disappeared into your kitchen, took your receiver off the TV, and hung it up. (So we don't get that constant *plank-plank* now.)

Well. So your son's a square, measuring so many annual dollars up each side: that's no cause to kill yourself, albeit without mess, though I haven't checked other rooms. Divorced wife Dorothy and daughter Lila, they're part of this, too. But I am not.

Except as receiver of some compounding energy which is now gathering through me through this place.

If you have come to life somewhere maybe now that you can you'll phone here.

But just after the first half of this confession was stolen, the detective tenor said as if in reply, "Oh it's got to be ruled a suicide," and then our super's deep voice said, "I can't believe it. He *wouldn't*."

The quality paperback on Egypt in his ripped hip pocket gives him more mileage than *The Autobiography of Malcolm X*, which the beautiful giraffe in jeans asked him about in the basement laundry room yesterday. "God," she said, "I was in the middle of *Malcolm* in April when my husband and I you know left for Greece and I couldn't put it down even to skim some book about the islands I bought for the plane." The super said he didn't want to discuss the Malcolm book on account of that low-life stuff in the first half, he couldn't see why they stuck all that in—"Why that's the best part," our lovely companion interrupted—and "this here," the super slapped the book in his hip pocket, "is more relevant to our real problems." Why, there was a Shadow Clock the Egyptians invented—"talk about your Greeks!"—it was over one thousand years before the Greeks got wind of this clock and stole the idea.

The beautiful homemaker had changed the subject to begin with and now she changed it back, to the pilot flame in the dryer: did the super know how to relight it? "Oldest clock in the world," he said to me, "two sticks all it was, set the crosspiece toward the east first thing in the morning, read the hours on the lengthways piece, then turn her round at noon so the cross-stick's facing west."

"The original clock-watcher," said the cameleopardess lounging against the dryer and bending me a smile as the super bemusedly pried up the panel right by her tight haunch and moved his lighter back in under.

"And Thutmose the Third to you," I said to her. The super brought the panel down again and said, "That's who it was all right, and that shadow clock ain't all he's famous for either."

Mileage on a Rootloose Outboard let's call Bob's memoirs. If I'm to leave them to him, better I not retaste Annette's dense, medium-rare beef liver of '68 in order to prophesy in rich retrospect that the upwards of three thousand dollars Bob got hold of to buy special, fine herring nets would return him a surprise. Maybe I'll leave *him* to tell that one, though his kind of patience is not for memoirs but for the rough interruptions life courts and absorbs. I'll let him explain, if he will, at length (though let me, on the keyboard of my exclamation-less Junior Corona, copy for him): how riding adrift slowly on the fragile night lid of his cove, and all alone, he saw down past the gunwale and then out everywhere the space below bursting with luminous bodies, and how also their slippery phosphorescence held him off with the odd funny-bone feel you got from John B.'s

Christmas magnets when you forced repellent ends together, but beautiful, in particular and in plenty: how instead of losing his money, his gross on one haul trebled it, even if he did have to wait a while, relying on islander reports; how with some experienced help—but this first try acting instinctively on what he'd heard said—he walled his weighted nets across the inner cove and at the crisis, moving two boats quickly together completed the trap's landward side and commenced narrowing; how the company steamer showed just after sunset and ten thousand dollars of big silver herring were sucked by a steady old engine up out of the cove into the two lighted holds.

After a nasty little discussion with Bob Petty (who then had private words with Bob and put a hand on his hip) would have let the boys stay for the haul and go aboard the steamer—whose name, Dom, is too symbolic to use here—and then sleep at the camp. But Bob got his professor pal to take her and the boys along when he crossed back to the mainland. We are on the ground of the '60s. We stood upon the granite shelf Bob's camp was based on above that black-green cove. Buoys marked the herring corral, and Bob said "that woman" picked only the busiest times to tell him she loved him when she knew damn well he couldn't drop everything; and once he'd told her to get her timing right.

"I guess I almost give her what she wants," but the straying tone was because he was watching a man way over on the nubble. It didn't matter. We had a drink and Bob told how he and the company men would finish the job and how close in the steamer would have to come to get its hose into the trap, and we had another drink and I thought maybe the steamer was going to have to run over one of the lobster buoys beyond the entrance to Bob's cove, but Bob said *Oh* no.

The earth-turn was making it harder to see the man on the nubble; and because of the Land Rover, whose cab we could just see over the far dune, and because after all how many other people did I know around Portland and the bay area however you measured it, I thought I knew who that man was at the other end of that distance.

Then I didn't know why I'd come up to see Bob and Petty and that didn't matter either. Bob stood up from the two-and-a-half-inch chuck steak he was charcoaling and said he'd like to get hold of that fellow's Land Rover, and we both laughed. In the new offshore breeze it didn't matter to me and in fact was pleasant that it was all the same to Bob who he had supper with. I mean only that he'd have been equally curious about that lobsterman who was one day soon afterward to throttle his outboard up too suddenly and fall drunk over the stern into the bay knocking the tiller around, equally curious about (say) a lonesome savant bookseller smelling the watery world, or about his friend Leo's pivotal rise in the regional chapter of something (now running for President; never missed a meeting; won Blue-Chip All-State fund-raiser award; has two lovely children, a five-year-old (adorable) girl Kimberley and a seven-year-old boy James; running on two main planks, Membership Seminar and Program to Secure Sponsors for state and federal programs), or equally curious about "what in the *hell*" I was doing exploring "displacement of food/energy parabonds by intellect/energy parabonds in the wilds of the biotic city." Bob didn't mind the brokerage business. He liked manipulating Leo in a small way who for his part thought he was doing statistical follow-ups that—and here Leo wryly lowered his voice—Bob wouldn't have done so efficiently.

After this beautiful evening of profit, those expensive nets that in one use had paid for themselves remained in Bob's mainland cellar behind the bags of cement. (My Junior Corona, after that awful April Saturday in 1946 when it was stolen from my father, turned into a grown-up portable which among other things had a back-spacer.) But waiting for the mammoth steak to get done and waiting for the little steamer to appear and interrupt the natural settling of dusk, I let the liquor's rich smoke ask in my weightless chest the question, "Why did Robby, leaving the island only a shade less reluctantly than John B. and always making it obvious I was a very special favorite with him, say to me over the Brandeis economist's gunwale as I tossed some mollifying quip to Petty amidship, 'Cy, you should get married.'" For he'd just witnessed a harsh difference of opinion between Bob and Petty and for that minute or two he and John B. had gone back to the heterogenous stationary vehicle they had shoved together out of crates and drift timber, and had tried to be busy till the difference of opinion was resolved. "What a funny thing for Robby to say to me"—Bob stood up and side-stepped the steak smoke—"he said I ought to get married."

"Robby's only a child," said Bob looking out toward where we were expecting the steamer to appear. Petty had bought that steak for four or five of us; she'd thought the boys would stay the night, though she herself would have to get back home to the mainland to the baby.

"Maybe he's only a child, but he's spooky."

I have just returned, Dom, to your kitchen to check that list of penciled excuses above the white phone I hung up, and since while there I had another look in the fridge though I knew what I'd find, I thought of the liver Ev served me tonight and of all that biotin—also known as Vitamin H (H for Hepatoscopy perhaps?)—spreading through the field of my system. But unlike ancient seers I foretell the past.

"Nothing spooky *about* him," Bob decrees. "I just wish he wouldn't mope around the hi-fi and fiddle with the changer. Petty says he's musical."

"What if he is?"

"Robby's only a child."

"What does his know about you?"

Bob squatted by the grill staring into his drink. "What's there to know?"

: that a week or so before the Heights fight (which was probably two weeks *after* my Junior Corona disappeared from the downstairs entrance of our apartment house where my father had set it down to run across the street and help Mrs. Bolla get out of a cab with a carton) Perpetua Pound told Bob's father of an event she knew only from me. Now, as I neared the end of my step-by-step account of the April afternoon Bob fired his boomerang northwest off the Brooklyn Bridge and it rose athwart a gusty southwest breeze and wheeled back toward the cable network between us and it, I took a breath and prepared to describe the concluding arc of that proud Christmas gift from his father that I had duplicated (except mine had a strip of adhesive tape) with Christmas money from none other than Uncle Cooley. But Pet's open mouth found words to enter my pause—"It came *back!* It came *back!* Bobby got it *back!*"— and looking at her dark lashes and her tongue curling preoccupied up against her lip, I drew a line of neutral energy through this field of living chance by saying only, "Yeah, *it* came back all right," and thought what the hell, that was the end of that particular story. So when Petty ingratiated herself with Bob's dad by telling all about it the next day at a cocktail party her "Pappy" gave in honor of his friend Mrs. Bolla's substantial return from Tucson, the received version was that the Christmas cross-stick had closed a wild loop returning incredibly to the boardwalk of the Brooklyn Bridge pedestrian way. It was at least true that a moment later Bob and I were traced there by Hugh and Freddy on information from Stingy Bill. That very night Petty visited me, she was having trouble with her Latin teacher. Bob phoned just after I tried to tell her the boomerang story, and she waved at me not to tell him she was with me, which later she smiled happily over, saying she'd surprise him with the fact tomorrow; but he didn't come to her father's cocktail party. Will *your* phone ring?

John (Zo-an, Zon, etc.) shakes a sandy-haired sixty-five-year-old head as I hang up some time, and says, "Cripes you old women gossip. If you had a brother to talk to maybe you wouldn't be on the phone all the time." I laugh and he says, "And if you weren't an only child maybe you wouldn't have such a swelled head." He gently cuffed it and I laughed long ago.

My time seems to lose its scale, and that step-grandfatherly complaint about the endless phone call of my adolescence perhaps through the agency of your space threatens with rough equivalence other words: Sue pricks her browning bird to test the clarity of its yellow juice and says, "They named you Cyrus so Cooley'd remember you when he died. Oh if your mother'd been able to have another baby." She slides the roasting pan back in along the blackened oven-rack and lets the door close gently, as my dearly honest and beloved step-grandfather John calls out, "Oh don't say that," and comes into the kitchen: "He'd leave him money regardless": And Sue sits down at her white table and says neatly, "Well I'm just quoting *you*, John."

Dom I may as well add (lest it be subtracted) that, as Dr. Cadbury had told me to one day when he was puffing up the stairs perhaps unsuccessfully trying to get away from me, I read Herodotus; and I found at the end of Book One what a certain general-mother-queen did to dead Cyrus because he'd tricked her own son captive and shamed him into suicide: after the action in which Cyrus was killed and his army decimated, she "ordered a search to be made amongst the Persian dead for the body of Cyrus; and when it was found she flung his severed head into a skin which she had filled with human blood..." and though I tried I couldn't see that this bit had anything to do with my own naming, though my mother once said she wouldn't mind having another chance to name a child.

No doubt these are questions from which my own two-and-a-half-year-old Emma keeping an eye on a TV ad for spray-Disneyvectors will not suffer. Nor Al, his first week on the *Barataria*, reading Herodotus in the fo'c'sle head but nagged by a Seaman First who's swabbing tiles around the very toilet Al is on and tells Al to hurry it up but when Al kicks the dank mop-strings aside that have fallen too close and looks up deadly alert, the boy backs down and, nodding at the book, says Did Al have two years college, and Al says And when I get out I'll have two more while you *ignorant* mothers are getting your hash marks. Can my nineteen-year-old Ted see that that the smooth sequence of carnage in Herodotus is not for heaven's sake some underground pacifist tract? No more than I for a long secret time could simply stand well-armed with my mercenary insight that Marathon at once must come but must wait, that in the grand casual handiwork of Herodotus the continuing narrative of Persian power and its knell was likewise a strangely coördinate field of tantalizingly stable custom and magnetic trajectories, of the delicately bruised myrrh the Egyptian embalmer uses and the living hand of Euphorion's son at the lasting instant before it was chopped off holding a Persian stern—and stop stop stop weighing the relative relevance to me of the twin events my father singled out as he powdered himself, namely the birth of Cyrus the Great, and the death. And then my father died and all I had to go on were the words he'd already spoken. "But like, how obvious can you get?" asks Darla Fasinelli before she goes on with unexpected intimacy of observation to reveal despite herself that perhaps your defenestration was not just a publicity jump. Talk about advertisements for yourself! what's more crudely obvious than the sign Darla's people hung out of their ninth-floor administrative office that Pacific day until a dark-sleeved arm that I still think may have been yours Dom reached out and yanked it loose:

THIS SPACE FORENT

What do I do if your phone rings?

Still no herring steamer, the lowering dusk seems to hold it back. Chewing barely seared steak we looked out to the north promontory. "Robby's always *doubting* me, if you really want to know," said Bob.

Al's Annette, a desomniac like me, wakes and for what seems a long and is a terrible time sees in the early light not fresh-laundered baby pajamas and kid's overalls draped airing over a Boston rocker but two empty bodies.

Ev periodically sleeps on her stomach to nip her incipient double chin.

Emma stops sucking, sets down her bottle on the long butcher block, and with a comfortable gasp asks the question she has been preparing perhaps all night but certainly since her conversation with Ev yesterday—she and I breakfast before Ev and Ted, it's early, it's raining against the pane, I must wash the windows someday: "Daddy was baby?"

Elsewhere with all the time in the world because I am with her, I hold her up sitting on my hand like some mechanical lift, to press the button for the west elevator, which the little articulator's plastic-bulbed clock-face just above the button tells us is already rising past the floor just below ours.

"*Quid est matrimonium?...*," Al might enjoy quoting to Bob from a letter Gray wrote to his sometime friend Walpole; "*Est coniunctio nunc copulativa, nunc disjunctiva.*"

Quare means "why" *and* "therefore." Perpetua Pound blinked respectfully when I went beyond my tutorial threshold and failed to excite her with what struck me then as a queer duplicity between interrogative and relative: *Why? Therefore.* Question and answer command a field of hazardous puzzles from (say) Lower Silurian to Lurid Iranian, from Taconic dives to submerged coronal engagements.

Now because the Medulla Oblongata, or Spinal Bulb, part of that three-point arc called the Vectoral Muscle, is incidentally the center of winking, I tried to link Tracy's tears of shyness with some anatomic dystrophy in her that I might be able to unearth—perhaps even vectoral, though I suspected that since she wasn't an only child and so probably lacked a vectoral muscle any such link would be in fact with mine.

The angle made by the Land Rover's windshield and hood was still visible, but not the man. Bob changed the subject. "Robby's right: what did happen with you and Tracy?"

That March weekend, after she said Al had made a pass the touching moistness—or you, Dom, would say (though of late you used this cool new clarity without conviction) the *measurable* moistness—around her eyes may have been mere loss. I said to her, "Right. Maybe I'm too tough. Tougher than you."

But I seemed to myself not to believe what I'd said. But now I see some inverse bravura made me *apparently* lie the *truth*.

All confessions are fantasies, though no less truthful. The man who will tell you he raped tells you so not simply to express guilt but to gild it to a local bloody shine; he's proud, and not secretly, of that force-fed laying-on of hands that he calls rape but that may have been just the successful palpation of her deep, just reluctance.

"You never want to kiss me unless it leads to something," Tracy lied.

Bob wound up and hurled a gristley red wedge of beef neither of us could manage, and a gull materialized out of the half-light and reached the meat as it hit the water. Above this near-point, running lights were now two miles off. "It's about time," said Bob.

Al hates leftovers, cold or hot, even for lunch.

Bob grabbed my boomerang just as Hugh shouted to us from the top of the steps leading to the main part of the Brooklyn Bridge pedestrian way. Did Bob see Freddy and Hugh coming into view before he grabbed my boomerang? In the anthrochron of friendship those are big questions, though in the field of probabilities—which is trying to engross my already smudging parabolas and my dystrophic dialectic of anthronoiacly keeping apart Al and Bob—these misgiving questions spread into tacit maturity. Bob fended me off and ran toward Hugh and Freddy, but then Freddy said to me, "Guess who's keeping tabs on *you*?" and Hugh said knowingly, "They all have claws, every goddamn one of them." Freddy meant that Tracy had begged him to come and see what we were doing on the bridge. We all started picking on Hugh and somehow my boomerang ended up that night on Bob's wall.

At the Pounds' next day Bob's father said chucking boomerangs off the Bridge was like dropping something out of a window— violated a municipal ordinance, didn't it? Rear Admiral Worth twitched a small smile and said gently that of course it was worse than that. Bob's father laughed, kept coming back to the achievement Petty had described, and laughed some more and said to Admiral Worth that Bob was co-captain of lacrosse. Admiral Worth said he hoped Bob hadn't been aiming for the Navy Yard, and Petty took him up and said Hey wait, Bob had aimed for the Statue, not the other way, and in the teeth of a stiff wind up there among the cables. Russell Pound entered the room with two old-fashioned glasses and called across to me Did my father have any clue who'd walked off with the typewriter.

I happen to know that this boomerang adventure eased things between Bob and his father.

(Elsewhere in tonight's often short-circuit field, that tough gruff gentleman heard from Russell Pound at Seneca's Sunday night Family Pot Luck Buffet (who had it from Mrs. Bolla who got it from Petty who had it from me) that Bob needed various thousands of dollars for the herring nets; so Bob's father phoned Bob station-to-station to offer a non-interest loan.)

For after I'd told Bob's father that Bob could have been class president if he'd campaigned the spring before, Bob's father challenged Bob on the matter: but this uneasy affection was received by Bob with such triumphant silence that his old man phoned me one night saying what was up with Bob, he was still planning on applying to Princeton, wasn't he? But though Bob had seemed to deliberately throw away that boomerang, he kept mine on his wall several weeks, I guess for his father to see. At school other guys were impressed by Bob's laconic confidence—his views on first dates with Catholic girls versus Jewish girls, and on what Torger Tokle's record at Iron Mountain had been; and because of Bob some of us thought seriously for several weeks of becoming seismologists on the west coast. To Bob class office was at best beside the point, he was a leader anyway. Akkie Backus told Bob that during lacrosse season he'd prefer Bob not to waste his time even on occasional contributions to the school paper. Bob's father was afraid that because of wrestling he'd end up at Lehigh.

"They certainly waited long enough," said Bob as the Land Rover's lights went on and we heard the motor. Bob stared at the steamer's running lights so neatly independent out there off the promontory.

"He a neighbor?" I asked, referring to the Land Rover.

"Him?" Bob murmured, moving down off the ledge. "He'll talk your head off. Married into an old Portland family. Ever hear of the Deerings?"

We were on the beach now and Bob was shoving a thin log under the bow to roll the rowboat down. He laughed. "*Damned* if I'd ask him over tonight." On the beach the Land Rover backed around and swung toward the island road. "'f he knew he's missing a herring haul," Bob chuckled, "*Je*sus he'll talk your head off."

But I've said Land Rover elsewhere tonight, Dom. Who was it I said meant to buy one? That famous vehicle appeared in those pages your psychiatrist son-in-law took from this antic table together with a typewriter repair ticket and no doubt a sly slip or two of your pen.

The white phone's been sounding in the kitchen.

It was Fred Eagle the Land Rover Fred Eagle. Is this the same vehicle? Footsteps to the elevator, no doubt fingers to the button—finger*tips*—eyes to the articulator, and then distinctly vague shuffling: nothing for three seconds but my phone still going off like an occulting alarm clock: another shuffle: are they kissing out there listening to this apartment ring? and perhaps each independently determined not to end their kiss at least till that phone stops. But if the elevator comes? The fine for tampering with your mailbox—if mere use is tampering—equals what Bob borrowed for his nets not of course allowing for inflation.

Bob dragged the roller out and down again to the stern. "He'd have had himself a couple three belts and told us what a lot of trouble his Land Rover turned out to be, and then told us how to get these herring."

"I doubt it," I said.

"You know, we should have had him over. He's a very funny man, and that's something."

"It was him or us," said Darla in '69 the morning of the Friday Bob flew down to New York and less than two days after your defenestration, "it was a live dichotomy. He wanted to upstage us for his own sake but he let himself down, he got confused. He poured himself some of our wine—well I didn't *really* mind, the ed and anthro departments sent us four jugs of Paisano and we should probably have boycotted it." As she spoke to me in New York, Bob was packing for the plane in Maine and he and Robby were arguing whether the noise cone came from the plane's bow or tail, a dispute confused at first because Bob thought Robby was talking—now they're talking out there as the elevator arrives—about a *nose* cone, and terminally interrupted when Robby said as he left his parents' bedroom, Well anyway Bob wasn't going by supersonic to New York, so who cared.

"A boy I just broke up with," said Darla, "was there with his zoom to photograph us holding the ninth floor and the crowd down below. He poured himself more wine and I said, Cool it, Ed, and took away his cup, I don't know why he let me, we weren't some fraternity party, I said. And Ed and I were just having it out, and he's saying Darley you're absurd and me saying our personal relationship was irrelevant to the overriding issue, when the great man was suddenly standing there, in a suit with a vest. One of my girls, Haya Watt, got stagestruck and told my guards outside to let him in.

"Nothing was negotiable, I said, so he laid a hundred-dollar bill on top of the dean's secretary's dicta-pol and said it was a contribution to the party. I told him to keep it, he'd need it for his own political career and he said would I meet him in Trinity Churchyard, Broadway and Wall, day after tomorrow—that's today, isn't it?—he was filming a TV spot he said between Al and Bob. Al and Bob? That's what he said. And Ed said, What's this Al and Bob? Well, some of the kids were settling down to enjoy him, and I had to go check the security of the rest of the floor and find out who let him past eight, but he was half fighting us half charming us—like, he said stop trying to purify and start studying just what it was that was supposed to be *being* contaminated, like what did we know about plankton and he went and hugged one of the guys who goes around in an old Arab skirt and a headband and told him not to think he was a freak but study, study, study—review the Cheyenne transvestites and their relation to the regular bravery, then he wheeled around and grinned and punched a fat kid in the shoulder and said to Ed, 'Al Hamilton, Bob Fulton.'

"So I told our great man he was right on schedule—he tried to interrupt me, '*Emotion* is time!' he cried out—and I said how could he be making a date with me in Manhattan day after tomorrow if he was planning as he said on the news to be involved with this protest situation as long as he was needed—'I'm *not* needed,' he said, 'that's the beauty of my being here'—but when he smiled taking off his jacket, Ed got hold of him and got butted in the stomach. So he got his jacket back on and then they were scuffling at the window and raising it, but that window wasn't the window he went out of, and when the great man knocked Ed onto a typewriter he looked over at me grinning and said he was only trying to make us less pompous; I have to admit I liked him, like a father (yes?) who's been away for a long time and you want to forgive him, but all of a sudden he was fielding questions right and left: yes he thought the technology generated by Viet Nam and the Space Program would develop ideas incidentally for transportation, nutrition, conserving space, etcetra etcetra; then, No indeed he wasn't interested in space exactly, space had no shape; and someone objected that—

"The fat kid told him what wasn't negotiable, who we want reinstated, who we want for black studies and that the dean responsible for the police emergency equipment outside had to go. But the great man went away to a window and raised it all the way up and leaned out. Then he came in again and his eyes were sort of watery and he looked his age, and he said, 'No, they're out there because of me.' You know, he's a shit but he's a nice man. He winced and he said, 'Ow, that wine,' and the fat kid said O.K. maybe he knew so much but in his last book what was his frame of reference, but Ed moved in, took his camera off and put it on a desk and took a couple of steps and the great man backed toward the window and five or six of the kids moved to break it up or something, and Ed swung and missed and then our guest in the vest was sort of sitting on the sill, and all but Ed dropped back away from the window, Ed was to one side and he turned and looked at me—at my breasts."

But Dom, the triangle collapsed to a kind of eclipse-line. I asked Darla how big that room was and she couldn't tell me. Is one of Ed's pictures in the box of slides in your bookcase right there behind the screen? Ed got several shots of the crowd below.

You sent Richard your *Suicide* when the paperback came out, and his neutral thank-you would have made you mad if I'd let it through. Long ago Richard rose beyond "attractive nuisances," Acts of God, and Mortality Expectancy Abscissae, to Quality-Probability curves. You learned that Richard had had a feeler from the Demographic Congress who were ready to make him a big research offer but he wasn't interested. If I hadn't this feeling that time's been temporarily solved tonight (if indeed "tonight" is not the wrong idea) I'd phone dear Ev now and apologize for this egregious breach of my legendary punctuality. In 1575 Costanzo (or Constantio) Varolio died in Bologna at thirty-two years of age, during at least the last three of which he was physician to Pope Gregory of the Calendar (the latter christened Ugo Buoncampagni, a professor of law at Bologna before Varolio was born and as pope an ambitious administrator for a decade after Varolio died). It was Varolio who noted that the cerebral cavities communicate, and it's only fair to say that if I'd never come across the properly memorial pons Varolii, Varolio's Bridge (that mass of nerves across the belly of the brain at the anterior end of the Spinal Bulb), I might never have located the Vectoral Muscle. No doubt one of the Field Pundits will answer the Televizier that yours was an instance of Anniversary Suicide. Listen, your life was so dense, *every* day was an anniversary. The dean's secretary is back at her Dicta-Pol high over the Pacific, and those occupation folk are elsewhere, and so the site though easily restored is hard to understand.

Petty was at the bedroom door as Bob snapped his case shut. She came and knelt on the other side of the broad bed facing him across the case he'd insisted on packing himself. She asked if he'd put a new blade in his razor, she was afraid she'd dulled the one he'd had in, doing her legs in the tub last night. He said he'd buy a dispenser of five when he got to New York. She asked what he had said to Robby, Robby just stamped out of the house and slammed the door the way he *never* does, and it was starting to rain. Bob said he'd always said Robby didn't know when to come in out of the rain and simultaneously as if by prearrangement Petty fell easily sideways off her knees onto her side on the bed much nearer Bob and Bob sat down, and the simultaneity produced an inertia that brought him right down to her face. She said, "But he went *out* in the rain; that's not the same thing." Her broad cheekbones and narrow nostrils should have excited him all over again, the faintly Indian strength opened for him but centered on a simple female secret he would have to ask for. ("Hey wait," you perhaps say, Dom, after three TN's too many, "what're you recommending, man, nose-fucking?" but normally you would have caught my sense.) Bob reached to put his fingers on a space of her neck below her ear but his hand stopped short of there and didn't touch her—or so he said in the bar that night over our second beer; and as he moved back to get up she got a hand on his hand before he moved it too, and she said she wished he'd let her pack for him for she was sure he'd forgotten something, and when he said there was hardly anything to put in it, it was practically empty, she said it was just as if he were packing that smelly old Austrian haversack they used to lug on one shoulder and he said he didn't see why. And at the airport in South Portland he told her it had been just some silly thing about noise cones and it was his fault, not Robby's. And Petty and Bob touched each other and paused. Petty said, "He's not a sissy, is he?" And Bob said, "Oh *Jes*us not *him*!" and laughed and opened the car door and got out.

Dom, at Cora's party last week where at last we really met, I might have been able amiably to say, "In case of disaster call me," or soberly that I'd seen at once that your deliberately dry suicide book wasn't trying to say something new but rather (and without humor) was a piece of the new measural experience. Or (before, having gazed past me, you walked around me as if I was a nobody and went to speak to the famous blind Negro actor) I was capable of saying and (as you may have recalled) *did* (succinctly) say, "I'm glad you reconsidered your space-program reservations and decided to take a close look at those guys." You murmured, "Reserve me a first-class on the next one out, man," and I heard Cora say, "Oh there he goes, I didn't know if they were speaking, but I couldn't not ask..." and a woman said very fast, "But Dom said the man was glad he'd waited till he went blind to do a black Oedipus; so maybe he'll forget Dom's new position on black militancy," and Cora said, "But he's *always* been blind, it isn't just the last few years." "But he isn't in Dom's league," the woman said, and Cora said offhandedly, "There are twenty *thousand* leagues nowadays, sweetie."

But at that opening and in the space of a mere handshake I couldn't very well tell you how months before I'd taken an interest in you as locus of violence and contemplation, how I'd even found similarities between us, and how I'd come to link our secret kinship with my ancient habit of not introducing Al and Bob. After you were stabbed in the calf by the black decathlon star who reached out from under a table, you told a reporter that the host (a traveling homosexual who kept a studio at the Chelsea Hotel) thought New York offered nothing better than the chance to throw a party at which two big shots would be brought together in order to rub each other the wrong way. Anyway last week at the opening I could not have demonstrated the relevance to what I'm saying tonight of sneaky Hugh's ill-advised challenge the Wednesday after Bob tested his boomerang off Brooklyn Bridge. It was May Day evening—I've checked it against the perpetual calendar in your almanac; the three of us were comparing our American History notes for a big exam; my notes were scantier even than Bob's but my knowledge was greater even than Hugh's, for I had a complex style of mnemonic encapsulations developed two years before when I was Dr. Cadbury's student. The key trick was to make a name contain a mass of data: thus, "Hammurapi" yielded "Babylonian Plain," from the alternative *p* and *b* spellings of that prudent king's name; it yielded "house" (from *H*), and hence building regulations and generally the famous Code of Laws which I ought to have mentioned before now; also (from *a*) "Amorites," whose Semitic tongue the Code was written in; *m* for Marduk; *r* for "religion" and Ishta*r*, i.e., my Asian Venus and the prime goddess of Babylon... Forgive me, this is of interest only to my father, who loved me, and to Tracy's brother Hugh, who did not. He'd been expatiating on my father's recollection about the stolen typewriter: namely, that Bohack Joey's delivery rig had been parked at the curb when my father went across the street to help the lady out of the cab but was *not* there when he returned to our apartment entrance and found my Corona gone. Hugh said I owed it to my father to do something about it, he was probably too nice a guy to. Ignoring Hugh and returning to history, I said today was not only May Day but Loyalty Day. We were in Bob's room, and Hugh had taken the boomerang off the wall. He said, Like hell it was Loyalty Day, there wasn't any such thing; and I said, Like hell it wasn't, and while Bob took the boomerang off the bed and idly looked at it and hung it up again, Hugh and I argued some more about Loyalty Day and I finally shrugged and said, "Act of Congress," gave the date of passage, picked up my book, and casually asked Bob if he thought our Intramural division at Poly between Blues and Grays was because of the Civil War. I went to the kitchen to make us a vanilla malted, and my mother, who had the entire contents of the refrigerator out on the table, said she would make it.

When Hugh and Bob and I met next morning, converging in the lower hall past a shot of tobacco smoke out of the master's room and then as the door of that floor's john came open and shut a whiff of lysol and entrail-methane, Bob kidded Hugh it wasn't Loyalty Day any more. But Hugh didn't take it. A friend of mine named Scheindlinger whose parents had just changed their name to Shane came up breathlessly and said, "How you gonna do, C.C.?" And ignoring him Hugh said to Bob (but poking *me* on the operative pronoun), "Your boomerang didn't have tape on it with *his* initials. You *lost* your boomerang off the *Bridge.*" Then Hugh preceded us into the history exam.

I've replaced your *World Almanac* on the low square parson's table where it lay beside what I happen to know Dot sent you for your most recent birthday: a *Time* Man of the Year cover suitable for hanging done in vinyl with a mirror occupying the main panel. I've had a look in it. My prints are all over this room; the kitchen too. Maybe it doesn't matter. Are Bob and Al here this weekend for a reason too simple for me to have thought of? Well, I never claimed it had anything to do with how badly Bob knew he'd done on that history test, or on Hugh's asking how he'd done as we trooped into Akkie Backus's study hall the next afternoon, or on my quick reply that it had struck me as a ridiculously fair test.

Wait: as Petty could have learned if she'd let me finish my story, Bob's boomerang indeed came back, but right over us through the cables and through the other side and on down as if at first toward the Navy Yard before it dropped onto an empty barge in tow of an outward-bound tug. But there was no point in explaining all this to Bob's father. After the Poly athletic director's report Friday night, Bob's irascible father would have concluded that Petty's boomerang story was Bob's lie, but I've gone too fast, we aren't quite yet into Akkie's Friday study hall. I find I'm reaching the end of these Sphinx 8 1/2 by 11's of yours, Dom.

No question, you knew just where the rescue mat was, when you exited through the window onto the twilight. But you knew it wasn't exactly a trampoline down there you'd be hitting. Did you simply not want to descend by the same route you'd come up?

Darla had fallen into her story. She no longer had an idea, but only what she thought she'd seen. You were half out the window and Ed looked at Darla's breasts or so *she* saw the trajectory of his focus: "Yes, I knew the situation had been like a triangle—don't get me wrong, you know what I mean; I don't have to explain, do I?—a triangle just at the instant it became just a line—me, Ed, and him in a line. I said at the airport press conference it was no defenestration—he wasn't pushed—that's what I said. You look at me as if I don't believe what I'm saying. Oh how do *I* know how you're looking at me."

I interrupt her pursed lips—courtesy of my now almost unrecognizable parabola softened by a field of distances equal only to some marvelous second-strength in my old, only-child's vectoral muscle—to bend you toward Akkie's study hall the early afternoon of May 3rd, 1946.

Still waiting for me in 1942 by the white picket fence outside her beloved stone heart house that she and my father stopped going to in 1950, my mother says, "You're a worrier like your father; my goodness, so Gail threw Al's sneaker into a field, so what?" And as I leave her in the kitchen May Day night of 1946, to make our malted with soft ice cream and to finish defrosting, she calls to me, "I saw Joey in Bohack today and asked him if he'd seen your typewriter downstairs by the other door, we knew he'd been there."

And in 1942 Al's first sight of the sea—so far as one sees the sea through Boston Harbor—could not have been from the Mystic River Bridge, for the MRB Authority didn't begin construction till '48 (the year of Al's car accident): any more than nine-year-old Gail could have sensed from such a distance and through a shimmering kitchen screen, that day in 1938 her dad came and fixed our old Kelvinator, my sudden stupor looking at her profile out there in the pickup and my prickling inkling of her closeness to the man. Al's big hand gets two cans of Colt 45 out of my memory's growing refrigerator Saturday afternoon of 1968 and says flatly, "Dad never fixed a Kelvinator gas refrigerator because Kelvinator never made one. And the Mystic Bridge changed its name to Maurice J. Tobin Memorial."

Robby wrote me the whole ordinary thing—its ordinariness fluent and wise: Bob and Robby dropped John B. and Petty at Cub Scouts. Then, though Robby wanted to get back home Bob decided they'd drive the five miles to the landing and check the outboard mooring. Robby said there was no need to, and when Bob said it wasn't as if they were going out to the island and asked what Robby had to do home, Robby didn't say he wanted to consult the Columbia Encyclopedia I gave him because he doubtless didn't, but just said, "Things," and shut up; and when Bob said, "Why in hell'd you come along then?," Robby continued with his murder mystery there in the front seat though Bob had said he was ruining his eyes reading that crap in the car; and Bob I believe was in the strangely weightless feeling of not knowing whether in the next five seconds

he'd forbid Robby or drop it. He said he'd need him when they got
to the landing but Robby knew Bob would do it all himself, row
the punt out, bail with the blue Maxwell House can if there was
anything to bail, and relash the outboard cover. But a mile shy of the
landing Bob suddenly turned in at some second-hand bookseller's
sign—did he mash and displace a trough of gravel cornering so
sharply?—and when he parked in front of the barn who should be
practically run down coming around its corner but the sinewy little
lobsterman who was apparently killed only a few months later when
his boat was sighted out in the bay going round in circles empty.
He jumped back but then got up on Bob's hood and crawled to the
windshield and Robby had to stop reading and laugh. And since
the lobsterman was headed back to the landing and Robby said he
didn't care about going in to look at books, Bob gave the man a
lift and he took them out to Bob's mooring and the three of them
sat for an hour and Bob never did get into his own boat but just
had a look. But at the end of that considerable period of rocking in
the dead chill of March, Robby's moroseness dispersed and though
he could never tell Bob because it was so vague he himself didn't
understand it, he became for a while quite happy.

Not because his dad gave him a bitter, luke-cold swig of beer
from the quart the lobsterman produced from under a thwart. Not
because the lobsterman told a funny story about a dragster cousin
up the coast who had too big a tongue so his mouth sometimes
looked full of it—indeed from crown to tip it measured a good four-
and-a-half inches, but was wide as hell too, and he bragged about
what he could do with that tongue, and some of the girls said he
really could, but he didn't have a steady girl but spent a lot of time
driving around the new school's parking lot, but now the tongue
was too big, too damned big, the lobsterman said, and people said
there was going to be an operation at Maine General but it might
cost too much.

Nor did Robby's mood change because the lobsterman said,

"What'd you do'th all them herring nets," and Bob smiled challengingly as if he had some tricky secret about those nets, a masculine
misdemeanor or a wild stinking joke, and then said quietly, "Oh I
still got 'em," and the men looked archly at each other and after a
moment laughed.

No: the fact is that Robby, a shivering skin-and-bones twelve-
year-old dead set against joining the Scouts, didn't like all this man-
to-man crap. But what he couldn't then or perhaps ever see—nor see
that the lobsterman himself didn't see—was a virgin dogma inside
Bob his father that said: "Fuck 'em all: *I* know there's a beautiful
bullshit mystery in these waters, Cassius Clay came to Lewiston
scared shitless, so scared he won; and that crazy fisherman I meet
out there sitting hunched in his slicker he takes a long look at me,
hand steady on the tiller, and maybe he raises his hand, maybe not,
but he's on his way by Christ someplace, checking traps or going
somewheres maybe you'll never guess in a year of watching him,
maybe going home to jump his wife on the kitchen table, and these
down-east, sardine-packing, mainiac independents are better than
poets because by Jesus they own that beautiful bullshit mystery but
don't know what it is and don't need to know; 87 percent of the
state's in forest, and 98 percent of that's privately owned, 98 percent!,
but you take all you ever thought you scratched up out of a book
or heard some scared, ball-less, tuneless, shitless people say in your
New Yorks and all the rest and puke it up into a cloudy southeast
wind for the seagulls and then you get your ass out into the bay't
those rocks and get hold of some lumber, and you tarpaper you a
roof and sit under it on a great gray afternoon and mister you don't
need any breaks, you got something and nobody's going to touch
you. I don't think I *want* to get hold of that mystery, but it's here."

No, what made Robby almost happy—though he didn't say
so in this letter (for he didn't quite understand)—was what Bob
finally said to the big-nosed little lobsterman who had stood up
with his back to the deserted landing to pee mostly over the side

moving his back a little with the stirring of the boat. Thought he was ending that stage of the discussion by stating that religions were all the same—only to be curtly gainsaid by Bob. Went on to ask Robby if he was going to be a millionaire college broker like his daddy; and after Robby said Bob didn't like being a broker and they really didn't have a lot of money—to which the lobsterman quietly retorted "I bet"—Bob poked Robby and said, "This one's going to be a vagabond like me."

In the letter Robby said he almost fell in between the boat and the dock later but Bob swung him up and over by an arm. They had a between-meals triangle of pizza on the way home and almost as soon as they got home and Robby had left the murder mystery on John B.'s bed because he'd decided to give it to John B. because John B. said he was stingy (though their mother disagreed), and Robby had raided the freezer with Petty's new ice cream scoop, it was almost time to go back to Portland. Robby looked up "vagabond" in his encyclopedia but didn't find anything. When he looked it up in the downstairs dictionary he didn't mind that the word didn't really seem to cover his dad. On the way to town, Robby started thinking again how Bob was always saying John B. would be President someday.

Whether that barn and house belonged to Fred Eagle and what the lobsterman could conceivably have come in from the island to do there are questions that recede like your suicide, Dom, blocked for a second by an equally unimportant equivalence I now see between Bob's view of summer people and Al's of people who don't know their facts, or between Bob's view of Ben Sedgwick and Al's of—if there isn't a parallel there (interior angles, binomial taxonomy, but I'm running out of paper and must write smaller), at least there *should* be: for Bob and Al are perhaps as strangely alike as, Dom, you are to me identifiably mysterious.

For, interrupting Darla's pursed lips I find again her tongue—a tongue still whole and bemused into the poetry of accident, for she has not yet realigned upon its agile unconscious the dialectic which gives rigor to her ideology today much as yesterday it did to her I.U. grad linguistics program to which she has promised her parents she'll return. But now, toward the end of my interview with her the day you, Dom, did that TV filming in Trinity churchyard, she isn't thinking of the tiny taste domes along that moist muscle or its root at the neck's hyoid bone or, midway to its pink waving tip, its corona (or blade); nor is she thinking of all those trigeminal nerves she learned about one night at I.U. that make their bitter-sweet exit through our old friend Pons Varolii. No, her beautiful memory embraces whatever of that restless line she can embrace...her: and Ed: and (at the window sill nine floors above the police rescue mat and a growing crowd now including me) you.

Akkie's radiator-rattling study-hall wasn't as big as I recall it, but I promise you it was on the third floor. I feel aisles longitudinal and rows transverse, and east door and west door. Of the eight aisles Bob's and mine are third and fourth from the north or clock wall, and our desks are next to each other in the rear transverse row. I feel the five rattley windows along the south wall tantalizingly sectioning the green of the athletic field's further reaches and beyond them and below the sky the then slowly rising V.A. hospital which when complete would block like a premature door one rectangle of those New York waters between on the far left Gravesend Bay (washing the parabolic shore of that Jewish enclave which you lived in as an adolescent, Dom, Seagate, which is a contiguous westward extension of, though anciently and gravely and by fence and private police discrete from, Coney Island), and on the right the Narrows (long before Verrazano Bridge—I mean long before it was built—I am writing smaller and smaller—I'm running out of paper—your paper, and I feel at floor-level of that old room but above floor-level too a hundred-odd invisible vectorways diagonal in two or three dimensions). Akkie's long face absorbed twitching from top left to bottom right of a sports page seemed upon his low podium to be high above us. Little Mr. Cohn came in, looked ironically round the room and stepped on the podium to have a word with Akkie: who smiles and keeps looking down as if at his *Times*, then at the punch line looks up sideways at Cohn and they both laugh. Hugh Blood says rather loudly, "Horny Cohn" and looks back at Bob and me, but Bob shrugs and says, "I got nothing against him," and suddenly Cohn is looking sharply at us over that great distance: Akkie and Bob had an understanding. It was that Bob could do or say anything so long—

Wait, wait—they all say Wait, and I too say Wait, Tracy's face at the Welcome party in '53 says Wait and Gail's says Wait through the screen door with her still wet light hair tight back from her forehead line and slick-massed down behind her ear and below her neck: and even dear strong bland undemanding recently deflowered Perpetua says it to fortify an absent Bob against Admiral Worth and his Navy Yard—"Hey wait, Bobbie aimed at the Statue of Liberty"—

And if Darla (formerly Darlene, from the Philadelphia area) did not actively *say* it just before or as you left the fenestral rectangle and gravely and without a peep much less an epic whoop came down to us hard like an authentic fast ball suddenly swollen past the space of time in which one's wrists might have snapped the bat through to meet it, she did surely *feel* that word Wait in all its intimate fear (I don't care what Darla now at the end of our talk adds about well of course all she really cared about was like interrupting the whole ideological momentum and like profile of the Occupation-Protest): Ed moved between her and you: he was in profile and very close to you and for an instant she could not see you straddling the sill: Ed glanced at her, then wheeled around to his right toward you: while simultaneously one of your arms stuck out from behind Ed: whose right shoulder then moved so that his hidden right arm appeared to be in action: you shouted "Hey"; but it isn't clear if Ed gave you an unprovoked shove (if you can even conceive of provocation being absent) or Ed shoved (or lightly pushed) in answer to a shove (or

feint) from you: or there was nothing and you just shouted Hey!—
and, so to speak, shoved off and went below: but Darlene, Darlink,
Darla, Darley, Darla just before she briskly recovers her official self,
has declined to a slow dream of uncertainty and as she betrays the
doubleness of your defenestration, nay a far *more* than double field
of human chance in which that gross event must be gauged, she
forgets herself enough to lay her hand on mine. Having said already,
I believe, in the sheets that your scientific son-in-law appropriated,
perhaps I don't need to prove all over again that (a) the vectoral
muscle is rare even among its principal possessors, Only Children;
(b) if you have it, you can perceive Field-State; but (c) only if
you have a V.M. can you come down with the dreaded Vectoral
Dystrophy which shrinks Field to Dichotomy. The relation of this
result to problems of parabolic locus should by now be clear.

    If, as the detective tenor said to the nervous woman, you are
killed and you did it yourself, I can't call it the anniversary of Doug's
suicide: only the anniversary of its eve: or if a Field-Rear Agnostician
insists upon an anniversary, then say tonight was the calendar night
Doug and I had it out while Al looked on embarrassed, and thus it
is the anniversary of one of the three or four days on which Emma
could have been conceived.

    But that isn't tonight any more.

    Hugh saw it with his eyes before I did, but I *felt* it: but I felt
it together with (at various distances, none equal): Akkie's scissors
poised open undecided whether to clip an article or not; Freddy
Smith turning the plastic-enveloped contents of his fat black wallet
from Lauren Bacall to Ann Sheridan to Bogart though thinking
of my own Tracy Blood; Bernie Scheindlinger's solemn red-haired
daydream about the tennis team's match tomorrow above what I
was almost certain was his *Problems of Democracy* book (memory
course, one-term course, sure A); and I felt too the minute-wand
of the old clock on the north wall as it jerked up a notch nearer
the hour-ending bell; and believe me felt so much else that you

couldn't donate enough reams of paper for me to etch in all that moment's vectors and vectresses. Akkie had raised all the windows and I could smell the impinging wholeness of grass and ground and the stretched, shiny-dyed cloth of bookbindings and even the clean ropy odor of new fuzz on a Dunlop ball and somewhere ink with its medicinal and promissory order.

But Bob was running for the middle window, not the usual outside window that was almost on a line from his starting point behind his desk; so he was at an angle when he cut around the rear end of the last lengthways aisle and took three strides to his new take-off. Ye gods there was nothing wrong with his calculations and he could not have been thrown off by Hugh's shrill but meaningless whistle which Akkie was too alerted to locate for punishment.

First, I saw Bob only from the waist up, over the heads, and then his feet left right kicked his legs out and as he passed through the middle window and his arms were up like a symphony conductor's preliminary sign, the original angle of approach had been bent almost straight.

But at a slight cost in momentum.

Yes, that may have been it. Or it may have been a stray vector mistaking him for an only child and saying, "Middle window or outside window, you've been here before, Champ, and your old man wants you to go to Princeton and from what Cy said you missed maybe half the short answers yesterday from Meade and Sedgwick to Jubal Early and the states covered by the Emancipation Proclamation (which you know was 1863 but weren't asked), and you're probably kidding yourself about the essay question."

I need not interrupt this scene; it interrupts itself. Since Bob's feet-first proneward flight passed a hair more slowly than heretofore into the window's area, his ready palms met the high-raised bottom edge of wood with insufficient force for him to ram himself back in across the sill. Instead, when Bob made contact and pushed, he succeeded only in making the window slide down a foot—and sensing that it might now come all the way down on his neck or chest leaving the rest of him outside the window arched and bent and maybe with a cracked back, he let go the moving window and flipped over, nearly losing the sill, and in our amazement at seeing all but his fingers and large white knuckles disappear, all fifty-odd of us sat still enough to hear in the fragrant air outside, that powerful long "Aoaww" of our harsh-tongued but much-beloved athletic director who had looked up to see not his air space violated by Bob's flannels but an unmeasurable threat to another space in his soul, some hygienically toughened schedule in his school mind joining us to the athletic afternoon which would begin at ten to, and joining us with no other or better future than that: well of course it was measurable, what he saw, all of Bob hanging, and hanging three floors above a space of ground near but not near enough the in-any-event not soft enough broad jump/pole vault pit, and I imagined wrongly that our athletic director rushed for this place either to catch all one hundred seventy-five pounds of Bob or just to be there.

And then as I rose sideways out of my desk Bob's hands lost grip and were not there.

A record number of vectors shot in like auto-retractable steel tape measures, but now for a timeless instance all Intention spread dissolving through my body from my quick neck and sharp shoulder blades down my able back through my butt to the inside bend of my knees under the old desk with its carvings and ink doodlings, and not a drop of Intention was left in my head and I was content and believed I could hold every one of us right on up to Akkie and his hound's face right where they were, and this I did for what would have been quite a time if the instance hadn't been timeless. Then, like a spatial extension of this helpless and intentionless magic, there were two voices below and it seemed impossible our athletic director was bawling Bob out, cawing right under our windows (in the wrong sequence no doubt because he was stricken with his own irrelevance), "Got a *game* tomorrow.

Hey whadda you think you're doing!"

You thought only the thirsty media cared for you, Dom—to drink you down and piss you out: the meteoric you at San Gennaro taking a flap in the face from one of those flag-exposing twin guinea hens who run Empire Hardware while yours truly watched through the fence with Joseph and Mary and their boy behind me; or you not quite upstaging sweet Seeger on the Hudson babbling huskily over your bourbon to a black news-chick while the skipper and his banjo sang us down the stinking tide; you bleeding right onto a hand-mike a raincollared TV reporter darted to you like an electric prod, against a field of dark Barrio stone on the edge of live gunshots one summer night when you were supposed to be not in Spanish Harlem but giving a big birthday party for Dot in Edinburgh; you getting mugged all alone on Brooklyn Bridge a month ago by three kids who it turned out didn't know who you were then or even by name later in some station house; you vomiting on a TV talk show, pointing at the eggy pool and calling it "Magma," and after mopping your mouth and tongue-tip, answering the host's original question straight and mild.

Are those excuses posted in the kitchen for any and all callers? And what about "EARTH = SPACECRAFT"? That addendum hardly seems an excuse for anything. Would you use it to put off a media representative? Or is it a hot-line excuse for the President of the United States to whom if he phoned you to congratulate you on being you you could say, "Sorry, can't talk now: the earth is a spacecraft." I'm losing you, Dom, though along with you also my fear that maybe I'd been in part responsible for your evacuation tonight. I have used you during what was tonight, Dom, but in order to dig away at less spectacular puzzles.

To save paper I've just for the last few moments been merely talking not writing.

Why write? to remember? or to give? or at last to forget. But soon after I opened my mouth and spoke I heard someone out by the elevator.

Ev says it's all a phase, my quest for an exit from my well-paid foundational anthroponoia, anthropolymetry, indeed even from my after-all-well-subsidized inquiry into the changes in the ceremonial geometry of the residential ground-grid of Brooklyn Heights. Dear Ev calls it a phase.

Ev can't know that Al did tell me about phoning her. Last year Al said, "You really should have brought Ev along this weekend, we expected her. You're a lucky man to have a woman like her. Did you know she took the trouble to phone me and ask me never to tell you she knew about that horror show with her first husband? She was afraid of what you might think she thought."

But did Ev find out about my nasty run-in with the doomed Doug from Doug himself? He hired his suicide car the next morning; did he phone her to tell her what I said to him? She brings together unlikely people, but would she phone Al out of the blue to open a discussion of the incident? Must I ask Al?

I must ask Al out of the blue. Ev won't have asked Al and Bob over from the motel, for if they've phoned she'll have wished to cover my absence and has probably told them she thought I'd go *there* as soon as I was done at the foundation, where I was let's say working late.

"Gossip," says my step-grandfather John from his grave which in the cinereal air is somehow just as far from my clean but no longer weightless parabola as other curiously important lines whose course or point may have made me what I am but whom tonight I haven't time to evoke.

There was no need to delineate for you your own living room: if I'd succeeded in bringing you here, you could see for yourself; if I'd failed to make you materialize, then what would be the point? Nor is it possible to measure this night in the old way. Yet if, then, I've made a paraphase here, maybe your room (including that blatant space on the east wall where the super says Dot removed a long narrow blank gray canvas) constitutes a para-site.

"You just do your work, boy," says old fisherman John, "you'll get ahead."

And all interruptions and rates of time and spaces of lapse collapse into even script, though now more cramped because you've so little paper left.

I confess I don't embrace *all* interruptions. I embrace Emma, but her silky cheek and the crumb of apple in the center hollow of her chin are hard to conceive of as interruption. And because she walks so slowly, we often miss lights and stand curb-bound staring through the cabs that fly by and seeing something very special across the intersection that we might have missed and the impatience in my tight forehead and the sockets of my eyes dissolves in the sights we see like tourists to these ruins of a city. Say it's afternoon around our TV, it's last summer and we're about to go away, and with Emma on my lap I nostalgically watch the Moon's pale world recede in the frame of the spacecraft's window through which the NASA lens witnesses the recession. But where am I? Emma squirms to get off me, and succeeds. At once our TV set experiences mechanical difficulty: the interruption isn't this channel's fault, I switch in vain to others.

One day I'll put a raft of these intersectional interruptions together as if they were one life and all the *rest* were interruption. I'll type it up and put it in Emma's safe-deposit box downtown right on top of her deed to a hundred acres of northern Canada that cost me a hundred dollars through an agency in Winnipeg by which I bypass the trickier, New-York-approved people. I've shown Ted *his* deed, but he's too busy bucking rid of dialectic to care, his psychiatrist asked if Ted had a picture of me but Ted said No of course not, and the shrink said Why do you say "of course"?

But now I remember: the ribbon-spools on my Junior Corona wouldn't reverse, and if I did it by hand they still wouldn't feed to the right. And one night doing a paper for English I just picked up my

Corona and chucked it back over my head, but from the living room my father heard only my oath, for the infuriating machine landed on my pillow. I retrieved it when I heard his steps and when he came in without knocking asking me what the devil I thought I meant using language like that he found me holding the old thing in my arms. Subtly I ignored his rebuke and asked in piteous exasperation if he could fix the spool-reverse, the ribbon would stop moving and I'd chew a hole in it before I realized it had stopped. My father said he didn't trust our neighborhood shop on Montague Street, but when he went to Manhattan in the morning he'd take it to the place around Wall that his firm used.

But my mother stayed in bed the next morning and I heard them talking behind the closed bedroom door for what at that hour of the beginning day seemed a long time. I left my Wheaties bowl with a trace of sweet milk in the bottom of it in the sink and looked in on them to say goodbye and left; but my father when he went off to Wall Street forgot my typewriter. And next day he was so concerned about my typing my English paper and one I was even surer of entitled "The Filibuster: Freedom or Tyranny?" that even though it was Saturday he took my Corona over to Wall Street. Ever been in Wall Street on a weekend morning? I took the subway out to school to play tennis.

Wait. Wait.

The only way to be sure if Ted knows of my brush with Doug his father the night before that post-marital suicide is to tell him. I should have tonight, or what was tonight. Instead tonight I let him bow to me and look with Ev's blue eyes rather than his father's gray coolly through my forehead like a laser targeting ten feet behind me. And I should have countered his terrible terrible statement with an opener honesty that unlike his wouldn't mean to stop talk but to recomplete the circuit even if that did mean going round and round. So when Ted then slipped out the front door I called to Ev combing her hair in the bathroom that I wanted some andirons in the basement, and as the door fell to behind me and I was in the hall looking at the near elevator and at Ted (who now made the physical mistake of turning back and gazing into me as if daring me to dare to leave the apartment), I heard dimly Ev's puzzled but tolerant "Andirons?" and hardly had time to wonder how Ted's terrible statement struck her or be glad she hadn't stepped out of the bathroom with her hair half-unpinned to intervene, for at the elevator door now Ted couldn't hold his gaze. Should I have given him a break and looked down? On the dark marble floor lay unrinsed swipes of an unrinsed mop, swift gray arcs and loops. With a prissy left-flank-*Harch* turn Ted made for the door to the stairs.

But Dom: Ted and I often do get along. Maybe I failed to interest him in the parabola principle—ye gods maybe to demonstrate conic section I should have drawn a few living cones like Gail's early breasts mole for mole, or the quarry pool which fear and desire told my cold-pressed diving eyes would spiral to a deep central point and thus prove even more conical than those truncated markers the bright ominous monuments to the man her father. Even at a gap of three or four or five miles that day of the dive he was making his force felt in the buoyant water even if accelerating up some secondary blacktop in his pickup, he was unaware that he was with us and unaware of the kiss and unaware of Al in his jeans exploding into the water to come to somebody's aid.

But if I failed with the parabola, I did one night succeed with Ted when I told about my half-mislaid accumulation of silly tales about Interfear perhaps part-inspired by that birthday gift in '38. Ted almost liked them, those I could recall.

Interfear! My God, I didn't expect to be here, Dom; yet the only child's room in Brooklyn Heights where in September '40 I (a natural speller learning to touch-type) keyed a word so it came up "interfear" was as real a scene of the difference between Al and Bob as this living room of yours was, Dom, hours ago when in some other state I got in here fresh from Ted's rebuke: he said if he and I were going to quit kidding ourselves we'd see that to him I'd always smell a little like a betrayer however much I did the father bit.

Being a natural speller I couldn't stand to leave the error right there in front of me in the machine. But having X'd out "interfear," I got thinking what it meant.

Well, until I was fifteen or sixteen I wrote Interfear Mysteries. And I was ahead of my time.

A blue-jowled giant, a genius named Darius Dominion, would create and cable anywhere on the planet any sort of fear required, so long as the person who ordered it for his own use or to blow someone else's fuse was bright and original. Darius Dominion didn't need a home; he simply lived inside his own great head, which had rather shocking knots and ridges down its back, for Uncle Cooley had given me Dr. Bernard Holländer's turn-of-the-century treatise on the higher phrenology. Uncle Cooley called it a real eye-opener; but there were things in it that meant much more to me than its level-headed distinction between Gall's bumpographic cranioscopy and Gall's real bequest to the study of cerebral localization. Many a night I sat handling my head as I read Holländer and imagined I had persecution mania due to injury of my temporal lobe's posterior, or ye gods a sexual desire "exalted" (as they used to say) by some perversion of my gray matter. But I'd have been ashamed to tell Ted all this about how Darius Dominion's bumps arose.

My father dismissed those Interfear Mysteries—but if that had nothing to do with our unhappy bout the Sunday morning I said God was just someone to tell your side of the story to, why do I bring together that Sunday encounter when he was feeling so badly, and those silly mysteries that I probably should have tried out on Ted tonight to ease him? But in those sheets that the Hungarian removed so long ago, didn't I somewhere say Ted has trouble with Betsy now? He started to phone her back and I walked past the phone and for some reason grinned at him. Did he go out to the phone booth on the corner across from the framer's to call her in private? But someone ripped the new gray receiver out of that booth, and it hasn't been replaced. But Ted could have gone in the hotel down the block. I do not know. I do know I was harsh, Dom, to Ev one early morning when I'd just pivoted from my delusion about her potholder to the real thing and warm against my shoulder came her voice saying, "I'm worried about Ted," and then, "Do we know any psychiatrists?" and I said to phone up Hugh Blood, he'd been shopping around for years. When Ev said, "I hardly know him," I said, "That doesn't usually stop you," but she was nice enough to ignore that and say, "I don't really know him. Would you?" I moved my shoulder blade back against her mouth.

Al said he thought he knew the boy in my rented back seat but not the girl, and if he could identify a photo in the Dean's Office file he'd report him for molesting a faculty guest. Al was quite serious. He was taking his two oldest to a birthday party, and before he left, I and Annette urged him to forget it, if he went after the boy he'd get him suspended. "Oh I couldn't get him sus*pen*ded," said Al.

Annette may have been embarrassed. We sat on the couch to look at her album. The third little girl was upstairs, Al's special favorite who bawled him out for eating before it had cooled one of the sugar-dough stars she'd baked in her toy oven, and bawled him out for not giving her a Valentine, and for losing a patch of hair in back that Annette called his tonsure.

Annette and I stared at a snapshot of Al asleep on a bed beside a baby. Annette said, "He just feels the students are rude, that's why he gets so upset; he says they want more than they're prepared to give—they don't know any facts."

There was a picture of Al's parents sitting formally relaxed on this very couch that Annette and I were sitting on. The house was quiet. Annette said, "*Those* two used to fight. But I guess she was devoted to him."

"Well, there was trouble," I said. "But...what the hell..."

"Bound to be," said Annette, crossing one knee over the other.

"The old man got to dislike me," I said, looking at the top of her top knee gleaming in its nylon.

There came a rattly knock at the kitchen door, the boy to mow the lawn.

It was one a.m. after the company steamer had scoured up into its two holds that dark field of silvery fish, all but those that flipped over the finally narrowing corral of expensive nets; and it was one, after Bob and I had left the outboard on its mooring and rowed the dory twenty-five yards in to the beach; and it was one before we'd divided most of the Jim Beam in slugs interrupted by minutes of silence and friendly but cautious and at one point rather tense talk, and it was after one before we'd said what the hell and killed that fifth and I took it outside and left it on a rock glimmering dully in the touch of a small moon.

During all this space of time sitting at a candle-lit spool table under a tattered American flag that a brother-in-law of Bob's had brought back from the Bulge, we had a few laughs—all roughly equal. They were about:

on one hand, the difficulties of coitus interruptus with a Bucks County girl in her brother's pup-tent in her farmer-pappy's dew-damp back yard probably watched through a distant screen door by a quiescent old Golden Retriever,

and on the other, Bob's feat with the cross-stick boomerang— "Well it sure as hell came *back*," said Bob, "I thought it was going to scalp me"

on one hand, Hugh Blood's strange whistle when Bob was about to leave his feet for the window, and Bob said he'd known way up in front of his mind that that whistle was Hugh's—

and on the other, Petty's dad's old friend Mrs. Bolla, recuperating in Presbyterian after having her veins done—each fine leg wrapped from ankle to ass—slowly reading an Updike novel brought by Bob's mother who once said to mine, "For an Italian she seems awfully restrained; but *he*, of course, was supposed to have been a bit on the cold side—all involved in natural gas geology":

while Bob—for it seemed throughout that this other force of Robby his oldest son preoccupied him or hung near like a power to which these outer, equidistant recollections were raised—with the dure pique of a good man who can't see why his warmth and abruptness are not accepted as a kind of leadership albeit temporary—Bob at several points recurred to Robby: "Said sucking a run of herring up out of the cove with a machine wasn't *real* fishing, and I said to him God who said it was! Well this is a kid who sits around reading electronic catalogues. One day I started mowing the lawn but then I was out of gas and when I said, 'Robby, get me the five-gallon can in the garage beside the skis,' he waited a second and looked at me: just blank. And yesterday I was alone in the house, or thought so, and I phoned Ben Sedgwick—*you*'ve met Father Sedgwick—I suddenly had to ask him what he *really* thought about Bonhoeffer going back to Germany in '40—wasn't it really suicide? and after I dialed I think I said a phrase or two in advance and I waited with this dead phone in my hand and then the line was busy and I held on, *I* don't know why I held on, and then I knew I was being watched and I looked off through the hall door across a corner of the living room through another door to the new living room and there was Robby just staring at me, it was like night and he made me feel like a fool, a lunatic, and do you think he looked away or said a word?"

"You mean you were scared?" I asked after a while as Bob pushed the bourbon across almost upsetting it on the table's central bolts.

Mild eyes framed in gold circles peer at me as if I am some distinctly odd question—the face opens and writhes in violent laughter and the whole pen assembly on my private seismovec gashes right off the drum, in fact up right off my Rictus Scale—the noise as suddenly turns off, and Bob says quietly, "'*Course* not."

"Come in here," my father said from his bed in the room to my right as I stood in my pajamas in the hall facing the bathroom and with my bedroom behind me. My morning muse had been Camille a moment before when I was sitting on the edge of my Sunday bed thinking about the party she'd taken me to. Now in the hall my morning muse had risen to the height of Tracy: I don't know what I expected my father to say but I delayed obeying him and said I'll be out of the john in a second.

Well he was mad in that sunny room. As I must have said in those pages removed by the Hungarian—I don't know which page but the phrase was in the lower right third—my father was sitting up in bed. You could see great gray-and-white platforms of ice in the water off the near docks; a tug crossed my path as I ran that ice-strewn Brooklyn slip straight across the East River to the ferry landings. On the floor of his open closet I saw the black-and-white saddle shoes he bought the summer we went to the shore instead of the stone heart house in Heatsburg. My father had my prominent nose, though not my height; eyes gray, face delicate and square, mouth precise but responsive. My mother had replaced the empty tumbler from last night and instead of that acidophilus milk I dreaded being near, there was water beside the three short brown bottles.

It was my saying God was just someone to tell your side of the story to.

The scene has less meaning now then earlier in this confession when it was a mere glimpse equidistant from Camille's father's Bahama duck marshes.

My father's being in bed sitting up against the ramp-like wedge of my mother's lemon satin invalid pillow that he'd bought her made his daunting finality immeasurable. He was not harsh but he was certain, though less terrible after he'd worked himself up a bit, for he thought my seeming taciturnity was gall.

What do you mean by saying such a thing? What were you

thinking of? Now you're in college you're free, is that it? I know
you don't tell me a lot of things. And I tell myself I don't want
you to. Listen: how dare you speak of God as *"just"* *any*thing? just
some pal to tell some petty tale to? What do *you* know? Now that
you're a freshman in college you can spout the difference between
Augustine and Bonaventure. You've been taught how to drive a car
because I knew you'd break the college rule and drive this year and
I wanted to make sure you knew how. You know Cyrus E. Dallin
sculpted Indians. You knew more about the Bible than any other
boy in your ancient history class four years ago, maybe more than
Cadbury. Well you don't know nothin'. And someday when you have
to earn a living—

(I've smoothed it here, Dom, he was hesitating as he got mad,
and I've eased his slight breathlessness.)

—and when you make some *big* mistakes instead of all these
little ones, come back then and tell me about God.

Dom, I'd been a bit flip but I didn't deserve what I got. Yet maybe
it's the uncalled-for things that say the most, am I running out of
space and is someone going to walk in on me here?, by uncalled-for I
mean the unfair blurts you should have done without. In the middle
of his ejaculations I felt affectionately insane and nearly asked him
what God's last name was, I'd often wanted to know. I wanted to be
weaker before my father that Sunday morning than I was; but even
in my gaping pajamas I didn't know how. Then my father said, "He
is so close, I don't see how you can't feel Him." My mother said, "It's
a phase."

Betsy and Ted were to have gone to a film tonight, and you know
that just as I could describe to you the gap Dot left vacant on this
east wall behind the white leather couch, so if I chose I could tell
you the theater Betsy and Ted went to and what was on and even
the price per head, which was why they were going there, and even
delineate the furniture emporium diagonally across the street. But
now I don't know if they went together or apart, or not at all. If not,

they found something else to do.

Dom, among some Indian tribes of Brazil the chief holds his numerous women partly because his important trances can be homicidally volatile, and somebody has to be around to keep him from killing perhaps even himself. Now at least in Dot's caustic wit if not wholly in your mind, you were a chief; so maybe you're a suicide because you let that pregnant secretary and other secretaries go, you let Dot go, Kit go, and whom else I don't know enough about you to know. Richard let you go.

There it is, hero. Yours is the ultimate insurance. Stunted by publicity, you've emerged at fifty-two into mystery.

Unlike me. I'm on the line registering under my own name in public space.

Bob was incredibly standing when we looked down. Seeing him we then swung our gazes away and back like a pendulum; he had a smudge of new-mown green on top of his crewcut, and we all heard him tell our athletic director he knew what he could do with the lacrosse game tomorrow.

Almost three floors he'd dropped. Now he walked away and he was placing his feet carefully. "You could be a parachute-jumper right now without a single day of training, Bobby," the athletic director called after him. But Bob just warped out of sight into the locker room, and the hapless athletic director who could not punish him glared up at us but didn't say a word to us and followed Bob inside.

Bob wouldn't let him drive him to the subway.

I was puzzled. Bob might well have made that window-leap in any event, but I did not tell my parents about it and about the miracle of his safe landing. At the time, it seemed a corollary miracle that my parents never heard about the feat from anyone else. I'm sure they never did. Sometimes you don't hear about things— especially without our old friend ye vectoral muscle. But you can bet Bob's father heard all about it from our athletic director, who as if to keep it all from being true by staying on the phone in the face of

Bob's father's stoic courtesy kept saying the same things in varying sequences: A fine clean guy. Could have killed himself. He was a good boy, no one's fault. Backus wasn't at fault. Bob was enough shaken up so he forgot the game tomorrow. He landed just enough off balance, and with enough basic thrust, to tumble. The game tomorrow. A good clean boy. It was unprecedented.

I had told Hugh his whistle hadn't done Bob any good. Hugh ignored this and asked if it had been a thirty-foot drop, and I said Less.

Bob wouldn't see any "medicine man," but his dad called Doctor Field anyhow and according to Petty, who wasn't really there, when that excellent laconic man came up to Bob's top-floor room Bob was very seriously taping his knees and looked up blankly like a king.

"But how *could* Al's dad like you?" Annette said lightly returning from the back door. Then, as if finding reasons for something she hadn't really meant, "All that hocus-pocus about newspaper puzzles? And the old man and Gail were driving past that antique shop of course when you were unloading your encyclopedia and later Al didn't believe his father but Gail said it was true. But so what? Al didn't care. He said he *wanted* the books. There's no puzzle in that."

"Exactly," I said.

"You might say he needed you, Cy. Don't think badly of him for that."

We share life, even our attempts not to.

Is it possible that I won't or can't explain to you, Dom, how Al and Bob happen to be here this weekend? If you were here perhaps I'd not risk it. Fred Eagle coughs and coughs, grinning helplessly; then he stops and hoarsely says, looking into his handkerchief but not at either of his visitors: Someone I want you to meet:

Al and Bob shake: and Fred's shelves and shelves of stock are comfortably around them, and on an old table a gallon of Gallo and a partly carved turkey: Fred tells the joke about the Renaissance Jew who in his lonely wanderings came at last to Rome and seeing the utter corruption of the clergy but concluding that this church, having survived it, must be indeed the true church, became a Catholic.

Al said, "He should have been content just to know his true enemy."

Bob said, "If you feel so strongly you ought to read Simone Weil."

A moment interferes in which A and B elect to be friendly.

Ev may not have gotten on to the cops; she may have just figured I went, and will come back.

Al checked Bob's name and origin, then said, "I wasn't invited to your Welcome Home party in '52 or '53, whenever it was."

No surprise from Bob: "Neither was I. I mean, *we* didn't go."

"But you were invited."

"Matter of fact, it was a surprise party, so I wasn't. But why would *you* have been asked to my parents'? Did you know someone?"

I am mentioned and Bob privately wonders why I let Al think the honored couple *had* turned up for the Welcome Home, for Al neglects to tell Bob it was not I from whom he learned where I really went that night in '53. And of course Al was awake enough to note that I came home with my mother, and my mother was heard to say the Vande Lands' Dutchman was a lot of fun even if he hadn't been a Resistance hero. He had talked about Europe's coming demands for energy and had been quite fascinating on the subject of natural gas in the Netherlands.

Dom, long ago I should have done you a floor plan of my parents' apartment on Brooklyn Heights, but for that matter a plan of our Heatsburg house too, including the upstairs room where on Sunday mornings early my father would sometimes sit with his dark brown Brokers Special pencils and long yellow pad, first outlining ABCD. For thus these spaces could have been around us throughout this night of time that seemed urgent one way when I came in your unlocked door but now spreads like an inestimably charged field ever, yet, within the coördinates of this room, to a mode like time, but solute—a paraphase.

As on the educational channel last week my small Emma was watching the thin man Mr. Rogers from his own private outer space end his kids' show "You make each day such a special day. You know how. By just your being you," the gossip column Eagle Eye said that your wife Dorothy had got her final decree but that you were sitting around these days enjoying life in your "vast elegant" living room running your slide collection round and round your Carousel projector—mostly "candid news shots involving himself."

I don't think that from our brief meeting at Cora's you recognized me in the Think-Tank shot or in Ed's overhead zoom of the Defenestration Crowd waiting. But are those even *in* your slide box against that far bookcase-wall above and to the right of the styrofoam?

I'll have enough paper, and even though as I write this, to my surprise I vector one of the elevators up its shaft and I divine footsteps preparing to come into existence, I will have time enough as well as paper, for I'm now into my proud paraphase. Let me subtract from that, rather than add, that instead of the dreaded Vectoral Dystrophy, I've got Writer's Cramp. And looking into your newly insured past though no longer divining by means of liver because Ev says even our high-priced butcher admits that liver is apt to be polluted nowadays, I think I can tell who it is in that east or west elevator coming here. He will not get to your floor until we're ready.

You learned Spanish after the War. Did I say you were an only child earlier tonight?

You were not an only child, though you said America was.

You said you didn't fear overcopulation any more: you said every great human test is new and its right solution unimaginable at first: the day you resigned from the primary to throw your support elsewhere, you said the secret of future solutions resided in the idea of spacecraft. After tonight you'll never know if spacecraft will as you predicted turn out to be earthcraft—if life-sup-portable microfields designed for interstitial vector-treks and vacuum-strolls can feed and house our ordinary unlaunched future too, and even space us far enough apart so we can like each other. Mmm...spacecraft is to politics, as—

One reporter asked if you'd said "statecraft" and you said No, and then incredibly another reporter, a girl, asked politely if you'd said "statecraft," and you stared at her but spotted your shrink son-in-law standing five spaces down from me and hailed him but he slunk sideways among the crowd. I think he'd been observing me.

You have done a lot for me, though you never knew it. I'm trying to reciprocate.

The TV cameras were still on you when Eagle Eye—in real life Valerie O'Doul—asked what you were going to be doing with yourself now: you said, "Val, if I could only, like, drop down a few floors and live an ordinary life."

I think I'll incinerate my file on Heights hors d'oeuvres.

At twelve I returned. Bernie Scheindlinger's mother drove me all the way from school to the 36th Street subway, so I skipped seven stations and because 36th is an express stop I could bypass four more local stations by catching a Sea Beach to Pacific Street, where just as its doors were closing I caught my 4th Avenue Local. When I sprang into the front car there was Hugh Blood with his feet up along one yellow straw seat reading the ads. He'd been at school that Saturday morning working on the newspaper.

My father hadn't been able to make the match. He was in the kitchen with my mother when I came in, sitting with his hand on *The Peloponnesian War*. To his eager question I replied that we'd been "vectorious." My mother had on a dark blue hat and a lighter blue—or was it gray—wool suit. She reminded my father that Joey would be delivering her order from Bohack, and my father wondered if Joey'd taken offense when she asked about the typewriter the other day. She was about to leave to go to Manhattan with Russell Pound to see some "abstracts" by a young westerner he was interested in who'd gotten very excited reading Pappy Pound's remarks on paint-perishability in his Ryder book. My father wanted all the scores of the match, singles and doubles. He was wearing his new light brown slippers and a gray cashmere sweater. He always looked young. His teeth were good, they hadn't worn blue at the end, and his hair was good too, he parted it in the middle; and he had a quick smile that was full of surprise and respect. Later, when he was really dying, he looked for a time even younger. My mother said, "I'm off," and they touched lips. But I'd forgotten about the lacrosse game, I'd meant to phone Bob from school to see if he was coming out for it.

Damn!, and I had a paper to write that I'd have to hand in in longhand. My mother now said, as she went into the hall, that Bob had called. My father had the refrigerator open and turned to say that my step-grandfather had phoned to ask me to go to the Museum of Natural History with him that afternoon; my father said he'd promised I'd call back. I have not told John's (Zo-an's, Zon's) story here, Dom, but I now think it makes an absence. Displaced from New England at twenty, never quite making it back except for a month in the summer and never for longer even in his long, neatly ordered widowerhood, he was now six months away from retiring; he would leave New York and go back up north; he had until now always made me feel I was smart, but he was getting dogmatic. All these details won't bring you back, Dom. Even to ask (say), "Who was that Sue you mentioned?, where does she fit in?" I don't think even Bob knows about her even though she was my great-aunt—which is something else Al has in common with Bob. My mother, from the hall and holding the front door open, had to tell my father twice to please shut the refrigerator, she'd defrosted it only two days ago. If Bob was going to play lacrosse after all maybe I could get a ride back out with him and his father. I should have phoned from Poly.

My father made two fried egg sandwiches, and if it would bring you back into this former space of yours, Dom, I'd describe the gold-gray damp of the grease coming into the Pepperidge Farm white. He said, "You can't wait till your birthday for a new typewriter." It sounded Jewish, but I wasn't perfectly sure what he meant. He said he was going into the bedroom for a nap. He took Thucydides from the kitchen table.

I have to finish this ancient history now or it will last for the rest of my average life-span. One day a man came out of the psychiatrist's inner office, shutting the door, and stood at the coat rack and talked to Ted: three insurance firms seemed to have got this man's name all at once and one of them just chuckled and said, "You've got a sense of humor" when the poor, irascible guy demanded of the salesman why he was trying to sell somebody who had only six months to live and no company would insure him and he didn't want insurance anyway. Despite the salesman's chuckles, it was true, yes, six months the man's doctor had given him. And Ted wondered why he was seeing a psychiatrist (and then for a second if that was what he meant by "doctor") but Ted didn't say anything except, sympathetically, "They're stupid," but the man stopped with his coat half on, arms pinioned, and said, "They are not stupid." Ted tells me things. He says he wants *someone* to get something out of all that shrinking money. Ted is in group dynamics at college. Group dynamics, it sounds like a stock. As my father turned to leave the kitchen I unaccountably rose with my mouth full of yolk and bread and asked if he wanted to go to a movie, but he said thanks he would read Thucydides, and when he walked into the dining room we both remembered and in unison said, "Bohack!" having forgotten for a second that we couldn't·both go out. Of course the suspect Joey could leave the carton on the doormat but there was danger of theft—maybe even from Joey—and anyway my father wanted to stay in. He'd been away on business the weekend before and since he couldn't possibly get back for Russell Pound's party he'd stopped in Washington to see Cooley. My father was born in 1900, Cooley in 1896. Cooley is not a close relation, but I called him Uncle. As

soon as my parents' bedroom door closed, Bob and Petty rang our
bell. I saw my father bundled dead into Joey's deep silver carrier and
the big lid banged down. That Junior Corona—if it was a Corona—
softens in recollection: its carriage and keys and the black center lid
over the type-bars become almost soft, malleably soft, as a new crisis
hardens out into undue clarity: I mean the injustice to me three years
before of Dr. Cadbury, who Akkie had just now told us was having
an operation on his gut; but I really mean my mere urge to expatiate
toward the end of Cadbury's midterm three years before. It was at
first the expatiation of a pupil so free in his knowledge and syntax
that the exam question turned into an invitation to art or play; in
essence, all I said was that in some later Assyrian reliefs the figures
could have been freed by first cutting away a small tissue of stone
but for some reason were not, and after all it wasn't as if they'd been
on the sea floor waiting for Captain Nemo. Cadbury rebuffed me
sorely in the margin; my father phoned him and complained; I was
embarrassed; Cadbury and my father both backed off, and I was left
with an A minus. My pyramids don't soften, I can tell you: they are
greater than ever: greater far than that well-known entrepreneur's
plan for a poured-concrete facsimile in California one foot higher
than the *great* pyramid.

When I opened the front door Bob and Petty were hand in
hand—no Joey—and she said, "Bob didn't play in the lacrosse
game." They looked married. "His father was terrible to him," said
Petty, "and so were the people at school; if he slipped off the window
sill, it could happen to anybody. I think I was rude to his father, but
it's funny, he sort of gave up; he took it."

I stood aside. Vectors everywhere, then and now. I now believe
the elevator I'm guiding up here is the near one, the west. Its
acceleration is wholly controlled by vectorcraft. I have switched on
your late TV but my trip to the foyer and kitchen is invisible on
this 8 1/2 by 11 Sphinx bond of yours. Your Hungarian son-in-
law wondered where your typewriter was. Is there an answer in the

words to which I have led myself? But so many of those have been removed by him. If you aren't dead after all, I didn't do that either. When my father died in '52 he'd been reading Lawrence's letters and hoping to go to New Mexico to recuperate. But if you're alive in the two parts of my confession, I guess I did do that. In the kitchen your TV screen is a bright blank.

But Petty and Bob and I didn't enjoy sitting around in my living room discussing what Poly would do about Bob's cutting the game and what his father would do if Bob went through with his abortive vow to abjure Princeton. We took a long walk. They were sober and dull and they needed me there with them maybe to have someone to exclude. The Heights was bigger twenty-three years ago. We moved past the famous Gothic exterior of Petty and Tracy's school, and we got all the way to the Greek Revival colonnades on Willow Place and a Gothic Revival house Petty pointed out with recessed spandrels over and under the windows later used in—

My block returned like an idea, after an hour, and Hugh appeared from the Bloods' brownstone on the corner and there were some others, Freddy Smith and Wit Holmes and North the minister's son and Angus Moore and the Negro superintendent's ten-year-old Abra (for "Abracadabra")—her real name I think was (with the *a* as in "saber") Sabra. She had a ball and she was dying to play, and I got a broomstick from her father.

We had played three innings by the time Joey came slowly into the long block with, on the sidewalk but walking beside his bike-cart, two guys I'd seen with him before.

Ted's no groupy and neither is his girl. But I think they're out of phase now. I feel I should keep pot as well as booze. It's only polite. You, Dom, smoked for your blood pressure. Its effect on the vectoral triangle is not known.

We didn't usually play in this street. My father's shade was down. For home we used the sewer cover up opposite the Historical Association's brownstone. I was glad not to bother my father if he was asleep. On a spring evening five years before when I'd had my supper of liver and bacon and gone out again to have a catch on roller skates with Freddy Smith who was still Bart Smith then, my father came home after working late. And, for some reason I half divine now long after, and long after I began this private confession, I called across the street, "Hi, Dad; soused again?" and Arnie the Good Humor Man standing with that rear icebox-door of his white truck open reaching in to find a burnt almond or a sundae for one of the kids who were around him with their money in their fists, turned to look, though his arm was still inside; but he saw merely a man in a gray worsted suit, a gray fedora, and black (not wing-tip) shoes, with his New York *Sun* twice-folded under his arm. At my weird words my father started to smile with a puzzled frown then interrupted himself and turned in the door of our apartment house. My father came back out before he'd even gotten to the elevator and asked me to please come in, he wanted to speak to me: for my father was barely even a social drinker, the doctor eventually had to urge him to take a drink before dinner: and as for me, I had never even imagined him drunk, had never seen him drink too much and knew I never would because *he* never would: unlike Bob's father and old Eben Smith, whose dragging guffawing chat and sweaty untrussing of sentiment and distrust seemed to me when I was nine or ten to close their bodies—there, yes, I've come upon the right word for the first time in my life, Dom, on your Sphinx bond paper, *"close"*—yet also loosen and coarsen and supplant those great laborious bodies. It must have been all of eight o'clock the evening after the boomerang incident that my father and the others were talking about Europe's future and Russell Pound asked my father if he still thought history a succession of moral lessons—when Eben Smith interrupted, "a succession of moral lessons no less" and then said to Bob's father and Russell Pound (though not within earshot of the glamorous guest of honor just back from the Arizona sun) that Mara Bolla's estranged husband was basically a perfumed fart. Russell Pound's mouth was

at once governed into an immobility the resultant of two vectors
which (even if this isn't very good physics—and I confess I learned
physics on my own) were directed one horizontally smilewards the
other vertically talkwards, the tolerant male chum (which actually
Russell Pound never was with those two if with any man) countered
by a lover's loyalty (though indirectly on behalf of the man Mara
had walked out on). He did point out (with a bright hospitableness
no doubt nourished by the sight of Bob's mother in her gray Persian
lamb approaching with Bob's father's dark blue overcoat over her
arm and doubtless herself debating whether they'd get as far down
Fulton as Gage and Tollner's lamb chops and the dear hierarchy
of epauletted Negro waiters, or stop at Joe's for Long Island duck)
that hardly four years ago Signor Bolla served on one of the famous
Italian subs that, approaching the Gibraltar passage between Punta
de Europa and Punta de la Almina, would cut the engines and in
the mysterious westward current deep deep below the great Atlantic
eastward influx, would ride silently out past the British listening
posts. I interrupted to say that the ancients had wondered why the
Med doesn't overflow, and Bob's father, the glow of Bob's boomerang
fading, said, "Balls."

Russell Pound's model ships were rigged to the last stay and
their lacquer personally dusted by Petty. They were all over the
library as if independent of each other and of everything else there:
they were in glass boxes, there was one out on a table under the
rare little portrait of a Colonial militiaman (paint cracking on his
musket); there was another ship on top of a display case full of
Indian things. The Pueblo mugs reminded Bob's father of German
steins, and Bob's mother thought the prairie dog vase was darling.
On a wall was a faded Navaho rug, patterned from those fluid, calm,
vulnerable dry-paintings poured in powdered sandstone color by
color upon smooth ground, made and destroyed while the sun was
up but exactly remembered by medicine men who no doubt saw to
it that to let evil spirits escape, the rug-weaver left a break in the

design—in the yellow blossoms of the sagebrush, or in the stubborn buffalo, or in the god. My father made a point of remembering what Russell Pound told him, from the Navaho swastika to Albert Ryder in New York not knowing what his bathtub was for.

Mrs. Smith's first name was Lydia.

I've gone to the near john: left at the foyer, and left again: on the tub's yellowed porcelain bottom that in the '30s for decoration more than safety they ribbed longitudinally with wavy parallels, a slivery oval of translucent amber lay among a dozen dark hairs at the far end from the drain. The water in the toilet keeps swaying in and then out like the water in our west toilet downstairs, as if on the other side of a ragged valve an open ocean moves, or some passing craft. In the cabinet are a bottle of Measurin with the cotton still in the neck, a punctured plastic sheet holding now only three Contac capsules, and a four-inch unsqueezed aluminum tube on whose red-framed label "Apply Externally" has been penned by (I believe) our own cut-rate man two blocks down. Recrossing the foyer's white and black diamonds—and for the second time in the choice acre of my life coming upon the thought (though now accepting it) that it must have been my father who created those latter puzzles in the *Hour*, the frigate and the ziggurat and those others that in turn made mild trouble in that Heatsburg family that once preoccupied me so—I have to confess to myself that there's a limit to what any of my outgoing vectors can do to that elevator rising in its own, other time; yet faced with '46 and the Joey Neurohr Three advancing at one end and my father's third-floor shade down at the other end, I'm nonetheless here to say that quite as if adolescence brought with it some breakdown like my grandmother's pre-fatal aphasia that at seven I'd knowingly discussed with my mother when it got her down, Hugh Blood would think Bob had it in for him if Bob failed to greet him enthusiastically. Hugh made the same mistake with yours truly though I corrected it; he didn't make this mistake with silent Wit

Holmes, who was a loner, but he did with Binocular Bill Smith
who called Hugh "You" and once in a while when they sighted each
other would neglect to share with Hugh their regular hog-holler
borrowed from some movie, "Suey! pig pig piggy!" Dom, in this
same earlier time maybe a year past Pearl Harbor, imperturbable
Petty stopped playing with us. She might—or might not—spare
half an hour Saturday before she went off hand in glove with her
"Pappy" to the Manhattan galleries. And she suddenly developed
an indiscriminate sweetness with Bob and Hugh and the Smith
twins and once Joey too and of course me which I happen to know
Bob in private told her to knock off for it was phony and which
to me bespoke some inescapable bounty of which she had made
up part. Joey had dark down on his upper lip when he was only
thirteen, and he rooted for the Giants. Where was Tracy? She
didn't like sports. The handsome creature in our basement laundry
room here in this benighted building asked the Super if he gave up
booze for Ramadan. He looked at her and moved toward the door
then halted—*suddenly*, so you were reminded that as usual he'd
been limping. Then with his back to us head down he said, "I guess
you might say we've put the salaam back into the salami," and she
said as if on cue, "Is that black humor?"

But it's the Irish-Italian axis my Austrian neighbor fears, some
decentralized outer Mafia. On the other hand, she smells very real;
she smells of (as the big button next to the green "KISS ME I'M
IRISH" in the stationery shop window says:) "SEX NOW": she
isn't quite Utah clean under her quilted sleeves or in her demanding
non-committal drawl "How you doing today?" That's not exactly the
password kids by custom exchange on the Hello Walk of Utah U.
perhaps locatable most vividly as the east third of a promenade that
bisects the campus's oval park. If I can't decelerate the elevector I
can retard the footsparks when they come into the echoing hall. Yet
maybe, too, I should welcome the chance to ask if, in law, suicide
invalidates a Whole Life policy. For it's Richard your son coming.

It has to be.

Let me insert into the record lines Tracy wrote in the book she sent me out west for my sixteenth birthday, *A Bell for Adano*:

Therefore I gladly trust
My bodie to this school, that it may learn
To spell his elements, and finde his birth
Written in dustie heraldrie and lines;
Which dissolution sure doth best discern,
Comparing dust with dust, and earth with earth.

I cannot feel the paraphase field come around me without it constellating into sentences which are as framing as the blindly momentous syntaxes I leveled at Al's father a generation ago. "Love is style," I must have said in the sheets the psychiatrist took away. Thank God I don't have to read them over to see if I've been consistent. Did he think they were your suicide note overlooked? If love is style, then is style love? Hugh Blood (no relation to Governor Henry H. Blood who in the '30s fostered the Utah U. art collection) winces: but not like Bob in front of Petty's medicine cabinet—but Hugh can't call my contagious equation dirty. My syntax in that parlor Al's mother hung with three big picture calendars was the truth if I could only get to it instead of laboriously hosting Al and Bob in the living room of a moderately famous American I hardly knew.

Parabolabuster. Absentee vote-pairings in Congress.

That Saturday in March of '53 I imagined Trace wasn't using anything, so I went ahead, I unearthed her and then in time (though stylishly) withdrew. Bob and Al would laugh and say Retracted the old landing gear. Well, after that, her whole body beside me was puzzling back beyond the strangeness to the spasms which she had once upon a time haltingly told me were like her vertebrae turned into little attacking hearts of electric blood sliding down one by one through her living womb and back. But now she began to shake and when I drew the covers up I found she was moving her fingertips through what I had left of myself on her. So style isn't necessarily love, O.K.? I had made her lose her grace, and I forgot then whether Al could have heard us from his snoring room and I thought only that guilt teaches nothing. But if Earth = Spacecraft, may not Space = Earthcraft?

The freaked-in cloud-hanger, his plane long gone, looks up for silver and feels the earth out there, and but half-willing to think of himself as just one more paratrooper, himself vectoring the drag and lift and their aerodynamic resultant vector which brother had better be equal to your downward weight, puts off deciding whether to yank his ripcord: but suicide? like, spend the rest of your life *dead*? Space is something to get through, to come from. It's how you use your earth.

Leave your lock off and someone's going to come in and suicide you.

The elevator came and the steps began and then stopped; and doubting the power of my paraphase I went to the peephole to look. And it *is* your son as I thought, but he is not magically moving in another time; he is standing halfway down the hall looking at the key.

What time is it?

*Once upon a night a lonely former witch
sat alone in her huge house. By the light
of one naked bulb she was poring over
a tome of old dead spells, when suddenly
down the hall the kitchen Minute-Minder
started clicking. Had Darius Dominion
returned?*

Is he operating independently of his curator? Einstein may in a way have rescued Lavoisier and Lucretius. My father said so. He said Einstein was twenty-six at the time of his break-through. Russell Pound up on the tarred roof of our apartment house (guarded above the brick barrier by odd cement parapets we tried to hammer off, the night of Poly graduation) looked at the spring sky and the field of harbor lights, the slow glow of Jersey City, a moving ferry bearing its tiers of lights behind a barracks on Governor's Island—and you know Dom, if I wanted to I'd tell you which constellations my father and his friend pointed out and followed, but at this juncture of my now shaky paraphase the names would seem to mean too much, and I (if not my trivia-scorning step-grandfather) prefer the fact that the roof right across the street from their star-watching is where stingy Bill Smith sold two-minute binocular views of the harbor and, as Tracy told me, had his glasses trained on the Bridge at the moment the famous boomerang was hurled through that diamond cable-weave, and saw the whole thing. And the day of the fight, ditto—though even with his binoculars he couldn't have seen what happened to Petty, to Bob, to Joey, and to me in the vestibule above those twelve august stone steps though he may have made out something on the face of Hugh Blood who half-reached in but never really did get where he later said he'd wanted to get, namely right into the vestibule.

"But you can't have everything," my mother said one evening four or five years after my father died. I'd explained how I would interpret rather freely the Foundation's understanding of my activities in those alien areas of Brooklyn—Brownsville and Williamsburg—and my mother said, "We're just ordinary people." But I bet that meant (say) the "1834" plaque on the Vande Lands' brownstone. In answer to her I nearly said like a blind soothsayer, "But I see tuxedoed adolescents ambling under eucalyptus trees, I see black nannies seated on benches and rocking prams and watching toddlers in Miss White's exclusive Garden" (an ancient immeasurable area now the mere base of an aging contemporary cube) "and I see a dangerously unorthodox anthropologist himself a Heights native lecturing your women's club Civitas": but what I really said to her was that, instead of a people, I was unearthing the customs of a person, whose slowly prospering parents had moved from Brownsville to a small apartment house in Williamsburg, then to Bay Ridge, then to Sea Gate, and who himself had found violent means to maintain yet vary inherited identity myths. My mother said it didn't sound like anthropology to her, and who *was* this person. But I said her remark was shrewd, Dom.

I take the measure of my Heights street's space partly by my two-sewer line-drive which Hugh Blood backpedaled to catch without coming within thirty yards of the harbor-view dead-end whose lamp-post and black-iron fence were roughly in the same plane as the street window of my parents' third-floor bedroom to my right and Binocular Bill's station on the roof to my left. As the space of your screen in your late kitchen showing at this hour the Educational Channel's bright blank can't be measured apart from your throwaway option to last night's audience involving your now approaching son Richard: so the space between me and Bob can't be traced by the down-then onward-bouncing trajectories of my trick pitch to Bob apart from his swinging third strike's coincidence with the "Look out!" bawled by one of Joey's pals as if for a car. Who could have foreseen the effect of that interruption on Bob's anger at striking out and taking such a cut that ten-year-old A.B. let it right through her dark legs and almost forgot to chase it seeing Bob instantly move with his stick toward the Joey Neurohr Three? And Joey dismounted on the sidewalk side.

All three had dark hair, darker than Al's. Joey's pals were a big-eyed Italian and a Puerto Rican kid apropos of whom my Irish doorman had said spics don't use toilet paper. Joey's broad-boned face built around small eyes could well have used more than its now-arrested adolescent mustache. Joey lowered his forehead eying Bob, the other two raised their chins. Even I could not have foreseen that the vectoral elite, of whom I must have been the sole representative there, pay for their strange power to receive incoming vectors, with a virtually gravitational impulse to launch vectors indirectly perilous to themselves: for without thinking, I called, "You wouldn't have hit that pitch in a million years"—*I*, who believed that German Joey Neurohr could well have hooked my Corona as a joke (and a joke with that ending). But I then said, "Don't worry about these sneaks, they only robbed you of a base-hit."

Bob said he was not worrying. Joey said to me, "Who robbed *you*, buddy?" and Bob clattered our broomstick into the gutter and put a hand on Joey's steel carrier and was about to do something, as Joey's pals moved in on either side, but a short braking skid whistled our eyes around toward A.B. who, looking back at us had run right into a car that fortunately had already come to a stop after whipping into our block as if headed for the far dead end.

"So don't worry about some of your friends who—" my father two years later eased off into other words he now saw would not ease our bedroom scene about God—"who expect you to get off these unclever quips. Now I don't mean Camille, or even Bob, or anybody special. It's just that I hate to see you get to be a wise guy. Even if you don't go to church any more. You see, Cy, God is exactly *not* the one you can tell your petty little *side* of the *story* to, He's beyond that." My mother had paused in the kitchen long enough—I bet at least fifteen pages of this Outer Paraspace, but because of time there's no more chance to check than to check all those pages your son-in-law took—and my mother now came audibly to the hall and was about to join us, and my father said with quiet precision and a deadpan wave, "Your pajamas are wide open," and then, "Maybe you know your Bible but you don't know Solomon's concubines," I subsequently found he was thinking of Solomon's favorite Abra— quite a Sunday joke for him.

Did you know, Dom, that Richard would get wind of your public remark about TV screens and him? But he probably didn't read your odd words. But it's unlike him to come without phoning the police, and they'd demand his key, wouldn't they?

Or is Richard just coming? That is, just to be here. I could tell him a thing or two about this space and how it's become mine to become itself.

Abra ran around the car slapping its front fender and chased the ball. The car jumped, and we all divided, and it pushed Bob right up against Joey's steel carrier with the insignia that Bohack had asked him to take off. Petty and I and some others came across in the wake of the car.

I must get home to Ev in order to wake early, but after tonight perhaps like you Dom I'll sleep late. That's what some of us need—a new federal, state, and local Program Oversleep. I'd hoped that my paraphase would be a break-through. Into the unimpeded field beyond the sway of ordinary light: Beyond that foully funny dream in which you Dom ask me to be your Secretary of Field-State and I consent as, simultaneously, though in another congruent kit of coördinates, I frown down on my father's powdered cheeks that are roughly at right angles to the casket's satin pillow, and I say, "But I was God."

yes, Beyond even paraday and night: to what you may have meant when you agreed with but would not support those who counsel emergency Silence, for you wanted (what can I name it but) Paraspeech. But I have not on this Sphinx bond paper of yours created Parawrite after all, have I. On the way back from the Hillsdale station and drawn in a kind of pressure between his family and the trees, my father listened to me tell about Al's father, how he'd bought us ice cream Thursday and how tonight we'd done the Heatsburg puzzles, and how Tuesday he was taking us to a Legion game. And my father asked my mother what progress *she* had to report, and she tilted her head humorously and said she and Emily were giving a recital after all on the Labor Day weekend, and my mother talked about how Emily's cousin who ran the *Hour* was depressed about costs and didn't know how long he could keep going. My words to you have taken me unexpected places where, though no one is waiting to receive me, it was something just to get there, or here. The Puerto Rican said to Bob lucky for him he had his girlfriend to back him up, and as the Italian with an eye on us picked the stick out of the street and leapt back to the middle of the sidewalk as Petty came around the front end of the delivery rig, Petty and Bob spoke words that began and ended together and had the same number of syllables: "He doesn't need *me*" and "She's not *my* girlfriend."

"I *seen* you with her," said Joey, "she got nice tits." But gallant Perpetua Belle Pound over her own words had heard Bob's "She's not *my* girlfriend," and Bob knew she had, and yet Bob hadn't exactly meant it. And so he jumped through Joey's bike frame and as he and Joey shoved each other's shoulders I raised my guard and moved around the rear of the bike and in on the Puerto Rican.

I was jabbing him up onto the first few steps of this brownstone stoop that was an absolute home ground though we didn't happen to know who lived there, but as on impulse I turned to see Petty clout Joey's ear from behind, I caught our stickball stick on my left arm right to the bone, which was better than getting it in the back which was what the Italian had tried for, and when the little Puerto Rican came off the steps to grab me from the side thinking I was occupied with Ginzo, I got the Puerto Rican and heaved him round so Ginzo had to let up as he went to swing on me again.

Where *was* everyone? But it was a few seconds, no more.

Wit Holmes—a brave guy whom my parabola has had to use now here only as a mere equidistance in order to make any headway at all, but a man whose tragic story I vow I'll tell you or someone someday, Dom—Wit Holmes, seeing the Italian wind up on me, cut in behind Petty (for Wit wouldn't have thought of doubling up against Joey, who'd been smashed in the face by Bob) and as

Joey turned on Petty and gasped "Fuckin' cunt," the Italian saw Wit
Holmes and elbowed his swing in so that as Wit fell forward to
make a diving tackle the stick caught him in the head for extra
bases. But Petty had backed away from Joey to the stoop and as
Hugh said jokingly, "Unhand her, sirrah" as she was approached by
Joey who'd had enough of Bob (and Bob said, obviously to Hugh,
"Oh *that's* what we need, that's a *big* help")—she scooted right up
past the Italian to just outside the vestibule and called that she'd ring
"their" bell but Bob said with that oddly paternal leadership voice,
Don't you dare.

Joey was up after her; and now the Italian halfway up the stoop
tried with the stick to duel Bob back down but Bob got against the
opposite railing and eluded the stick sidestepping up the stoop after
Petty and that poor jerk Joey; and then I got under the Italian's stick
and lifted him by the knees right over the other railing and dumped
him stick and all ye gods backward a hell of a clattering drop into
the next areaway. Joey and Petty were jumping around inside the
vestibule, he had his hands on her, and Bob got into the doorway
and said, "Kraut crud" and when I saw just their legs and Petty said
with an astounding semblance of calm, "There's a knife," I swear
in the back of my head the two secret vector-fontanels (neither of
which ever has grown together like the one on top and neither of
which I've ever told any of my various doctors about) saw Hugh
put a hand on the stair railing at sidewalk level and say, "Let's fight
fair," and in the corner of an eye I found a tall Trace in a sleeveless
daffodil frock walking and running down the sidewalk calling, "Cy,
what did you *do* to him!" Thank God nothing happened to Abra. My
father wanted once to know why we called her Abra, and I said we
call her A.B. too.

If, earlier, I had tried to parallel (a) my rush up into that
clambering vestibule and (b) the position of the young Cyrus when
because of his childhood survival he became the reason Harpagus
lost his only son, I could have done it. But I can't now. I know the

two histories, one verbatim in the graceful English of Herodotus, the other poly-vectored in my doomed memory. Neglecting royal orders, Harpagus hadn't seen personally to the murder of the infant Cyrus, whom soothsayers had foretold would supplant the king. Therefore, Harpagus's only son was cut up, variously cooked, and served to his dad while the other guests got mutton. And when he had eaten his fill—and I speculated to Cadbury's distaste that Harpagus found future and past in the boy's living liver—he was brought a platter and told to lift the lid. I felt Stingy Bill's field glasses on me down that long angle from his roof at the far, dead end of my street and looked and saw him at a parapet like a sinister sentry.

You can see, Dom, my ancient history wasn't unimaginative. Dr. Cadbury had to sit by in my narrow margins and grumble at the Alexandrian longitudes and Pythean latitudes by which I caught in intersection the kindred ways (say) in which "those two fabulous travelers, the monarch from Macedon and the astronomer from Marseilles, made a Mediterranean world o'erflow east to the Hindus and north to triangular Britain." My father and my teacher must have been right to worship fact even when in Herodotus the fact was really the man, who (let's add) is to be pitied for having lived a century too soon to tell us the truths about where Phocean Pytheas really went, north from Gibraltar. Cocky was I, but now I see. And better to have seen too late than never to have seen at all. If I'm not arrested for entering your open apartment and occupying (though not exactly stealing) your typewriter paper I'm going up to the marine nutrients station next week to carry on your interest in the phytoplankton breakthrough. It will cost me more than my farm camp savings and the money Bob lent me that summer of V-J Day that I sent off to a famous writers correspondence course. But I've journeyed to your screen-lit kitchen to look at your excuse-list again, and I'm even surer that in the beginning *I* was the one meant to hear your off-the-hook phone, study that maudlin script, and thence come to EARTH = SPACECRAFT.

On my return journey to this table there were two sets of steps, mine inside and someone else's outside. After mine got lost in Dot's vast acrylic carpet the footfalls outside turned to tiptoe, Richard taking out some hugger-mugger insurance that my steps would not hear his. But the tiptoes stop—maybe ten feet from your door. In a second I'll forecast Richard's next moves but before I do I must tell what I see for the First Time Ever about my old ancient history: I see that whether from an only child's insulation or some other costive formula, I was overconfident in fact about the *lack* of bearing all that stuff had upon my life: so I could and would in my expatiations blithely abduct from context and casually charm contraband into my locus: for I was Utmosis the Last.

I wish I could be Forgetorix the First, and leave behind me a mass of Past as merciful as Gail's plaid case that Al started to take but I said we'd pick up later.

I turned back into my apartment after Ted snubbed me tonight, and with her hands out toward me Ev came from the bathroom but came and spoke hastily because we had people arriving, and said, "It's inevitable, *you know* that," and she smiled at my sad stupor and said, "Well he doesn't know about all you said to Doug, and he never shall, because he couldn't understand." And I kept from asking how the hell *she* knew but then saw of course it'd been my friend Al.

Abra was juggling her ball and talking to two women with grocery bags, who must have been on the far sidewalk. The Italian was crying in the areaway where he'd wrecked his shoulder lighting on the raised handle of a garbage lid.

Which as I reached into the vestibule was so far from the issue I'm surprised it comes back.

As I reached for Joey, who was on his knees with his back to me, he dodged Bob's ladle uppercut whose follow-through sliced *my* check and shook me sideways into the one of the two inner doors that didn't open, and there was Petty inside the house on the other side of the door that was ajar having got it open and slipped through to the hall, and she was pulling hard against the door-closer's piston-resistance, as Bob grabbed that door as Petty gave it the final pull and it shut on his fingers. Joey was a mess but so was Bob, as I hope I described in those pages Richard's brother-in-law whom he doesn't like took away. A pair of good chinos were slit and there was dark soaking one khaki leg.

Joey staggered up between me and Bob, Bob groaned trying to get his white-knuckled fist out of the door that Petty thought she was pulling against Joey, who turning around toward me saw his switch-blade at my feet and with a glance of authentic apology as if for bad manners bent his bloody head and reached, and Bob kicked him in the ass and I swung and I just missed Joey's mouth but hooked his septum and as I recall his nostrils broke out and up and between Bob and me we lifted him right off that marble floor. And then all he could think of, all Joey could think of, to say was, "I din't *take* your typewriter." But Bob, who was panting so hysterically fast he retched for a second, dropped to his knees and as if continuing a quite other conversation said to me with a breathless half-belch, "So why'n hell'd you let her believe that crap about the boomerang?"

And at last now after more than twenty years I recall not only my consequent *feeling* but my *words*. On cue I said, "Why the hell didn't I throw that pitch right over A.B.'s head? Why didn't I stop you from doing that stupid window-stunt? Why didn't I *keep* my boomerang?" Well, I didn't have to underline my point, if you can underline a point. And Joey crawled out of the vestibule past Hugh, crying, "I didn't touch any fuckin' typewriter." I thought I vectored hatred on Bob's cracked face. Petty opened the front door again and said, "Do you know there's no one home—my God *Bobby!*—and they left the door unlocked. Your head!" And then Bob got hold of her and I went down the stoop to see about Wit and I saw the daffodil yellow dress in the areaway, Tracy looking at the Italian's shoulder but now at me in needy bewilderment.

Petty's police never came. But did she phone?

"Simple," my step-grandfather would have said if he'd learned of the fight and my feelings about it: "You lost your tempers."

But how much did Ev hear about the tongue-lashing I gave Doug?—who you may recall was Ev's first husband.

Well there's no point in killing yourself rehashing all this.

My parents were oblivious of me. I mean three years before.

Richard's key is in your lock, Dom, and my paraphase is about to close.

I was thirteen, and after half an hour of their strange bickering my father's voice rose on a rush of absolute reasonableness and my mother's broke into a hardness that wasn't firm; he wanted to go to the shore for the summer, she wanted Heatsburg and thought he wanted the shore because of Heights people and business, and when he said she'd have music galore she said with the wrong intonation, Oh you're *very fair!* I've always said you're *very fair!*— so that one of my vertebrae started getting dry-ice signals from Ultima Thule—then the voices were low but worse, until I turned out the light and stared not unhappily at the intimate fire of the Statue's torch out beyond Governor's Island. (I made a mental note to write down if I could ever figure it out who she was carrying the torch for.) Then my father cried such a nightmarish No! No! that I tiptoed in my stocking feet to my door and slowly into the hall whence I could see the piano and the Seth Thomas metronome. There was nothing and I didn't move. There came material against material, and I snuck to the living room entrance and peeped past toward the couch and as far as feet, then further; and they were kissing in a position there's no more point in graphing here than there is in prophesying the past.

Richard will enter. Looking into the dark kitchen at the far window like the one Ted looked through one early morning, Richard will find reflected part of the TV screen. Seeing the back of your portable Admiral just inside the door to his right, he'll perhaps put a foot over the threshold. He may not know the wall phone is only a few inches away. But since I took the phone-receiver off the TV and hung it back up, Richard won't connect the TV with the excuse list above the phone, and hence not with EARTH = SPACECRAFT, which he'd not have understood anyhow. He'll turn away to the living room and he'll look in the desk for bank books and such, not for his sake but for expedition's.

He'll spot these 8 1/2 by 11 sheets that I've made mine, and he'll peruse the last one or two, which are on top, and he'll straighten the pile and roll it and, finding a rubber band in a desk drawer, he'll take this second part of my convection with him. But he won't dare look (say) behind my curtain by the long window. Through the window I see that the red EXIT in the great workroom of the nightgown company across the way is dimmer now as morning nears and the containing edifice itself shapes forth its towering stone verticals. But you didn't assume your son would come before morning, so maybe you didn't think it would be dark and you thought he would indeed connect himself, by cathode ray, with SPACECRAFT and thence to the body's volume and the cubic habits of the heart and your love for your only son. But that link is left to me.

What brought the cops so quickly long ago? All that kind of thing will come out in the wash. Richard will almost think the steps he heard came from another apartment, even from the penthouse where he doubtless does not know you used to trampoline. He will extinguish the light over this table. He will keep his key; he will dart his eyes about seriously, to make himself feel better. Departing, he will open the door slowly, stand a safe moment in case what he has percentally ignored betrays itself (though what would he do if it did?). He will step to the mat, and he'll think What's all this about someone's mother seeing a Puerto Rican kid pedal a delivery rig past in the opposite direction with a skull and crossbones on it and her thinking what's happened to Joey? and as Richard descends the west shaft he'll wonder who it was that Joey didn't deliver to which lost him his place at Bohack's though Monday after school he went to work for A&P on Montague Street; and then who is this Bob on an island at night?—to whom someone says it takes a thousand pounds of phytoplankton to produce a hundred zooplankton to produce ultimately ten pounds of herring, and this Bob says back to this someone "So *what!*" still irked that this friend or companion or whatever he is offered advice about Bob being gentler with one of his sons.

Then, Dom, I will sincerely leave. And your door will be unlocked once more.

Acknowledgments

Thanks to Mike Heppner for invaluable help with the text of this second edition.

JOSEPH McELROY is the author of nine novels, a novella, and a volume of short fiction. A volume of his essays, *Exponential*, has been published in Italy and in expanded form will be forthcoming as an e-book from Dzanc. A nonfiction book about water approaches completion. Three short plays are forthcoming. He received the Award in Literature from the American Academy of Arts and Letters and fellowships from the Guggenheim, Rockefeller, and D.H. Lawrence Foundations, twice from Ingram Merrill and twice from the National Endowment for the Arts. He has taught at numerous universities. McElroy was born in Brooklyn, New York, in 1930. He was educated at Williams College and Columbia University.